SHADOWS ACROSS THE VEIL

SHADOWS ACROSS THE VEIL

JOHN D JENNETT

Contents

For my wife Christy, who held the light when the world went dark and never let me forget why stories matter.

1

The Aftermath

Maya surfaced slowly.

At first there was only the faint awareness of motion, tiny shifts of fabric against her skin, the soft sigh of conditioned air, a steady pattern of beeps keeping time with something inside her chest. Light pressed against her eyelids, warm but muted, nothing like the brilliant green-white glow of the Weave.

A whisper of fear threaded through her.

Am I back?

She forced her eyes open.

The ceiling above her was too white. Too flat. Too human. The overhead fixture hummed quietly, the sound dull and lifeless compared to the harmonic symphony she had drifted in moments, or ages, ago.

Her breath caught as she realized where she was.

A hospital room.

An IV line trailed from her arm. A monitor blinked quietly to her right. A chair sat beside the bed, its cushion bent in the shape of someone who had been sitting there far too long.

Maya turned her head.

Alex was there.

His posture was slumped forward, elbows on his knees, head bowed, hands cradling hers as if he were afraid she might disappear if he let go. His hair was an unruly mess, and dark circles smudged the skin beneath his eyes. Dust still clung to the creases of his jacket.

He looked like he hadn't slept in days.

Her voice came out thin. "Alex?"

His head snapped up.

"Maya." A breath, half-laugh and half-break, escaped him. He sat straighter, his hand tightening around hers. "Thank God. You're awake."

She swallowed, her throat sore and dry. "What... what happened?"

He dragged a hand over his face, and for a moment the effort of holding himself together showed in every line of his expression.

"You've been out for three days," he said softly. "Completely unresponsive. Not even a twitch."

Three days.

She tried to remember, but the last thing she recalled was,

Light.

Threads.

Voices older than memory.

None of that fit into words.

Alex took a deep breath. "Let me explain."

He shifted closer, his knee brushing the side of the bed, and for a moment simply looked at her, like he needed to confirm she was real.

"It started when the Talisman chamber collapsed," he said. "The whole place went insane. Threads tearing, resonance screaming, like reality was trying to fold in on itself."

Fragments of sensation flickered at the edge of Maya's mind: the floor trembling, air fracturing, a flash of ash-light from the Talisman.

"You tried to blink us out," Alex continued. "But the harmonics were unstable. Every time you anchored a jump point, the corridor buckled. So I..." His voice faltered. "I forced a grounding field around us. It was stupid. It nearly snapped me in half. But it held just long enough for you to grab me and blink."

She stared at him. "You could've died."

"Yeah," he said quietly. "I know."

The room hummed around them. A distant PA announcement murmured through the halls. But Alex didn't look away.

"When we hit the surface, you collapsed. Completely gone. Your resonance was," he searched for a word, ", burned out. The ground was vibrating under you like the Weave was still trying to pull you back inside."

She shivered, though the room was warm.

"I tried to wake you up," Alex said. "Nothing worked." He swallowed. "And then... Ethan appeared."

Her heart stuttered.

"Ethan?"

"Not the way you saw him in the cavern," Alex said. "This was... different. Fractured. Like he was barely holding together. Light, not a body. But he looked right at *you*." Alex's voice dropped to a whisper. "And he said:

'Find the others. The Convergence isn't a prophecy... it's a deadline.'"

The words struck Maya like a sudden plunge into cold water. A chill crawled up her arms.

"What happened after?" she asked.

"He vanished," Alex said. "Just blinked out like static breaking apart. And HECATE teams were already closing in, triangulating the surge from the collapse. I carried you out before they got a clear visual. I didn't know where else to go, so I brought you here."

He let out a long breath and finally leaned back in the chair, exhausted.

"I didn't know if you'd wake up," he admitted. "Every hour they checked you, but your scans were... weird. Not coma, not normal sleep. Just, out." His fingers gently brushed the back of her hand. "I stayed. I wasn't leaving you."

Maya stared at the ceiling for a long moment.

Three days unconscious.

Her body here.

Her mind elsewhere.

And in that elsewhere,

She remembered threads glowing with life.

Merlin's calm, curious eyes.

Beagron's stone-deep voice.

Kemen's warmth wrapping around her like a steadying hand.

The Fifth Covenant forms.

She had heard those words.

Felt them.

But none of this was something she could explain. Not yet. Not when Alex's world was still grounded in what he could see and touch.

She turned her head, meeting his gaze.

"Alex... something happened while I was out."

His posture straightened. "What do you mean?"

The room seemed to tighten around her. She wasn't ready to talk about the Weave or the Immortals or the word that still trembled faintly in her chest, *Walkers.*

"Just, stay with me a little longer," she said.

He nodded instantly, as if the request itself steadied him.

"I'm not going anywhere."

And with Alex's hand holding hers, Maya let herself breathe, her mind drifting in the space between worlds.

The Weave was still humming in the distance, waiting, calling.

And she knew with absolute certainty, everything had changed and this was only the beginning.

2

Elara

Miami's humidity clung to Elara's skin like a second layer, thick enough to taste every time she drew in a breath. She pushed open the rooftop door and stepped into the night, letting it slam behind her. The muffled sound of her roommate still shouting drifted up through the stairwell window, but she shut it out and walked toward the edge of the roof.

A puddle of rainwater rippled beneath her sandals. Her reflection shimmered in it: red hair, wavy and bright even under the washed out glow of the security light; strands stuck to her cheeks where sweat gathered; green eyes rimmed with exhaustion, unfocused and too wide. She looked like someone who had been running without stopping. Someone afraid of what she might see in the mirror.

She hugged her arms around her small frame and tried to steady her breathing. Her hands trembled anyway. Anger gnawed at her from the argument downstairs. Embarrassment too. The candle she had been lighting earlier had flared up by itself, scorching the wall. Her roommate's expression had shifted from annoyance to fear.

Another burning episode, they had called it.

She hated that word.

Neon lights flickered along the street below, painting shifting colors up the building. A warm ocean breeze brushed her hair, but it did nothing to cool the heat rising beneath her skin. It felt as if a fire waited there, trying to claw free.

Elara lifted her hands and stared at her palms. Too warm. Hotter than before. She wiped them on her shorts, then froze when she noticed the tar beneath her sandals begin to soften.

"What is happening to me," she whispered.

Her stomach tightened. Fear surged, sharp and electric. Anger rose beneath it, tangled together in a way she could not separate. The emotions fed each other, growing stronger.

Her heart thudded once, then again.

A pulse of green white light blossomed behind her eyelids. Not from the city. Not from the sky. From inside her. Something aware.

She blinked rapidly, startled.

For a moment she felt as though someone had breathed her name. She froze.

The humid night air pressed in around her, yet something colder slipped through her mind. A sudden flash of green white light filled her vision, bright enough to make her stagger.

She pressed a hand to her forehead as the rooftop tilted. She caught herself against the low concrete wall.

It was not pain.

It felt like her mind had been pulled toward something distant and alive. A rhythm beat inside her skull, steady and warm, almost familiar.

Recognition.
That was the strangest part.

She had no idea what she was recognizing, yet the sensation settled deep in her chest like a hum that did not belong to her.

Her heart sped up. She swallowed.

"What was that?" she whispered.

Miami continued as if nothing had happened. Lights blinked. Cars crawled through distant intersections. A siren wailed somewhere far off. Everything looked the same.

Fear rose sharply. The pulse inside her did not fade. It strengthened, meeting her fear head on. Heat flickered across her palm.

She looked down.

A tiny spark crossed her fingers like a living ember.

Her breath hitched.

And her power reacted.

Heat rushed into her palms so fast she gasped. It felt as if a fuse had been lit beneath her skin, fire racing up her arms in a violent sweep. She held her hands out, fingers splayed, as if distance alone could stop it.

The air shimmered. Pebbles on the rooftop glowed faint orange, pulsing like dying embers. A wave of distortion rolled outward from her feet, bending the light and making the night ripple.

A low metallic groan sounded behind her.

She turned toward it.

The vent pipe a few steps away glowed dull red. Heat rippled off its surface in waves. Smoke curled from the base where it met the roof.

"No, no, no. Stop. Please stop," she whispered.

She backed up. Every step sent another burst of heat through her hands, like her body was answering a command she could not hear.

A spark drifted from her fingertips, small and bright.

It burst.

A thin ribbon of fire shot through the air and struck the vent with a sharp hiss. The pipe ignited instantly. Flames spiraled upward in a twisting rush, dancing like a torch caught in sudden wind.

Elara screamed and stumbled backward. The fire chased her terror, climbing higher as her fear grew. The tar below bubbled and split.

This was not control.

This was raw emotion turning into fire.

A stronger wave of heat burst from her core.

Flames rolled outward across the rooftop, catching on anything too slow to resist them.

The air thickened, alive with heat. Tar blisters swelled and burst, releasing the sharp smell of burning rubber. Fire curled upward in twisting waves, reaching for the sky.

Elara stumbled back, eyes wide. Flames chased her retreat. She tore off her jacket and swung it at the fire, trying to smother it.

It did nothing.

The flames roared higher the moment the fabric touched them, feeding on her fear. The jacket blackened. She dropped it and backed up until her spine hit the concrete wall.

"Stop. Please stop. Just stop!" she screamed.

The fire did not stop. It roared louder, heat rolling across her skin in waves that seemed to come from inside her.

Color flared beneath her skin, streaks of gold and red twisting along her arms like veins of living flame. Her hands glowed brighter than the vent pipe. She pressed them against her thighs, trying to hide the light, but it bled through her fingers.

"Oh God," she whispered. "I'm doing this. I can't control it."

For the first time, she understood the fear in her roommate's eyes. She was becoming exactly what they feared.

Her heartbeat spiked. Flames surged again, climbing the night like a wave trying to swallow the sky.

Far above, a satellite captured the sudden heat spike.
The rooftop burned bright enough for HECATE to see it clearly.

Inside the HECATE Operations Center, a technician leaned closer as his thermal display surged. A sharp bloom of heat filled the screen. The center pulsed in precise intervals no natural fire produced.

He frowned, tapped a command, and watched the AI analysis appear.

Walker Probability: 73 percent
Class Unknown

He pressed the alert button. The data streamed directly to Senator Hargreaves private feed.

Hargreaves sat alone in his office, lit only by the glow of monitors. The alert chimed. He lifted the tablet, scanned the data, and narrowed his eyes.

Another one.

He opened a secure line.

"Trace the source," he said. "Keep it quiet. I want eyes, not a confrontation."

He ended the call and stared at the pulsing thermal image. It moved like a heartbeat. He knew exactly what it meant.

The rooftop alarms shrieked as smoke poured into the stairwell. Elara spun and bolted for the door. Her foot slipped on softened tar. She caught herself with one hand and pushed off, running through the stairwell entrance.

She stumbled inside. Her chest heaved. The metal railing rattled beside her. Thin ribbons of flame followed her down the first few steps before fading.

They were following her.

She grabbed the railing, then jerked her hand back as smoke curled from her fingertips. Her skin glowed faintly. She pressed her hand to her chest, terrified.

"What is happening to me," she whispered.

The fire did not fully enter the stairwell. The further she moved, the weaker the flames became. They were reacting to her.

Cold understanding settled inside her.

Her power was emotional, not random. Her breathing slowed. The smoke around her fingers thinned. Then another pulse hit her. Warm and bright, it rushed through her mind. She grabbed the railing, steadying herself. It was not her pulse. It came from somewhere else.

Elara froze on the landing. Warmth spread through her chest, gentle and comforting, as if someone had placed a hand over her heart.

She closed her eyes.

Green light flickered behind her eyelids. Threads of it drifted across her mind in weaving patterns. A distant silhouette stood at the center, blurred and human.

Someone was reaching for her. Someone she had never met. Someone familiar. Her voice came out soft. "Who are you?"

The light dimmed. The silhouette faded. The warmth receded, leaving only the echo.

She opened her eyes, shaken.

The alarm blared. Screams filled the floors below. Elara wiped her palms on her shorts and pushed through the next door. She joined the flow of residents rushing toward the street.

Smoke drifted around them. People coughed and shouted. No one noticed her hands glowing faintly.

She reached the sidewalk and pulled away from the crowd. Emergency vehicles crowded the street. Firefighters rushed inside. Flames danced on the rooftop above.

She tugged her hoodie up and slipped between two parked cars.

Her hands tingled. Golden light flickered beneath the skin. She clenched her fists and shoved them into her pockets.

Her breath shook. Every inhale tasted of smoke and guilt. Every exhale felt like fire waiting to escape.

"I can't stay here," she whispered.

She moved away from the chaos, then ran. Neon signs cast shimmering reflections across wet pavement. Music thumped from nearby clubs. The city pulsed with life, but Elara felt completely alone.

She ran until her legs ached and her lungs burned. She didn't know where she was going. She only knew she needed to get away. From the fire. From the alarms. From the questions she could never answer.

Fear settled deep inside her.

She was afraid of herself. But something else was coming. Something she could feel.

A faint harmonic pulse stirred in the air, the same thrum she had felt twice before. She stopped on the sidewalk, heart racing.

Hundreds of miles away, Joe Biggs felt the same spike while Elara shivered and pulled her hood tighter, disappearing into the Miami night.

3

Joe Biggs

Joe Biggs sat hunched over his cluttered desk, the glow from his cheap lamp casting harsh shadows across the cramped office. The place smelled like old coffee and dryer sheets drifting up from the laundromat downstairs. He had been there since early evening, long past the time any sane person would have called it a night.

He ran a hand through his messy brown curls and squinted at the monitor. His reflection in the darkened window stared back at him. Late twenties but already tired around the eyes, a scruffy beard that made him look like he never quite finished shaving, and a build that suggested he walked more than he slept. He looked like someone who had lived out of his office for weeks. Maybe he had.

The video on his screen looped again. Another cheating-spouse case. A married guy slipping into a motel with someone he wasn't supposed to. Joe paused the footage and sighed.

"This is what I get for not taking the police exam," he said under his breath.

He tried to focus on the case, but something else kept tugging at him. A low hum at the back of his skull, steady and insistent, like a note he couldn't locate. It had started small weeks ago, barely noticeable. Recently it had grown stronger, almost musical. Tonight it was impossible to ignore.

Joe pressed two fingers to his temple. His head ached, a dull pressure that had been building all night. The hum sat beneath it like a second heartbeat.

He didn't know what it meant. He only knew it made him uneasy.

Sometimes the hum sharpened when he spoke to clients who weren't telling the full truth. Sometimes it shifted when he watched security footage, as if his brain was reacting to something he couldn't see. He had stopped mentioning it to his doctor after the man suggested less caffeine and more sleep.

Joe exhaled and leaned back, chair creaking under him. The laundromat machines thumped below, steady and mechanical. The only real comfort he had was that consistency. Everything else around him felt slightly off-kilter tonight.

Like the world was holding its breath.

He rubbed his forehead to push back the headache, but it only grew tighter. The hum rose with it, gaining a faint tone. He tried to shake it off.

Then something shifted inside him.

A sudden click, sharp and definite, like a puzzle piece snapping into place.

Joe stopped moving.

The hum turned into a clear note. Not loud, but pure. It rang through him in a way he didn't have words for. His breath caught as the tiny office seemed to tilt, like gravity had changed direction for a heartbeat.

His pulse quickened.

"What the hell was that?" he whispered.

The note didn't fade. It waited, like something out there had just opened its eyes.

The click inside Joe's skull had barely settled before something far stronger slammed through him. It hit without warning. A deep vibration shuddered through his body, so abrupt and powerful that he thought an earthquake had rolled under the building. His chair rattled, his coffee mug tipped, and he grabbed the edge of the desk just to stay upright.

A sharp pressure wave surged through his mind. Not sound, not sight, something else, something he had no name for.

The air in his office stayed still, yet the world felt like it had twisted a few degrees sideways.

Joe blinked hard, trying to steady his vision. The lamplight bled at the corners, bending in a way that made his stomach lurch. He squeezed his eyes shut and opened them again, but the sensation clung to him.

His heart hammered. Sweat prickled along his hairline.

Then everything around him went quiet.

Not the physical world. He could still hear the dryers downstairs tumbling and clanking. Cars rolled by outside. A siren wailed in the distance.

But something deeper went silent.

The faint background buzz he always felt around lies and half-truths snapped out like someone had yanked a plug from the wall. The quiet hit him so hard he doubled over slightly, hands on his knees, breath caught in his throat.

Then the quiet broke. A pulse struck him from the east. It wasn't sound, but it sure as hell felt like it. A low, steady thud against his senses, like a heartbeat he wasn't supposed to hear. It pushed at him, distant but unmistakable.

Before he could recover, a second surge hit him. This one came from the south. Hot. Wild. Sharp enough to make him flinch.

Joe staggered back against his desk. The two forces clashed inside him, sending a violent jolt up the back of his neck. The room swayed for a moment, and he had to brace himself on the edge of the desk to keep from collapsing.

His headache spiked into something worse. Something alive.

"This isn't normal," he said through clenched teeth. "This is really not normal."

The pulses faded, but they didn't disappear. They left traces, threads of sensation crawling beneath his skin, as if the world had reached inside him and left fingerprints behind.

His truth-sense flared again, painful and sharp. Someone out there had changed. Someone had awakened. Maybe more than one. But Joe had no idea how he knew that. And he had even less idea what to do about it.

Joe's pulse hadn't settled. The aftershocks of whatever had slammed through him still crawled beneath his skin, restless and electric. He pushed away from the desk and crossed his cramped office to the filing cabinet, opening the bottom drawer with a shaky hand.

Behind a stack of overdue billing forms sat a small black lockbox. A strip of masking tape across the top read: SALERNO. The name wasn't real. The case was.

He carried the box to the desk, set it down, and hesitated before opening it. Outside the window, Chicago glowed under streetlamps and refinery haze, quiet and indifferent. But Joe couldn't shake the sense that the world had shifted while he wasn't looking.

He unlocked the box.

Inside lay the material he had collected after the Salem blackout. Printouts, screenshots, scribbled notes, a thumb drive filled with news clips that had vanished from the internet within hours. The most striking image sat at the top: a young woman collapsing on a sidewalk outside a Salem warehouse, her eyes faintly lit just before the camera glitched to static.

Joe had never meant to chase this story. He had come to Salem on a missing-persons job, tracking a runaway teen who'd been seen near the blackout zone. But then the videos started spreading. People online talked about strange electrical surges, a man who "glowed," and a woman who disappeared from a hospital hallway for three seconds while the security feed distorted.

Joe hadn't believed any of it.

Not until he felt it.

He lifted the printout gently. The moment his fingertips touched the paper, a ripple of sensation rolled through him. The same tingle he had felt when he'd watched the viral clips. The same spark that had hit him earlier tonight.

And the same sharp, gut-deep reaction he'd experienced the one time he had actually seen her. It had been brief, barely a moment.

He'd been standing in the ER lobby at Salem Memorial, talking to a nurse about blackout injuries, when a man burst through the entrance carrying an unconscious woman in his arms. The man had shouted for help, and the staff rushed him toward a trauma bay. Joe didn't know who they were. He only knew that when the woman passed him, pale and barely breathing, something in Joe's mind lit up like a blown transformer.

A snap of pressure behind his eyes.
A jolt through his gut.
A feeling that she mattered in a way he couldn't explain. He had pretended it was exhaustion. Stress. Too much coffee. But when he reviewed the viral footage later, the sensation hit again. Now, tonight, it had returned stronger than ever.

Joe traced the corner of the printout. The same strange imprint clung to the paper, like an emotional fingerprint burned into the fibers.

His truth-sense pulsed, steady, insistent.

"It's her," he murmured.

He wasn't sure what he meant. He didn't know her name. He didn't understand what his instincts were trying to tell him. But his body recognized her signature tonight the same way it had in Salem.

Fear tightened his chest. Not fear of her, fear of the pattern forming around her. He leaned back, exhaling slowly, trying to quiet the pounding in his skull. A sharp chime broke the silence.

Joe turned toward his laptop. A new alert blinked across the screen. His scraping program, which monitored fringe-government channels and local emergency networks, had flagged an unusual cluster of activity. His stomach sank. He crossed the room and clicked the alert. The same kind of anomaly that had dragged him to Salem earlier this week

had just appeared again, and this time there were two.

His scraping program worked quietly in the background most nights, pulling everything from emergency response chatter to low-level federal memos. Ninety-nine percent of the time it fed him junk. Tonight it threw sparks. A string of classified feeds blinked onto the screen. First was a thermal anomaly tag. A heat bloom over a Miami rooftop. Rapid onset. Sharp edges. The kind of spike a wildfire never produced.

Joe zoomed in.

The center pulsed in perfect intervals. "That's not electrical," he murmured. "Not an accident." Before he could process it, a second alert populated the queue. Seismic distortion. Colorado, shallow depth, localized, not tectonic. The waveform made no sense. It wasn't geological. It was something hitting the ground in a way his system could not categorize.

The pressure behind Joe's eyes tightened.

Another pulse, another direction. As he watched, a third file slid into the stack. This one from a private federal channel his program had only cracked once before. The memo header read: **SILENT PRO-TOCOL: Escalation Review Pending**

Joe's pulse jumped.

Silent Protocol was the same classification tag that had appeared during the Salem blackout. He didn't know who authorized it or what division ran it, but whatever it was, it had teeth. It erased media. It locked down witnesses. It rewrote reports.

And now it was back.

He leaned closer to the screen, scanning the metadata. Three events in three states. All within the last thirty minutes. Joe exhaled slowly.

"They're already tracking them," he said.

The words tasted wrong on his tongue. He didn't know who "them" was supposed to be. But he felt the same pressure in his head that had hit him when he saw the viral Salem footage. The same weight that slammed him tonight when the pulses came from the east and south.

The program pinged again, a quiet chirp that felt like a countdown. Joe dragged his laptop closer and opened a new window. He pulled up a map of the United States and pinned the Miami thermal bloom. Then the Colorado distortion. Then Salem. Then the Chicago spike he had felt in his own skull a moment earlier.

Lines began to form in his mind, quiet and insistent. He felt his heartbeat answer them. Something was happening across the country, something big and Joe was the only one who could feel it.

Joe pushed his chair back and stood, pacing once around the tiny office before stopping in front of the blank section of wall where he usually tacked missing-person timelines. Tonight it felt like the only place he could breathe. He grabbed a stack of sticky notes from the corner of his desk and a pen that had seen better days.

He wrote SALEM on the first note and slapped it high on the wall.

Then MIAMI, pinned several feet to the right.

Then COLORADO, lower, near the corner.

He stepped back and stared at them. The buzzing in his skull grew stronger. Each note seemed to vibrate in the air, faint but undeniable. It wasn't the paper. It wasn't the ink. It was something beneath his senses, humming the way a power line hums in the cold.

He grabbed another sticky note and hesitated.

He didn't have a name for the signature he had felt from the central pulse in his head. It hadn't been a location so much as a presence, pressing close but not geographically close.

He wrote CENTRAL PULSE and placed it left of center, slightly above Salem.

The hum intensified.

His breath caught.

One more.

The strongest pulse he had felt tonight.

The one that kept dancing around the edge of his awareness, never still, never clear.

He wrote UNKNOWN SIGNAL and held the sticky note for a long moment.

It tingled against his skin.

He placed it near the center of the wall.

When he stepped back, the arrangement didn't look random anymore. The notes formed the loose shape of a triangle, with Salem, Miami, and Colorado forming the corners. The central pulse sat just inside the shape, glowing faintly in his perception. And the drifting signal hovered at the center, refusing to stay put, the edges of the connection slipping just out of reach.

Joe frowned and rubbed the back of his neck.

He didn't understand what he was seeing. He didn't even know how he was seeing it. But his instincts screamed that these events were connected. Not by geography. Not by coincidence. By something deeper. Something pulling these people toward each other.

He stepped closer. His fingers hovered near the middle note where the drifting pulse had nearly knocked him out of his chair earlier. The hum rose behind his eyes, almost like a warning. Or a promise.

"Something's happening," he whispered. "Something big."

He touched the center note.

A sharp resonance tore through him.

He staggered back with a curse as the room snapped into focus, brighter and sharper than before. The pulse slammed into him again, stronger than the two that had hit earlier. The invisible pressure filled his skull and rolled down his spine like a wave.

His knees nearly buckled.

Whatever this was, it wasn't over.

It was accelerating.

The humming in Joe's skull had just started to settle when the office lights flickered overhead. Once. Twice. A faint buzz rolled through the wiring, sharp enough to make him wince. He lifted his head, eyes narrowing at the ceiling.

"Come on," he muttered. "Not again."

The lights steadied, but the air shifted in a way he couldn't define. It felt like the entire room drew a long breath, holding it for a heartbeat.

Then everything exhaled through him.

Joe gasped and braced himself against the wall. His truth-sense sharpened so suddenly it felt like a needle driving behind his eyes. The sticky notes on the wall vibrated in his peripheral vision, as if reacting to something outside the building, outside the city, maybe outside anything he understood.

A pulse hit him from the south. Fear, hot and panicked. It crashed into him like a wave, wild and bright, and he stumbled forward under the weight of it. His breath came fast. His hands shook. He felt heat racing along his skin even though the room was cool.

Whoever had sent that pulse was terrified. Before he could recover, another pulse struck him. This one from the east. Confusion. Soft. Disoriented, like someone struggling awake in a place that didn't feel real. The sensation brushed against him gently, almost apologetic. It stole the tension from his shoulders for a second before fading.

He recognized it. It was the same signature from Salem. The same presence he had seen in the ER and felt on those corrupted videos.

The third pulse came from somewhere closer. Not in distance, but in feeling. Strain. Steady and grounding, but pushed to its limit. Someone holding too much weight and refusing to break. It pressed against Joe's mind like a warning.

All three signatures slammed into him at once, weaving through each other in a way that made him drop to one knee. His breath hitched. Sweat rolled down his spine. The sensation was too layered, too heavy, too human to be anything logical.

He squeezed his eyes shut. The fear. The confusion. The strain. It was all rising. All connected.

"This isn't random," he whispered. "They're waking up."

The pressure receded slowly, leaving him chilled and shaking. He forced himself to stand and wiped his palms against his jeans. The map on the wall pulsed faintly, each sticky note humming like a struck chord.

Joe stared at the center of the triangle. He didn't know what was happening. But he knew where it started. And he knew who he had to find.

"I need to get to her," he said to himself.

He didn't know who "her" was. Not fully. But the truth sat in his chest like a quiet weight waiting to be spoken.

Joe stayed still for a long moment, hands resting against the cluttered desk as the last tremors of the resonance faded from his skull. His breath finally steadied, but his mind didn't. The sensations he had felt were too real to ignore. Too sharp. Too human.

They were people. Whoever they were, whatever they were becoming, they were people.

And one of them had reached him before. A woman he had only seen once. A woman he now knew he had to find. He grabbed his jacket from the back of the chair and shrugged it on. The fabric smelled faintly of old coffee and winter air from earlier that morning. He crossed to the metal locker bolted into the corner of the room and twisted the combination with practiced ease.

Inside sat his old military duffel, folded and ready. He yanked it out and set it on the desk. Dust rose from the canvas as he unzipped it. He packed fast: burner phone, backup ID, a small first-aid kit, flashlight, and a portable battery.

His hand paused when it reached the small wooden box tucked in the corner. He hesitated, then opened it.

Inside lay a strange little device the size of a pocket watch. A brass disc etched with concentric rings and a sliver of clear crystal embedded in the center. He had taken it from a HECATE storage cabinet two years ago, back when he hadn't fully realized what he was stealing. The thing had hummed the moment he touched it, a soft vibration deep enough to pass as a heartbeat.

It hummed now.

Joe closed his fingers around it. The warmth settled into his palm.

"You're coming with me," he said under his breath.

He slipped the compass into the duffel and zipped it halfway. Then he moved back to the laptop and typed quickly. The digital trail left by the Salem blackout was nearly gone, scrubbed and buried under official explanations, but he had copies of everything that mattered. Including her name.

Maya Rodriguez, Salem Memorial Hospital.

He stared at the line for a moment, the enormity of what he felt pressing in on him again.

"If she's awake," Joe muttered, "this whole thing's about to change." He closed the laptop with a soft click.

The office was dim and quiet now, the hum of the dryers below fading as the laundromat switched to its overnight cycle. Joe slung the duffel over his shoulder, turned off the desk lamp, and stepped to the door. He paused with his hand on the knob. He didn't know what he was walking into. He didn't know who the pulses belonged to. He didn't even know why he could feel them. But he knew one thing. He was already too late to stop it.

Joe stepped out into the cold Chicago night. Snowflakes drifted through the glow of the streetlamps, settling on the pavement in quiet patterns. Somewhere far from here, the world had started unraveling. And he was finally moving toward the center of it.

4

Released

Morning light filtered through the thin hospital curtains, warm and soft, the kind that should have felt comforting. Instead it pressed against Maya's senses like a weight. Every machine in the room hummed with a strange undertone she shouldn't have been able to hear. Each monitor emitted a faint shimmering pulse that crawled along her nerves, rising and falling like a whisper trying to form words.

She lay propped against the pillows, pale and unsteady. Her hands trembled where they rested atop the blanket. She felt awake, but not entirely present. It was as if part of her still drifted somewhere else, somewhere bright and deep and far too vast.

Two figures stood at the foot of her bed reviewing a tablet. Their voices were quiet, but every tremor in their tones carried straight to her.

"It's not a seizure pattern," the technician murmured.

"It isn't any pattern," the doctor said. "Look at this."
A fingertip tapped the screen. "Neural spikes with fluctuating heat signatures... but her temperature is normal. And this haze around the EEG traces..."

"Interference?" the tech offered.

"Interference from what?" the doctor whispered.

Maya listened, heart tight. She could hear more than their words. The doctor's stress vibrated at the edge of her vision, a faint static that flickered in his shadow. The technician's worry pulsed in little stuttering echoes behind him.

She pressed a palm to her temple. The fluorescent lights above buzzed with a soft harmonic wave that rose in sync with her breathing. She flinched as a burst of green white shimmer flickered behind her eyelids.

Alex stepped out of the corner, expression stiff from lack of sleep. Dust still clung to his jacket. His eyes flicked between her and the doctors, protective and unyielding.

"She's leaving today," he said. "You've run every test you can."

The doctor frowned. "We're seeing neurological irregularities we don't understand. She needs monitoring. Rest. Another night, at least."

"She's not staying," Alex said, voice low but calm. "She needs quiet and space, not more fluorescent lights."

Maya managed a thin smile. "I'm fine. Really."

It was a lie. The hum in the machines was growing stronger. Reality itself seemed too loud.

The doctor hesitated, then sighed. "We'll finalize discharge. But if anything changes, you come back. Immediately."

When the staff left, the room finally settled. The echo in the machines softened. But the dread didn't fade. Something inside her was still vibrating, still listening.

Alex stepped closer. "Ready?"

She nodded, but when she swung her legs off the bed, they nearly buckled. Alex caught her instantly.

"Easy," he murmured. "Let me."

He guided her into a wheelchair. The moment she sank into it, the world steadied, not completely, but enough for her to breathe. Alex took hold of the handles and wheeled her toward the door.

As they crossed the threshold, something shifted.

A flicker of green-white light flashed in the corner of her vision. She snapped her head toward it, but nothing was there, until an orderly hurried past, and for a heartbeat a second shape peeled off him like a lagging shadow, half a second behind the real one.

Maya gasped.

The hallway looked wrong. The air seemed double-exposed. Light smeared along the walls, creating faint duplicates that hovered before snapping back into place.

Her pulse sped up. "Alex... it followed me out."

Alex slowed the chair. "What did?"

She pointed with a trembling hand. An echo flickered behind a nurse, thin, trembling, jittering with the woman's stress. The janitor who trudged by carried a second outline behind him, slumped with exhaustion, as if even his after-image was tired.

"It's the Residuum," Maya whispered. "It learned from me."

Alex moved in front of her and crouched. "Maya. Look at me."

She forced her gaze off the flickering echoes and onto him. His outline stayed solid, steady, unbroken. His presence pushed back the static in her head. Her breathing eased.

Alex stood again and pushed her forward. The echoes stayed behind, watching, swaying with the movement of the people they mirrored, but they no longer surged toward her. His grounding field muted them enough to keep her steady.

They reached the elevators. The doors opened with a metallic clang that bent oddly at the edges, warping like sound passing through heat.

Maya flinched. Alex squeezed the handles. "Almost there."

Inside the elevator, the overhead light buzzed softly. The moment the doors closed, the light began pulsing, slow at first, then perfectly in sync with Maya's heartbeat.

Her breath caught. "Alex..."

"I see it."

Her reflection in the metal wall shimmered. Then split. One layer blinked behind the other, slightly out of phase. The back reflection lifted a hand while the front stayed still.

"Not again," she whispered.

Her vision flickered. The elevator walls wavered like heat haze. The reflections slid apart as if preparing to peel into two realities.

Alex knelt beside her and placed his hand over hers. "Stay with me. I've got you."

His stabilizing presence pushed across the Weave like a warm ripple. The distortions hesitated, then folded back. The reflections merged.

The light steadied.

Maya let out a shaky breath.

When the elevator reached the ground floor, the bell rang. The doors slid open.

Normal sounds filled the lobby, beeping pagers, rolling carts, conversation. But Maya could still sense the faint distortion beneath it all, like a cracked note in a song.

Alex pushed her toward the exit. The glass doors parted automatically, letting a wave of warm air wash over her.

And then it hit her.

Two pulses.

The first burned, hot, frantic, wild. The emotional signature tasted like flame and spiraling fear.

The second pulse slid into her senses like a low thrum, steady but shaken, overwhelmed with confusion and sharp pressure.

Maya stiffened. "Someone else... someone's scared."

Alex froze behind her. "What did you feel?"

She swallowed. "Two people. Far away. Both... waking up."

Alex said nothing, but his hands tightened on the wheelchair.

Cars rolled by outside, unaware that something had trembled just beneath their reality.

Maya felt it settling into her bones, the knowledge she wasn't alone, and that her world was no longer just hers.

"Let's get you home," Alex said softly. "Then we find who needs us."

She nodded, gripping the armrests as he pushed her into the sunlight. The pulses faded behind them, but not completely.

They were still there.

Waiting.

Calling.

And Maya knew:

Whatever had begun in Salem was no longer an isolated fracture.

It was spreading and she was part of it now.

5

First Backlash

Alex's apartment was quiet in a way that felt wrong. The walls didn't hum like the hospital. The air didn't shimmer with echoes. Nothing flickered in the corner of Maya's vision. But the silence didn't comfort her. It felt like the world was holding still so it wouldn't set her off.

Maya sat on the couch with her knees drawn up, a blanket wrapped around her shoulders. Her hands still trembled, though she tried to hide it. She'd been awake for less than a day and already felt like she was wearing someone else's body.

Alex paced the living room, restless energy running through him in tight, sharp lines. "You don't have to do this right now," he said. "We can wait."

Maya closed her eyes. "We can't wait forever."

He stopped pacing. The look on his face told her he hated agreeing with her.

She shifted, letting her feet rest on the floor. "I need to know if it still works."

Alex crouched in front of her. "Then I'm right here. If anything feels wrong, you stop."

She nodded, though wrong had become her default.

Maya drew a breath and reached inward, searching for the thin, bright threads she'd once been able to grasp without thinking. Her fingertips twitched.

For a moment, she felt it. A tremor. A familiar tilt in the world, like gravity hadn't quite committed to a direction. The air around her thickened, shimmering faintly.

Then pain stabbed behind her eyes. The shimmer snapped into a warped green tear three inches in front of her face, as if reality had cracked like thin ice. The apartment walls wavered. The coffee table rattled. A bowl edge skidded toward the floor. Maya pitched forward.

Alex lunged, catching her before she hit the carpet. Her vision darkened at the edges, and she felt something warm trail from her nose. Alex swore under his breath and pressed a sleeve to her face.

"Hey, hey, it's okay. I've got you."

She blinked until the room steadied. The tear in the air sealed itself with a faint hiss, leaving behind nothing but a faint smell of ozone.

Her voice shook. "I can't do it. Something's broken."

Alex rested a hand on the back of her head. "Then we don't do it. Not until you're ready."

But that wasn't the part that scared her.

Her power hadn't just failed. It had fought her. Twisted. Reacted like something unfamiliar had slipped into the spaces she once understood.

Maya leaned against him a moment longer, pressing her fingers to the bridge of her nose. The pain faded slowly, but the dread didn't.

It settled in her chest like a stone. She sat up straighter without realizing it. The air in the room shifted, subtle and sharp. Something tugged behind her ribs, faint at first, then stronger, like a plucked wire vibrating through her entire spine.

"Maya?" Alex asked.

She lifted a hand, breath trembling. "Wait."

A second tremor pulsed through her, not inside her, but somewhere far away. A flicker of heat. A rising pressure. A signature shaped like fire and fear wrapped tightly together.

Maya gasped and grabbed the couch cushion. "Someone's calling. Not like a voice. Not words." She pressed a hand to her chest. "Threads. They're pulling at me."

Alex moved to her side. "Tell me what you're feeling."

"It's a girl," she whispered. "She's burning."

The phantom heat licked up her spine, frantic and bright. Her senses flickered outward in a way she didn't fully control, and for a second she saw it: a distant point to the south, crackling like a flare thrown into the dark.

Her breath hitched. "She's terrified."

Alex's face tensed. "Is this the same pulse you felt at the hospital?"

"Yes." Maya swallowed. "Stronger."

The tremors didn't stop. They rippled through her hands, her shoulders, her breath. She curled forward, trying to hold herself still, but the shaking only grew.

Alex crouched in front of her again. "Maya, talk to me."

Her voice came out broken. "If I try this again, I might tear something open."

"Then don't," he said. "We'll walk if we have to. Drive. Crawl. I don't care how long it takes. But we're going."

She pressed the heel of her hand hard into her brow. "What if moving sets it off? What if I'm dangerous just by being awake?"

"You're not dangerous," he said. "The Weave breaking wasn't your fault."

"It feels like it was."

"No," he said firmly. "What you're feeling now, this connection, you didn't choose it. But you can choose what you do next."

The flare in her senses surged again. A scream without sound. Heat curling tight. Elara's fear rising like a wildfire catching wind.

Maya's breath caught. "She's getting worse."

Alex stood and offered his hand. "Then we move now. No blinking. No shortcuts."

Her fingers shook as she reached for him.

But she reached.

He pulled her gently to her feet. Her knees buckled from weakness, but he steadied her immediately, an arm wrapped around her waist until she found balance again.

For a long moment, she just leaned against him, waiting for the trembling to stop.

It didn't.

But the fear shifted, edged by something else. Resolve.

"Let's go," she whispered.

Alex grabbed his keys and her bag. "We'll find her."

Maya nodded, though the flare under her ribs pulsed hard enough to make her wince.

As they stepped into the hallway, Maya felt the world tilt again. Not breaking. Not collapsing.

Calling.

Someone out there was burning.

And Maya knew they were already running out of time.

6

Silent Protocol

The room was too cold for comfort and too dark for anything but bad news.

Senator Victor Hargreaves sat alone at the head of a narrow conference table, one hand wrapped around a mug of cooling coffee. The only light came from the wall of screens opposite him, their glow painting the room in shifting blues and whites. Washington's skyline glittered faintly beyond the tinted glass behind him, but he kept his back turned to it.

The city could sleep.

He did not.

On the central screen, a paused video frame showed a warehouse district in Salem, Massachusetts. Grainy security footage from a traffic camera. The surrounding buildings were dim. The warehouse itself was a washed out rectangle in the middle of the shot.

At the bottom of the frame, the timestamp blinked patiently.

Hargreaves tapped a key.

The video rolled.

First came the blackout. Streetlights popping off in a wave. The warehouse flaring with sudden internal light. A faint corona of distortion rippled outward, warping the edges of the image like heat off a desert highway.

He had watched this footage a dozen times, maybe more. It still made the back of his neck prickle.

"Advance to frame two thirty four," he said.

The system obeyed. The video jumped forward.

A man stumbled into view, carrying an unconscious woman in his arms. The camera's angle was too high to see their faces clearly, but Hargreaves knew their names.

Alex Caldwell.

Maya Rodriguez.

He watched the way Alex moved, shoulders hunched, protective. He watched the way the woman's arm dangled, fingers slack. Blood streaked her temple. Her head lolled when Alex shifted his grip.

They looked human. Fragile, even.

Then the image glitched.

A wash of static cut across the screen. For three frames, the woman in Alex's arms blurred, her outline smeared sideways as if she were being pulled in another direction. Her body vanished completely in the next frame, leaving Alex holding nothing at all.

In the frame after that, she was back, slightly out of alignment, the fabric of his jacket wrinkled differently under her weight.

As if the universe had changed its mind about where she belonged.

"Pause," Hargreaves said.

The frame froze on Alex's face, caught mid shout. The distortion still clung to the edges of Maya's body, a fine halo of interference.

"She phased," he murmured.

His voice sounded flat in the empty room. "Even for half a second, she phased."

The door behind him opened quietly.

"Sir?" a voice asked. "You wanted me."

Hargreaves did not turn right away. He took a sip of coffee that had gone lukewarm, then placed the mug carefully on the table.

"Come in," he said.

The HECATE tech director stepped into the room, closing the door with cautious care. He was mid forties, lean, with a receding hairline and deep shadows under his eyes. His name was Dr. Aaron Lyle, and he looked like he had not gone home in three days.

"Sit," Hargreaves said.

Lyle obeyed, folding himself into a chair halfway down the table. He glanced at the frozen frame on the screen and winced faintly.

"I keep hoping that will start making sense," he said.

"It will," Hargreaves said. "If we live long enough."

He tapped the keyboard again. The footage rolled past the glitch, through the chaos outside the warehouse, then faded out. Another file loaded automatically, labeled INTERNAL FEED 07.

"Same night," Hargreaves said. "Inside Salem Memorial Hospital."

The video was poorer quality. Grainy security footage from an ER corridor. Nurses rushed in and out of frame. Patients on gurneys rolled by. Then the double doors at the far end burst open.

Alex again, carrying the same woman, both of them smeared with dust and blood. He shouted for help. Staff ran to meet him.

For three seconds, the feed distorted. The woman's body flickered in and out, as if she existed in two locations at once and the camera could not decide which one to record. Then she stabilized.

Hargreaves paused the video and zoomed in on the last clear frame.

"There," he said. "You see it."

Lyle rubbed his eyes. "Yes, sir. The resonance distortion."

"Not resonance," Hargreaves said quietly. "Displacement."

He sat back, fingers steepled.

"When I was a young man," he said, "I watched an apartment building come down. Gas leak. Faulty sensor. Twenty seven dead. You know what the first responders looked like when they realized half those deaths could have been prevented?"

Lyle swallowed. "Sir?"

"They looked like this." Hargreaves gestured toward the frozen image of Alex and Maya. "Stunned. Angry. Helpless."

He let that hang in the air.

"We missed something in Salem," he said. "Something big. And now it is spreading."

The tech director cleared his throat. "We have new data on that, sir. That is why you called me in, I assume."

Hargreaves nodded once. "Show me."

Lyle pulled a tablet from his bag and tapped through several screens. The main display shifted away from Salem, replaced by a series of graphs and schematics.

"Starting with containment attempts," Lyle said. "I know you wanted an update on the Disruptor Pack field tests."

"I wanted results," Hargreaves said. "Did you get any?"

"Not the kind we were hoping for."

Lyle brought up an overhead image of a concrete test chamber. Several mannequins stood inside, each rigged with sensors. In the corner, a faint outline of a human figure flickered, first in one position, then another.

"We replicated the Walker signatures we recorded in Salem," Lyle said. "We used Ethan Moore's energy event as a baseline and overlaid Rodriguez's displacement harmonics."

"I know what a Walker is," Hargreaves said mildly. "Tell me why we still cannot stop one."

Lyle winced. "The Disruptor Packs overload, sir. They work for two, maybe three seconds, then burn out. The node locks destabilize harmonics briefly but do not hold them. And the field scramblers are... inconsistent at best."

"Inconsistent," Hargreaves repeated.

"They work on one kind of signature, then fail on the next," Lyle said. "If all Walkers expressed the same way, we could tune the tech. But they don't. Some bend fields. Some push heat. Some phase. We are fighting an entire spectrum with single frequency tools."

Hargreaves studied the jittering outline on the monitor. "What you are telling me is that if one of these people decided to walk into a federal building, we could not keep them out."

Lyle hesitated. "At present, sir... no. Not reliably."

Hargreaves felt that same cold weight settle in his chest. The memory of drifting smoke. The sound of distant sirens. The knowledge, learned early and hard, that failing to act when you had the chance cost lives you could never get back.

"Then we stop trying to play catch-up," he said. "And we stop thinking about this as a tactical problem."

Lyle frowned. "I am not sure I understand."

Hargreaves tapped a key. The central screen split into three sections. Left: Salem's blackout incident. Center: a thermal map of Miami. Right: a waveform graph labeled COLORADO ANOMALY 02.

"We already lost the hardware race," Hargreaves said. "These people evolve faster than our devices. So we stop focusing on the moment they act."

He pointed to the Miami image.

"And we start focusing on everything that happens before."

The Miami thermal map brightened as he zoomed in. A block of rooftops appeared, each outlined in pale orange. One building in the center flared white hot, then blazed into a sharp yellow core.

"This is the rooftop fire?" Hargreaves asked.

"Yes, sir," Lyle said. "Raw satellite thermal feed before the incident was reclassified and the public report edited."

The heat bloom pulsed in perfect increments, almost like a heartbeat.

"The pattern is wrong for a normal fire," Lyle continued. "The temperature jumps in discrete spikes, not a smooth curve. Whatever ignited up there did not spread like combustion. It flared. Like someone feeding a pulse into it."

"Walker probability?" Hargreaves asked.

"Seventy three percent," Lyle said. "Higher now that we have a Salem baseline."

On the right-hand screen, the Colorado anomaly played in a loop. A shallow seismic reading, localized and sharp, like something heavy had dropped onto the earth from a low height.

"Depth?" Hargreaves asked.

Lyle checked his notes. "Less than a kilometer. No tectonic movement. No fracking. No recorded explosion. Just the hit and the ring."

On the second screen, a classified memo header appeared.

SILENT PROTOCOL: Escalation Review Pending.

"That tag appeared in Salem," Hargreaves said. "It appears again now. Connected events."

Lyle nodded slowly. "Our internal classification system flagged them as harmonic anomalies of interest. That is all Silent Protocol has been so far. A label."

"Then we change what it means," Hargreaves said.

He stood, the motion deliberate, and leaned both hands on the table. The glow from the screens turned his lined face into a study in shadow and intent.

"Get me Carter," he said. "And Ops."

They arrived eight minutes later.

Dana Carter, operations director for HECATE, entered first. She wore a gray suit and the expression of someone who had rehearsed her objections on the way over. Behind her came a younger officer with a secure tablet tucked under his arm, his HECATE badge clipped neatly to his lapel.

"Senator," Carter said. "We were not expecting a full briefing tonight."

"You were not," Hargreaves agreed. "That was my mistake. I should have made this urgency clear days ago."

She went still at his tone.

He gestured toward the chairs. "Sit. Both of you."

They did. The junior officer carefully set the tablet on the table, screen still dark.

Hargreaves pointed back to the wall of displays.

"We have three events on the board," he said. "Salem. Miami. Colorado. Three Walker-level anomalies in a matter of days, maybe a week."

"Salem was bad," Carter said carefully. "But the narrative held. Power grid failure. Gas line issues. The public bought it. Miami was written up as faulty rooftop wiring. Colorado is tagged as a minor seismic burp. There was no visible Walker activity on the ground that civilians noticed."

Hargreaves smiled without humor. "You sound like a press release."

A faint flush touched her cheeks. "My point is, sir, we have managed perception so far. No mass panic. No widespread belief in any... supernatural explanation."

"And that is exactly why you need to understand what comes next," he said. "The public's calm is not proof of safety. It is proof they are blind."

He nodded to Lyle.

The tech director tapped his tablet. The memo header enlarged on the central screen: SILENT PROTOCOL.

"This classification tag was created after the Salem blackout," Hargreaves said. "Meant for internal tracking of events we could not fully explain but did not want on standard channels. Until now, it has been little more than a label."

He turned back to Carter.

"I am activating it."

She frowned. "Sir, Silent Protocol has no defined operational framework. It is just a flag. If you want a formal response, we should route through Homeland, or create a joint interagency—"

"No," Hargreaves said. "The more people touch this, the less control we have. Silent Protocol remains in HECATE. But its scope changes."

He took a breath, then laid it out.

"We stop chasing Walkers with toys that do not work. We stop trying to pin them down with visible force. That only teaches them how to avoid us. Instead, we watch. We interfere quietly where it hurts them most. We remove their advantages before they know they have them."

The junior officer shifted uneasily. Carter tilted her head.

"What does that look like, concretely?" she asked.

"It looks like this," Hargreaves said.

He nodded at the young officer. "Open the Silent Protocol framework. New directive."

The officer swallowed and began typing.

"Under Silent Protocol Level One," Hargreaves said, enunciating each word, "we identify all suspected Walkers and their immediate associates. We audit their digital footprints. Financial. Communications. Travel."

He lifted a hand, ticking the items off on his fingers.

"We place quiet flags on their IDs. We introduce friction into their lives. Small delays. Lost reservations. Flagged transactions. Credit freezes where we can justify them. Nothing overt. Nothing that pushes them into hiding on purpose."

Lyle frowned. "You want to harass them into making mistakes."

"I want them off balance," Hargreaves said. "If they are busy fixing their bank accounts and rental agreements, they are not jumping across cities without warning."

Carter stared at him. "That is... extrajudicial, sir."

"So is reality tearing open over Salem," he snapped.

Silence fell for a beat.

He eased his tone back down. "We are not arresting anyone. We are not freezing assets without legal cause. We are simply slowing them. Watching where they go. Who they call when their cards stop working. Who fronts money for them when their accounts glitch. Every response they have to our pressure reveals their network."

Carter exhaled slowly. "And you believe this will help us contain them long term."

"I believe brute force will fail," he said. "And I believe time is our ally as long as they do not know we are using it against them."

He paced once along the length of the table, the movement deliberate.

"Right now, they are improvising," he said. "Scared. Disorganized. They think the danger is whatever is chasing them through the sky and under the ground. They are not looking at us yet, not really. They see us as an annoyance. A nuisance."

He stopped and looked each of them in the eye.

"Let's keep it that way."

Carter folded her hands. "You realize if this ever surfaces, we will have little defense."

"If this ever surfaces," Hargreaves said, "it will be because we failed. And when that happens, the question won't be why we froze a bank account or flagged a plane ticket. It will be why we did not do more when we still had a chance."

He gestured back at the frozen image of Maya phasing in the ER corridor.

"That woman dropped off the grid the moment she left that hospital," he said. "Her scans make no medical sense. Her movements do not match known physics. And wherever she is, anomalies are starting to light up around her. Are you prepared to explain to the families of the next Salem that you did not want to inconvenience her?"

Carter's jaw tightened. The junior officer stared fixedly at the table.

Lyle spoke up quietly. "What about Miami, sir?"

Hargreaves shifted his gaze to the thermal map.

"The rooftop event," he said. "Yes. Let us talk about that."

The Miami footage expanded. The building glowed hot in the center of the cluster of rooftops, then dimmed, then flared again.

"Report," he said.

Lyle cleared his throat. "Cause listed as faulty rooftop wiring. But the first thermal spike predates any recorded electrical fault. Fire crews reported localized ignition that did not follow fuel patterns. Neighbors reported seeing what looked like a column of fire that vanished too quickly to blame on accelerants."

"Casualties?" Hargreaves asked.

"No deaths," Carter said. "One resident treated for smoke inhalation. Several displaced."

"Witness statements?"

"Confused," she said. "Some claimed they saw a girl running from the building. Red hair. No clear ID yet."

Hargreaves felt something coil in his chest. "And the pattern?"

Lyle swapped screens. The Salem and Miami data sets displayed side by side, overlaid with frequency graphs.

"The harmonic signatures are not identical," he said, "but the spikes line up in the same bands. Whatever happened on that rooftop responds to similar stresses as Salem's incident."

"Stress," Hargreaves repeated.

"We believe it is emotional," Lyle said. "Or at least influenced by the Walker's state of mind. Fear, anger, panic. The spikes are sharper when they are under duress."

"So we have a frightened, untrained asset wandering around Miami who can ignite rooftops when she has a bad night," Hargreaves said. "And a displacement-class Walker who can vanish out of hospital corridors. And something hitting the ground in Colorado hard enough to register underground."

He turned back to Carter.

"Do you still want to wait for a joint interagency task force?"

Her lips pressed into a thin line. "What do you need from us, sir?"

"Implementation," he said. "Silent Protocol Level One, effective immediately."

He nodded at the junior officer again.

"Pull all flagged Walker files," he said. "Known and suspected. I want travel, banking, employment, medical insurance, phone records, any system we can access without raising external oversight. We do not show cause. We show curiosity."

Names and data began scrolling down the secondary screens. Ethan Moore, listed deceased. Maya Rodriguez. Alex Caldwell. Several others flagged with partial data. Joe Biggs as a peripheral contact. A handful of unknowns tied to anomalous locations.

Hargreaves watched the list grow.

"We will not move against them," he said. "Not yet. No arrests. No raids. If any field agent gets overeager, they are done. Understood?"

Carter nodded once.

"We monitor," he said. "We inconvenience. We confuse. We give them the sense that the world is turning slightly against them, but not so much that they realize it is deliberate. When they shift routes, we track. When they change phones, we log. When they seek help, we find out who answers."

"And when do we escalate beyond Level One?" Carter asked.

"When we have a clear picture of their network," he said, "and when we know exactly how much damage each one can do if we misstep."

He shook his head slowly.

"These people are not simply weapons," he said. "They are fractures. Every time they act, reality bends a little more. Our job is to keep that bending from becoming a break."

The room was quiet again by the time Carter and the officer left. Only Lyle remained, hovering near the doorway with his tablet in hand.

"Sir," he said carefully, "do you really think this will hold them?"

"No," Hargreaves said. "Nothing will hold them forever."

He returned to his chair, lowering himself with more care than he liked to show. His knees ached. His back twinged in protest. Getting old, he thought, would have been easier in a world that stayed within expected parameters.

"But I think it will buy us time," he said. "And time is what we never had in Salem."

Lyle hesitated. "If I may ask... do you honestly believe they mean us harm?"

Hargreaves stared up at the frozen image of Maya in Alex's arms.

"I believe they will," he said. "Even if they do not intend to. Power without control always does."

He gestured toward the Miami thermal bloom.

"That girl on the rooftop did not mean to set that fire," he said. "But she did. Imagine what happens when there are a dozen of her across the country. A hundred. All frightened. All unstable."

He picked up his mug, realized the coffee had gone cold, and set it down again.

"People like to think the world will always be the same shape when they wake up tomorrow," he said. "My job is to make sure they are right."

He looked back at Lyle.

"Make sure Silent Protocol stays quiet," he said. "No leaks. No hints. If any of our targets realize we exist before we are ready, we lose the one advantage we have."

Lyle nodded. "Yes, sir."

He left.

Hargreaves waited until the door clicked shut behind him, then turned once more to the wall of screens. Miami's rooftop burned in looping silence. Colorado's waveform spiked and fell. Salem's corridor froze on Maya's blurred outline, caught between being and not being.

He reached for the controls and dimmed the room lights even further.

On another screen, almost as an afterthought, a fresh notification appeared.

UNREGISTERED DATA SCRAPE DETECTED. SOURCE: CHICAGO, IL.

QUERY: SILENT PROTOCOL / SALEM / HARMONIC ANOMALY.

A small indicator flashed red.

Hargreaves narrowed his eyes.

"Who are you," he murmured.

The system flagged the IP, traced it to a private investigator's office above a laundromat.

Name: Joseph Biggs.

Hargreaves tapped the Silent Protocol tag beside the listing.

"Add him," he said quietly.

The system complied.

Outside the glass, Washington's lights gleamed on.

Inside the dark briefing room, the net began to tighten, invisibly and without fanfare.

The Walkers had taken their first steps.

Now, finally, so had he.

7

The Warning

The hallway outside Alex's apartment was dim and narrow, lit by tired fluorescent bulbs that hummed just a little too loudly for Maya's raw senses. Her legs felt unsteady beneath her, and she leaned into Alex as they stepped out of the apartment. He kept one hand on her back and one steadying her arm, the way someone might guide a recovering patient down a ship's trembling deck.

"We'll take it slow," he murmured. "If you hear anything strange..."

"I always hear something strange now," Maya whispered.

The hallway wavered at the edges of her vision, like reality was breathing too softly. The faint harmonic pull in her chest, the one that felt like heat and panic, tugged again, pointing somewhere south. Not a direction so much as a gravitational pull on her nerves.

They needed to leave. The girl she kept sensing, the one burning at the edges of consciousness, didn't have much time.

They made it three steps before a voice cut through the quiet.

"Caldwell."

Alex froze. Maya's breath hitched.

At the far end of the hallway, a man stepped out from the stairwell landing, the door drifting shut behind him. He wasn't dressed like HECATE or law enforcement, jeans, jacket, messenger bag slung over one shoulder, but there was something in the way he stood, something deliberate and coiled, that made Alex shift in front of Maya without thinking.

"Who the hell are you?" Alex demanded.

The man raised his hands, palms open. "Name's Joe Biggs. Before you decide to punch me, let me get this out: I'm here to warn you."

Alex didn't relax. "You followed us."

"Yeah," Joe said. "For two days."

Maya blinked, confused. "How? Why?"

Joe exhaled. "Not the way you think. I started with the hospital. You gave your name when you brought her in, so I ran it. Your DD 214 isn't sealed. Neither's your VA file. That led me to your brother in Toledo."

Alex stiffened. "You called Michael?"

"Yeah," Joe said. "He told me you left Salem fast and weren't answering anyone. Said you'd been staying with some guy named Santiago. When he said that name, I felt it. Same signature I picked up the night she flickered out of reality in that ER hallway."

Maya's breath caught.

"So I staked out the apartment," Joe continued. "Figured you'd swing by for something you left behind. And when you did..." He motioned down the hallway. "...I followed. Quietly. Nothing fancy."

Maya's pulse quickened. Joe wasn't lying, she could feel truth the way other people felt heat. His resonance wavered around him, jagged and earnest.

Alex stepped farther between them. "You need to leave. Now."

Joe didn't move. "Look, I'm not your enemy. If I wanted to hand you over, I would've called someone before I knocked on your door."

"We didn't hear a knock," Alex said.

Joe nodded once. "Didn't get that far."

Maya tightened her grip on Alex's arm. "Why did you track us?"

Joe slipped his hand into his jacket pocket and pulled out a folded set of papers. "Because whatever happened in Salem didn't stay in Salem."

He held the papers out. Alex didn't take them. Maya did.

The first page was a news clipping. The headline read ROOFTOP FIRE IN MIAMI, NO CASUALTIES. The byline timestamp was less than forty-eight hours old.

Another page showed a blurry thermal still, rooftop white-hot at the center, surrounded by cooler shades. Someone had highlighted three thermal spikes in red pen.

"The original satellite images disappeared an hour after they went up," Joe said. "The local report got rewritten. And the thermal leak? Gone from every public channel."

Alex's eyes narrowed. "This isn't proof of anything."

Joe gave a humorless snort. "It's proof someone's cleaning up. Same way they cleaned up Salem. Same way they're about to clean up whatever you two do next."

Maya's chest tightened. She felt the heat-thread again, sharp, panicked, hot, pushing against her ribs like a fist from inside.

"That rooftop..." she whispered. "Something happened there."

Joe nodded slowly. "A girl ran from the scene. Red hair. Witnesses disagreed on everything except that she was terrified."

He didn't know her name. Maya didn't either. But they were both sensing the same thing.

Joe shifted his weight. "I don't have the whole picture. I'm not inside whatever machine is doing the cleanup. But I know the pattern of buried stories when I see it. You're not on a list yet. But they're building one. Quietly."

Alex drew a slow breath. "Who's 'they'?"

"I don't know their name," Joe said. "But they're federal, they're organized, and they don't want attention. Which means they're scared of you. Or the girl in Miami. Or both."

Maya looked down the hallway, as if expecting something to step around the corner. "They're watching," she said softly. Her voice shook. "They're already watching."

Joe's expression softened.

"You're not alone," he said.

Maya lifted her eyes. For a heartbeat, she felt warmth at the idea. Relief, even.

Joe's voice dropped.

"And that's the problem."

Silence filled the hallway, thick as smoke.

Joe continued. "Two spikes in days. Salem. Miami. And I felt both. You're linked whether you want to be or not. And whoever's tracking this... they'll find her first. Unless you get to her before they do."

Another pulse slammed into Maya's chest, bright, terrified, burning. She held the wall to stay upright.

Alex immediately steadied her. "Maya. What is it?"

"Her," Maya whispered. "She's scared. She's so scared."

Joe stepped back, giving them space. "Whatever you're feeling, she's putting out a signal even I can pick up. And whatever's chasing her? It won't stop to ask questions."

Alex helped Maya straighten. "Then we move. Now."

Joe nodded once. "I'll go my own way. Last thing you need is someone else slowing you down. But if anything changes..." He slipped a card to Alex. "That number gets to me. Eventually."

Alex glared. "If you bring anyone to us,"

"I won't," Joe said. "They don't need me to find you. They already started."

The hallway felt colder at that.

Joe turned and headed down the stairwell, footsteps fading fast. Alex watched him go, jaw set, shoulders tense.

Maya took a shaky breath, clutching the railing as the burning pulse struck again, harder this time, like a flare in the dark.

"We have to go," she whispered.

Alex nodded and gripped her shoulder. "We will."

Together, they followed the pull into the unknown, leaving the flickering hallway and the first warning behind them.

8

The Search Begins

The cold morning air hit Maya like a breath of clarity and threat rolled into one. She had barely stepped out of Alex's apartment building before her vision wavered again. The concrete walkway trembled at the edges, light bending in thin sheets like heat off summer asphalt. Alex tightened his grip on her arm, ready for her knees to buckle the way they had twice already.

"You with me?" he asked quietly.

"Trying," Maya whispered.

They moved slowly across the lot toward Alex's car, but Maya stopped halfway, her body going rigid. A flare ripped through her chest. Not pain, not pressure, something brighter and hotter than either. It felt like a spark catching in dry brush, a burst of emotion so intense it stole her breath.

She sucked in air and grabbed Alex's sleeve. "Wait."

He turned instantly. "What is it?"

Maya pressed a hand to her sternum as if she could trap the sensation, but it pulsed straight through her palm. Heat rolled up the inside of her ribs, frantic and sharp. Fear. Not her own.

"She's there," Maya whispered, her voice thin with shock. "The girl. The one I felt in the hospital. She's burning again."

Alex pulled her closer. "Where?"

Maya didn't point. Couldn't. This wasn't a direction on a map. It was a pull from beneath her ribs, a thread tugged toward a distant flare of panic.

"South," she breathed. "Far. But close enough to feel."

She closed her eyes and saw a smear of red and orange behind the lids, like a wildfire trapped in a glass sphere. It throbbed with the rhythm of a heartbeat.

Alex steadied her shoulders. "You said she was scared before. Is it worse?"

Maya nodded. "She's not just scared. She's coming apart."

Alex's voice hardened with resolve. "Then we find her."

Maya opened her eyes. "I don't know if I can blink again. Not after last night. Not after the elevator. It's like something's broken in me."

"Then we fix it together," Alex said. "If you jump, I jump. I'm not letting you do this alone."

Her vision blurred for a moment, but not from distortion. Emotion tightened her throat. She swallowed it back and let him guide her the last few steps to the car.

Inside the vehicle, the world felt too quiet. Maya's breath shuddered once, then steadied. The flare inside her chest rose again, urgent, frantic. She could feel the girl's panic spike in uneven bursts, like matches striking stone.

Alex rested one hand over hers, grounding the tremor in her fingers. "Tell me what you need."

Maya exhaled shakily. "I need to reach the Weave. Just enough to anchor us. But the fractures are still there. If I push too hard, it might tear something open again."

"Then don't push alone. I can help hold the line."

She met his eyes. There was no fear there, only determination. Whatever she had become, whatever she was breaking into, Alex wasn't running.

She nodded once. "Okay. Hold on."

She closed her eyes and reached inward. The Weave was thin and sharp today, like glass stretched too tight. Threads shivered under her touch, flickering in frantic pulses that matched the flare she felt from the south.

The air in the car thickened. Light bent slightly as the first edges of a corridor tried to form. A green shimmer cracked across the windshield like frost, splintering into a dozen unstable strands.

Her breath hitched. "Too fast."

Alex wrapped his hand around hers, firm and steady. "Focus on me. Use my resonance. Don't let it run away with you."

She centered herself on the feel of his presence. Solid. Grounded. Human. Not a force screaming for her to follow but a point to anchor to.

The corridor steadied, just enough to hold shape. A thin ribbon of Weave-light curled outward from the car door, like a crack opening into a different world.

Maya tried to guide it, but her pulse spiked and the corridor buckled. Light warped, shadows peeled back, and for a moment she saw the Residuum crouched along the edges like a whisper waiting to pounce.

"Stay with me," Alex said sharply. "Stay here."

She latched onto his voice. Onto the warmth in his palm. Onto the breath he steadied for her.

The corridor firmed again.

Her vision cleared enough to see a hotspot ahead of them, a flare so bright it felt like touching fire.

"That's her," Maya whispered. "That's where she is."

Alex squeezed her hand. "Then take us there."

She let the flare pull her forward. The corridor snapped wider, swallowing the edges of the car. Green and white light spiraled around them as they fell sideways through reality. Maya felt Alex's grip tighten, felt his resonance locking with hers, their harmonics slamming into alignment with a force that made her gasp.

The corridor flickered dangerously, trying to collapse, but Alex's grounding steadied it again.

"We've got this," he said.

The flare grew hotter and brighter, so close Maya could almost see the flames licking at the edges of her mind.

Then the corridor lurched violently and spat them out into blinding sunlight.

Maya stumbled, barely catching herself. Heat hit her first. The smell of smoke hit second. They stood on a rooftop, the early morning sky streaked with haze. Somewhere below them, someone was screaming.

Alex scanned the surroundings. "We're in Miami. That's the building from the report Joe showed us."

Maya's chest tightened. The flare was no longer distant. It was here. Close. Burning.

"She's inside," she said.

And this time, she wasn't only afraid for the girl.

She was afraid of what would happen if they were too late.

Inferno

Elara jolted awake with her shirt clinging to her skin, soaked through with sweat. For a moment she lay perfectly still, staring at the ceiling as her breath came too fast. The air in her bedroom felt thick and heavy, warm enough to fog the edges of her windows. She pushed the blankets off and felt heat rising from the mattress as if someone had left a space heater running under it.

Her lungs tightened. Not again.

She sat up slowly, pressing a trembling hand to her sternum the way her counselor had taught her. Four breaths in. Hold. Four breaths out.

It didn't help.

The warmth inside her chest spread, a slow bloom of heat that matched the panic curling through her nerves. She shut her eyes and tried again.

"One breath at a time," she whispered to herself.

Her heart only kicked harder. Every strong emotion she had felt in the last week had done this. Panic attacks, the doctor said. Stress. Hormones. Trauma. Pick an excuse. None of it explained why the room always got hotter when she was scared. None of it explained why the vents blew warm air even when the AC was set to sixty.

She swung her legs over the edge of the bed and stood on unsteady feet. "Cold water," she said, as if naming it would make it work.

The bathroom tiles felt warm under her toes. She twisted the faucet on and cupped her hands under the stream, but the water that hit her skin wasn't cold. It wasn't even cool. Within seconds it warmed to match her palms.

Elara jerked her hands away. "Stop it," she said, voice shaking. "Just stop."

The lights above the mirror flickered. She froze. One bulb popped with a sharp crack. Then another. Tiny shards clinked against the sink, glittering like sparks.

Her breath stuttered. The heat in her chest surged again, harder this time, like something inside her was trying to fight its way out.

"No, no, no," she whispered, backing into the hallway.

The air smelled wrong. The faintest bite of smoke curled into her nose, so thin she almost doubted it. Almost.

She turned toward her bedroom just as a thin line of flame licked out from beneath the door. It trailed across the carpet like liquid fire, catching in two places at once.

Her heart slammed against her ribs.

The flames surged as if they'd heard her fear and answered.

Elara stumbled back, coughing already. The smoke thickened. Heat rolled across the hallway in a wave that made her eyes water. She grabbed the doorknob, instinctively trying to shut out the fire, but the metal seared her palm and she cried out.

The floor vibrated under her feet. A burst of light exploded beneath the crack of the bedroom door.

She was trapped.

The flames didn't spread like normal fire. They moved in sharp, deliberate lines, racing along the walls in bright streaks that glowed like molten veins. Every place the flame touched seemed to ignite instantly, as if the apartment itself had been soaked in gasoline. Heat punched through the hallway, forcing Elara to stagger back.

Smoke rolled toward her in thick waves. It filled her lungs before she could turn her head, stinging her eyes, burning her throat. She coughed hard enough to double over, her palm scraping the wall as she tried to keep her balance.

"I need help," she rasped.

Her voice barely made a sound. The smoke swallowed it whole.

She stumbled toward the living room, each breath sharper than the last. The air felt alive, trembling, as if it were reacting to her panic. She reached the window and fumbled with the latch, coughing so violently she could hardly see straight.

Her fingers slipped twice before she managed to wrench it open. A blast of humid Miami air hit her face, but the smoke poured out faster than she could lean forward. She tried to scream, to shout down to the street, but the moment she pulled in a breath, her throat seized and she choked instead.

Her pulse hammered. The flames answered.

A sudden burst of fire shot up the wall behind her, flaring in rhythm with her heartbeat. Another pulse surged across the ceiling. The light bulbs exploded in rapid succession, showering the room with sparks that vanished before they hit the floor.

"What's happening to me," she whispered, though the words were barely sound at all.

Her skin felt fever-hot. Every inhale made her vision dim around the edges. The fire pulsed again, faster, brighter, as if it were feeding off the fear rising in her chest.

The floorboards groaned. The hallway behind her roared with flame. The apartment filled with smoke so thick it felt like drowning standing up.

Elara sank to her knees, one hand braced against the floor. Her vision flickered. The heat pressed in from every direction. She tried to drag herself toward the window, but her arm gave out and she collapsed sideways, coughing weakly.

The fire surged toward her.

Her heartbeat thudded once, twice, then faltered.

And just as her vision went black, something tore open in the center of the room. Light split the air like a crack ripping through glass, spilling green and white sparks across the smoke.

Elara didn't see what came through.

She only felt the sudden rush of cold air and the violent twist of reality as she slipped away.

The corridor spat Maya out like it was rejecting her.

She stumbled through the rift and into a wall of heat so fierce it felt like someone had pressed a burning iron against her face. The blink behind her wavered, the green shimmer cracking like a pane of stressed glass. The corridor wasn't collapsing in one piece. It was tearing at both ends, like something inside the fire was pulling against it. She tried to pull breath into her lungs, but smoke filled them first.

She doubled over, coughing hard.

The apartment was an inferno. Flames crawled up the walls in jagged lines, racing along the ceiling and bursting outward in sharp, rhythmic pulses. They didn't move like fire. They moved like something alive.

She lifted an arm to shield her face, the skin prickling instantly from the heat. Her eyes watered, but she pushed forward anyway, squinting through the swirling smoke.

A shape on the floor caught her attention.

Someone was curled on their side, half-hidden by rolling firelight.

"Elara," Maya choked out, though she didn't know how she knew the name. It just rose in her mind, tied to the burning harmonic she had felt for days.

She fought toward the girl, stumbling over a fallen lamp that melted under her touch. Her fingertips burned. Her vision swam. The blink behind her gave another violent crack, shrinking fast.

"Hold on," Maya rasped. "I'm here."

She reached out, but the moment her hand moved, the flames surged as if drawn to it. A burst of fire shot toward her, licking up her arm. She jerked back, gasping as the heat seared through her sleeve. Panic flared in her chest. The flames answered, brightening with a terrifying hunger.

"I can't do this," she whispered, voice breaking. The heat was too much. The air was too thin. The corridor was collapsing behind her, and she felt her resonance slipping, unraveling one desperate strand at a time.

She pressed her back to the wall, coughing until her vision blurred.

"Alex!" she shouted, voice cracking in the smoke. "Alex, I need you!"

The corridor behind her screamed in a high, electric whine. It bent inward, trying to close, sparks spraying across the burning apartment.

Maya reached for it with trembling hands, her knees threatening to give out.

"Alex!" she called again, throat tearing with the effort. "Please!"

The crack in the air widened for one last second.

Then Alex forced his way through, teeth gritted, shoulders pushing against the failing corridor as if he could hold reality open by sheer will alone.

The blink corridor nearly crushed him on the way through.

He stumbled into the burning apartment with a gasp, one hand braced against the collapsing shimmer behind him. Heat struck him like a physical force. Smoke clawed at his throat. He could barely see Maya through the rolling flames.

"Maya!" he called.

She was crouched on the floor, one arm up to guard her face, reaching for a girl curled in a tight ball near the center of the room. Fire snapped toward her like it recognized movement and wanted more of it.

Instinct took over.

Alex dropped to one knee, slammed both palms against the scorched floor, and pulled.

His shielding harmonic roared up his arms, a force like thick air suddenly solidifying around him. The barrier snapped outward in a rush, forming a shimmering sphere that wrapped around Maya, the girl, and himself.

The flames hit it instantly.

They bent backward like a hurricane wind slamming into a pane of glass, curling and thrashing against the curved shield. The fire didn't behave like normal flame. It struck in sharp pulses, each one aligned with the frantic thud of the red-haired girl's heartbeat.

Alex clenched his teeth. The shield flexed hard under the pressure.

"Got you," he growled, though it was unclear if he meant Maya, the girl, or himself.

Maya looked up at him, her eyes red from smoke. "She's burning from the inside. It's her panic."

Alex forced his focus into the shield, stabilizing its edges. It was like trying to hold a bubble underwater while a storm raged above it.

"Then we get her out now," he said. "Grab her. I'll hold the line."

Maya nodded, crawled to Elara's side, and hooked her arms under the girl's shoulders. Elara's skin radiated heat, her whole body trembling with fear so intense it vibrated through Maya's grip.

As Maya pulled, the fire harmonic erupted again.

A ring of flame burst outward from Elara's body. It slammed into the barrier so hard Alex gasped. His shield buckled inward, sparks shooting across its surface. Sweat broke over his brow. The apartment lights blew out, one after another, tiny explosions snapping in the dark.

"Alex," Maya yelled over the roar. "The corridor!"

He twisted, seeing the blink fracture dwindling behind them. It was seconds from sealing shut.

He pushed everything into the shield, extending one foot backward until it touched the trembling edge of the corridor. His harmonic flared, grounding both protections at once. Reality groaned like metal under strain.

"Move!" he shouted.

Maya dragged Elara toward him, her teeth clenched, her burned forearms shaking. The shield shrank around them as the fire grew more violent, hammering again and again.

Alex's legs trembled. His vision went blurry at the edges. He felt the corridor slipping.

"I can't keep this open much longer," he warned, voice raw.

"You're holding it," Maya said, breathless. "Just a little more."

Together they crossed the threshold, Alex maintaining the barrier in one hand and the collapsing blink with the other. The moment their feet hit the shimmer, the fire behind them surged in a final, furious wave.

The shield convulsed.

The corridor buckled.

Alex forced a roar from his lungs, shoving his harmonic outward in one last surge of strength.

The blink collapsed outward in a burst of heat and light, swallowing all three of them whole.

And the burning apartment vanished behind them.

The world slammed back into place.

Concrete under her hands. Hot air rushing across her face. A thin ocean breeze she did not expect. Maya collapsed to her knees on a rooftop across the street, the blink dropping her so hard her vision went white for a moment.

Beside her, Elara rolled onto her side and coughed, each spasm violent and tearing. Smoke poured out of her mouth. Her whole body shook as if she were freezing, though the heat still radiated off her skin in waves.

Alex fell to one knee, one hand gripping the roof gravel to steady himself. His other hand went immediately to Elara's throat.

"Her pulse is racing," he said, breath rough. "But she's alive."

Elara flinched at his touch, but she was too weak to pull away. She stared up at the sky with reddened eyes, panting like someone who had sprinted through fire for miles.

Behind them, a deep boom shook the air.

Maya turned.

Elara's apartment erupted.

Flames shot out the living room windows like a dragon exhaling. Glass burst and rained down onto the street. Smoke belched upward in a thick black column. Sirens wailed from every direction. Fire engines swerved into the intersection below, lights painting the surrounding brick buildings in frantic red and blue.

Maya's heart hammered. People would be watching. Cameras too. They had only minutes before someone looked up and saw three figures who had no business being on this roof.

"Maya," Alex said sharply.

She looked back.

Elara was staring at her.

Not at the fire. Not at the smoke. At Maya.

Terrified. Disbelieving. Lost.

Her lips trembled as she struggled to speak. "What... what's happening to me?"

Her voice cracked on the last word. Tears cut clean lines down soot-streaked cheeks.

Maya crawled closer, ignoring the way her hands shook or the way the rooftop kept tilting at the edges of her vision. She reached out, stopping just short of touching Elara's shoulder.

She didn't want to overwhelm her.

She didn't want to lie to her either.

"You're not alone anymore," Maya whispered.

Elara blinked, and a fresh sob tore loose, small and raw.

Alex shifted closer, his presence steady as always. "We need to move. Sirens are on top of us."

Maya nodded, but she kept her gaze on Elara for one more heartbeat. The fire inside the girl had quieted, but it hadn't left. It pulsed beneath her skin like a caged sun.

Maya knew that feeling too well.

She squeezed Elara's hand gently. "We're going to help you. I promise."

Below, car horns blared. Voices shouted. A helicopter thumped in the distance.

The world was already closing in.

Maya steeled herself, rose shakily to her feet, and helped Elara stand.

The first rescue was over.

But everything after this was about to get much harder.

10

Three in Flight

Sirens were already rising from the streets below, a frantic mix of wails and overlapping echoes that climbed the walls of the buildings around them. The beat of helicopter blades swept across the sky, cutting through the early morning haze in heavy rhythmic thumps. Maya tried to breathe, but the air on the rooftop still tasted like smoke and adrenaline.

Alex steadied Elara against the low ledge while Maya forced herself upright. Her legs quivered beneath her, part exhaustion, part the fading shock of the flames she had pulled herself out of moments ago. Her own resonance felt unstable, stretched thin and jittering like a frayed wire.

She closed her eyes and reached inward, searching for the green shimmer that usually rose to meet her. Instead she found a fractured hum, sharp and uneven. Her pulse stuttered. The Weave resisted her touch, as if scorched from the inside out by the fire harmonic they had just escaped.

Alex stepped in close and gripped her shoulders. Warm, grounding pressure flowed from his hands into her arms. His presence steadied her fractured resonance, pulling her back from the edge of collapse.

"I've got you," he said quietly. "You're alright. Just breathe."

Behind them, Elara coughed again, the sound raw and thin. She was shaking so hard her shoes scraped on the gravel. The heat still radiating from her skin made the air ripple faintly. She stared at her own trembling hands as if terrified they might ignite the moment she blinked.

"I don't want to burn anything else," she choked.

"You're not going to," Maya said, though she did not trust her voice to stay steady.

The sirens grew louder. A helicopter banked toward their block, its view searching the rooftops. Maya felt a strange pressure then, not on her skin but in the Weave itself, as if something unseen was turning its attention toward them. It was the same cold weight she had felt outside Salem Memorial, the sense of being observed by something that did not stand in any physical place.

"Someone is looking for us," Maya whispered.

Alex's grip tightened. "Then we need to move now."

Maya nodded and reached again for the Weave. Her hands trembled, but she pulled anyway, dragging the first threads into a corridor shape. The air shimmered, reluctant and uneven. The forming blink buckled, shuddering like a sheet ripping down the middle. Light cracked along the edges, green and white trying to hold together against the strain.

"Come on," she whispered, as much to herself as to the corridor. "Please hold."

The rift widened, thin and unstable, bending at both sides as if the fire harmonic still clung to her. She felt Alex pull Elara close behind her, steady and ready to shove all three of them through before anyone on the ground could look up.

The blink flexed, warped, and finally peeled open.

It held.

Just barely.

"Go," Maya said.

And they stepped into the trembling light.

The moment the corridor opened, Alex felt the rooftop shudder beneath them. Sirens wailed below, echoing between the buildings, and the distant thump of rotor blades rattled the metal ducts nearby. There was no time to wait.

"Go," he said, pushing Maya forward.

She staggered into the shimmering tear in the air, still pale from the fire. Elara followed, barely on her feet, coughing hard. Smoke smeared the air behind them as Alex shoved both women fully into the blink and then stepped in after them before the rooftop filled with eyes and sirens.

Inside the corridor, the world narrowed to a trembling tunnel of light. At once, Alex felt the pressure shift.

Three harmonics collided in the same tight space.

Maya's signature rippled along the walls in fractured green-white light. Her resonance had been unstable before the fire rescue, but now it flickered like shards rotating inside a broken prism.

Elara's pulse lit the air in red-orange bursts. Every flare matched the girl's heartbeat, sharp and hot, like sparks jumping across oil. Her panic spiked again as she looked around the corridor, and the red pulses surged violently.

Alex felt his own harmonic rise in response, a deep blue pressure spreading from his chest and down his arms. It pushed outward, trying to anchor the space, trying to keep the corridor from collapsing.

The walls bent inward anyway.

The corridor shivered like soft metal being squeezed from both ends. Light warped. Shadows thinned. Alex braced one hand on the nearest wall, feeling it ripple like liquid under his palm.

"Maya," he warned, "you have to steady your side or this is going to fold in on us."

She tried, he could see that, but her entire resonance was fractured and vibrating out of sync. Every time she pulled the threads together, Elara's panic burst again and sent a shockwave through the tunnel.

"I'm trying," Maya said, voice thin. "She's burning again."

Elara flinched at the sound, then pressed her hands to her skull as another pulse ripped through her. Red-orange sparks shot from her fingertips and scattered like embers against the corridor walls. The blink shuddered violently in response.

Alex felt the shift instantly.

Traveling with one Walker was hard. Traveling with two unstable ones was almost impossible. The corridor responded to all three harmonics at once, and none of them matched. They were pulling in different directions, vibrating at different frequencies, clashing in ways he had never experienced.

"Elara, look at me," he snapped.

She tried, tears streaking through soot on her cheeks.

"You're not on fire right now," he said. "You're safe. Just breathe. Don't push your resonance."

"I'm not trying," she choked. "It's just doing it."

Another pulse. The corridor flared bright red, then lurched sideways, nearly throwing all three of them off balance. Alex grabbed both women and pulled them close, forcing his own harmonic outward in a tight, grounding ring around them.

The corridor trembled. Cracks of white light forked through the green shimmer above them like lightning trapped inside glass.

Alex gritted his teeth.

Traveling with multiple Walkers was more than dangerous. It was exponential. Every extra signature multiplied the instability tenfold. If they lost control here, the corridor would not spit them out somewhere safe.

It would tear them apart.

"Hold on," Alex said through clenched teeth. "The walls are going."

Light fractured. The corridor rippled in a violent shudder.

And then the cracks spread.

The world around Elara was a tunnel of shifting light, rippling like heat on pavement. She had no idea how she had gotten inside it. One moment she was choking on smoke, the next she was falling sideways into a place that felt alive and wrong at the same time.

Her breath hitched. Her palms burned. Her heartbeat thudded painfully under her ribs, sending bursts of heat racing down her arms.

Then she saw Maya.

The girl stood only a few feet away, bracing herself against the trembling wall of light. Elara blinked, once, twice, trying to clear the tears from her eyes. But the glow around Maya didn't fade. It clung to her like threads of green and white fireflies swirling around her skin. It wasn't fire, not like the flames that had chased Elara across her apartment. It was calmer, almost musical, pulsing in soft irregular waves.

Elara stared, stunned. "You're glowing."

Maya didn't answer at first. Her jaw was clenched tight, hands trembling as she fought to steady the collapsing corridor. Shards of pale light broke off the walls and spiraled toward her like sparks drawn to a magnet.

Elara turned toward Alex next.

He glowed too.

His outline shimmered in deep blue, steady and rhythmic, like a heartbeat projected into the air. His presence softened the tremors in the corridor whenever he moved closer, as if his very existence pushed the chaos into order.

Elara's throat closed. Tears blurred her vision again. "You're like me."

Maya finally looked at her. The green-white sparks dimmed and steadied. "No," she said softly. "You're like us."

Something inside Elara cracked. Not the frightening heat that had threatened to rip her apart, but something smaller, something that had been knotted tight for days. The certainty that she was broken, dangerous, wrong.

Maybe she wasn't.

Maybe she wasn't alone.

Her breath shook. "I thought I was dying."

"I know," Maya whispered. "I thought I was too."

Alex shifted closer, grounding both of them with a firm hand on Elara's shoulder. The blue glow around him pulsed once, and Elara felt the pressure inside her chest loosen just enough to breathe again.

But the corridor didn't care about any of that.

A crack of white light ripped through the air above them. The walls convulsed, bending inward in a violent shudder. The ground under their feet tilted as if the floor had dropped an inch all at once.

Maya's eyes snapped toward the distortion. "I have to pick a landing point."

Elara grabbed her arm, terrified. "I don't know how to stop it."

"You don't have to," Maya said. "Just stay with us."

The corridor buckled again, forcing Maya to choose before it tore itself apart.

The corridor was coming apart behind them.

Maya felt it in the way the air thinned, in the way the light flickered like a dying filament, in the way the harmonics around her strained against one another. Elara's fire pulse was spiking again, sharp and frantic. Alex's grounding pressure fought to hold it down. Maya's own fractured shimmer trembled like cracked glass.

Another tremor rippled through the corridor. The walls bent inward, warping shapes and shadows.

"We're losing it," Maya gasped.

Alex tightened his grip on both her and Elara. "Pick a landing point. Anywhere."

The corridor buckled again, snapping a hairline crack down its center. Maya didn't think. She reached for the first stable anchor she could find, the closest place that wasn't burning or under surveillance. A flicker of Miami outskirts brushed her senses.

A cheap roadside motel. Two floors. Peeling yellow paint. Wide parking lot.

Not safe. But safer than here.

She pushed toward it, forcing the Weave to catch the anchor before the corridor tore completely.

The world twisted.

Then it spat them out.

Maya hit asphalt so hard her bones rattled. Air punched from her lungs. Her vision exploded in white spots, then fractured into strobing after-images of the motel sign above her. The sickly neon tube flickered with each blink, doubling and tripling like the world couldn't decide what shape it was supposed to be.

Beside her, Alex landed on his side and rolled, dragging Elara with him so she didn't crack her head on the pavement. He took the hit on his shoulder with a grunt and pulled the girl into his arms, shielding her from the ground.

Elara groaned weakly. Her skin was still too hot. Her pulse skittered like a frightened animal.

Maya tried to sit up, but her arms shook under her weight. She felt hollow, drained, like half her resonance had been scraped raw by the collapsing corridor.

Alex crawled to her the moment he knew Elara was still breathing. "Maya. Hey. Stay with me."

She forced her gaze to focus. Alex's outline flickered once in her vision, then steadied.

"I'm fine," she whispered, even though she wasn't. The parking lot tilted under her. The motel sign buzzed overhead, too bright, too loud.

Alex touched her cheek, checking her pupils. "You're barely conscious. Just breathe."

She did. Slowly. Carefully. Elara coughed beside them, each breath thin and wheezing.

"We made it," Maya managed. "That's what matters."

Alex nodded, but his jaw was tight. "Barely."

Maya closed her eyes for a heartbeat.

And felt something.

A faint pulse. Far away but sharp enough to cut through the ringing in her skull. Not Elara. Not Alex. Not the fire they'd escaped.

Someone else.

Someone searching.

Maya's eyes opened fast. "Alex."

"What is it?"

"We're not alone out here." She swallowed hard. "Someone's looking for us."

The neon light above them buzzed again, flickering in and out.

And somewhere in the Weave, a distant harmonic shifted in their direction.

Fifteen minutes later, the motel room smelled like bleach, old carpet, and a hint of mildew. It was the kind of place people passed by without a second glance, which was exactly what Alex needed right now.

He dragged both women inside, one arm around each of them. Maya was half-conscious, her legs barely cooperating. Elara trembled under his grip, heat rolling off her skin in waves that made his palms sting. He nudged the door shut with his foot and locked it, then shot the latch across for good measure.

"Easy," he said, guiding Elara to the nearest bed.

She hesitated at the edge of the mattress, staring at it like it might burst into flames if she even breathed wrong. Her eyes were wide and red-rimmed. Smoke still clung to her hair.

"I can't touch anything," she whispered. "I'll burn it."

"No, you won't," Alex said, though he was not completely certain. "Just sit. Slow breaths."

She perched on the edge of the bed, pulling her knees tight to her chest and curling her arms around them. The springs creaked under her small weight. The heat radiating from her skin began to soften, fading from scorching to simply warm.

He turned to Maya.

She had slid down the wall and now sat on the floor with her back against the chipped plaster, legs stretched in front of her. Her breaths were sharp and uneven. The blinking after-images were still fading from her eyes. She looked like she could fall unconscious any second.

Alex crouched beside her. "Talk to me."

She swallowed hard. "The Weave followed us."

His stomach tightened. "Followed us how?"

"I don't know," she whispered. "It felt like something stepped into my wake. A ripple. Not HECATE. Not Elara. Not you. Something new."

Alex's jaw tightened. "Could it track you?"

"I don't think so. But it noticed us. And that's bad enough."

He scrubbed a hand across his face. They needed rest, time to think, time to regroup. Instead the world was tilting faster with every hour.

Maya leaned her head back against the wall and closed her eyes. "If we stay here long, someone will feel the distortion again."

"We just need time to breathe," Alex said. "Ten minutes. Maybe fifteen."

Elara curled tighter on the bed, watching both of them with fear and something else. Wonder. Confusion. Hope and dread tangled together.

"You two," she whispered softly. "You glow."
Her voice cracked on the last word.

Maya managed a tired smile without opening her eyes. "You do too."

Elara's breath hitched. For a moment she looked like a girl who had been pulled from the center of a nightmare and was not yet convinced she had woken up.

Alex rose and checked the windows, pulling the curtains tight. No sirens close. No voices outside. Just the hum of an air conditioner that could barely fight the Florida heat.

He turned back toward the room.

That was when he felt it.

A tremor in the air. Soft, but unmistakable. A harmonic unlike the three already tangled in the room. Not fire. Not shielding. Not Maya's fractured shimmer.

Something deeper. Older.

Maya's eyes snapped open at the same moment. "You felt it too."

Elara sat up straighter, alarm flickering in her gaze. "What was that?"

Alex exhaled slowly, the weight of the moment settling over him.

"Someone else," he said. "Another Walker just woke up."

And somewhere out there, the world shifted again.

11

Joe Arrives

Morning light leaked through the thin motel curtains, painting the cracked walls in pale strips. The room was quiet except for the soft wheeze of the ancient air conditioner and Elara's uneven breaths. She sat curled at the foot of the closest bed, her knees to her chest, hands buried in the blanket as if afraid they might heat up again.

Maya was dead asleep. Not resting, not dozing. Out cold. Her legs were still half-tangled in the motel's thin sheet from when Alex had lowered her there a few hours earlier. Harmonic exhaustion had wiped her out completely, and even in sleep her resonance flickered faintly under her skin.

Alex stood near the window, watching the parking lot through a small gap in the curtains. Cars moved in and out of the lot. Strangers came and went. No police. No fire crews. Nothing that screamed HECATE.

For once, a few minutes of stillness.

Then he heard it.

Footsteps on the concrete walkway.

Not heavy. Not sprinting. Slow and deliberate.

Elara's head snapped up. Her fingers tightened in the blanket.

Alex held up a hand for silence.

The steps stopped right outside their door.

A calm, quiet knock followed.

Not a cop's knock.

Not hotel staff.

Not a panicked stranger.

Wrong rhythm. Wrong confidence.

Alex moved instantly, placing himself between the door and both girls. His harmonic rose without asking, humming under his skin. He didn't unleash it yet, but he was seconds away from a full shield if the door burst open.

He leaned toward the peephole.

A man stood outside. Alone. Hands visible. Shoulders tense.

Joe Biggs.

Alex whispered under his breath, stunned. "How did you find us?"

As if hearing the unspoken question, Joe didn't knock again. He spoke softly through the door, voice low enough that only Alex could hear.

"You left a wake in whatever that was last night," Joe said. "And they're already tracing it."

Alex's jaw tightened.

They weren't safe.

Not even close.

He unlatched the door and opened it just wide enough for Joe to slip inside.

Voices pulled her toward consciousness.

Muted at first, then sharpening as her mind fought its way through a haze of exhaustion. Maya blinked hard. Her limbs felt heavy, her pulse slow and thick. Her body had not recovered from the corridor collapse. Every part of her hummed with raw fatigue.

She pushed up on her elbows.

Alex was near the door, posture guarded. Elara sat stiff on the corner of the bed, blanket draped around her shoulders, eyes wide and alert.

And standing just inside the doorframe was Joe Biggs.

Maya's breath caught. For a heartbeat fear stabbed through her. HECATE found them. They traced the corridor. They sent someone.

She forced herself upright, ready to blink even though she knew she couldn't manage a stable one.

Alex turned toward her. "It's alright. He's alone."

Joe raised both hands slowly in a show of peace. "I'm not here to hurt anyone. I'm trying to keep you three alive."

Maya didn't relax.

Joe stepped forward only when Alex nodded. He set a battered messenger bag on the stained carpet and crouched beside it, moving with deliberate, careful motions. He opened the bag and began pulling out papers.

Not weapons, not restraints, files.

Stacks of them. Hard copies, redacted PDFs, printed memos, even a few satellite images. He spread them across the floor between Maya and Alex.

"I've been trying to follow these events for weeks," Joe said quietly. "I kept seeing patterns. Reports wiped clean within hours. Fire scenes sanitized. Camera feeds erased. And the same team shows up every time."

Maya's stomach twisted. "HECATE."

"Yeah," Joe said. "Them."

He pushed a clipped packet toward her.

Thermal anomalies across the country.

Florida.

California.

Tennessee.

Another sheet showed the official incident report for the Miami apartment fire. It had already been rewritten. Electrical fault. Overheated wiring. No mention of a girl screaming for help. No mention of flames that moved like living veins.

Elara flinched at that one.

Joe kept going.

He pulled up an internal memo, its header partially blacked out. The remaining text read:

"Emergent Resonant Individuals. Classification under review."

Maya swallowed hard. Resonant. They didn't know the word Walker. Not yet. But they were hunting for something close.

Joe opened one more file. This one was thinner, the pages wrinkled like he had handled them often.

"This is their early list," he said. "Pulled from internal scans, incident reports, and whatever their sensors are picking up."

Maya scanned the first page.

"Walker Manifestation Candidates — Priority Review"

Her name was near the top.

Maya Rodriguez

Flagged: Unconfirmed Salem Anomaly

Status: Active Observation

Below that:

Elara Whitcombe

Flagged: Thermal Spike 0019

Status: High Interest

Elara's breath caught. "They know my name?"

"They will soon," Joe said. "The fire you walked away from was impossible to miss."

Joe sat on the edge of the motel's battered desk chair, elbows on his knees, eyes fixed on the worn carpet as if the threads might rearrange themselves into answers. He hated talking about this part, but he owed them honesty. They deserved to know why he was here, why he had followed them across two states, why he had walked straight into whatever this was.

He lifted his head slowly.

"There's one more file you need to see."

Maya tensed on instinct. Alex shifted slightly, enough to block Joe's line of sight to the girls. Elara clutched her arms tighter around herself, heat still rising off her skin in faint waves.

Joe opened his messenger bag and pulled out a thin, redacted document. It looked old only because it had been printed ten times too many, passed between hands that didn't want to leave a digital record.

He placed it on the bed near Maya, then sat back.

"I didn't understand what I was looking at until a few weeks ago," he said quietly. "Not after Salem. Not even after Miami. But when everything started lighting up at once, I went back through the older anomalies HECATE tagged."

Maya frowned. "Older? I thought nothing happened before Ethan."

"Nothing public," Joe said. "Nothing explosive. But after the fracture, HECATE retroactively flagged a handful of incidents. Events they couldn't explain before, but suddenly matched the same kind of… whatever this is."

Elara swallowed. "Like mine."

Joe nodded once, then tapped the file.

"This one is the worst. Richard Barrett. Age fifty-four. Colorado."

Alex narrowed his eyes. "What kind of anomaly?"

Joe met his gaze, and his voice dropped into the tone he used when delivering bad news with no soft way to say it.

"He changes things."

No one responded, so he continued.

"HECATE calls it material-state fluctuation. The report from the first incident says rock turned to slurry. Metal lost cohesion. Wood flash-dried. Then everything solidified again like nothing happened. They thought it was seismic at first, but sensors kept failing when he was nearby. Ground-penetrating radar. Thermal imaging. Even structural load scans. Everything shorted or spit out void data."

Maya's eyes widened. "That's not a normal Walker signature."

"No," Joe agreed. "That's why they classified him differently from the rest of you. Everyone else gets a hazard class between one and three. Barrett is the only one tagged Level Five."

Elara whispered, "Level five what?"

Joe hesitated. "Hazard. They think he's volatile enough to collapse a building without meaning to. And according to this, the more distressed he gets, the worse it becomes. Like the resonance amplifies through him."

Maya's breath hitched. "He awakened after the fracture?"

"Yeah. First week of April. A mine collapse in the foothills. He was the only survivor. The details get fuzzy after that. HECATE scrubbed local records, pulled emergency reports offline, and sealed witness statements. Two of those witnesses... vanished. No transfer orders, no forwarding address, nothing."

"HECATE erased them," Alex said, voice flat.

Joe nodded.

He leaned forward, elbows braced on his knees again.

"I don't know what Barrett can do. I don't know what any of this really is. But I know the pattern. They move faster when they think they're losing control of a subject. And his file scares them more than yours."

He tapped Barrett's name again. This time his hand shook, only for a moment, but enough for Maya to notice.

"Look," Joe said quietly. "You need to understand something. If HECATE finds Barrett before you do, he won't survive it."

His eyes flicked to Elara.

"And neither will anyone near him."

The motel room fell silent.

Elara flinched the moment Joe stepped closer to the bed. Heat rippled over her skin in a soft wave, barely visible but enough for Alex to move instantly. His hand rose, instinctive and protective, a discreet shield forming around Elara before she could flare again.

Joe froze in place.

"Easy," he said softly. "I'm not here to hurt anyone."

Elara's eyes were wide and frightened. The heat under her skin pulsed again, but Alex's grounding harmonic steadied her before it could spike.

Joe swallowed and lifted both hands a little higher, fingers spread in a gesture that was more surrender than caution. "I don't want to fight you. I want to help you stay off their list."

Maya watched him carefully. Not with her eyes. With the fractured shimmer that rose behind them, the same sense that let her feel fear and truth in the same breath. Joe's resonance was jagged and tense, but it carried no intent to harm. Only worry. Frustration. And something deeper that felt like fear for them instead of himself.

He was telling the truth.

Maya let the tension ease from her shoulders. "He's not lying."

Alex held his shield in place one more beat, then lowered his hand. Elara exhaled shakily and pulled her knees closer, watching Joe through smoke-reddened eyes.

Silence settled in the room, thin and fragile.

Elara was the one who finally broke it.

"Are there more," she whispered, "like us?"

Joe hesitated. Not long. Just enough for the truth to hurt.

"Yeah," he said quietly. "There are more."

Elara's breath caught.

Maya leaned forward slightly. "How many?"

Joe reached for his bag again, slower this time so Elara would not panic. He pulled out a folded packet of papers, a rough stack of printed maps and marked-up notes. He laid them on the motel bedspread between them and flattened the top sheet with his palm.

"Six signatures," he said. "That we can confirm. Spread across the U.S. All within the last three weeks. All suppressed in public records within hours of happening. Only one of them is you two. And only one of them is flagged Level Five."

Richard Barrett.

Maya felt her chest tighten, but Joe wasn't done.

"There's another one," he said. "Detected this morning. Pacific Northwest. Strong pulse. Very strong. The kind that makes sensors glitch and comms drop out."

Maya's blood went cold.

She had felt that pulse in the parking lot. It had rippled through her bones like a warning. Not close enough to threaten them, but close enough to notice.

She nodded once. "I felt it."

Alex stared at her. "When?"

"Right after we landed. It was brief. A vibration inside the Weave. Not fire. Not shielding." She looked at Joe. "Not me."

Joe grimaced. "Yeah. That matches what I've got."

He spread out the papers fully now, creating a rough map of the United States across the motel blanket. Red ink circled several locations. Miami. Salem. Tennessee. Colorado. A new circle near Oregon.

Finally, he tapped the largest circle. The most heavily marked. The one labeled only with a timestamp and the initials R.B.

"Barrett's last known position," Joe said.

Maya leaned closer as if the ink itself pulled at her.

Joe's voice lowered.

"If you want answers, we start with him."

The room fell silent again, but this time it was not fear.

It was the beginning of a choice.

A dangerous one.

And the first hint of an alliance none of them fully trusted yet.

1 2

Fractures

Maya woke with a sharp jerk, her breath catching as the world snapped back into place. For a moment she did not know where she was. The cracked ceiling above her wavered, the air conditioner hummed, and the thin motel air smelled faintly of bleach and damp carpet.

Then the resonance hit.

A thin pulse rippled through her body, faint but unmistakable, like a storm rolling somewhere far across the horizon. Barrett. She did not know how she knew it was him, only that something in her recognized the signature.

She pushed upright, wincing as her ribs protested. The motel room swam into focus. Alex sat on the far bed tying his boots. Elara sat against the opposite wall, knees pulled up to her chest, her arms wrapped around them so tightly her knuckles had gone white. She stared at the floor, refusing to look anywhere else.

Maya cleared her throat gently. "Morning."

Elara did not answer.

Maya tried again. "How are you feeling? Any heat spikes?"

Elara lifted her head just enough for Maya to see the fear in her eyes. "You don't know what's happening to me."

"I'm trying to help," Maya said softly.

"You can't," Elara snapped. "Every time I breathe wrong something burns."

The heat in Elara's body flared in a faint shimmer. Maya felt it, a hot pulse brushing against her senses. She swallowed hard, choosing her words with care.

"I went through something like that. Not the same, but close. If I can teach you how to anchor the surge, it might..."

Elara cut her off. "You say that like you understand everything. Like you're in charge."

Maya stiffened. "I'm not trying to lead you. I just know a little more about the Weave."

Elara barked a short, humorless laugh. "There you go again. You think that makes you better than me."

Alex stood quickly, stepping between them before the tension could snap. "Alright. That's enough. Everyone's tired. Everyone's scared. No one here is trying to hurt anyone."

Elara looked away again, shoulders trembling. Maya felt a cold knot twist in her chest.

Elara did not trust her. And Maya had no idea how to fix that.

A soft knock came at the door. Joe's voice followed.

"Got food. And some things you need to see."

Alex exhaled through his nose. "Great. Just what we needed."

The moment broke, but nothing inside it was repaired.

Alex held the door for Joe and watched him set two grocery bags on the desk. Maya was trying to breathe evenly, but her eyes still had that overbright shimmer that meant her resonance was unstable. Elara sat rigid on the bed, heat rolling off her in thin waves.

Both girls were pulling on him again.

Maya needed grounding to stabilize her fractured harmonic. Elara needed grounding to keep from igniting the room.

Alex had become the bridge between two storms, and the strain burned through him like a low electric current.

He rubbed a hand across his face. "I'm gonna grab a minute."

He stepped into the bathroom and shut the door. The sudden quiet hit him harder than he expected. He braced his hands on the sink and stared at himself in the mirror.

His reflection stared back with dark circles under the eyes and a tension in the jaw that had not been there a few days ago.

He turned on the faucet and splashed cold water on his face. His hands were shaking. He closed them into fists until the tremor eased.

"I can't do this alone," he whispered.

But he knew he would try anyway, because the alternative was letting both women fall apart. And that was not an option.

A knock sounded at the bathroom door. Joe's voice came through low and steady.

"Alex. You need to see this."

Alex dried his face, straightened, and stepped back into the pressure he could not escape.

Joe spread the documents across the motel bed with slow, precise motions. There was no point softening the truth. Not anymore.

"This is HECATE's new directive," he said, laying a printed memo flat. "Silent Protocol Level One. Active monitoring."

Maya leaned forward, still pale from exhaustion. Elara inched closer but did not touch the bed.

Joe tapped the bullet points one by one.

"Travel disruptions. Credit freezes. Identity flagging. Surveillance expansion. That's only Level One."

Elara's breath hitched.

Maya asked quietly, "Level Two?"

Joe looked her in the eyes. "Targeted removal."

The room went still.

Joe continued. "They're not ready to act yet. They don't know what you are, and they're terrified of making the wrong move. But you're leaving trails behind you. Every blink, every flare, every time one of you loses control."

Maya swallowed hard. "They'll come for us?"

"Yes," Joe said. "One by one. Because you're not a team yet."

He reached into his bag and unfolded a hand-drawn map. Thin lines crisscrossed the country, red circles marking incident points.

"Elara's spike in Miami. Maya's surge in Salem. Barrett's signature near the Rockies. And this one."

He pointed to a new ring drawn near Oregon.

"This signature woke up this morning."

Maya's face drained of color. "I felt that."

Joe nodded. "I figured you did."

The air in the room grew heavy, the weight of the coming threat settling over all of them.

Elara's voice trembled, but her words hit with force. "You almost got us killed twice. First the elevator. Then the fire. You're reckless."

Maya's eyes flashed. "You think I wanted any of that? I'm doing my best to keep you alive."

"You don't listen," Elara shot back. "You just drag us after you and hope we survive it."

Maya stepped forward. "You refuse to learn anything. If you'd let me help you control your harmonic, that fire might not have..."

"Don't say it," Elara warned.

Alex moved instantly, stepping between them again. His grounding harmonic surged under his skin. The motel walls vibrated like someone had pressed a tuning fork to the air.

"Stop," he said. "Both of you. We're not doing this."

Elara wiped her eyes with the heel of her hand, glaring at the floor. Maya turned away with a frustrated breath.

Joe watched all of it without speaking, his jaw tight, his hands clasped in front of him. When he finally stepped forward, there was nothing calm or gentle left in his voice.

Joe slammed his files shut and the sound cut through the tension like a blade.

"Enough," he said. "If you don't unite, Silent Protocol will crush you separately."

They all looked at him.

He spread Barrett's file across the bedspread.

"You're fire," he said to Elara.

"You're displacement," he said to Maya.

"You're shielding," he said to Alex.

Then he tapped Barrett's name with finality.

"And he is something else. Alone. Unstable. Scared. If HECATE gets to him first, they'll treat him as proof that all of you are too dangerous to live free."

Silence fell like a weight.

Maya looked at Elara.

Elara looked at Alex.

Alex exhaled slowly, shoulders sinking under a burden he had not asked for.

Joe folded the map, his voice low and sure. "If you want answers, we go to Colorado. We start with Barrett."

No one spoke, but the decision was already made.

The motel room filled with the rustle of bags and the scrape of boots as they began to gather their things. The air carried tension, fear, and something that almost felt like resolve.

Four people, barely united, barely trusting, Moving toward a storm they could not comprehend.

13

The Colorado Node

The sun had only begun to bruise the horizon when Richard Barrett stepped through the rusted chain-link gate and into the abandoned mining site outside Boulder. A cold wind sifted through the foothills, carrying dust and the faint smell of old timber soaked in decades of rain. The mountains loomed like dark ribs against the morning sky.

Richard moved slowly, one hand trailing along the tunnel's jagged wall. The rock felt wrong. Too warm. Too tense. As if something inside it was holding its breath.

He opened the journal tucked under his arm and flipped through pages of erratic sketches. Spirals that never completed. Lattices inside lattices. Shards of geometric shapes drawn so hard the paper tore. He didn't understand any of it. Not consciously. The drawings came when his mind drifted or when the pressure in the rock became too much to ignore.

Today the pressure hummed through the tunnel like a heartbeat.

"It called me," Richard whispered. "Not the other way around."

His breath fogged in the cold air, though the rock beneath his palm radiated a faint heat. He rounded a corner into a natural cavern where the ceiling opened like a cracked shell. A line of quartz veins webbed the far wall, catching the rising sun and scattering pale light across the chamber.

The node.

He didn't know the word for it, but he felt it. A place where the world was thinner. Where the pressure was stronger. Where something waited for him.

The hum rose again, deep and resonant. Richard pressed his trembling hands to the quartz.

"I can relieve it," he told the stone. "I can let it out."

He closed his eyes.

And whispered the fractured sound he heard in the back of his skull.

A sound he'd never spoken aloud before.

The quartz vibrated immediately, shivering under his touch like something alive trying to escape its cage. Richard gasped as heat flooded his palms. The stone beneath his fingers softened, its crystalline edges sagging into viscous motion.

Rock liquefied into silt.

The metal support beams nearby flaked into powder, disintegrating in slow, rippling waves.

Richard's eyes glazed. He watched the transformation with horror and awe tangled together. He wasn't shaping the stone. He wasn't choosing. The reaction poured out of him in a current he couldn't turn off.

"Tighten it," he whispered to himself. "Focus. You have to hold it."

Pain hit like a hammer. A nosebleed trickled down his upper lip. His hands shook violently. A tremor ran up both arms. His emotions spun out of phase inside him, like parts of his mind no longer agreed on what he felt.

The cavern rumbled.

The node responded.

The Weave pulsed outward from Colorado in a shockwave that tore through the world like invisible thunder.

And far away...

Maya bolted upright in the motel bed, a green-white recoil stabbing behind her eyes.

Elara gasped as heat burst across her skin.

Alex swayed where he stood, feeling the harmonic floor of reality drop beneath him.

Joe froze mid-breath, dread twisting through him without knowing why.

Back in the cavern, the quartz veins dimmed, then flared, then dimmed again, flickering like a dying star trying to relight itself.

Richard staggered back.

The stone rippled in a final unstable wave... then something inside the crack stirred.

Something watching.

Something waiting.

The chamber's temperature dropped all at once. Breath turned white. The flickering quartz threw shadows that didn't match the angle of the light.

Richard backed away, heart pounding. "Wait. No. That's not... that's not mine."

Negative-space crawled along the walls, thin ribbons of mimicry peeling away from the stone as if the darkness itself was learning how to shape limbs. Echoes of his outline rippled along the quartz surface. One lagged behind him by a heartbeat, moving after he moved.

Richard's stomach flipped.

"No. Stop. I didn't mean to wake you."

He slapped both palms against the floor and strained to reverse the shift. Rock solidified under his hands, jerking back into place in violent spasms. The transformation snapped shut like a trap, sending a crack through the cavern wall.

The quartz sealed. The shadows recoiled—

And the shock knocked Richard clean off his feet.

He hit the ground hard. Pain exploded across his skull. The mimicry dissolved into static flickers that slipped back into the cracks of the Weave.

The node steadied... barely. But the flicker would be felt across the entire lattice.

And it wouldn't be forgotten.

Richard's eyes rolled back.

Darkness swallowed him.

Above the mortal lattice, in a space without shape or time, five Immortals regarded the disturbance as if watching ripples in a pool.

Kemen stood first, tall and radiant, light coiling around her like a living mantle. She touched a hovering thread that showed the Colorado foothills. The flicker distorted beneath her hand.

"The weave is weakened," she said. "Ethan struggles to maintain the wound."

Vilya's eyes glimmered with memory. "The Threadweaver walks toward her awakening."

In another shimmer of layered images, Maya Rodriguez moved through the motel room, her hands shaking as the recoil struck her.

Cylian watched Barrett's unconscious form beneath the mountain. "The Transfigurer strains the lattice. He will break before the node does."

Beagron did not speak. His heavy presence radiated burden and inevitability. The echoes climbing the cavern walls disturbed even him.

But the Immortals remained still.

Their oath held. The Weave trembled beneath them like a wounded animal and they simply watched.

Richard woke hours later, cheek pressed to cold stone, mouth filled with the taste of copper. His nose had dried blood across it. His hands felt bruised down to the bone.

He pushed himself upright with a groan. The cavern around him was wrong.The stone he had softened had re-solidified in twisted shapes, frozen mid-wave like liquid caught in the instant of turning solid. Beams curved like melted wax. Quartz veins spiraled in unnatural patterns that hadn't been there before. And something had whispered his name while he was unconscious. Not aloud. But inside the stone.

Richard grabbed his journal with shaking hands and stumbled toward the tunnel mouth. His heartbeat echoed too loudly. The air carried faint vibrations that crawled down his spine.

Every shadow felt too deep.

Every noise felt too close.

He hurried faster.

By the time he burst through the mine entrance and into harsh daylight, he was gasping.

He leaned against a shattered fence post, shaking uncontrollably.

Far beneath the soil, the node hummed once more. A low tone that vibrated through the soles of his boots. A warning. Richard closed his eyes.

"Something in the stone woke up today," he whispered to himself. "And it knows my name."

14

❦

Splintered Paths

Morning found Maya, Alex, Elara, and Joe gathered in a single fragile silence.

Pale sunlight pressed through the flimsy motel curtains, laying thin gold stripes across the carpet and over the worn sheets where Maya sat cross-legged. Her head still throbbed from Barrett's catastrophic pulse. Every time she blinked, she felt the faint echo of it, like a pressure behind her eyes.

The motel room was quiet again, though not the brittle kind of silence they had woken to. The sun had dipped behind the building, leaving the air dim and soft. Elara sat in the center of the floor, her back against the foot of the bed, arms wrapped tight around her ribs. Every breath she took quivered with the heat rising beneath her skin.

"I can't do this," she whispered. "Every time I feel anything, it gets worse."

Maya knelt across from her, palms resting lightly on her own knees. "You're not breaking," she said gently. "You're resonating. Your flame listens to you even if you don't know how to speak its language yet."

Elara shook her head hard. "You don't get it. I almost killed all of us."

Alex moved from where he'd been leaning against the dresser and lowered himself beside Maya, steady and calm. "And we're still here," he said. "Which means you didn't lose control. You survived it. That counts."

Elara's gaze flicked to him, desperate and uncertain. "What if next time I don't?"

This time Joe stepped forward, slowly, so she could see every motion coming. He crouched beside her, forearms resting on his knees. His voice was low, but it carried the weight of truth the way only Joe's could.

"Elara," he said, "I can feel when someone's lying. You're not lying to us... but you're lying to yourself."

Her breath caught.

"Your fear's real," Joe said. "But the story it's telling you? That you're dangerous and alone?" He shook his head. "That's false. I can feel the false note in it."

Elara blinked fast, tears rising but not yet falling. "How do you know?"

"Because the truth is louder," he said simply. "And you feel it too. You just don't trust it yet."

Maya extended her hand, not touching, just offering. "Let us show you."

For a long moment, Elara didn't move.

Then her fingers uncurled, trembling, and she placed her hand in Maya's.

The Weave stirred.

Not with the violence of flame or the fracture of panic, but with a soft hum rising around the four of them. Maya exhaled slow, letting her own resonance unfurl in a thin ribbon of green-white light. Alex steadied it, grounding each vibration so it didn't spike too fast. Joe's harmonic, quieter, subtler, pulled the false notes away, letting only the truth ring clear.

Elara gasped as warmth pulsed in her chest, not heat, but something steady and bright. A small spark flickered behind her ribs, rising in answer to the glow in Maya's palms.

"Do you feel that?" Maya whispered.

Elara nodded, eyes wide. "It's... listening."

"It always was," Alex said. "You just needed space to hear it."

Joe leaned closer, voice soft. "You're not a danger to us. You're one of us."

The spark in Elara brightened, unfurling like the first breath of a flame that finally found its shape. It didn't lash out. It didn't burn. It hovered, gentle and warm, weaving itself into the harmonics around them.

A single moment of balance.

For the first time since awakening, Elara breathed without fear.

The four of them stayed like that, hands linked, harmonics intertwined, as the spark settled in her chest like a small sun that finally knew where it belonged.

Maya smiled faintly. "See? You're not losing control."

Elara looked at each of them, Maya with her quiet strength, Alex with his steady heart, Joe with his unyielding truth and something inside her shifted.

"I'm not alone," she whispered.

"No," Alex said. "You never were."

And the Weave hummed in agreement, binding the four of them in a resonance that would carry them into whatever came next.

A short while later Joe had claimed the only chair, and the small motel table was buried under maps, printouts, and files. Barrett's name appeared again and again, circled in ink that looked more desperate the longer she stared at it. Alex stood near the window with the curtain cracked just enough to see the parking lot. His posture told her everything.

They were already being hunted.

Elara sat at the far edge of the room, her back pressed to the wall, arms wrapped around her knees. Her eyes were red from both smoke and exhaustion, but the deeper trembling in her hands had nothing to do with fatigue.

Joe rubbed a hand over his face. "Barrett's signature from this morning pushed half the continental sensors into overload. HECATE is going to tighten the net. If we stay in one group, we'll get pinned."

Maya's stomach sank. She knew he was right, but the words still hurt. "Then we split."

Elara's head snapped up. "No. No, we just got away from the fire. From them. You can't make me leave now."

"I'm not sending you away," Maya said gently. "But we'll be harder to track if we break into two teams. Two smaller signatures instead of one giant one."

Elara shook her head, eyes glossing with panic. "You don't know what's happening to me. Every time I breathe wrong something burns. How am I supposed to go with him?" She jerked her chin toward Joe as if he had personally offended her existence.

Joe held up both hands. "I'm not trying to take you from anyone. I'm trying to keep you off the list. You come with me, you pull heat away from Maya's trail. Literally and figuratively."

Maya crossed the room and knelt in front of Elara. "We can't let HECATE follow us to Barrett. They're scared of him. If they catch him first, they'll use him as proof that all of us should be contained."

Elara flinched. "Then you two should go with him."

Alex finally turned from the window. "No. Maya and I have to track Barrett. She's the only one who can navigate the kind of distortion he's creating. And I'm the only one who can keep her stable long enough to get there."

Maya felt heat rise in her cheeks. Not from Elara. From the truth of Alex's words. She needed him more than she wanted to admit.

Elara hugged her knees tighter. "So I get sent off like a decoy."

Joe cleared his throat. "More like bait in the wrong direction. HECATE's already watching transit hubs. If we move through them in a way that looks suspicious enough, it'll draw attention. They'll think the Walkers are with me, not Maya."

"You want me to pretend to be a terrorist," Elara whispered.

Joe winced. "More like a glitch in the system they can't ignore."

Alex stepped closer to the two women. "No one is abandoning you. Maya wouldn't let that happen."

Elara looked at Maya, eyes shining. "Then why are you sending me away?"

Maya touched her hand again, whisper-soft. "Because if we stay together, we won't just get caught. We'll get crushed."

Elara didn't speak. She only breathed, shaky and uneven, the heat under her skin flickering like candle flame.

A soft knock interrupted the tension. Joe walked to the door, checked, then returned with a brown paper bag. He set a ring of keys on the table. "You'll need a way out of Florida that doesn't leave a digital footprint. It's clean, bought with cash, and nobody is looking for it. Here are some supplies. Water bottles. Burn cream. Snacks. A prepaid phone."

Elara wiped her eyes with the back of her hand. "So this is happening."

Joe nodded. "Yeah. And quickly. HECATE is running wide sweeps. Every hour we wait, the harder it gets."

Maya stood slowly. Her knees felt weak, but her resolve did not. "Alex and I will take the back way out. You two leave first. Joe, keep her out of crowded areas unless you have to. Elara, listen to him. He understands more of this than he admits."

Elara exhaled sharply, a tear slipping down her soot-stained cheek. "I don't trust him."

Maya touched her hand again, whisper-soft. "Trust yourself. Just for a little while. I'll find you again."

Elara seemed to fold inward, then nodded once, small and broken. "You better."

Alex gathered their few belongings as Joe tightened the straps on his messenger bag. When he stepped to Elara's side, she flinched at his proximity, but didn't pull away when he gestured toward the door.

"You ready?" he asked.

"No," she said honestly. "But I'll go anyway."

Joe gave Maya one last look, something like respect flickering through his expression. Then he led Elara out into the morning light.

The motel door shut behind them with a hollow click.

Maya stared at the empty doorway. Her chest felt heavy in a way that had nothing to do with exhaustion. Alex stepped beside her, shoulders steady and warm. "You did what you had to."

She nodded. "That doesn't make it easier."

"It's not supposed to be easy," he said. "It's supposed to work."

For a moment, they simply breathed in the narrow room.

Then Maya lifted her head. "We should move. Barrett won't stay still."

Alex opened the door, checking for watchers. The edge of dawn felt sharper than usual, as if the whole world was waiting on the next step they took.

"Colorado," he said quietly.

Maya followed him out. Two paths diverged behind them. One toward danger and one toward misdirection. Both toward fate.

And somewhere deep under the mountains, a broken man who could unmake stone whispered to the Weave again.

15

Tracing the Weave

The highway unspooled ahead of them in long gray ribbons, stretching north out of Florida toward miles of open country. Dawn had passed hours ago, but the sky still held a faint gold haze that softened the edges of the world. Maya watched it absently through the passenger window, one knee drawn up, the other foot braced against the floor. Alex had been driving in a steady silence, only the low hum of the tires grounding them in the present.

She had just opened her mouth to speak when something inside the Weave buckled.

The distortion hit her so hard she flinched sideways, one hand flying to her sternum. A sharp gasp tore from her throat. At the same moment, the car's dashboard flickered, the radio cutting in and out with a burst of static.

Alex jerked the wheel. "Maya? Talk to me. What is it?"

She couldn't answer yet. The Weave rolled through her in a jagged wave, threads folding over themselves like a crumpled sheet. Her vision blurred, then snapped into a strange double-focus. She felt stone grinding against itself, the echo of pressure pushing outward from some distant underground place.

"It's Barrett," she managed, breathless. "His resonance is... wrong. It's sinking."

Alex frowned. "Sinking?"

"Like something heavy is pulling the threads down," she whispered. "Like stone trying to remember water. It shouldn't feel like that."

A fresh pulse tore through her. She nearly doubled over, her forehead hitting the edge of the dashboard. The jolt rattled her bones.

Alex swore under his breath and pulled off the highway onto a narrow shoulder. He threw the car into park and leaned across the console, gripping her arm. "Stay with me. You're shaking."

She felt it too, the tremor in her limbs, the static clawing along her spine. Her resonance sputtered uncontrollably. Every time she reached for stability, the distortion yanked her sideways again.

Then something warm brushed against her awareness.

A soft white-gold pulse, familiar and steady, like a hand pressed gently against the inside of her mind.

Ethan.

He didn't speak. He never had, not in words. But his presence steadied her resonance enough to pull a thin breath into her lungs.

Maya closed her eyes, swallowing hard. "He's alive. Barrett. But he's hurting the Weave. I can feel it folding. If he keeps doing that, the whole lattice could tear."

Alex's jaw tightened. "Can you track him?"

"Yes," she whispered.

The truth settled like lead in her chest.

"I can track him... but it's ripping me apart to try."

Alex pressed a hand to the back of her neck, grounding her with slow, even pressure. "Then don't push yourself alone. Let me help."

Maya nodded, but the moment she tried to follow the distortion again, the threads twisted sharply and yanked her deeper than she intended. Her breath caught. Her vision flashed white.

"Maya?" Alex's voice sounded distant, muffled.

She wasn't hearing with her ears anymore.

The Weave pulled her under like a riptide.

And she slipped too deep.

The moment Maya slipped too deep, the world folded away. The highway, the car, Alex's voice, all of it peeled back like paint washed from glass. She dropped into the Weave.

Only this time it did not welcome her.

Threads twisted around her in jagged spirals, vibrating with strain. They did not form a corridor or a path. They pulled into a shape she had never seen before, a vast, circular impression that felt older than language.

This was not a vision sent by the Immortals.

This was memory.

The Weave remembered.

Light bled into form around her. She stood in a smoky chamber lit by torches that flickered in strange rhythmic patterns. Runes painted in deep pigments spiraled across the floor. They were arranged in segments that looked almost familiar, like the sigils she had seen in Barrett's distorted pulse.

But these were whole. Balanced. Meant to harmonize, not tear apart.

Shadows shifted. Someone moved through the chamber.

A man with silver-streaked hair, a long mantle, and hands stained with old pigment leaned over a wide stone slab. Not Immortal. Human. Yet the air bent slightly around him, as if the Weave braided itself more tightly in his presence.

Maya knew his name without needing it spoken.

Merlin.

He traced a finger along a lattice carved into the stone. It resembled a map, not of land, but of harmonic nodes. Lines intersected at key points. Small glyphs marked what must have been ancient gate sites. Her breath caught when she recognized one of them.

Colorado.

A Guardian gate once lived beneath those mountains.

Merlin turned, reaching for something resting beside the stone table. A small block of black mineral, covered in grooves that pulsed faintly with inner light. Rougher than the talisman Maya had seen before, but unmistakable all the same.

Beagron's Talisman, in its earliest form.

Voices drifted around her, blurred and distant, like hearing someone speak from underwater. Merlin's lips moved, shaping words she could not quite grasp. The chamber trembled as if the Weave strained to maintain the memory, to let her see what she needed and nothing more.

The distortion surged.

Barrett.

His destabilization slammed against the memory like a stone striking glass.

The echo-shadows flickered wildly. The pigments on the floor peeled up and dissolved into dust. Merlin blurred into streaks of gold and violet. Threads twisted, snapping back and forth between past and present.

Then a single phrase broke through, clear and sharp.

"...the Transfigurer must never touch the node..."

The entire memory shattered.

Light ripped apart. Threads snapped violently, recoiling in every direction. The force hurled Maya backward through the Weave, tearing through her senses until her mind felt raw and exposed.

She screamed as she was thrown out of the vision.

The world crashed back. Cold air struck her face. Gravel dug into her palms as she convulsed on the roadside shoulder, her breath broken and frantic. Alex was kneeling beside her, arms wrapped around her shoulders, trying to keep her upright.

"Maya. Maya, breathe. Look at me."

She clung to his shirt, shaking uncontrollably. The memory still pulsed behind her eyes. Rune circles. The talisman. The Colorado gate. Merlin's warning.

Her voice cracked as she whispered, "The Weave remembers."

Alex held her tighter as she trembled against him, and for the first time she understood the full truth of her power.

She could walk not only through places.

She could walk through the history held in the Weave itself.

Maya's light was the first thing he saw.

It sputtered around her like a broken filament, thin flashes of green and white snapping across her skin in uneven bursts. Every time she tried to breathe, the air near her face warped, bending like heat over asphalt. Alex caught her shoulders before she tipped forward again.

"Maya. Stay with me. Look at me."

Her pupils were blown wide, her skin clammy. Threads of light shimmered at the edges of her outline, too bright, too sharp, as if her entire body was slipping out of sync with reality.

"I can't hold it," she whispered, or tried to. The words fractured around her, distorted by the ripple bleeding out of her aura.

Alex felt the instability before he saw it. The harmonic pressure pressed into his chest and teeth, a deep vibrating tension that made his whole body want to recoil. He braced himself and pushed his grounding resonance outward, trying to wrap her flickering signature in something steady.

The moment his harmonic touched hers, Maya gasped and arched forward. The flickering light steadied for a heartbeat, then sputtered again, more violently. Alex gritted his teeth, forcing his resonance closer, compressing the dissonance until the spikes softened.

This time, the strain hit him like a weight across his ribs.

He had never felt Maya this volatile. She was unraveling. And he was barely strong enough to pull her back from it.

He tightened his grip on her arms. "We can't keep doing this. You're burning out."

Maya's breath hitched. She shook her head, and the motion sent another ripple spiraling through the air.

"No," she said, voice thin but fierce. "Barrett is near a node. I saw it. If it collapses, the Weave goes with it. Ethan can't hold everything forever." She swallowed hard. "We have to get to him."

Alex shut his eyes for a moment, fighting against the instinct to say no. Every protective instinct he had screamed that she needed rest, that she would tear herself apart if they pushed further. But the memory of the pulse that hit Miami, the vision that ripped her out of the Weave, and the tremors still quaking across the harmonic lattice told him she was right.

Barrett was a threat none of them were ready for. And they were the only ones who could reach him in time.

Alex exhaled slowly. "Alright. We keep going. But you stay centered on me. I mean it. You drift even a little and I lose you."

Maya met his eyes. Fear flickered there, but something steadier rose behind it. Trust. Resolve.

"I won't drift," she whispered. "Not with you holding the line."

The words struck deeper than she probably meant them to. Alex felt his own resonance tighten, pulling into alignment with hers, stabilizing her flicker for a few precious seconds.

Her light smoothed. The distortions around her face eased. For the briefest breath, she looked like herself again, grounded and present and whole.

"Good," Alex said, voice low. "Hold onto that."

Maya nodded and closed her eyes. His hands remained firm on her shoulders as her aura steadied to a faint pulse. She reached again for the Weave, her fingers curling in the air as if grasping threads only she could see.

Alex braced himself, ready for whatever came next.

The moment stretched, silent and tense.

Then Maya inhaled sharply as the world around them began to shimmer.

She had stabilized just long enough to reach for the Weave again.

Maya pressed her palms to her knees and tried to breathe through the tremor still shaking her chest. Alex's grounding resonance wrapped around her like a warm pressure, steady and constant. Without it she was certain she would have slipped straight back into the distortion's undertow.

"Alright," Alex said quietly. "I've got you. If you reach again, you stay tethered to me. No drifting."

She nodded once, then let her eyes fall half-shut.

The Weave opened with a shimmer under her skin.

Not gently. Not cleanly. It unfurled like a cracked sheet of glass catching sunlight, sharp and bright and unpredictable. Maya reached anyway, threading her perception through the lattice one fragile strand at a time while holding Alex's stabilizing pulse at her back like a lifeline.

The distortion was easy to find.

It pulsed through the Weave like the aftershock of an earthquake, jagged folds radiating outward from a single point far to the northwest. Each pulse rattled the threads, bending them in unnatural patterns. Maya followed the vibration deeper, feeling it tug against her ribs, sharp enough to sting.

Alex's grip tightened on her shoulders. "You alright?"

"Yes," she whispered, though her voice shook. "Keep holding."

Her awareness stretched, sliding across the lattice until the world around her narrowed into visions pressed against her mind like thin, translucent layers.

She saw quartz caverns lit from within by a pale blue glow.

She saw rock twisted into shapes that did not belong in nature, as if something had pushed through it and left the stone struggling to remember what it once was.

She saw dust swirling around a figure kneeling in the dark.

A man. Shoulders rigid, hands pressed into the earth. Whispering to stone the way others prayed.

Richard Barrett.

His presence throbbed through the Weave like a wrong note struck too loud. Matter bent under his touch, threads warping and recoiling as he tried to force them into shapes that did not belong to them. The fractures in the lattice spread like resin cracks crawling through old clay, reaching far beyond the cavern. Reaching toward her.

Her breath hitched.

Barrett's head snapped up.

He froze, eyes widening, not physically at her but at the sensation of being perceived. Maya felt his awareness brush the lattice, searching, hunting for whatever had touched him back.

He sensed her.

Maya jerked out of the Weave so fast her vision shattered into static. She gasped and grabbed Alex's arm, heart hammering.

"Maya," he said sharply. "Talk to me."

She swallowed hard, the taste of dust and cold stone still clinging to her breath. "He is awake," she managed. "He is fully awake."

Alex frowned. "And?"

She forced the next words out, each one shaking. "And he's not alone in there."

Alex went still. "You mean more Walkers."

Maya shook her head. "No. Something else. Something he stirred up. It was watching him." She wrapped her arms around herself. "I think it was watching me too."

Silence pooled in the car.

Then Alex reached for the keys and started the engine, his jaw tightening with resolve.

"Then we go now."

The tires crunched over gravel as he pulled them back onto the road. Maya leaned into the seat, still trembling.

She had Barrett's location.

But the truth settled heavy in her chest.

Tracking him meant he could feel her tracking him.

The car rolled back onto the highway, the tires humming against the asphalt as sunlight flared off the windshield. Maya tried to steady her breathing, but something in the Weave kept pulling at her awareness like a faint tug on a thread she had not meant to touch.

She leaned her head against the seat. "Just keep driving," she murmured.

Alex nodded, eyes fixed on the road. "I am. Focus on breathing, not on pushing."

She was trying. She really was.

But the Weave disagreed.

It shivered again, a flicker that ran across her vision like static crawling over a screen. At first she thought it was a leftover echo of Barrett's pulse, another recoil from his failed ritual. Then she felt it more clearly, a harmonic sliding under her skin, thin and tight like wire drawn too far.

A whisper formed inside the threads.

Not words.

Not a voice.

A presence.

Maya gasped and grabbed the dashboard just to stay upright. The plastic warped under her hand for a second as her resonance flared uncontrolled.

Alex shot her a sharp look. "Maya. What did you see?"

She swallowed hard. Her chest rose and fell too fast. She pressed her palm against her sternum as if she could steady the pounding behind it.

"Something is moving in the Weave," she whispered. "Not Ethan. Not the Immortals. Not Barrett either."

Alex slowed the car instinctively, his knuckles whitening around the steering wheel. "What do you mean something? What kind of something?"

Maya shook her head. "I don't know. But it felt like... static being shaped into intention." She closed her eyes, the echo still ringing faintly inside her skull. "Like the Weave itself was thinning. Like something was pressing from the wrong side."

Alex exhaled slowly. "Whatever Barrett started."

Maya opened her eyes, pupils wide with fear she could not hide. "It is only the beginning."

For a long moment the highway stretched ahead of them in a long silver ribbon, empty and shimmering in the heat. The world outside looked normal. Cars passed. Trees waved in the breeze. Nothing suggested the tremor spreading under reality.

But Maya felt it.

And when she looked toward the distant horizon, Colorado felt less like a destination and more like the edge of a storm they were already too close to outrun.

Alex pressed the accelerator.

They drove north, racing toward a man who could unmake stone, and away from something far worse that was beginning to wake beneath the threads.

16

Fire and Lies

The industrial outskirts of Miami smelled like rust and wet concrete, a dull mix that clung to the back of Elara's throat as she followed Joe between rows of abandoned warehouses. The early heat of the day already pressed at her skin, but the warmth inside her chest was worse. It coiled and tightened with every step, waiting for something to go wrong.

They rounded a corner into a narrow service alley littered with broken pallets and scraps of metal. That was when she heard it.
A faint electric whine overhead.

Joe stopped sharply and lifted a hand for silence.

A surveillance drone drifted above the alley mouth, its camera swiveling with insect like precision. Red tracking LEDs flared as it scanned the ground. Elara felt her heartbeat spike. The warmth in her chest surged toward her throat in a panicked rush.

Joe leaned close. His voice was barely a breath. "Don't run. They'll track motion before heat."

She tried to swallow the fear back down, but her skin was already prickling. Heat shimmered around her face as though the air itself were bending away from her. She stepped backward until her shoulder hit cold brick.

Another drone slid into view above the first one, its rotors spinning in slow, controlled arcs.

Her pulse flared. The warmth inside her flickered dangerously.

"Joe," she whispered, "I can't hold it."

"Yes, you can," he said. "Just breathe. Nice and slow."

But she couldn't. The fear pressed too hard. The heat pushed higher, frantic, wild. She squeezed her eyes shut and braced for the fire to erupt out of her in one violent burst. She had seen what that looked like. She had nearly burned her apartment to the ground. She had almost killed them all.

A sharp whine sliced the air. The nearest drone locked onto them.

Elara gasped.

And instinct moved before thought.

She inhaled sharply, then released a breath so hot it rippled visibly in front of her. The heat shot upward in a narrow column, a single focused pulse that struck the drone square in its undercarriage. Circuits warped. Plastic curled. The machine let out a strained electronic squeal as its rotors seized.

It dropped like a stone, hitting the asphalt with a smoking thud.

The second drone jerked, sensors scrambling to adjust to the sudden thermal spike.

Joe stared at her, stunned. "Elara... you aimed that."

She opened her eyes slowly. Her hands were trembling, but the heat inside her was settling. Not gone, but quiet. Contained.

"I didn't mean to," she whispered.

"Doesn't matter. You did."

Sirens began to rise several blocks away, quick and urgent.

Joe grabbed her arm and pulled her deeper into the alley, weaving them behind a stack of rusted barrels. "We need cover. Now."

Elara followed, her breath still unsteady, but her pulse calmer than she expected. For the first time since the fire, she felt something other than fear.

She felt control. And that scared her almost as much as the drones did.

Joe guided her into the shadows as the sirens grew louder, chasing the smoke she had left behind.

They moved fast and quiet, cutting through a maze of empty loading bays until Joe spotted a boarded-up storefront across from an abandoned parking lot. The front windows were cracked but the interior looked empty enough. More important, the building offered clear sightlines in every direction.

He ushered Elara inside, then crouched behind a dusty metal shelf. "Stay low. I need a minute."

She hugged her arms, heat still rolling faintly off her skin. "I thought we were running."

"We are." Joe slid his bag open and pulled out the stolen HECATE scanner tablet. "We are just running smarter than they are."

The device flickered to life with a soft beep. A digital map unfolded across the screen, dotted with shifting heat signatures and pulsing search grids. Joe's brows pulled tight as he watched the perimeter tighten around their node.

"Alright," he muttered. "Time to lie to people who lie for a living."

Elara blinked at him. "What does that mean?"

"It means we give them exactly what they expect to see."

He tapped several quick commands onto the tablet. The scanner chimed, then sent a pulse through the network. On the map, a bright flare appeared three blocks away near a dumpster behind a shuttered restaurant.

Elara leaned over his shoulder. "Is that... us?"

"No. But they think it is." Joe smirked faintly. "Walkers panic. At least, that is what they think. So we make a trail that looks panicked."

Another few taps, a swipe, and a second thermal burst lit up near the docks. The HECATE grid shifted instantly, squads redirecting toward the false signals. Drone markers peeled away from their quadrant and zipped toward the decoys.

Within two minutes the entire search pattern had fractured, pulling away from them in a messy scatter.

Elara stared at the map, stunned. "You can do that?"

Joe shrugged. "I can see the lie in their pattern. So I tell a better one."

For the first time since the alley, Elara's expression changed. The panic softened. Something like respect flickered behind her eyes, cautious but real.

Joe powered down the tablet and slipped it back into his bag. "Come on. The window is small."

He pushed open the back door, and they slipped into a narrow service alley just as sirens roared past the intersection. The search perimeter collapsed behind them, moving exactly where he needed it to go.

Joe glanced at Elara. "See? We are not trapped. We are just getting started."

She followed close, this time without shrinking back. They disappeared into the shadows before HECATE realized the trail was a lie.

The machine shop smelled like rust and old oil, the kind of place time had forgotten long before she and Joe ducked through the side door. Broken belts hung from the rafters. Dust coated the concrete floor in a thin gray film. It should have felt safe. Instead, Elara stood in the center of the empty space with her hands shaking hard enough to ache.

Her breath came too fast. Heat pulsed under her ribs in sharp, angry bursts. She pressed her palms against her thighs but the trembling only got worse.

Joe watched her from a few feet away, careful not to step too close. "You're alright," he said softly. "We shook them off."

She curled her fingers tight. "Stop saying that. I am not alright."

Joe said nothing, but the silence only made something snap inside her.

"Why are you helping me?" she demanded. Her voice cracked high, sharper than she intended. "You barely know me."

Joe did not flinch. He slid his hands into his pockets and leaned his shoulder against an old drill press. "Because I know what it is to be scared of your own head."

Anger flared up her spine. "You don't have fire inside you."

"No," Joe said. His voice stayed low, steady. "But I have truth. And sometimes that is just as dangerous."

His resonance flickered, subtle but unmistakable. Elara felt it ripple through the air like a soft vibration. He was hearing her fear as distortion. She hated that he could.

Joe pushed off the machine and took a slow step toward her. "Elara, listen. You think the fire is trying to hurt you. That is the lie."

She went still.

Joe lowered himself to one knee so he could meet her eyes without looming. "The truth is different. The flame is reacting to you, not attacking you. You are not a bomb waiting to go off. You are a signal that has not learned its own shape yet."

Her throat tightened. "You do not know that."

"Yes," Joe said, and the word hummed with unbearable certainty. "I do."

Elara's chest stuttered with a breath she did not mean to let out. For the first time since the apartment burned, her walls slipped. Not much. Just enough to let in the possibility that she was not doomed to destroy everything she touched.

Joe's gaze softened. "Let me show you the truth in it."

She swallowed hard. "How?"

"By helping you release it on purpose," he said. "Not in a panic. Not because it is breaking loose. Because you choose to."

Her hands trembled again, but this time she did not pull them away.

"Will it hurt?" she whispered.

"It will scare you," Joe said honestly. "But I will be right here. And I will tell you what is true every second it happens."

For the first time, Elara did not run from the fear.

She nodded.

Joe rose slowly and asked, "Then let me guide you into a controlled flame release."

Joe crouched near a pile of scrap and picked up a broken metal pipe, its edges jagged and rusted. He set it on the concrete floor between them, the hollow ring echoing through the dim machine shop.

"Alright," he said, stepping back. "Heat this without melting it. Just enough to change the color."

Elara stared at the pipe as if it might bite her. Her chest tightened. "I can't. I will start something on fire."

Joe raised his hands, palms open, giving her space. "You will not. We are not asking the flame to explode. We are asking it to speak."

"That is supposed to help?" she muttered.

"Yeah," Joe said lightly. "Believe it or not."

Elara wrapped her arms around herself, then forced them down again. The tremor in her hands had calmed a little since earlier, but fear still pulsed under her ribs like a second heartbeat.

Joe watched the micro flickers around her aura, reading the tension the same way other people read facial expressions. He took a slow step forward, careful not to touch her. His voice softened. "You are not controlling fire. You are listening to it."

Elara shook her head. "It never listens."

"That is the lie," Joe said. "The truth is in how it responds to you. So breathe. Not deep, not dramatic. Just breathe the way you did when you could feel our harmonics in the motel."

Elara closed her eyes. She tried to inhale without the heat pushing too far. Her breath trembled, but she caught the rhythm on the second try. Warmth rose under her skin, but it did not surge. It curled inward instead, a quiet ember waiting for direction.

"There you go," Joe murmured. "Now guide it to your hands. Not out. Just in place."

Elara lifted her palms a few inches above the pipe. At first nothing happened. The fear clawed at her, telling her she was seconds from losing control again.

Then the metal darkened.

A faint shimmer pulsed along its surface, like heat haze on a summer road. The pipe warmed to a muted orange, slow and steady.

It did not melt.

Elara opened her eyes. "I did that?"

Joe smiled, not the sarcastic kind she expected, but something warm and real. "Yeah. You did. I told you it listens."

A small spark of pride rose in her chest. The first clean feeling she had felt since the apartment fire. Not fear. Not shame. Something close to hope.

She let out a shaky laugh. "I can't believe that worked."

"I can," Joe said. "Because the truth in you is louder than the fear. You just needed to hear it."

Elara met his eyes. For a moment, something settled between them. Not trust exactly, not yet, but the start of something that felt like solid ground.

Before she could speak, a mechanical whir buzzed faintly overhead.

Elara stiffened. Heat leapt under her skin, primal and fast.

Joe reached toward her, stopping short of touching her arm. "Not this time. We walk away calm. Let them chase ghosts, not fire."

She swallowed hard, nodded, and stepped back from the glowing pipe.

For the first time, she believed she could. They slipped out the far door as the drone drifted past, its camera searching for a panic that never came.

They slipped out the back door of the machine shop just as the drone drifted overhead. Joe kept one hand lightly on Elara's elbow, guiding her toward the narrow gap between two storage buildings. The air smelled like rust and old coolant, the kind of industrial stink no one questioned on Miami's edge.

They had almost reached the next block when a sharp voice cut through the alley.

"Hey! You two. Stop right there."

HECATE.

Elara froze. Heat punched through the air around her, a sudden spike that made the humidity sharpen into a shimmer. Joe felt the surge like a punch to the ribs. If she flared now, half the block would light up like a signal flare.

He stepped in front of her before panic could take hold.

The agent jogged forward, one hand near a holstered scanner. He looked alert but not aggressive yet. Joe saw the caution in his shoulders, the suspicion in the tight set of his jaw.

Joe smiled calmly. "You looking for the leak too?"

The agent blinked. "Leak?"

"Yeah," Joe said, letting certainty color his voice. "We just came from the next block over. Folks said you had some kind of gas leak situation."

A ripple of doubt crossed the agent's expression. Joe felt it hit his Walker sense like a tiny harmonic shiver. Not fully convinced. Not fully rejecting it.

Adjust the lie.

He leaned in slightly, voice low and practical. "We smelled it too. Pretty strong. You might want to check the southeast vents."

The agent hesitated, glanced toward the direction Joe indicated, then clicked his radio. "Possible gas leak near the southeast HVAC vents. Checking it now."

Joe nodded as if relieved. "Good. Better safe than sorry."

The moment the agent turned his back, Joe grabbed Elara's hand. "Now we run."

They sprinted down the alley, their footsteps splashing through puddles and kicking up grit. Elara kept pace beside him, her breath ragged but controlled, the heat under her skin contained by sheer will.

Sirens flared somewhere behind them, but the sound grew fainter as they slipped deeper into the industrial maze.

Joe did not let go of her hand until they ducked behind a rusted dumpster two blocks away.

Elara pressed her back to the wall, chest heaving. She stared at him, eyes wide. "You just lied to a federal agent."

Joe shrugged once. "He needed the lie more than we needed the truth."

A shaky laugh escaped her. Not quite humor. Not quite disbelief. Something in between. "I thought my power was the problem. But you... you just turned that whole search net sideways."

Joe met her gaze, steady and sure. "Your fire saved us from the drones. My truth tilted the agent. We do this together, Elara. You and me, we make a different kind of damage."

Her expression shifted. Understanding. Recognition. The smallest flicker of pride.

She whispered, "We are dangerous in completely different ways."

Joe nodded. "And HECATE has no idea how to handle that."

They moved deeper into the maze of alleys, two shadows slipping past a hunt meant for an army, learning that survival was easier when their strengths aligned.

They did not stop moving until the old bus station rose out of the heat haze like a forgotten skeleton, empty and sun-bleached. Graffiti curled across the cracked walls. The benches were rusting through. No buses had stopped here in years.

Joe pushed the door open and scanned the dim interior. "Clear," he said quietly.

Elara stepped inside and finally let her back hit the cool tiled wall. Her lungs still felt too tight. Her hands trembled with leftover fire she had not let loose. She slid down the wall until she was sitting on the floor, arms wrapped around her knees.

The adrenaline ebbed. The fear followed slower.

Joe sat a few feet away, not touching, not crowding her.

The silence stretched between them until she felt something in her chest unclench.

"I thought I was broken," she whispered.

Joe looked at her, eyes steady and warm in a way she had not expected. He shook his head. "You're waking up, Elara. There's a difference."

Her throat tightened. No one had said it like that before. No one had made it sound like something other than a curse.

She looked at him, really looked, and felt gratitude rise through the exhaustion. "Thank you," she murmured.

Joe's voice softened. "We'll find Maya again. For now, we learn to survive."

Elara nodded, a slow, trembling breath falling out of her. She pushed herself to her feet. Joe rose with her. They stood there for a moment in the dim quiet of the abandoned station, two shadows caught between fear and something that almost felt like purpose.

They walked toward the far exit together.

Not strangers anymore.

Not a team yet.

But bound by fire and truth, moving into the uncertain light beyond the cracked glass doors.

17

Echo Selves

The highway rolled beneath them in long gray waves, Georgia stretching out in pale morning light that shimmered across the asphalt. Maya pressed her forehead lightly to the passenger window, half awake, half drifting in that strange state where the Weave tugged at her thoughts even when she tried to ignore it. Alex drove with one hand on the wheel, the other resting casually near the gearshift, steady and calm as miles unfurled behind them.

She should have slept. She wanted to. But every time her eyelids drooped, the Weave rippled under her skin like something whispering for attention.

A thin tremor moved through her chest.

Then another.

She frowned and straightened slightly. The threads around her vision were fraying again, edges flickering in faint green-white pulses. Barrett had damaged a node. She had felt the shock of it hours ago, but the aftershocks were still echoing through the lattice.

Alex glanced over. "You doing alright?"

"Yeah," she lied, swallowing against the tightness in her throat. "Just tired."

She wasn't. Not exactly. It was something else. Something hollow pressing along her ribs.

The Weave shivered again, and Maya's breath hitched.

A second presence brushed her awareness.

Not Alex.

Not Ethan.

Not Barrett.

It felt like her, but distant. As if her own resonance had peeled away and was humming somewhere outside her skin.

Maya blinked hard. "Alex, slow down a second."

He eased off the gas, concerned, but she didn't finish the thought. Her vision pulled sideways, drawn toward the window. She couldn't help looking.

For a heartbeat she saw herself.

Walking along the roadside, keeping pace with the car.

Same clothes. Same hair. Same posture.

But not quite right.

The figure jerked forward in uneven skips, like a video buffering in the wrong frame rate. Its head turned toward the car a second too slow, and its eyes—

Maya inhaled sharply.

The Echo-Self flickered, broke into static, and vanished.

Alex hit the brakes. "Maya! What is it?"

She forced her breath steady and pressed a hand to her forehead. "Nothing. I just... I thought I saw something. I'm tired. That's all."

Alex didn't look convinced. "That wasn't nothing. You jumped like you were hit."

"I'm fine," she insisted, then softer, "Just tired."

She felt him watching her for a long moment before he eased the car back into motion. He didn't push, but the silence between them thickened.

Maya curled her fingers into her palm, grounding herself against the warmth of her skin. Her heart thudded too fast. She knew what she had seen. That wasn't exhaustion. That wasn't imagination.

It had been her.

Or something wearing her shape.

The Weave shivered again, faint but sharp, brushing her mind like cold fingertips.

Warning her.

Whatever she saw wasn't alone and neither was she. Maya turned her face toward the window again, but she didn't let her eyes drift shut this time. The Weave felt too thin. Too open. Too watched.

The gas station sat alone on a stretch of rural Georgia highway, its awning buzzing with tired fluorescent lights. Alex pulled the car up to the pump, killed the engine, and exhaled. They had been driving for hours, and though Maya insisted she was fine, her eyelids had drifted half-closed more than once.

He stepped out into the humid air and reached for the fuel pump.

That was when it hit him.

A strange density pressed against his skin, almost like static before a lightning strike. Not painful, but wrong. The hairs on his arms lifted. His jaw tightened as a faint buzzing crawled across the back of his neck.

Instinctively, he tried to ground himself.

The moment he opened the harmonic channel, something yanked at him.

It was subtle at first, like a tug on a loose thread. Then it pulled harder, draining the stabilizing pressure he released. Alex gasped and gripped the top of the car to keep his balance. The pump nozzle slipped from his hand and clattered against the metal.

His breath came shallow. His ribs felt hollowed out.

"What the hell," he whispered.

He forced another grounding pulse, this one weaker and more controlled, but the same draining sensation pulled at him, siphoning off a piece of his harmonic field as if something invisible had hooked into him and would not let go.

The static around him eased only when he cut off the grounding reflex entirely.

He leaned against the car, fingers tight on the doorframe.

Inside, Maya's eyes snapped open.

She pushed the door open halfway. "Alex? You alright?" Her voice was tired, but alert.

He swallowed, still dizzy. "Stay inside." His hand shook slightly as he finished refueling and set the nozzle back in place. Then he got into the driver's seat, forcing calm into his breathing.

Maya turned toward him immediately. "Something's wrong. I felt a pull through the Weave, like a thread got scraped." Her gaze lowered to his hands. "Alex... what happened?"

He tried to steady himself, but the lingering hollow pressure behind his ribs made it hard to speak.

"Something took a piece of me," he said quietly.

Her expression changed instantly. Fear sharpened her features. Without hesitating, she reached out and brushed his shoulder, not to comfort, but to read the harmonic residue clinging to him.

Her breath caught. "There's static on you. It feels like cold ash. Like something fed on your harmonic when you grounded."

Alex nodded once, jaw tight. "Yeah. I felt it. That wasn't normal static."

She closed her eyes, following the residue deeper, tracing the faint echo still clinging to his ribs. When she found it, she flinched.

"It's connected to the thing I saw on the roadside," she whispered. "The hollow version of me. The Echo." She swallowed hard. "Alex... it touched you."

"Can it do that?" he asked.

"I didn't think so," she said.

He rubbed a hand across his face. "Shields are supposed to push static away, not feed it."

"It didn't feed," Maya whispered. "It stole."

The air in the car felt too small suddenly, too close.

Alex stared out at the empty road, fighting the feeling of something watching from somewhere they could not see. "We should move."

Maya nodded, but her voice trembled. "Alex... please don't ground again unless you have to. If the Echo is siphoning from you, it'll get stronger."

He started the engine, trying to pretend the hollow ache was fading.

"Yeah," he said. "No more free meals."

They pulled back onto the highway.

Both of them pretended they were fine.

Neither of them believed it.

The afternoon sun slanted across the dashboard, turning the cracked plastic into a pale shimmer of heat. Maya leaned forward to adjust the air vent, her fingers brushing the dial.

And froze.

Her reflection in the windshield had moved before she touched anything.

The breath caught in her throat. She lifted her hand again, painfully slow. Her reflection followed a fraction too late, its motion jerky, like a skipped frame in a video.

No. No, no, no...

The figure stared back at her with her own face, but drained of color, hollow where the eyes should have been. Threads of pale green light bled backward into the glass instead of reflecting out.

Her Echo-Self.

The same presence she had sensed along the roadside. The same cold tug she had felt in the Weave.

The Echo lifted its hand. Slowly. Deliberately.

It pressed its palm to the inside of the windshield, but from the wrong side, as if the glass were a thin barrier between two realities.

Maya jerked backward so fast her seatbelt bit into her shoulder. A small cry escaped before she could stop it.

Alex's head whipped toward her. "Maya? What is it?"

She stared at the glass, struggling to breathe. The windshield had fogged, a faint outline where the Echo tried to touch the world. But the figure itself was gone.

She shook her head hard. "You didn't see it?"

"See what?" He leaned forward, sweeping his hand across the fogged patch. His fingers passed through empty air. "Maya, talk to me."

Her pulse hammered against her ribs. "It was me," she whispered. "A wrong version of me. It moved before I did."

Alex went still. Not afraid. Worse. He looked like someone who had just heard confirmation of his worst suspicion.

"Maya," he said quietly, "how long have you been seeing this?"

She hesitated, her throat tight. "Since Georgia. Maybe earlier. I thought it was stress, or exhaustion. But it wasn't just a shadow or a reflection. It looked right at me."

"And the static that hit me at the gas station," Alex said, voice low. "It wasn't random."

Maya closed her eyes as the last echo of the figure dissolved from her memory, leaving only the cold behind.

"It isn't just copying us," she whispered. "It's watching us."

Alex swallowed. "No. It's feeding."

They sat in heavy silence, the road humming beneath them.

The Echo had touched the glass.

Next time, it might reach further.

The road stretched ahead in a silver blur, but Maya barely saw it. Her hands were clenched in her lap, her pulse still thudding from the moment in the windshield. Alex drove in tense silence, checking her every few seconds without saying a word.

Finally, she whispered, "It wasn't a hallucination."

Alex kept his eyes on the highway. "I figured."

"No," she said quickly, shaking her head. "I mean it wasn't anything we have seen before. Not illusion. Not a Weave memory. Not residue from a blink." She swallowed hard. "It wasn't me. It was something trying to be me."

Alex's grip tightened on the steering wheel. "You think it copied you."

"It used my harmonic signature," Maya said. "That distortion the Weave keeps pushing through. The strain in the lattice. Barrett's pulse opened something and the Shadow Current crawled through it." She pressed a hand to her chest. "It grabbed whatever trace of me it could find. My outline, my resonant shape... all the pieces I leave behind when I blink or when I touch the Weave too hard."

Alex exhaled slowly. "So it built an Echo version of you."

"Not built," she corrected. "Birthed. Pulled from the wrong side of the threads."

The word hung between them, cold and heavy.

Alex's voice dropped even lower. "If it can copy you, it can learn you."

Maya turned toward him sharply. She had thought it, but hearing it aloud made her breath stutter.

"It followed my movements," she said. "But it wasn't guessing. It was matching me, learning where I would be a second before I got there. Like it was trying to sync up."

Alex nodded grimly. "And failing. Which means it will keep trying."

A tremor rippled through the Weave, soft but unmistakable. Maya inhaled sharply.

Alex looked at her. "What is it?"

She closed her eyes. "There is more than one."

He cursed under his breath. "More than one Echo?"

Maya nodded, her fingers digging into the seat. "They are forming in layers. Flickering in and out like static trying to become shape. Some are ahead of me. Some are behind. None of them are stable yet, but they are trying to be."

Alex's jaw set. "And if one of them stabilizes..."

"It could pass for me," Maya whispered. "Or worse, it could shadow me. Follow me. Mirror me until it knows enough to act on its own."

A long silence followed. Neither of them breathed easily.

Alex finally said, "We need to regroup. Now."

Maya opened her eyes and nodded. "There was a rest area ten miles back. Another one should be close."

"Next exit," Alex said, already checking the signs. He flicked the turn signal and eased into the right lane.

Maya stared at her reflection in the side mirror. Her own eyes stared back.

But for a split second, just before she looked away, the reflection lagged behind.

The rest area was nearly empty. A few picnic tables sat crooked in the shade of tall pines, their branches rattling softly in the rising wind. Maya paced near the curb with her hands pressed to her temples, trying to steady the tremor in her aura. Alex stood a short distance away, scanning the tree line.

His instinct kept pulling at him. Something was wrong with the air. It buzzed faintly, like static caught under the skin.

Maya's breath hitched. "Alex, the Weave is thin here."

"I know," he said quietly. "I can feel it."

He took a slow step forward, eyes narrowing at a patch of shadow between the trees. At first it looked like nothing more than a darker shape inside the branches. Then it shifted.

A figure stepped out.

Alex's heart slammed against his ribs.

It was Maya.

Same posture. Same hair pulled over one shoulder. Same expression she wore when she was trying not to panic. She stood perfectly still, watching him without blinking.

"Maya," Alex called softly.

Behind him, the real Maya jerked her head up. "What?"

He raised one hand in warning. "Stay back."

The silhouette turned its head toward the sound of her voice, the movement just a little too sharp, a little too delayed. Then it looked back at him.

Alex felt his harmonic surge on instinct, a protective rise of pressure that enveloped his chest and arms. The Echo shimmered at the edges, then rippled like a sheet of water disturbed by a stone.

And it changed.

His breath caught as his own face stared back at him.

Not a clone. Not a trick of the eye. A perfect mimicry. His height, his build, the way his shoulders squared when he tried to look calm. It was all there.

Except the eyes.

They were empty, flat like glass with no reflection.

"Alex," Maya whispered behind him. "That is not me."

The mimic took one slow step forward. Alex's shield rose higher, his harmonic spreading like a pressure wave in front of him.

The Echo responded instantly.

It drank the shield in.

The static collided with his resonance and pulled at it, sucking threads of energy straight through his ribs. The drain hit so fast he nearly collapsed.

Alex dropped to one knee with a harsh gasp. "Maya... it is feeding on me."

The mimic moved again, jerkier now, like it was learning how to walk by watching him fail to stand.

Maya sprinted toward him. "Keep breathing. Do not fight it alone."

She grabbed his shoulders, grounding her pulse through his collapsing harmonic. Green-white light spiraled across her hands, sinking into his chest and pushing the static back. Her heartbeat synced to his in one hard rhythm.

The Echo recoiled.

It flickered violently, its outline shredding into thin ribbons of static that whipped backward into the trees. Maya pushed harder, her grounding pulse flooding the air like a shockwave.

The mimic tore apart.

It dissolved in a burst of pale ash and vanished into the wind.

Alex sagged forward, catching himself on both hands, chest heaving. Maya knelt beside him, one arm around his back, steadying him before he could fall.

"You all right?" she whispered.

He shook his head. "It took something out of me. Not much, but enough. If we had been a minute slower..."

Maya swallowed hard. Her hands trembled against his shoulders. "Echo-Selves are not shadows. They are feeding forms. Learning forms."

Alex lifted his head. Fear flickered across Maya's face in a way he had never seen. She looked toward the trees as if expecting another version of herself to step out.

"We have to warn the others," she said.

Alex nodded, pushing himself upright. "They are too far already."

Maya gripped his arm, helping him stand. "Then we find Barrett fast. The longer the Weave stays strained, the stronger these things get."

Alex steadied himself, breath slow and ragged. "Then we keep moving."

They walked back to the car together, neither looking behind them. The wind stirred the trees once more, and for a moment the shadows flickered like something still trying to take shape.

Maya got Alex back into the car with his arm slung over her shoulder. He was shaking hard, his skin pale and cold in a way she had never felt from him before. Shields were not supposed to be drained like that. They were the ones who held the line.

She closed the passenger door gently and hurried around to the driver's side. The moment she sat, her breath caught. The Weave pressed in on her awareness, restless and thin.

"Maya…" Alex murmured, rubbing a hand over his face. "Just drive."

She gripped the steering wheel but did not start the engine yet. The Weave was already pulling at her, threads vibrating in jagged pulses that made the air swim.

She exhaled and let her senses open.

The world dropped away.

Cold light spilled across the lattice, unraveling in long streaks that trembled under the strain. Barrett's destabilization had not just fractured one node. It had shaken the entire network. The aftershocks radiated outward across the continent, and in their wake something new had slipped through.

Dozens of phantom impressions.

Some barely formed, just silhouettes flickering like candle smoke. Others sharper, pulling themselves together around stolen harmonic shapes.

Echo-Selves.

Not just hers. Not just Alex's.

Something about Barrett's ritual had opened a door the Shadow Current had been waiting centuries to push against.

Her breath hitched as one of the impressions sharpened. A shape pulled free from the surrounding distortion, stepping into clearer focus within the lattice.

Her.

But not her.

This Echo did not mimic her posture or her expression. It stood as if it had been waiting. As if it had anticipated the moment she would look its way.

Slowly, it turned its head toward her.

Its mouth stretched into a smile that was not a copy of hers. It was an interpretation. A prediction.

Wrong. Intentional. A smile meant for her alone.

Maya jerked out of the Weave with a strangled breath and gripped the steering wheel so tightly her knuckles whitened.

Alex turned his head, still weak. "What happened?"

She stared through the windshield at nothing, every nerve shivering.

"Alex," she whispered. "We are running out of time."

He tried to sit straighter, grimacing. "Tell me."

"The Echoes... they are not just reflections. They are forming across the Weave. Dozens of them. Maybe more. Something pushed through when Barrett destabilized the node." She swallowed hard. "They are not copying us anymore. They are learning us."

Silence settled over the car, heavy and cold.

Alex reached for her hand. His grip was weak, but steady. "Then we move faster."

Maya nodded. She turned the key, and the engine rumbled to life.

Colorado was no longer just a place they had to reach. It was the heart of a race against something born in the dark, something using their own resonance as its blueprint.

She pulled onto the road with her pulse trembling in her throat.

Ahead of them, the highway stretched out like a thin thread.

Behind them, Echo-Selves flickered in the Weave, each one sharpening into something with purpose.

18

Silent Protocol II

The command center three stories beneath the Capitol had no windows, no clocks, and no sense of day or night. Fluorescent lights hummed overhead with a faint metallic buzz that matched the tension in Senator Victor Hargreaves's jaw. Screens lined the walls in a broad semicircle, their sharp blue glow reflecting off polished floors and the dark sheen of HECATE uniforms.

Hargreaves stood before the largest display, hands clasped behind his back. The map of the United States flickered with colored points, some pulsing red, others dissolving into gray static as quickly as they appeared. Anomalous heat signatures. Sudden surveillance gaps. Erased camera grids.

Resonant disturbances.

The room smelled faintly of ozone and recycled air.

A young analyst cleared her throat. "Sir, we have confirmation that the Miami incident has been fully sanitized. Public narrative is holding."

Hargreaves barely nodded. His eyes tracked a pulsing dot near Colorado before it blinked out entirely. Another signature. Another loss of control.

Control.

The one thing he could not afford to lose.

"Silent Protocol Level Two is active nationwide," the operations chief reported from a nearby console. "We are pushing travel alerts through DOT channels, tightening air and rail tracking, and expanding misinformation campaigns in all major markets."

Hargreaves spoke without turning. "Phase in civilian compliance measures. Claimed security threats. Infrastructure concerns. Give the public a reason to trust fear."

"Yes, sir."

Another screen shifted to a list of doctored news copy. Draft headlines scrolled by in tidy bullet points.

Strange Heat Phenomena Linked to Faulty Power Grids
Surge of Gas Leaks Across Florida Under Investigation
Federal Agencies Respond to Unconfirmed Threat Reports

Narrative.
Shape the story and you shape the people.
Shape the people and you shape the response.

He finally spoke, voice steady and cold. "This is not terrorism. It is contagion. And containment begins with narrative. If we control the frame, we control the threat."

The room stilled. Even the analysts who disliked him knew better than to push back.

"Sir," another operator said carefully, "Silent Protocol Two authorizes targeted disruption of communication networks. Some agencies are concerned about overreach."

Hargreaves glanced at him, expression unreadable. "If these individuals can disrupt infrastructure, break physics, or erase their presence, then overreach is the only appropriate reach." He turned back to the primary map. "We act before they do. That is the entire point of Silent Protocol."

A fresh wave of static rippled across the displays. Several red markers blinked out as if swallowed by the dark.

The operations chief swallowed hard. "Sir, we lost three signatures in the last sixty seconds."

"Then find them," Hargreaves said. "And if you can't, build something that can."

He stepped away from the table, coat settling sharply against his legs. His shoes echoed across the floor as he walked toward the far end of the chamber, where a reinforced door waited under the guarded sign:

ENHANCEMENT WING — AUTHORIZED PERSONNEL ONLY

The biometric lock clicked open before he touched it, already synced to his clearance.

He paused in the doorway and looked back at the room of analysts, soldiers, and screens.

"Begin national coordination," he said. "Every state, every agency, every tool we have. Silent Protocol Two must operate as if we are already at war."

No one breathed as he stepped inside the restricted wing.

The door sealed behind him with a heavy, deliberate thud.

And the hunt for Walkers deepened.

Dr. Caulfield was already waiting for him when the elevator doors slid open.

The lower HECATE wing did not advertise its existence. No secure signage, no brass plaques, just a concrete corridor with recessed lights and a biometric scanner that hummed softly as it read the pattern in his palm. The air felt cooler down here, dry enough to sting in his nose.

"Senator," Caulfield said. She had the tired, wired look of someone who lived on caffeine and classified briefings. "You came quickly."

"You said you had something operational," Hargreaves replied. "Not theoretical. I respond to that."

She allowed herself the smallest flicker of a smile. "Then you're going to like this."

She led him through a security door and into a long observation gallery. One wall was solid concrete. The other was glass, thick and slightly darkened. Banks of monitors lined the back of the room, some cycling through heat maps, others tracking vitals and chemical read-outs. Below, in the chamber on the other side of the glass, a dozen soldiers stood at attention.

They wore no insignia. No unit patches. Just matte gray uniforms that hugged too close to their skin.

"Division Gray," Caulfield said.

Hargreaves stepped closer to the glass. The soldiers were in their twenties and thirties, but there was something old about them already. Their skin had a faint sallow cast, like they had not seen sunlight in weeks. Muscles tense. Eyes too still. A few had a barely noticeable tremor in their hands.

"What am I looking at?" he asked.

"Your first field-ready counter-Walker unit," Caulfield said. "They're trained to operate in high-static zones. They can maintain formation and weapons discipline inside conditions that scramble un-modified neural pathways in under thirty seconds."

She tapped a control on the console. A diagram appeared on the central monitor, overlaying the chamber view. Human silhouettes lit up with glowing points along the spine, sternum, and base of the skull.

"We've implanted stabilizer nodes at key junctions," she went on. "Synthetic harmonic dampeners. They bleed off low-level resonance before it can overload their nervous systems."

Hargreaves studied the diagram, then looked back at the soldiers. The faintest flare of gray light pulsed beneath their collars and along their wrists, barely visible against their skin.

"And the chemicals?" he asked.

"Neurochemical cocktails," Caulfield said. "Timed microdoses. They mimic Shield-class resistance patterns, at least in effect. Reduced emotional volatility. Sharpened focus. Blunted fear response." She hes-itated, just slightly. "Some motor jitter as a tradeoff. You'll see that more under live static exposure."

One of the soldiers blinked hard, jaw tightening as his fingers twitched against his thigh, then went still again.

"They look exhausted," Hargreaves observed.

"They are," Caulfield said. "They've been through three weeks of high-static simulation. Their bodies are adjusting to the implants and the drug cycles. They're still within tolerances."

"Will they hold up in the field?" he asked.

"For a time," she said. "But they're not built for long-term use, Senator. The implants stress the cardiovascular and endocrine systems. There will be cognitive drift with extended exposure. Organ damage, eventually."

He watched one of the Gray soldiers shift his weight, expression flat, eyes focused on something only he could see.

"Then we rotate them out," Hargreaves said. His voice stayed even. "We knew from the start this wasn't a marathon. It's containment. Short engagements. Hard strikes."

Caulfield studied him for a moment, weighing how much truth to press. "You understand the cost."

He turned his head just enough to meet her gaze. "Doctor, the threat we're facing is rewriting physics in front of cameras. It killed a man in Salem, almost took down a hospital, lit a Miami rooftop like a controlled burn, and fractured something under Colorado your own sensors can't chart."

His eyes went back to the soldiers. "They're not built to last, I understand that. But the threat isn't meant to last either."

He paused, voice sinking into something colder. "This is not endurance. This is containment."

She exhaled slowly. "Division Gray can deploy inside Walker resonance events. They can hold a perimeter when normal units would break. They're not meant to replace your armies. They're meant to stand in places no one else can."

"Then they're exactly what we need," he said.

Down in the chamber, an alarm tone chimed softly. A voice spoke over the intercom, calm and clipped.

"Division Gray, prepare for live demonstration. Static density at forty percent. Target release in ten seconds."

Hargreaves watched the soldiers as they moved. Their formation tightened with mechanical precision. Hands flexed. Stabilizer nodes pulsed in unison, a faint synchronous glow that made them look almost inhuman for a heartbeat.

He set his palms on the railing, the glass cool under his fingers.

"Show me," he said.

Caulfield nodded to the technician at the console. "Begin demonstration."

In the chamber below, something crawled into being at the far end, where the lights were already starting to flicker.

The containment chamber hummed beneath the fluorescent lights, its reinforced glass vibrating with a low mechanical rumble. The operator stood at his console, tablet steady in both hands, watching the anomaly crouched inside the room. It twitched like a glitching frame in a corrupted video, flickering in and out of shape. Whatever it had once been didn't matter. Now it was just static dragged into something that resembled a body.

"Bring in Gray Team One," the commander said.

The side door slid open. Six soldiers marched in with perfect synchronicity, their boots striking the floor in the same instant. Their skin held a washed-out pallor, the kind that suggested exhaustion or illness. Thin stabilizer nodes lined their spines, glowing faintly with a muted gray light. They moved with the flat precision of machines, not men.

Dr. Caulfield tapped her wrist console. The stabilizers brightened. "Chemical sync engaged. Neural alignment stable."

It didn't look stable. Each soldier's fingers shook in tiny, involuntary spasms. One blinked too slowly, as if his eyelids were struggling to obey.

Inside the chamber, the anomaly scraped itself across the far wall. A warped, broken sound rippled through the speakers, more distortion than voice. It threw itself sideways, smearing into a streak of static before snapping back into shape.

The soldiers advanced at once.

Static pressure dropped sharply as their dampeners activated, drawing the distortion toward them in a tightening funnel. The anomaly convulsed, its outline breaking into jagged shards of light. The stabilizer nodes along the soldiers' spines pulsed harder, straining to keep the resonance contained.

One soldier jerked violently. His jaw clenched. Blood beaded at his nostrils.

Dr. Caulfield turned sharply. "They're over-threshold. Pull them back or you're going to—"

"Maintain formation," the commander said without looking at her.

The Gray soldier didn't fall. None of them moved out of sync. They absorbed the anomaly's thrashing resonance until the creature finally ruptured inward, collapsing into drifting flecks of ash that skittered across the chamber floor like dying sparks.

The stabilizers dimmed. The room fell silent except for the harsh breathing of the Gray team.

"They're at collapse margins," Caulfield snapped. "They can't sustain another second in that environment."

"They don't need another second," the commander replied. "Three minutes is enough."

Enough for a field strike. Enough to suppress a Walker long enough for containment to begin. Enough to die doing it.

The operator's tablet buzzed.

A new alert flashed across the screen:

Resonant signature detected.

South Florida region.

Pattern consistent with two emergent Walkers.

He stiffened. "Sir. Fresh spike. Miami corridor. Probability index rising fast."

The commander scanned the data, his jaw tightening. "We should deploy Division Gray. This one's active."

Medtechs hurried in to stabilize the trembling soldiers. The operator didn't miss the quiet panic in their movements, or the faint static crawling under the skin of the Gray team.

They were already burning out.

And someone out there was about to be hunted by them.

The glass wall of the command floor reflected rows of analysts, each hunched over glowing monitors that streamed real-time resonance maps, satellite telemetry, and classified civilian feeds. Hargreaves stepped into the center of the room and clasped his hands behind his back, the way he always did before delivering an order that would ripple across the country.

"Status on the Miami signature," he said.

A tech glanced up, nervous. "Two moving heat vectors, sir. Intermittent distortions consistent with early-stage Walkers. We think they're traveling together."

Incorrect, but no one here knew that yet.

Hargreaves nodded once. "Deploy Division Gray to the Miami perimeter. Quiet approach only. I don't want a public footprint."

Another tech hesitated. "Sir, that will put them in high-exposure range within the hour."

"Good," he said. "Let's see what the investment produces."

He turned toward the operations matrix, watching lines of code cascade down the main screen. "Initiate expanded transit monitoring. Flag any unusual pattern within two hundred miles. If someone changes buses twice or pays cash more than once, I want it logged."

"Yes, sir."

"And start civilian data scraping in the Miami corridor. Cell pings, purchase patterns, emergency calls. Pull everything."

A third analyst swallowed. "Do we issue a misinformation package, Senator?"

Hargreaves didn't look away from the screen. "Increase it. Push controlled leaks through the usual media contacts. Words like gas leak and faulty infrastructure work well. If there's smoke, blame aging buildings. If someone reports heat flashes or strange lights, blame electrical faults." He paused, then added, "Walkers aren't the story. Containment is."

The room hummed with activity as commands rushed through federal systems.

A predictive model opened on the primary display, bright white lines mapping probability arcs across the southeastern United States. The software began generating likely future movements of the two signatures.

Hargreaves leaned in and pressed his thumb to the authorization pad.

"Activate predictive capture models."

A tone sounded as the system accepted his clearance.

"No more Salem," he said quietly. "No more uncontrolled anomalies."

The analysts didn't respond. They never did when he used that tone.

Hargreaves stepped back. His reflection stared at him from the glass wall, stern, composed, already considering the next escalation. Silent Protocol II was in motion now, humming across the country like a rising pulse.

Behind him, a tech flinched as a new alert popped up in red.

"Sir?" the operator called. "Something else just registered on the long-range grid. Not a Walker. Not static either. Unknown signature."

Hargreaves turned with a slow, focused calm. "Unknown how?"

"It's an unknown anomaly in the Miami region, it's not human. It's... I don't know what it is."

Hargreaves's jaw tightened.

A new threat, emerging inside his perfect net.

"Track it," he said. "And don't take your eyes off it for a second."

The corridor beyond the demonstration chamber was colder, quieter, and dimly lit by recessed strips of pale blue light. Hargreaves walked with his hands clasped behind him, the echo of his footsteps the only sound until the security doors slid open and released a wave of antiseptic air.

Dr. Caulfield hesitated before following him inside. She knew what he would see, and what he would decide.

On either side of the hall, glass panels revealed small containment rooms. Each held a single figure strapped to a reinforced cot.

Prototypes.

Early failures.

The first attempts to push human biology into resonance-adaptive territory.

A soldier inside the nearest cell twitched under a thin blanket, his limbs jerking as static crawled across his skin like invisible insects. His eyes were open but unfocused, staring at a point far beyond the ceiling. Another convulsed softly, breath hitching with each ripple of distortion that passed through his nervous system.

Hargreaves paused at each window.

The bodies trembled, their implants pulsing faint gray light in unsteady rhythm. Some murmured fragments of words that made no sense. Others stared into nothing, pupils blown wide, as if they could see something that no unaltered mind was meant to survive.

Caulfield spoke quietly behind him. "These were early attempts. Exposure was higher than we understood. The neural structures couldn't compensate."

Hargreaves didn't respond. He watched one prototype grip the rails of his cot with white-knuckled intensity, his muscles spasming as though resisting some unseen pressure.

"These men volunteered," Caulfield added, voice tight. "We were trying to prepare for threats we didn't have language for yet."

He finally turned his head slightly. "And now we do."

Her expression faltered. "Sir—"

"They are casualties of adaptation," Hargreaves said, calm and absolute. He kept walking, examining each ruined body as if they were data points rather than people.

At the end of the hall, he stopped. The last prototype lay almost still, barely breathing, eyes half-open and drifting as though tracking something moving behind the glass.

Something only he could see.

Hargreaves studied the man for a long moment.

"If humanity can't adapt," he said softly, "it will be overtaken."

Caulfield closed her eyes, as if the verdict landed heavier than she expected.

A soft alarm tone chimed from the wall console behind them.

A tech's voice came over the intercom. "Senator, new resonance signature detected. It matches the Miami anomaly pattern. It's moving northwest."

Hargreaves didn't even turn. "Keep a trace on it. Notify the sector commander."

The intercom clicked off.

Outside the containment cells, the prototypes twitched in unison, as if reacting to something unseen.

The war he'd been preparing for had already begun.

The command floor was buzzing when the junior operator stepped forward with a tablet pressed tight against his chest, as if the data might burn through it. He approached Senator Hargreaves carefully. No one liked interrupting him when he was studying the field monitors.

"Sir," the operator said, voice low. "We have a live update."

Hargreaves turned just enough to acknowledge him. "Report."

The operator swallowed and held out the tablet. "Two signatures matching early Walker profiles were detected on the Miami grid. The readings are intermittent, but they line up with the individuals flagged in the Level One sweep."

"Elara Whitcombe," Hargreaves said, scanning the pulsing lines on the display. "And the man who keeps surfacing near her. Joe Biggs."

"Yes, sir. But there's something else." The operator tapped the screen, enlarging a cluster of jagged distortions. "Our static monitors picked up a pattern we have never catalogued before. Resonance mimicry. The system flagged it as unknown."

Hargreaves frowned, leaning closer. "Mimicry."

"It appears to be copying the harmonic signature of the targets," the operator said. "If the pattern is real, it might be learning them."

Hargreaves lowered the tablet, his expression tightening. "Then send Gray."

The operator hesitated. "Sir, Division Gray hasn't been tested in open conditions. The stabilizers might not hold if the distortions keep spreading."

Hargreaves gave him a look sharp enough to cut the hesitation in half. "If these things are learning, we learn faster."

The operator nodded and rushed off to relay the order.

Behind him, Hargreaves faced the shifting map again, the red pulses crawling slowly across state lines like a spreading infection.

Silent Protocol II was no longer containment. It was war.

19

St. Eligius

The foothills rose like dark, broken ribs against the Colorado sky. Cold wind scraped across the abandoned mining road as Maya and Alex climbed higher, the gravel crunching under their boots. Pines whispered overhead, but the Weave hummed louder than the forest, a constant low vibration that made Maya's teeth ache.

The deeper they walked, the worse it became.

Threads shivered in her vision, snapping in and out of clarity like frayed wires sparking under strain. Every few steps a pulse ran through the ground, sharp enough to knock her breath sideways. At the edges of her sight, hollow figures flickered and vanished, their outlines jerking like corrupted reflections.

Echo-Selves.

Not fully formed, not stable, but watching.

Alex paused to steady himself, one hand braced on a warped support beam half-buried in the dirt. The beam crumbled under his fingers like brittle sand.

"Maya," he said quietly, "I feel it pulling at my shield again. Like pressure under my ribs."

She nodded. The air around him shimmered faintly, his harmonic thinning each time the static tugged at him. The Weave here was wounded, and everything near it felt the strain.

Maya touched the side of a boulder where stone had softened and refrozen in strange, rippling waves. A transfigurer's mark. Richard's presence bled through every distorted surface, familiar but warped like a cracked bell struggling to ring true.

"He's close," she whispered. "He's trying to reshape something he doesn't understand."

Ahead of them, the St. Eligius mining complex rose from the foothills in jagged outlines. Old processing towers leaned at odd angles, some twisted into glassy spirals. Quartz veins along the rock face glowed with faint internal light, fractured in patterns that looked almost like runes.

Alex scanned the field with a soldier's caution. "This place looks wrong."

"It is," Maya said. "He destabilized the node. The Weave is trying to hold shape around it, but it's slipping."

A cold pulse ran beneath their feet. The ground vibrated as if something deep underground had stirred.

Maya drew in a sharp breath. "He's not just working here. He's opening something."

They stepped closer to the mine entrance, half-collapsed and rimmed with glittering quartz that pulsed like a heartbeat. Resonant pressure spilled out of the dark tunnel, thick and suffocating, as though the mountain itself was exhaling through a wound that never closed.

Alex tightened his grip on her arm. "Once we go in, we're committed. No easy exits."

Maya stared into the trembling darkness ahead.

"He's inside," she said softly. "And he's about to break something he can't fix."

The node trembles, the air thickens, and Maya feels Richard's harmonic drag her forward like a tide pulling at her ribs. They step into the mine, the darkness rippling around them. The confrontation has begun.

The tunnel widened into a cavern that felt too large for the mountain holding it. Alex stepped inside and stopped short. The air vibrated around him like a tuning fork struck too close to his skull. A metallic tang coated his tongue. Every breath felt charged.

Residuum shadows clung to the walls, slow and syrupy, as if the darkness itself was replaying the last few seconds of movement. When Alex lifted his hand, the shadow lifted a heartbeat later. When he let it fall, the shadow lagged behind, drifting back into place like a discarded afterimage.

Static lived here. It had roots.

In the center of the cavern, Richard Barrett knelt on the stone floor, surrounded by a rough chalk-and-quartz circle that pulsed with uneven light. Crystals were embedded in the ground around him, veins of fractured quartz that shimmered as if reacting to his touch.

Richard's hands were pressed flat to the stone, fingers splayed, knuckles white. His journal lay open beside him. The pages were covered in jagged lattice sketches, some incomplete, some repeated dozens of times, all drawn with a frantic intensity that made Alex's skin crawl. Richard had no training, no framework, no understanding. He was replicating the Weave by instinct alone, and instinct was killing him.

He muttered under his breath in broken harmonic intervals, a sound that wavered between chanting and sobbing. Each phrase bent the air around him, warping it like heat over asphalt. Threads of static crawled across the cavern floor, twisting toward the center of the node.

Alex felt the ground pulse. Not with life. With strain.

Maya stepped forward before he could stop her. Her voice was low, steady, threaded with fear she refused to show. "Richard. Stop. You're tearing the node apart."

Richard's head snapped up. His eyes were wild and red around the edges, but not frightened. Relief flashed there, raw and startling.

"You heard it too," he whispered. His voice cracked with something like awe. "The Weave doesn't want us small. It wants you open."

Alex moved in front of Maya automatically. His shield flared without conscious thought, a thin shimmer over his arms. Richard watched the motion with detached curiosity, as if the threat did not register.

Maya touched Alex's shoulder. "It's alright," she murmured. "He's not attacking."

Alex kept his gaze locked on Richard. He wasn't so sure.

Richard stood slowly, joints trembling. The quartz circle pulsed harder in response, as though his movements pulled too much current at once.

"Maya," Richard said, his voice rising with a brittle intensity, "you were chosen. You woke the moment the Weave cracked. I saw the light on the night of the breach. You're meant to open. You're meant to break through."

Maya flinched as the word break echoed through the cavern. The node responded with a low groan that made Alex's teeth ring.

"Richard," she said softly, "you're hurting yourself. You're hurting the Weave. You don't know what that circle is doing."

Richard smiled. It was not madness. It was certainty. The kind that frightened Alex more than a threat ever could.

"The Weave showed me," Richard whispered. "It showed me Echoes. Reflections that could become real. It showed me how small our forms are. You don't fix a vessel like that, Maya. You break it open."

Alex stepped forward, jaw tight. "You're wrong. She doesn't need to be broken."

Richard tilted his head, studying him with a strange, distant sympathy. "You think I want to hurt her. I don't. I want to free her."

Before Alex could answer, the floor shuddered. Hard.

The quartz veins webbed through the cavern pulsed bright white, then fractured outward like lightning trapped in stone. A wave of static rolled through the chamber, slamming into Alex's chest. He staggered back, shielding instinct overriding everything else.

Richard gasped and pressed his palms harder to the ground. "It's almost ready," he whispered. "It's opening."

"No," Maya said, horror tightening her voice. "You're channeling too much. Richard, stop."

Richard didn't stop.

He couldn't.

The ground trembled again, stronger this time, shaking dust from the ceiling. Echo-Selves flickered in the far edges of the cavern, thin outlines of Maya and Alex jerking in and out of visibility like broken reflections caught in strobe light.

Richard smiled at Maya, as if offering her a gift.

And the node screamed beneath them.

Richard rose slowly from the chalk-and-quartz circle. His movements were unsteady, as if every bone in his body protested. Static clung to him in thin threads of light, crawling along his arms and neck. His pupils had expanded until they looked like deep wells, swallowing most of the color in his eyes. He looked both fevered and hollow, like someone who had been staring into a storm for too long.

Maya felt Alex shift beside her, readying himself. The cavern pulsed with the strained heartbeat of the node, the air humming against her skin.

Richard lifted his hands as if trying to calm them. "Maya," he whispered. His voice cracked. "I didn't think you would come."

"Richard," she said carefully. "You're tearing the node apart. You must stop."

He laughed, soft and frayed at the edges. "Stop? I can't stop now. You didn't hear what it said when I collapsed. The node spoke. It finally spoke."

Maya's breath caught. "Richard, nodes don't speak. They resonate. They warn or pull, but they don't talk."

He shook his head violently. "You weren't here. You don't know what it showed me. The Immortals abandoned this world. They locked the Weave and left us with a system that can't sustain itself. Someone has to take their place."

He stepped out of the circle, wobbling slightly, but there was purpose in every step. The cavern light flickered in response, shadows bending as if drawn toward him.

"You're the Threadweaver," he said. "But incomplete. Still bound inside a body too small for what you're meant to carry."

Maya's pulse thudded in her ears. "I don't know what you think you saw, but you're wrong. I'm not meant to replace anyone."

"You are!" His voice echoed too loudly, and the quartz veins in the walls shimmered. "When I collapsed, the Weave flooded through me. It tried to reshape me, tried to open me, but I wasn't the right vessel. So I tried to help it. I tried to cut a path for it, to reshape myself and the node so the pressure wouldn't break the world."

Maya stared at the warped stone and melted beams around them. A cold certainty settled in her chest. "The Echo-Selves. You did that."

Richard's expression twisted with sorrow and awe. "Not on purpose. They formed when I pushed too hard. Fragments pulled from the wrong layers. Reflections searching for coherence." He lifted a trembling hand. "If I could have contained it, if I had been stronger, the Weave wouldn't have needed to break itself into pieces."

He stepped closer. Desperation sharpened his voice. "But you can. Maya, you're still closed. You're trying to hold all that resonance inside a vessel that can't contain it. You must be broken open to become what the Weave needs."

Maya recoiled. The words hit like cold water. Alex moved instantly, stepping in front of her with a shield rising in a shimmer of blue.

"Back away from her," he said.

Richard didn't flinch. He didn't even seem to see the shield. "I'm not trying to hurt her, Alex. I'm trying to free her. Don't you understand? Once she's open, she won't need protection. She'll reshape everything. She'll stabilize what the Immortals left behind."

Maya's stomach twisted. The sincerity in Richard's voice made it worse. He believed this. He believed tearing her apart was salvation.

"Richard," she said quietly. "If you try to break me open, you'll kill me."

"No," he whispered, eyes shining. "I'll transform you."

The ground shuddered, a deep tremor that rippled through the cavern floor. The node flared with a violent surge of static, and Richard turned back toward the circle with fevered purpose.

"You came at the perfect moment," he said. "Let me show you."

"Maya," Alex said urgently, "he's channeling again. We need to move."

Static erupted from the ritual lines like shattered glass. The cavern lights snapped and flared, and Richard dropped to his knees inside the circle, hands pressing into the stone as the ritual roared back to life.

The node screamed through the Weave.

And everything began to break.

The moment Richard laid his hand against the heart of the node, the cavern groaned like a living thing. A sharp tremor ran through the quartz floor, and Alex felt the resonance hit his ribs before he heard it. Light fractured across the chamber in overlapping waves, each one carrying a distorted echo of reality with it.

Richard's figure split into three shapes, then four, then five. Each version lagged half a heartbeat behind the real one, their movements stuttering in and out of alignment. For one nauseating instant, Maya split too, her echoes flickering through the same unreal rhythm, like the world couldn't decide where she belonged.

Alex swore under his breath and threw up a shield. The pressure slammed into him immediately. Blue-white static rippled across his arms and burst outward like sparks off a grinding blade. His shield crackled, flickered, then steadied only because he pushed every ounce of focus into it.

Maya shouted something, but her voice warped in the layered distortion. The chamber rippled like a pond struck by falling stone. Dust shook loose from the ceiling and drifted sideways instead of down.

Richard stood in the center of it all, eyes bright with feverish conviction. A surge of Transfiguration energy erupted from his hands, not aimed to harm but to twist the air around Maya, to force the resonance toward her like a hand trying to pry open a sealed door.

Alex felt the intent and braced. The force hit the shield hard. Static tore at the edges and clawed straight into his chest, pulling at the same place the Echo had drained days earlier. Pain flared behind his ribs, sharp and cold. His vision blurred.

He gritted his teeth. "Not again."

The shield wavered as another wave rolled through the cavern. It dragged at him, trying to siphon off more of his harmonic field. His knees buckled for a moment before he locked them again.

Maya lifted her hand to counter, but her aura flickered wildly, green-white light sputtering like a torch drowning in wind. She gasped and nearly doubled over as the energy snapped through her.

"Alex, hold it!" she cried.

"I'm trying," he forced out.

Richard didn't even look at them. He was murmuring to the node, his fingers buried in fractured stone that glowed a sickly amber. Lines of distortion spread outward from his touch, racing across the cavern walls and breaking the quartz into jagged planes. Every breath Alex pulled felt charged, thick with unstable resonance.

The echoes multiplied. Richard's shadows overlapped like shifting layers of glass. Maya's form blurred again, her edges fraying into thin luminous strands before snapping back.

Alex felt the moment the node began to unravel. The floor shuddered, then pulsed.

Something else pulsed with it.

A deeper vibration rolled through the chamber, low and cold and hungry. It wasn't Richard. It wasn't the node. It came from the dark space between the walls, from inside the fractures he had opened.

Maya's eyes widened. "Alex... something's coming through."

The Shadow Current focused, drawing close like a mind leaning over their shoulders.

Alex's shield trembled under the new weight. Sweat ran down his spine.

"Richard," Maya shouted, her voice cracking under the distortion, "stop the ritual. You're tearing the Weave open."

Richard didn't stop. He didn't even flinch.

The tremor deepened, a dark harmonic rising from the fractures like a predator scenting blood.

And Alex knew, with sick certainty, that whatever Richard had pulled toward them was about to arrive.

The cavern shuddered around her, the stone bending and unbending like something alive. Maya braced herself against the wall, but her vision fractured before she could draw a steady breath. Ancient runic circles flared across the floor, ghostly shapes that had no business appearing in the present world. Merlin's diagrams floated in the air for a heartbeat, transparent and trembling, as if the Weave was remembering itself through her.

A pulse rippled through her chest. Ethan's resonance flickered faintly, a distant spark, too weak to guide her and too familiar to ignore.

Her knees buckled. She caught herself, but the cavern spun and another version of her appeared at the edge of her sight, half-formed and flickering. The Echo pulled away from her body, jerking a few inches out of alignment, its empty eyes locked on hers.

Not now. Not here.

She forced herself upright, fighting the split. The world lurched as Richard stepped toward her, his hand reaching through the distortion with desperate intensity.

"Maya," he shouted, voice ragged, "let it break you. That's how you ascend!"

His face was lit by the fractured glow of the node. He looked terrified and certain all at once. The stone under his feet rippled as if it could no longer decide what it wanted to be. The air thickened, vibrating with energy that did not belong to the Weave.

Maya stared at the space around him, and her breath caught.

The Shadow Current folded inward near Richard's body, dragging the light around it as if tasting him. The mimicry that had stalked her along the roadside earlier throbbed here too, stronger, closer, drawn by his unraveling power. It was shaping itself around his resonance, learning him, feeding on him.

She understood in a single cold flash.

Richard wasn't channeling the Weave at all.

He was channeling the thing eating it.

"Alex, hold!" she screamed.

He braced his shield fully, sweat sliding down his temple, his teeth clenched as static clawed at him.

Maya dragged what was left of her focus together. The ritual circle under Richard's knees pulsed like a beating heart, and she felt the Current reaching through it. She pushed her hands forward, forcing her resonance into a single hard counterpulse. It tore through her ribs and skull like fire, but she didn't stop. She let it detonate outward.

The circle shattered.

The ground roared with harmonic backlash. Stone cracked like thunder. A wave of energy exploded through the cavern, slamming into all three of them. Alex was driven backward, shield flickering. Richard was ripped off his feet, hurled into the far side of the chamber where a secondary tunnel yawned in darkness.

Maya fell to her knees. Her vision bled white at the edges. Every thread in the Weave seemed to scream around her, then settle, then scream again.

For a brief moment, the node steadied. Its fractured light held still, trembling but intact.

Then it groaned with deep, ancient strain.

Dust drifted down from the ceiling and drifted through her hair. Maya forced herself upright, lungs burning, and looked toward the tunnel where Richard had struck the wall.

"Alex," she whispered, "where is he..."

But the tunnel was empty.

Richard was gone.

The cavern settled in jagged breaths, stone groaning as if it were trying to remember what shape it was supposed to hold. Dust drifted through the air in lazy spirals, catching the faint green shimmer still clinging to Maya's skin.

Alex pushed himself upright and stumbled toward her. She was on her knees, shaking so hard her teeth chattered. Her aura flickered in broken flashes, the green-white light sputtering like a bulb on the edge of burning out. Blood trailed from one nostril, bright against the pale smear of dust on her cheek.

He crouched beside her and slid an arm around her back. "Maya. Hey. Look at me. Stay with me."

She leaned into him as if she had forgotten how to hold her own weight. Her breath came in short, hitched pulls. When she finally lifted her head, her eyes were too bright, too wide, and not entirely focused.

"He thinks I need to be broken open," she whispered. "Richard believes it's the only way the Threadweaver awakens. He thinks my body's too small for the resonance."

Alex felt cold sweep through him, deeper than the static still crawling under his skin. "Stop. Don't even say it like it might make sense."

"He believed it," she said, voice trembling. "And the way the Weave reacted... Alex, what if he's not completely wrong about the pressure. What if I really am—"

"No." His hand came up and he cupped the side of her face, forcing her eyes to meet his. "You're not letting him inside your head. You hear me? You're not a vessel that needs to break. You're a person. And I won't let him do anything to you."

Her breath shuddered again, but she nodded. Slowly. Reluctantly. As if the fear had sunk deeper than she knew how to hide.

A pulse shivered under their feet. The stone trembled for a moment, and shadows rippled across the cavern walls. At first Alex thought they were Residuum remnants, but when he focused, he saw the shapes lagging behind themselves, sliding out of alignment before snapping back.

Echo-forms.

The node was still bleeding distortion into the chamber.

Maya clutched his sleeve. "He'll try again. And next time he won't just break the node."

Alex looked toward the collapsed tunnel where Richard had vanished. The rubble settled in a slow sigh, small fragments shifting down the slope. For a moment there was only silence.

Then a sound rose from somewhere deep in the stone.

A laugh.

Soft.

Wrong.

Delayed by a heartbeat, as if the cavern couldn't quite figure out how to release it.

Maya flinched. Alex tightened his grip on her.

That echo-laugh wasn't mocking. It wasn't triumphant. It sounded relieved.

"He thinks he's saving you," Alex said quietly.

Maya swallowed hard. "And the Shadow Current thinks so too."

Dust drifted again, stirred by some distant tremor. The air tasted metallic, sharp with static.

Alex helped Maya to her feet, feeling the weight of the weave settle on both of them.

They were no longer just chasing Richard.

They were racing a man who believed breaking Maya open was salvation.

And something dark in the Weave believed it with him.

20

Confrontation

The rubble did not move all at once. It settled first in tiny shifts, a soft rain of grit pattering down the slope of the collapsed tunnel. Then the air changed. Static crawled across Maya's skin in thin, stinging lines, prickling at the edges of her aura like a warning that had come too late.

She pushed away from Alex's shoulder and turned toward the blockage.

"Wait," Alex said, catching her arm, but her focus was already sliding inward, into the ripple of the Weave that trembled behind the stone.

The collapsed tunnel glimmered faintly. Not with light, but with distortion. Pale points of static flickered through the dust like insects trapped inside glass, stuttering in and out of existence. The resonance there was wrong, twisted back on itself, like a song played in reverse.

Maya's breath caught. "He's not gone," she whispered.

Before Alex could answer, the rubble shifted in a single, deeper heave. A slab of rock lurched forward, then softened at the edges. It did not fall. It slumped. Stone that had been solid moments before sagged like wet clay, sliding aside in slow, viscous folds.

Richard emerged from the distortion like he was walking out of a broken reflection. For an instant Maya saw three versions of him

153

at once, each one lagging a fraction of a second behind the last. The echoes snapped into alignment with a soundless jolt, leaving only one man standing there.

He looked worse than before. Color had drained from his face until his skin was almost gray. His hair clung damply to his temples. Static burn traced faint, darkened veins along his throat like smoke trapped under the skin. His eyes were too bright, pupils large and ringed with a pale halo of shimmer that made her stomach twist.

But he was not alone.

Echo-forms trailed behind him like stuttering shadows. They clung to the walls and floor, delay-images of his posture and movement, a heartbeat behind the real man. When Richard lifted his foot to step forward, three ghost-feet followed, dragging through the dust before snapping together with a faint crackle.

Maya's aura recoiled.

The Weave around him was shredded, threads knotted and pulled tight, humming with a sick, strained pitch. His harmonic signature had always had a weight to it, a grounded density like stone, but now she heard it in overlapping layers, three, four, maybe more tones stacked out of sync. It was like listening to one voice speaking in chords.

He lifted his head and looked at her.

There was no hate in his gaze. No gloating. No satisfaction in what he had done to the node or to himself. What she saw there made her chest hurt more than the static.

He looked at her the way a drowning man looks at a distant shore.

"Maya," he said.

Her name came out in overlapping echoes. The first word reached her ears, then a second followed a half breath behind, then a third. The same syllables, the same pitch, lagging, replaying. It sounded like a recording skipping against itself.

Alex stepped in front of her without thinking. His shield flared, a faint blue pressure wrapping across her chest and ribs. "Stay back, Richard," he said. "You're done here."

Richard did not seem to hear him. Or if he did, Alex's presence was secondary, something peripheral. His focus stayed fixed on Maya like she was the only solid thing in a world that kept flickering.

"You broke the circle before it could complete," Richard said. The chorus of his voice brushed over her skin, three versions of the sentence nearly in sync, one just enough behind to make the hairs on her arms rise. "You stopped the node from opening. You stopped yourself from opening."

Maya swallowed, her throat tight and dry. "You were killing it," she said. "You were tearing the Weave apart. You were letting that thing in."

His mouth tightened, not with anger, but with something like frustration. The Echo-forms behind him shivered in a slow, rippling wave, as if answering her words with their own soundless protest.

"You heard it," Richard insisted, taking a step forward. Dust fluttered around his boots, refusing to settle. "You felt the pressure. The node is choking. You are choking. The Weave does not want us small, it does not want you small. It wants you open."

Static jumped between his fingertips like faint threads of lightning. The Echo-forms leaned forward with him, stretched thin against the cavern walls. Maya felt the Shadow Current stirring inside that motion, a low, hungry interest coiling around his resonance.

Alex's shield tightened. "Maya, he's riding it," he said under his breath. "He's not just listening to the node. The Current has its hooks in him."

Richard finally seemed to notice the shield, the subtle distortion it cast through the air. His gaze skipped to Alex, then back to Maya, as if checking that she was still there.

"I tried to relieve it," he said. "I tried to take the strain into myself first. I thought if I could reshape the stone, bleed off the pressure, the node would hold. It spoke to me when I collapsed. It showed me what you are."

Maya shook her head. "Whatever spoke to you wasn't the Weave."

"It was." His insistence fractured across the cavern, the Echo-forms' mouths moving a hair behind his own. "You are the Threadweaver, but you are incomplete. You are still bound inside a body too small for the resonance that wants to move through you. It will tear you apart if you keep holding it in. You know that."

Images flashed through her mind in a painful rush: the Salem cavern collapsing, the half-formed corridors that had almost ripped her in half, the way her aura had shattered when she tried to blink after the hospital. The Echo at the windshield, smiling ahead of her. The green fractures that kept appearing whenever she reached for the Weave.

She did know it, some part of her. That did not make him right.

"The Echo-Selves," she said. "You created them."

Richard flinched, just slightly. The echoes behind him rippled again, some flattening, others sharpening as if listening.

"I didn't mean to," he said. "They were a side effect, a misfire. The node is trying to adapt. The Weave is looking for shapes that can survive what is coming. You are one of them. I tried to reshape myself first. I couldn't. The resonance slipped past me and took hold of my shadow. It learned how to echo through me, and when I reached for the node again, it... copied me. It copied you when you touched it. I saw it."

Maya's stomach dropped. At her side, Alex's breathing had gone tight and shallow.

"You're still closed," Richard said. "You must be broken open to become what the Weave needs. Let me finish what it began. I can help you ascend before this world tears you apart instead."

She took a step back. Alex matched it, his hand finding her wrist and anchoring her behind his shoulder.

"You're not helping," Alex said. "You're letting the thing that is eating the Weave use you as a conduit."

Richard's expression twisted in pain, as if Alex had struck him. "You think I do not know what I am standing in," he said quietly. "You think I do not feel it clawing at the lattice, learning our shapes. That is why we have to move first. We have to break before it does, by our terms, not its."

Alex lifted his shield another notch. The air thickened in front of them, vibrating with blue-white pressure that tasted like ozone on Maya's tongue. Her head pounded. The node hummed under the rock like a held breath that might turn into a scream.

"Richard," she said, forcing her voice to steady. "Listen to me. Whatever you heard in the dark is not the only voice in the Weave. You are not its chosen anything. You are a man who almost collapsed a node because he listened to the wrong frequency. You keep pushing, you won't just break me. You'll break everything."

For a heartbeat, something wavered in his eyes. The echoes behind him flickered, as if their attention faltered.

Then the moment passed.

"You broke the circle before it could complete," he repeated. "You stopped the ritual halfway. You tore the pattern apart, you did not let it finish. The Weave pushed. You resisted. That is why it hurts. Let me fix it."

He raised his hands.

The stone around them answered.

Maya felt it before she saw it. The floor under her boots softened, its solid weight turning strange and unsteady. The walls seemed to inhale. Quartz veins that had been frozen in place began to ripple inside the rock like liquid glass.

Alex swore under his breath. His shield flared brighter as the node's resonance surged again, roaring through the chamber like a buried river.

The cavern did not just shake.

It started to melt.

Alex felt the blast before he saw it.

The air tightened, pulled inward as if the entire cavern had inhaled at once. Then Richard thrust both hands forward, and the world tore open in a howl of raw Transfiguration.

Stone did not simply break. It liquefied, stretched, and snapped into razor-thin ribbons of crystalline matter. The cavern walls rippled like molten glass caught in a storm. A spiraling wave of refracted light and shattered mineral shot toward them, shredding the air in jagged spirals.

"Shield!" Maya shouted.

Alex was already moving.

The blast hit his barrier with a sound like a bell breaking. The force slammed into him, lifting his feet off the ground and throwing him backward across the stone. He skidded several yards before he dug his heels in and forced the shield to hold, sucking air through clenched teeth.

His arms shook violently. His vision blurred.

This wasn't the wild, unfocused power Richard had thrown earlier. This was controlled. Directed. He had shaped the eruption specifically to break something open.

Richard wasn't trying to kill him.

He was trying to peel Maya apart.

"She has to ascend!" Richard cried. His voice fractured, overlapping itself in warped echoes. "You can't hold her inside that shape forever. You're suffocating her!"

The shield buckled under the next surge. The pressure didn't slam outward so much as claw inward, scraping across Alex's ribs with a sickening familiarity.

The Echo attack.

Only now it felt like the cavern itself was learning how to eat him.

Alex's jaw locked. A thin whine threaded through his ears as the shield thinned to a translucent shimmer.

Maya lunged toward him, one hand gripping his forearm, the other pressed to his chest. Her grounding pulse snapped through him like cold lightning.

"Stay with me," she whispered. "I've got you."

Her resonance poured into him and steadied the trembling barrier just long enough for him to catch his breath. The crushing pull on his ribs eased, though it didn't disappear entirely.

Alex forced his focus outward. Richard stood framed in a swirl of warped stone and flickering Echo-shadows, his expression a fervent mix of desperation and belief.

He lifted his hands again.

The cavern answered with a deep, rising groan. Cracks spidered across the floor. Shards of suspended quartz lifted into the air like a constellation being torn apart.

"No," Alex breathed. "Not again. I can't take another one of those."

Richard drew the second wave together, larger, denser, coiling around him in tightening loops of fractured light.

The first strike had been an opening blow.

The next would be the one meant to break her.

The cavern dimmed around the forming blast, and Alex braced for a hit he knew he might not survive.

The moment Richard raised his hands; the Weave flared across Maya's vision in a violent rush of green-white light. It wasn't a clean glow. It was cracked, splintered at the edges, laced with thin fractures that pulsed like overstrained nerves.

The node beneath the earth groaned in her awareness. It warped under Richard's pull, threads grinding against one another like tectonic plates slipping out of place. The whole lattice felt bruised.

Maya gasped. "Alex, get ready."

A soft echo brushed her mind, familiar as breath.

Move, Maya.

Ethan's voice.

Or the memory of it.

She couldn't tell anymore.

Richard's second attack erupted before she could decide.

The blast spiraled toward them, brighter and denser than the first. It curled like a living thing, stone liquefying at its center, ribbons of quartz spinning like blades.

Maya didn't think.

She answered the harmonic.

A raw counterpulse tore up her spine and out through her hands, brighter than anything she had ever released. Light exploded from her in a green-white flash, uncontrolled and furious. The Weave screamed as it went.

The cavern shattered into layered realities.

For a heartbeat she saw everything at once:

Ancient runes burning across the stone.

Merlin's diagrams sketched in light, hovering like ghosts.

The Colorado node as it existed centuries ago.

A shape of herself that wasn't her, an Echo reaching out with a hollow smile.

The visions folded in on themselves as the two forces collided.

Maya twisted her counterpulse at the last second. Richard's attack veered off its path and slammed into the far wall, detonating with a roar that shook the chamber. Fragments of quartz burst like shattered stars, showering them in glowing shards.

The shockwave nearly ripped Maya off her feet. Her legs buckled. The world spun sideways.

Alex lunged and caught her before she hit the ground. His grip was tight, trembling, frantic.

"Maya. Look at me. Stay with me."

She tried. Her vision swam with overlapping images, the Weave still flaring uncontrollably behind her eyes. Her aura flickered in painful bursts, each one threatening to split her open from the inside.

She had saved them.

But the act felt like it had torn something loose in her chest.

Across the chamber, Richard staggered backward, arms dropping. For a moment he looked almost human again, exhausted and unsteady.

Then the darkness behind him shifted.

A low tremor rippled through the air, deep as a drumbeat in the bones.

The Shadow Current swelled upward, gathering behind Richard like a second presence wearing his outline.

Maya's breath caught.

The real fight was only beginning.

Richard staggered, breath tearing in and out of his chest as if each inhale scraped against broken glass. His journal hung from one hand, pages fluttering in the cavern's shifting air. When he looked down at it, the sketches he'd carved into the paper pulsed with faint static, lines writhing like they wanted to crawl off the page.

He flipped through the book with shaking fingers. Each diagram glowed faintly, fractured lattices, half-formed glyphs, circles that should never have been drawn by a human hand. The static clinging to the journal hissed softly, as if whispering instructions only he could hear.

"They left us blind," he murmured, voice hoarse. "The Immortals abandoned the world. They turned their faces away while everything collapsed."

Maya steadied herself on Alex's arm. "Richard, stop. Listen to yourself."

But he wasn't listening to her.

His gaze jumped from the journal to Maya, eyes fever-bright and lost. "Someone has to open the path again. Someone must finish what they started."

Above him, the Echo-forms crawled along the cavern ceiling like distorted marionettes. One held Maya's posture but bent wrong at the shoulders. Another mimicked Alex's stance, but its movements lagged by a heartbeat. A third flickered between both forms, uncertain which shape to steal.

Richard didn't seem to notice or care. His focus tunneled entirely toward Maya.

He lifted both hands. The ground responded.

The fractured circle he'd carved earlier reignited beneath him, lines of quartz and chalk glowing molten gold. The air thickened as the harmonic pressure surged, warping the cavern's shape.

"Maya," he shouted, voice cracking with conviction and terror. "The world cannot survive unless you're unbound!"

The circle brightened violently.

Light crawled up Richard's arms, weaving itself through the shaking pages of his journal, threading into the fractured stone beneath his feet.

The ritual reawakened.

And this time, it wasn't just following his will.

Something darker moved with him, guiding his hands. The Shadow Current curled like a hungry tide, ready to claim whatever broke first: the node, the cavern, or Maya herself.

The circle detonated in a blast of soundless pressure that hit Alex like a wall made of ragged metal. Harmonics scraped across his bones, a grinding resonance that felt as if someone were carving lines through his ribs from the inside. The air buckled. Stone shuddered.

Alex didn't think. He moved.

He threw himself in front of Maya and slammed his shield into place. The barrier flared into a trembling curve of green-white light just as Richard's energy tore through the cavern.

The impact cracked the shield.

A sharp burst rang through Alex's skull. His vision went white around the edges. He tasted copper as blood slipped from his nose and ran over his lip. His hands shook so violently he almost dropped the shield entirely.

"Alex, move!" Maya screamed behind him. "You can't hold that!"

"I'm not letting him touch you," he said through clenched teeth.

His knees buckled as the next wave hit. Richard's Transfiguration strike hammered the shield so hard it split into two overlapping arcs, each flickering wildly as Alex struggled to keep them from collapsing. The pressure lifted him off his heels, dragging him backward across the uneven stone. His boots scraped uselessly for purchase. His shoulders felt like they would tear from their sockets.

Richard cried out from the center of the circle, voice echoing in layered distortions. "She has to ascend! You can't hold her inside that shape forever!"

Alex's breath hitched. His arms trembled uncontrollably. The shield buckled inward another inch, then another.

He had seconds left. Maybe less.

Behind him, Maya's aura flared, unstable and fierce.

She placed a trembling hand against his back. "Alex... let go. I have to answer him."

He knew what that meant. He knew the cost.

And still, he held the shield as long as he could, until the world narrowed to shaking arms, burned lungs, and the desperate hope that she was fast enough.

The moment he faltered, her power surged.

She was preparing a counterpulse strong enough to break the ritual.

Or herself.

Maya's hands trembled as she pressed her palm against the cracked stone. She could feel the jagged edges of her own resonance tearing at her ribs, urging her to stop, warning her she was already too close to breaking. But Richard's power flooded the cavern again, shaking the ground beneath them, and Alex was seconds from collapse.

There was no choice.

She opened herself.

The Weave surged through her cracked harmonic like a river forced through shattered glass. Pain lanced through her chest. Her breath caught. For one impossible heartbeat the cavern went perfectly, terribly silent.

Even the Echo-Selves froze, their warped bodies caught mid-lurch, flickering in the stale air like half-finished reflections.

Maya felt the threads align. Not cleanly. Not safely. But enough.

She whispered, "Hold on, Alex."

Then she released everything.

The counterpulse tore out of her in a flood of green-white light that hit the chamber like a silent explosion. The ritual circle shattered first, cracking apart in a burst of quartz dust and broken sigils. The shockwave ripped across the stone floor, lifting Richard off his feet and hurling him backward into the far tunnel. His journal scattered in the air, pages twisting like startled birds before settling across the ground.

A deep groan rolled through the cavern. The node beneath them shuddered as if in pain, its harmonics bending under the force of her blast. For a breathless moment Maya feared she had broken it completely.

But the resonance settled.

Unstable, wounded, but no longer spiraling.

Her knees buckled. She fell forward onto one hand, gasping as her aura sputtered in violent, fractured pulses. Light crawled over her arms in jagged bursts she could no longer control. Her vision blurred in and out, the world tilting with each breath.

Alex caught her shoulder. "Maya. Maya, look at me. Are you alright?"

"No," she whispered. "I can't do that again."

The words shook with truth. Something inside her had cracked, and she knew it. If she tried another counterpulse, there would be nothing left to hold her shape together.

A faint rustle echoed from the tunnel where Richard had vanished.

Maya lifted her head just in time to see a cluster of Echo-Selves slip after him, their flickering forms stretching and contracting like hungry shadows drawn toward a deeper darkness.

Richard had escaped.

And he wasn't alone.

Maya closed her eyes for a moment, steadying her breath as her aura dimmed to a tremor. She forced herself upright with Alex's help, even though her legs felt hollow.

"He's going deeper," she whispered. "And if he reaches the next node junction before we do..."

Alex finished for her, voice grim. "He'll finish what he started."

They stood in the settling dust, the cavern pulsing with a faint, wounded resonance.

Maya had stopped him once.

She knew she wouldn't survive stopping him the same way again.

Alex pulled Maya upright, his arm firm around her waist as she struggled to find her balance. Her entire body shook, her aura flickering in faint, uneven pulses that barely held together. The cavern still hummed with aftershocks of the counterpulse, the air tinged with quartz dust and the metallic taste of static.

Maya's breath trembled. She stared at the dark tunnel where Richard had vanished, the last wisps of Echo-shadows curling after him like dying flames.

"He's not trying to destroy the world," she whispered. Her voice was thin, frayed. "He thinks he's saving it."

Alex turned sharply toward her, eyes tight with fear and anger. "He'll kill you trying."

She shook her head, slow and unsteady. "No. Something else will."

The shadows around the tunnel seemed to move with their own pulse, flickering in jagged patterns that didn't belong to Richard alone. Something deeper stirred in the stone, watching, learning.

Alex followed her gaze, and understanding hit him with a visible weight. "Maya... what did you see?"

"Not him," she said softly. "Not just him. The thing he's feeding. The thing feeding on us." She swallowed hard. "If he reaches the next junction, if he tears the node open the way he wants to, it won't be him that finishes it. It will be the Shadow Current. And it will take me first."

Alex tightened his grip on her shoulder, grounding her the way he always did. "Then we don't let him get that far."

Maya didn't answer. She simply stared into the dark, where Richard limped deeper into the mine with Echo-Selves trailing him like loyal ghosts.

They were no longer trying to stop Richard.

They were racing to reach him before he destroyed her.

21

The Immortals Speak

The cavern should have been roaring.

A moment ago the air had been full of screaming harmonics, quartz dust, and the ragged edge of Maya's counterpulse. Now it settled into an uneasy hush, as if the stone had decided it did not dare make another sound.

Maya stood with Alex's arm braced around her, her knees still trembling. Her aura flickered in thin green-white pulses that could not find a steady rhythm. Every breath scraped her throat. The mine smelled like scorched minerals and ozone. Somewhere deeper in the tunnels, water dripped in slow, patient beats.

Then the Weave went quiet.

Not quiet the way exhaustion made something quiet. Not the kind of quiet that came after a storm passed. It was a held silence, tight and deliberate, like a lungful of air refused its release.

Maya blinked, suddenly aware of how loud her own heartbeat was. The threads she usually felt under everything were still there, but they were not moving. They were suspended. Waiting.

Alex swayed beside her, his hand lifting instinctively as if he meant to raise his shield again. He stopped halfway, face tightening with confusion.

"What the hell," he murmured.

Maya opened her senses. The Weave did not answer her. It watched.

The Echo-Selves that had been lingering at the edge of the chamber were still for a heartbeat, their stuttering outlines frozen in mid-flicker. One stood half formed against the far wall, a pale imitation of her posture with the wrong timing in its breath. Another clung to the ceiling like a reflection that had lost its surface.

They did not lunge. They did not feed. They simply stopped, as if a command had been spoken in a language they could not disobey.

Then, without resistance, they unraveled.

It was not an explosion. Not a fight. With the Weave held, they couldn't maintain coherence. They thinned and collapsed into ash like static, dissolving into nothing like smoke pulled into a vacuum. The air cleared in seconds. The pressure that had been crawling under Maya's skin eased, not because it had left, but because something stronger had told it to be silent.

Alex inhaled sharply and stumbled back a step. He pressed a hand to his ribs, eyes squeezed shut as though he was trying to steady something inside himself.

"My shield," he said, the words rough. "I can't feel it."

Maya felt it too. The constant static tug that had been eating at his grounding reflex, the harsh grit that had lived in the space around him ever since Georgia, vanished in an instant. The absence left him dizzy, like a man who had been leaning into a storm and suddenly found himself standing in open air.

Maya's stomach rolled. Her body felt wrong, like gravity had shifted. She was weightless and pinned at the same time, as if she had become a nail hammered through the world.

"Alex," she whispered, not sure if she meant it as a warning or a question.

He opened his eyes. His gaze flicked over her face, her flickering aura, then scanned the chamber as if expecting Richard to step out again. Instead he found nothing but the silence pressing in from all sides.

"Maya," he said quietly, "are you doing that?"

She shook her head. The motion made her vision spark. "No."

The Weave did not move. It did not hum. It did not ripple with damage or strain.

It held.

Maya swallowed hard, tasting metal. She reached toward the threads like she always did, careful and tentative, and found something that was not thread at all.

Attention.

It was the sensation of standing in a dark room and realizing someone had been there the whole time, breathing with you, waiting for you to notice.

Her skin prickled. The fine hairs on her arms rose. Even the dust hanging in the air seemed to pause, caught in an invisible stillness.

Something had noticed them.

Not Richard. Not the Shadow Current.

Something older.

Maya's breath came shallow. She stared into the dim air ahead of them, where the last faint shimmer of her counterpulse still clung to the stone like a memory.

A light began to gather.

It did not bloom like fire or flare like electricity. It formed the way a chord formed, piece by piece, tone by tone, harmonics layering until the air itself seemed to become luminous. Thin lines of resonance traced patterns in the space around them, circles that were not drawn but implied, like geometry hidden inside reality.

Green-white, soft and steady.

Silver, deep and ancient.

A darker weight that felt like stone and oath.

A sharp sorrow that tightened Maya's throat.

A distant cold that did not feel cruel, only inevitable.

The lights did not come from fixtures. They came from the Weave.

Alex took a step forward, instinct dragging him between Maya and whatever was forming. His shoulders squared. His hand lifted again, but the familiar pressure of shielding did not rise. It was as if his body remembered how to protect her and the world refused to give him the tool.

"Maya," he said, voice low. "Get behind me."

She tried. Her legs almost buckled. The moment she shifted her weight, the air thickened, and the gathering light responded like a living thing.

Five presences stepped into shape.

Not flesh. Not bone. Not bodies the way humans understood bodies.

Resonance forms.

They were made of harmonics and memory, of pressure and light and the sense of something vast choosing to be seen. Their outlines shimmered with the quality of reflections on moving water. Their faces were not perfect, not fixed, but Maya could still recognize them as clearly as she recognized her own name.

Kemen stood first, tall and radiant, her auburn hair flowing as if stirred by a wind that did not exist. Her light carried warmth that did not comfort. It demanded.

Beside her was Vilya, older than mountains, his long silver hair and beard threaded with faint starlight. His presence pressed down like a deep ocean. He did not look at Maya as if she were small. He looked at her as if she were unfinished.

Beagron was burden given shape, the weight of choices and the consequences that followed. He felt grounded, steady, like a hand on a shoulder that reminded you the world did not bend just because you wanted it to.

Cylian's light was sharp, sorrowful, full of fracture. She made the air feel thinner. Her gaze carried the ache of watching something break over and over again and still loving it.

Antec stood slightly apart, distant and watchful. His resonance was colder, not heartless, but aligned with inevitability. He felt like a horizon you could not outrun.

Maya's breath caught and she sank to one knee without meaning to. The cavern floor was cold beneath her jeans. Her hands trembled.

Alex stood rigid, jaw tight, eyes moving from one Immortal to the next.

"What are you?" he demanded, voice hoarse. "What do you want?"

None of them answered yet.

The Weave stayed held, silent as a drawn blade.

Maya lifted her head, her throat tightening until it hurt to speak. She did not know where the courage came from. Maybe it was fear. Maybe it was the same stubborn instinct that had kept her alive this far.

"You've been watching," she said, the words barely more than breath. "All this time."

Kemen's expression flickered, and for a heartbeat Maya felt the edge of grief behind her radiance.

Vilya's gaze settled on Maya. The pressure of it was immense.

Beagron's resonance steadied the chamber like a brace.

Cylian watched Maya as if she could see every crack in her spirit.

Antec did not blink.

Maya swallowed. "Richard is tearing the node apart. The Shadow Current is learning. Echo-Selves are spreading. Alex is getting drained every time he shields and I can barely hold myself together. So tell me why you aren't stopping it."

The words came out sharper than she expected. They echoed faintly off the stone, then fell into the held silence like pebbles dropped into a well.

Alex stared at her, shocked she had said it aloud.

Maya did not look away.

For a moment, the five Immortals remained still, their resonance forms unwavering.

Then their voices aligned.

Not five voices speaking one after another, but a single chord, layered and harmonized, vibrating through the air and into Maya's bones.

"Not yet."

The words were simple.

They landed like a verdict.

Maya's throat tightened so hard she could barely breathe. She stared at them, disbelief rising hot behind her eyes.

"Not yet?" she whispered. "People are going to die."

Alex stepped forward, anger flaring. "She almost died. Twice. So you show up now and tell us to wait?"

Kemen's light shifted, and for an instant Maya felt fierce regret in her resonance.

Vilya's gaze did not soften. It deepened.

Cylian's sorrow sharpened, but she did not move.

Beagron held steady, as if he were bracing the entire cavern by will alone.

Antec watched them like a storm watching a coastline.

And the Weave remained held, silent, attentive.

Maya stared at the five resonance forms, her pulse loud in her ears, and understood something she did not want to understand.

This silence was not mercy.

It was restraint.

Power withheld on purpose.

Power that could act and chose not to.

The light around them gathered a little more, harmonic patterns tightening in the air as if the Weave itself was preparing to speak again.

Maya's hands curled against the stone. Her voice came out rough.

"Then when?"

None of them answered yet.

But the Weave, still held like breath drawn and not released, made it clear.

They had noticed her.

And they were not here to save her.

They were here to confirm the law holding them back, and to warn her what crossing it would cost.

Cylian stepped forward, her resonance sharpening the air until Maya's skin prickled. Her gaze held Maya's, sorrow threaded through every harmonic curve of her form.

"The Weave is still settling from your counterpulse," Cylian said. Her voice carried the echo of fracture and healing both. "What you did stabilized the node, but the lattice is strained. It is holding because it must, not because it is whole."

Maya swallowed. Her head still rang from the effort, from the way her power had cracked open and slammed shut again. "If it's holding," she said, "then why not finish it?"

Beagron's presence deepened, heavy as bedrock. When he spoke, the cavern felt steadier, as if his words anchored reality itself.

"Because intervention now would tear it wider," Beagron said. "The lattice cannot be forced closed while it is still redistributing strain. If we act, we do not heal. We rupture."

Alex let out a sharp breath, anger flashing across his face. "So you just let it get worse?"

Vilya turned his ancient gaze on Alex for a moment. The weight of it made Alex falter despite himself.

"The Fifth Covenant cannot be forced into being," Vilya said calmly. "It is not summoned by pressure or violence. It emerges when the conditions are met. To rush it is to break it."

Maya's chest tightened. "Richard thinks I need to be broken open," she said. Saying it aloud still made her feel hollow. "That the resonance won't fit unless I'm shattered first."

Kemen stepped closer then, her light warming without comforting. Her expression was fierce with sorrow, the kind that came from choosing restraint when every instinct screamed to act.

"He is wrong in his method," Kemen said. "And he is not blind to the truth. Timing matters. But breaking the vessel destroys what it is meant to carry."

Maya's hands shook. She stared at her own faintly glowing skin, at the way her aura still struggled to hold a steady shape. "So what am I supposed to do? Wait while he tears everything apart?"

Antec's voice answered, distant and cold as a horizon you could not outrun.

"The Shadow Current must be allowed to reveal itself fully," Antec said. "It hides when opposed too early. It adapts when pressed without understanding. Its shape must be known before it can be ended."

The words sank into Maya like stones.

She felt the truth of them, even as she hated them.

"You're saying I'm awakening correctly," she said slowly. "But if I open myself the way Richard wants, it'll destroy me."

Cylian inclined her head. "Yes."

"And he's wrong," Maya pressed, "but not completely."

Beagron answered this time. "He senses the coming threshold. He misreads what it requires."

Maya's throat burned. "And you can't help."

Vilya's resonance softened just a fraction. "We will not," he corrected. "Not until Veilfall begins."

The word settled heavily in the air.

Veilfall.

Maya did not know exactly what it meant yet, but she felt the shape of it forming somewhere ahead of her, inevitable and immense.

Alex shook his head slowly. "So this wasn't a meeting," he said. "You didn't come to help. You came to tell us to stay alive long enough for something worse."

Kemen met his gaze without flinching. "We came to warn you."

The Weave trembled faintly, not in pain but in acknowledgment. The held silence began to loosen, just slightly, like breath finally preparing to move again.

Maya bowed her head, exhaustion and knowledge crashing together inside her. She understood now why this felt different from every other encounter, every other brush with power.

This was not guidance.

It was permission withheld.

When she looked up again, the resonance forms were already thinning, their outlines softening as the Weave slowly resumed its cautious motion. Threads stirred. Pressure returned. The world remembered how to breathe.

The Immortals were gone and the warning they left behind weighed heavier than any intervention ever could.

22

The Surge

The silence did not fade.

It broke.

Maya felt it first as a release in her teeth, the way a held breath finally gave up and turned into a gasp. The threads that had been suspended around the cavern snapped back into motion all at once, not flowing but lashing, like someone had yanked a cord that should never have been pulled.

The air shuddered. Light pulsed along the stone in hard, strobing waves. A harmonic shockwave rolled through the chamber and punched into her ribs. Her knees buckled and she would have gone down if Alex had not tightened his arm around her waist.

"What's happening?" he rasped.

Maya tried to answer, but the Weave was too loud. It was not a sound. It was pressure, vibration, a chord so dense it made her vision warp at the edges. The dust in the air stopped drifting and then blasted sideways as if the cavern itself had exhaled.

Residuum thickened instantly.

It poured from hairline cracks in the walls and from the floor seams where the node's strain had been bleeding for days. It did not move like smoke, but it behaved like it, curling and rolling, swallowing the beam of the overhead work lights until the chamber became a dim, shifting haze. Maya's throat tightened. Every inhale tasted like cold metal and burned minerals.

In the fog, shapes flickered.

Echo-forms tried to pull themselves together again at the edges of her sight, late reflections desperate to become bodies. They formed for half a heartbeat, hollow and wrong, and then unraveled as if the surge kept tearing their seams apart faster than they could stitch themselves together. They shredded into pale static fragments that skittered across the air like sparks dying before they hit the ground.

Alex's hand lifted, instinct trying to throw a shield up. It wavered in front of them, a thin blue curve that sputtered and then caught, unstable but present.

He exhaled like he had been holding his breath for hours. "I can feel it again."

Maya did not feel relief. She felt consequence.

The Immortals had not fixed anything. They had held the world still long enough to speak, then let it go.

And now it recoiled.

The cavern floor trembled under her boots. Not a simple quake, but a layered ripple, as if reality had been folded into sheets and someone was shaking the stack. A deep groan rose from beneath them, the sound of stone trying to move in more than one direction at once.

Maya's gaze dropped to the ground.

Cracks were forming.

Not spiderweb lines. Wide, deliberate arcs that spread outward from the node's location like a compass drawing circles through rock. The fractures glowed faintly at the edges, green-white light leaking up between them.

Alex shifted, trying to brace them both. "Maya, we need to get out of here."

"I know," she whispered, but her voice came out thin.

The floor lurched.

Stone lifted in slabs as if gravity had forgotten its job. At the same time, other sections softened and sagged like wet clay. A support beam near the far wall began to bend, metal flowing the way wax did when held too close to flame. Quartz veins in the rock flared bright, then dulled, then flared again, each pulse timed to the surge building under their feet.

Alex's partial shield caught the first wave of flying debris, but it did not feel like it used to. It dragged. It stuck. Residuum clung to it as if the barrier were something solid and edible.

His face tightened. He pressed his free hand hard to his ribs.

"It's pulling again," he said through his teeth. "It's in my shield."

Maya could feel it too. The surge was feeding on anything active, anything that tried to push back. The Weave's motion was not random. It was hungry for harmonics, for resistance, for effort. It took the shape of whatever fought it.

Holding the line was making it worse.

Another shudder hit, stronger. The chamber lights flickered and then went out completely. Darkness folded in, broken only by the faint, sickly glow of the cracks in the floor and the occasional static spark as Echo fragments died in the fog.

Maya's pulse hammered. She reached for the Weave.

It snapped at her like a live wire.

Pain lanced behind her eyes. Her aura flared and sputtered. A cold sweat broke across her neck and spine.

Alex's grip tightened. "Maya. Don't."

"I have to," she whispered.

The surge was spreading outward from the node now. She could feel it the way she felt a storm front before the rain, only this storm lived inside the lattice of the world. Threads were collapsing, not breaking clean but folding into each other, pathways that used to lead somewhere now twisting into dead ends. The mine itself felt like a wound closing wrong.

A traditional blink would not hold. Not here. Not with the Weave convulsing under them.

If she tried a simple corridor, it would tear in her hands and take them with it.

Maya swallowed hard and forced herself upright. Her legs shook, but she planted her boots on the uneven stone and locked her focus on Alex's face.

His eyes were wide in the dim glow, fear and fury fighting for space. He looked like he wanted to pick her up and run, like running could outrun a world that was changing.

"We can't stay," she said.

"We're leaving," he snapped, as if his certainty could make it true. "Tell me how."

Maya drew one slow breath and tasted ozone and dust. In her mind, the internal line was cold and simple.

If she stays, the world breaks. If she runs, she might.

Her gaze swept the chamber. Residuum swirled. Echo-fragments skittered. The cracks in the floor widened another inch, then another, with a slow, hungry patience.

They were not alone.

The tunnel Richard had disappeared into had gone black, but Maya felt him as a smear in the Weave, an overlapping tone vanishing deeper into the mine. She could not get a clean lock on him. Not now. Not through this.

She would have to let him go for the moment.

Her stomach turned at the thought.

Alex followed her gaze. "He's gone."

"For now," she said. Her voice barely held steady. "We can't chase him through this."

Alex's jaw tightened. "Then what are we doing?"

Maya reached out and grabbed his forearm, not gently. She needed him anchored to her, not bracing against her. "We're jumping out. Both of us."

"Both of us?" His eyes flicked down. "You can barely stand."

Maya's mouth went dry. "I'm not doing it the clean way."

The ground heaved again. A slab of stone rose on their left, tilted, then dropped and shattered into a spray of sharp fragments. Alex's shield caught most of it, but the barrier flickered and bowed under the weight. Residuum smeared across it like oil.

Alex grunted, pain sharpening his breath. "Maya, don't do something that kills you."

She almost laughed. It would have sounded hysterical.

"I'm going to do something that doesn't kill us," she said. Then, softer, "Hold on to me."

"I am," he said, and there was no hesitation.

Maya closed her eyes.

She did not reach for a door. She reached for vectors.

The Weave was not a road right now. It was a storm of collapsing pathways, and the only way through was to grab two different strands at once and force them into alignment long enough to throw their bodies across the gap.

She anchored Alex first. His harmonic was a steady blue pressure under all the pain, the only thing in the cavern that still felt like stability. She wrapped that around her like a rope tied to her waist.

Then she anchored herself. That was harder. Her resonance was cracked, green-white light flickering in uneven pulses. Every time she tried to steady it, it slipped.

Residuum pressed at her senses, thickening, eager. It wanted a shape to copy. It wanted her.

Maya forced her focus deeper and found the memory of the Weave before the fracture. A cleaner chord. A steadier rhythm. It was faint, almost gone, but it was there.

She latched onto it.

Her aura flared, bright enough to paint the cavern walls. Alex stiffened beside her, his shield reacting, trying to rise and protect. The surge immediately tugged at it harder.

"Alex," Maya hissed, eyes still shut. "Don't push."

"What?" he snapped.

"Let me do it. You hold me. Don't fight it."

His breath hitched. Then he forced his shoulders to drop, forced his shield to stop surging outward. He became a brace instead of a weapon.

Maya took the opening and pulled.

A corridor tore open in front of them, but it did not look like her usual blink. It was not a clean green-white tunnel.

It was fractured.

Multiple exit points flashed in her mind, overlapping like transparencies. The Weave folded incorrectly, then tried to correct itself, then folded again. Maya felt the path split into three, then four, then five, each one promising escape and each one threatening to shear them in half if she chose wrong.

Her vision shattered even with her eyes closed. She saw the cavern from three angles at once. She saw herself standing a step to the side, out of sync. She felt an Echo-form brushing against her shoulder like a cold hand, trying to peel away from her body and become real.

No.

Maya clenched her jaw until it hurt and shoved her resonance inward, tighter, harder. She would not give the Echo a seam to pull apart.

Alex's body went rigid beside her.

For a heartbeat, his shield inverted. The barrier didn't shield outward anymore. It collapsed through itself, turning protection into a hollow pull that tried to drag the air, the dust, and Maya's breath straight out of her.

Instead of wrapping them, it slipped away. Cold air slammed into Maya's skin, exposing her to the surge in a raw, naked moment. She felt the Weave's pressure claw at her ribs and throat. Her stomach lurched.

Alex made a broken sound. "Maya, I can't, I can't hold it."

"You don't," she gasped. "Hold me."

His hands locked on her, iron grip, the only constant in the collapse.

Maya chose a vector.

Not the safest one. Not the cleanest. The nearest stable anchor she could sense outside the mine, a point where the Weave was thinner but not snapping. She grabbed it like a lifeline and pulled the corridor over them.

The world folded.

Noise vanished. Sound, gravity, breath, all of it dropped away. Maya felt their bodies flung through a space that was not distance but resonance. The corridor shuddered around them like torn fabric. Echo fragments streaked past in the dark, hungry and curious.

Then the Weave snapped again.

They slammed back into reality.

Cold air hit Maya's face. She tasted dirt instead of ozone. The ground beneath them was not stone but hard-packed earth and gravel. They had landed in scrub and broken weeds, the edge of an old service road somewhere outside the mining complex.

Maya's knees hit first. Pain flared up her legs. She barely caught herself with her hands before her face went into the dirt.

Alex hit a half-second later, twisting to take the worst of it, his body shielding hers by reflex even when his power would not cooperate.

"Jesus," he panted.

Maya tried to breathe and found she couldn't. The air felt too thin. Her aura flickered once, twice, then sputtered hard, the light snapping like a dying bulb.

She sagged forward.

Alex caught her by the shoulders and hauled her up enough to keep her from collapsing completely. His hands shook as if his muscles were struggling to obey. He looked past her, scanning the horizon and the trees, searching for movement.

"Where are we?" he demanded.

Maya's mouth opened. No sound came out.

Residuum drifted here too.

Not thick like in the mine, but present. It curled along the ground in faint gray wisps, slipping between rocks like fog that did not care about wind. It made the world look slightly out of focus at the edges.

Alex swore under his breath. His eyes narrowed. "It followed us."

Maya forced a breath. The inhale burned. "It's spreading," she managed.

Sirens rose in the distance, faint at first. A rising wail that meant roads, people, response. The world reacting to something it could not see but could feel in its bones.

Alex listened, then looked back toward the direction of the mine. He could not see the entrance from here, but the air carried a low vibration, a distant tremor that made the weeds shiver.

"That wasn't contained," he said.

Maya shook her head, too weak for anything else. Her vision swam. The edges of the world doubled for a second, and she saw herself sitting a foot to the left, out of sync, then the image snapped away.

She swallowed bile and blinked hard.

The Weave was settling into a new rhythm.

Not calm. Not stable. Different.

The pressure of Echoes felt more organized now, less frantic. The Shadow Current had learned from the surge. It was not simply mimicking. It was anticipating.

Something brushed her mind.

Not the Immortals. Their presence had been immense, deliberate, unmistakable.

Not Richard, whose resonance had always been a cracked bell, loud with desperate purpose.

This was quieter.

Colder.

Coherent.

It touched the edge of her awareness the way a fingertip touched glass, testing for a crack, and in that touch Maya felt intent. It wasn't just residuum in the air. It was a mind using the residuum as a nervous system.

She shivered violently.

Alex noticed at once. He pulled her closer, grounding her with the only thing he could still give. "Maya, what is it? What do you feel?"

Maya tried to answer, but her throat tightened. She stared at the air where the Residuum drifted and the world looked just slightly wrong.

"It's not over," she whispered.

Alex's jaw set. "No. It's just starting."

Maya's vision darkened at the edges. Before she lost herself entirely, one thought landed in her mind with brutal clarity.

The Surge did not end the fracture. It taught it how to spread.

***

Richard woke choking on dust and copper.

The surge had thrown him hard. He lay twisted against the stone, one arm numb, his journal crushed beneath his chest. The tunnel around him no longer looked like the mine he remembered. The rock had flowed and fused, seams sealed shut as if the earth itself had decided this passage no longer existed.

Residuum drifted through the air in slow, deliberate curls.

Not wild.

Watching.

Richard pushed himself onto his side and gasped as pain lanced up his ribs. His vision swam, then fractured. For a heartbeat he saw two tunnels. Three. One of them showed him standing, whole and calm, his hands glowing with perfect harmonic control.

The Shadow Current offered him the image like a gift.

You survived, it whispered without words. You were right.

Richard squeezed his eyes shut. His head rang. His thoughts felt crowded, layered with echoes that did not belong to him.

"No," he croaked. "That's not survival."

The pressure inside him shifted. Not anger. Not resistance.

Curiosity.

The Shadow Current did not push harder. It adjusted, smoothing the image, refining it. The false Richard smiled gently now. Reassuring. Patient.

You opened the way. You took the burden. She couldn't.

Richard's fingers dug into the grit-streaked floor. His journal slid open beneath his palm, pages fluttering weakly. The sketches inside were no longer just his. Lines had been corrected. Patterns sharpened. Harmonics he did not remember drawing stared back at him with unsettling precision.

Too precise.

His breath caught.

"You didn't show me the truth," he whispered. "You showed me what I wanted to see."

The Shadow Current paused.

It was not a silence like the Immortals' restraint. This was recalculation.

Richard forced himself upright, every movement sending sparks of pain through his spine. The pressure in his skull intensified, but now he recognized the sensation. Not guidance.

Feedback.

"You never spoke to the Weave," he said hoarsely. "You spoke through it."

Memory snapped into place.

The Echoes had not behaved like Weave phenomena. They lagged. Mimicked. Learned. They fed on response, not harmony. They grew sharper when opposed and thinner when ignored.

Just like this presence.

Richard laughed weakly, the sound tearing at his throat. "You're not the current," he said. "You're the leak."

The Shadow Current surged then, no longer patient. Pain flared as static clawed at his nerves, trying to collapse him inward, to reclaim the hollow places it had found so easy to occupy.

Richard screamed and slammed his journal shut, pressing it to his chest like a shield.

"No," he gasped. "I won't be your mouthpiece."

The tunnel trembled. The false image of himself fractured, lagging out of sync, its expression flickering with something that looked dangerously like irritation.

Richard did the one thing the Shadow Current had not anticipated.

He stopped channeling.

He let go.

The pressure recoiled violently, tearing free with a sound like glass ripping apart. Richard collapsed forward, retching, every nerve screaming as the borrowed resonance burned out of him.

When he could breathe again, the presence was thinner.

Not gone.

But no longer inside his thoughts.

The tunnel had split during the surge, a new fracture opening along one wall where the stone had buckled instead of sealing. Cold air seeped through, carrying the faintest echo of sirens and distant movement.

Richard dragged himself forward, half crawling, half sliding, his injured leg useless beneath him, intent on finding a way out. Each movement cost him something. Strength. Blood. Certainty.

Behind him, Residuum stirred.

Echo-shapes flickered briefly, then hesitated.

They did not follow.

They watched.

Richard was trying to stand when green-white light engulfed him. Maya's vector jump caught his harmonic by accident, snagging it like a loose thread and wrenching him through the collapsing corridor.

He broke free into scrub and shattered rock, the night air slamming into his lungs like a physical blow. Richard collapsed just beyond a jagged opening in the stone, chest heaving, face pressed into dirt that smelled blessedly, unmistakably real.

Somewhere nearby, alarms wailed.

Human sounds.

Richard lay there shaking, staring at the stars through blurred vision.

"I was wrong," he whispered into the earth. "But not about everything."

The Shadow Current lingered at the edge of his awareness, distant now, colder, no longer pretending to be benevolent.

It had lost its prophet.

But not its interest.

Richard Barrett closed his eyes and did not let it back in.

23

Division Gray

Miami had not cracked open like Colorado.

There were no collapsing tunnels, no green-white fractures bleeding light into the street. The skyline still stood where it belonged. Traffic still moved. The world still pretended it was normal.

But the air felt wrong.

Elara walked with her hands in the pockets of a borrowed hoodie, head down, hair tucked forward, as if posture could hide her from satellites. Joe kept pace at her side, his shoulders tight, eyes constantly scanning the spaces people forgot to look at. Alley mouths. Rooftop edges. Reflections in darkened windows.

The fallout here was quieter, thinner.

A haze that wasn't fog drifted along the low places between warehouses and loading docks. It didn't billow. It didn't swirl with wind. It clung to concrete like something that wanted to be part of the world but didn't know how. Elara could feel it prickling against her skin, raising tiny, involuntary chills on her arms. Residuum, but diluted. Aftershock residue, not a rupture.

Colorado bled. Miami trembled.

She hated that she knew the difference.

Joe slowed near the mouth of an abandoned service corridor that cut between a line of shuttered garages and a fenced industrial yard. A detour. A shortcut. A mistake waiting to happen.

Elara reached for the Weave, not to pull, not to flare, just to listen like Joe taught her.

The threads here weren't torn. They were unsettled, like a net that had been yanked hard miles away and was still vibrating from the tug. A new rhythm. Not calm. Not stable. Just different.

She didn't like different.

"Do you feel that?" she asked quietly.

Joe's gaze stayed on the corridor. "Yeah."

Not a yes to her question. A yes to everything.

Elara took one step forward and the hair on the back of her neck rose.

The quiet was too clean.

Not the kind of quiet that happened when a place was abandoned. This was organized quiet. Held quiet. The kind that came from someone making sure nothing moved without permission.

"Joe," she breathed.

"I know," he murmured.

Shapes emerged from the corridor with the timing of a machine.

Six figures. Then eight. Then twelve, spreading with practiced precision, cutting off angles without rushing, without a single wasted motion. Their uniforms were matte gray, no insignia, no patches, no rank markings. Their faces looked pale under the streetlights, not ghost pale, but drained, as if their blood had forgotten how to warm them. Their eyes were steady. Too steady.

They moved as one, synchronized in a way that made Elara's stomach tighten.

A hum threaded the air, low and faint, like a distant transformer under load.

Joe's jaw flexed. "They're not normal soldiers."

Elara didn't answer. She didn't need to.

One of the gray soldiers stepped forward half a pace. He didn't raise a weapon. He didn't bark a warning. No shouting. No threats. Nothing that would play badly in a leaked clip. He didn't do anything that would fit on a bodycam for public viewing.

He simply spoke, flat and measured.

"Elara Whitcombe. Joseph Biggs. You are to comply with federal containment protocol."

Elara's breath snagged.

They knew their names.

They knew enough to send something like this.

Her heat flared, reflexive, protective. It rose under her skin like a match struck in a sealed room. She didn't want to burn them. She wanted to make space. A wall. A warning. A moment to run.

"Back up," she said, voice low.

The soldier didn't react.

Elara lifted her hands and let the fire come.

It burst out in a controlled wave, a broad sheet of heat and orange light that rolled down the corridor like a living thing. It wrapped the first line of gray soldiers, swallowing them in flame.

For an instant, it looked right.

Then it didn't.

The fire didn't bite. It didn't catch. It didn't even push them back.

It spread around them like water meeting stone, and the heat drained out of it as if the flame itself had been convinced it had no right to exist.

The soldiers walked through it.

Not fast. Not desperate. Not burned.

The fire guttered, thinning to embers that clung for half a second to their sleeves before dissolving into nothing.

Elara stared, disbelief turning sharp and hot in her chest.

Joe's voice was a whisper beside her. "They're not just trained. They're engineered."

The hum in the air deepened.

The gray soldiers advanced.

Elara's hands shook. She forced herself to breathe.

"Okay," she said under her breath. "Okay, then."

She could do more than heat. She could do force. She could do pressure.

She started to pull again, reaching deeper, trying to find the seam where the world still listened.

And the air pushed back.

Not the way a wall pushed back. The way a hand pushed your face away and held it there.

Her flame sputtered in her veins.

The soldiers didn't slow.

The trap had been set for her.

And she had walked straight into it.

Joe's vision always changed before anything else did.

It wasn't like seeing the world in different colors. It was like seeing the part of the world people lied about.

The gray soldiers looked solid if he let his eyes stay ordinary. Men in uniforms. Boots on cracked concrete. Hands at their sides.

But when he let his sight slip into the deeper layer, the truth was brutal.

Their harmonics weren't natural.

They had been reinforced, stitched, pressed into shape with something that didn't belong inside a human body. He could see it in the micro fractures around them, hairline distortions that followed their joints and spines. Every step they took was accompanied by a faint stutter in the air.

Not enough for cameras. Enough for him.

Stabilizers.

Nodes under the skin along collar lines and wrists, pulsing faintly with a gray light that was almost invisible unless you knew how to look. The hum he'd been hearing wasn't equipment.

It was their bodies.

Joe's stomach rolled.

They were holding themselves together with a lie made physical.

The lead soldier lifted a hand. A device in his palm flashed once, and the air thickened.

A net, but not a net you could see.

Pressure slammed into Joe's skull like someone had pressed both thumbs into his temples. His teeth ached. His eyes watered. The world compressed, edges sharpening too hard, as if someone was trying to force reality into a narrower shape.

Elara made a strangled sound behind him. Joe didn't turn. He couldn't risk losing the pattern.

The net was a dampener.

Not to stop fire. To stop resonance.

To stop them.

Joe forced air into his lungs. His vision flickered. For a heartbeat he saw the gray soldiers as they really were.

Not invincible.

Burning.

Their organs glowed with strain. Their blood carried something wrong, chemical and cold. The stabilizers along their spines were not miracles. They were restraints, clamping down on biology that was trying to rebel. Joe could see fatigue in their muscles, not ordinary tiredness but a desperate depletion, as if their bodies were paying a debt that would come due soon.

One of them twitched. Just a tiny tremor in the fingers.

Joe's stomach clenched.

They weren't soldiers in armor.

They were men being used as tools.

The pressure behind his eyes increased. The dampener tightened, squeezing the truth layer, trying to compress it until it became noise.

That was the point.

If Joe couldn't see the cracks, he couldn't pry them open.

He swallowed hard and stepped forward, putting himself between Elara and the line of gray uniforms.

The lead soldier's gaze fixed on him.

"Joseph Biggs," he said. "You will comply."

Joe stared back and let his sight sharpen until it hurt.

He saw the lie inside the soldier's posture. The rehearsed steadiness. The rewritten obedience laid over fear like paint.

Joe's pulse hammered.

He didn't need a speech.

He didn't need to persuade.

He only needed to say one true thing in the right place.

Joe locked eyes with the lead soldier.

The pressure in his skull screamed at him to look away. The dampener pulsed again, tightening the invisible net, but Joe held the soldier's gaze like a handhold.

He saw the soldier's truth.

A name buried under protocol. A flicker of panic under chemical calm. A body running on borrowed time.

He saw the stabilizer nodes pulsing, not steady but frantic, as if the device had to work harder every second just to keep the man upright.

Joe's throat went dry.

He spoke anyway, quietly, almost gently.

"You don't want to be here."

The soldier didn't blink.

But his harmonic did.

It stuttered.

The formation around him shifted by a fraction, not a step, not a break, but a micro delay, like a machine catching on a gear tooth.

Joe pressed in, voice still low.

"You're dying."

The lead soldier's fingers twitched.

For a heartbeat, his eyes changed. Just a flicker. Something human trying to surface.

The stabilizer at his collar flared brighter.

Then it stuttered.

A sharp, ugly pulse rippled through the line.

The synchronized hum in the air faltered.

Elara sucked in a breath behind Joe. He heard her, even through the pressure, like a match being struck again.

Joe felt the dampener react, a tightening squeeze meant to crush the truth back down.

He fought it and paid for it instantly.

Pain exploded behind his eyes. His vision blurred. He tasted blood.

But he saw the crack.

He saw the lie failing.

And he knew exactly what to do with it.

"Your orders aren't courage," Joe said, louder now, forcing the words through the net. "They're fear with a uniform on."

The lead soldier's jaw clenched.

His knees softened.

His formation broke.

Not by choice. By truth.

The gray line hesitated.

Just long enough.

Elara didn't waste the opening.

The instant the formation faltered, she moved.

Heat snapped through her hands, not a broad wave this time, but a tight, focused surge aimed at the crack Joe had made. She drove the fire into the split rhythm, into the stuttering stabilizer pulse, into the moment where the soldiers' artificial harmony couldn't hold its shape.

The lead soldier convulsed.

The gray light under his collar flared, then flickered, then surged in a frantic burst. His mouth opened in a sound that wasn't a scream so much as a body discovering it was allowed to feel.

He dropped to one knee.

The soldier beside him reached automatically, not in concern, but to preserve formation. His stabilizer pulsed harder as if it had been ordered to compensate.

Elara's fire caught the strain and pushed.

The air flashed orange.

One gray soldier collapsed fully, shaking, hands clawing at his own throat as if trying to pull the wrongness out of himself.

Joe staggered.

He swayed like his bones had turned to water, one hand pressed hard over his nose. Blood ran between his fingers.

"Elara," he rasped. "Now."

She grabbed his sleeve and yanked him backward.

They ran.

The gray soldiers did not pursue with panic. They did not scatter. They did not break into chaos the way normal men did when something went wrong.

They regrouped in silence.

Two of them knelt beside the fallen soldier with clinical precision, hands moving to stabilize nodes and inject something into his neck. The others turned their heads in the same direction at the same time, watching Joe and Elara disappear into the maze of industrial shadows.

Recording.

Marking.

Learning.

Elara dragged Joe behind a rusted shipping container and shoved him down into a crouch.

He tried to breathe and failed. His eyes were glassy, unfocused. His face had gone gray.

She pressed a hand to his cheek. "Joe. Hey. Stay with me."

He blinked hard, swallowing pain. "They weren't immune," he rasped. "They were held together."

Elara's throat tightened.

"Yeah," she whispered. "And you just pulled a pin out of them."

Sirens rose somewhere in the distance. Real ones this time. Not just her imagination. Not just nerves. The city reacting to something it didn't understand.

Joe wiped at his nose and smeared more blood across his knuckles. His gaze lifted, distant, as if he could still see the gray line through metal.

"They didn't chase us," he said.

Elara's stomach sank. "Because they didn't need to."

Joe's voice went flat with realization. "It was a test."

Elara's hands tightened into fists. "And we passed."

They moved again, slower now, deeper into places the city forgot. Elara kept her fire low, just a simmer under her skin. Joe kept his eyes half unfocused, letting truth-sight come and go in careful pulses.

The air still held that thin Residuum prick, a reminder that something far away had changed the rules everywhere.

Miami hadn't shattered.

But it had shifted.

Joe's chest ached with every breath. His nose still bled in slow stubborn drips. He wiped it away and stared at the smear on his palm like it could answer him.

"They know what we are," he said quietly.

Elara glanced at him. "They've known."

Joe shook his head once. "No. They know how to fight us."

Elara's face hardened.

Joe's gaze drifted toward the industrial corridor behind them, toward the place where gray uniforms had stood without hesitation and walked through flame like it was weather.

Fire hadn't stopped them.

Only the truth had.

And even that had barely been enough.

Top of Form

24

Convergence Begins

Maya tasted smoke before she saw it.

Not the thick, oily kind from burning rubber, but a thin chemical bite that clung to the back of her throat and refused to go away. It rode the wind across broken scrub and torn rock, mixing with the copper tang of blood and the sterile sharpness of disinfectant drifting from the direction of the road.

Somewhere beyond the low ridge, emergency lights strobed through the night in hard pulses. Red. Blue. Red. Blue. Like the world was trying to pretend this was still a normal kind of disaster.

Maya kept her head down and her hands tucked close to her chest as she moved, careful with every step. The ground was uneven, scattered with gravel and jagged fragments of stone that looked wrong in the way they caught the light. Not glossy. Not wet. Just too sharp, like the earth had been cut and never smoothed over.

Alex walked half a step behind her, close enough that she could feel him without looking. His presence did not calm the air anymore. Not fully. After the Surge, his field was there in ragged edges, like a blanket with burns through it.

Still, it was something. It was him.

"Keep left," Alex murmured.

Maya nodded. She did not answer out loud. Voices carried out here, even when there was no one nearby.

Especially when there was no one nearby.

The Residuum hung thin around them, barely visible unless she let her perception tilt sideways. Then it became a haze of almost light, a shimmer that did not move with the wind. It clung to low places and cracks in the stone, gathered in shallow pockets, and made the air feel slightly too cold against her skin.

Colorado bled. The rest of the country trembled.

Out here, it still bled.

They crested the ridge and dropped into a shallow basin littered with brittle brush and blackened patches of dirt. Maya slowed, feeling the Weave beneath her feet like a net pulled too tight. Threads quivered. Motion. Memory. Energy. Everything strained as if the world had been yanked hard and was still deciding whether to snap.

Ahead, beyond a line of stunted trees, a road cut through the dark. A cluster of vehicles sat on the shoulder with hazard lights blinking. A few figures moved in reflective vests. A stretcher. A portable floodlight.

Maya pulled Alex down behind a boulder and crouched low.

"We can't go that way," she whispered.

"I know," he said. His voice was rough, like he had not slept in days. "We swing wide. Stay out of the light."

Maya nodded again, then stilled.

Something shifted.

Not footsteps. Not a voice. Not the movement of people on the road.

The air itself stuttered.

For half a second, the Residuum around them went sharp, like someone had plucked a single thread and made the whole net vibrate. Maya's skin prickled. Her vision tightened. The world felt like it had skipped a heartbeat and then tried to pretend it had not.

She sucked in a breath and tasted cold.

Alex's hand closed on her sleeve. Not a pull, just contact.

"You feel that?" he asked.

"Yes," she whispered. Her eyes scanned the basin. "It's like... a hiccup."

Alex's jaw flexed. "Pressure changed."

Maya did not look at him. She did not need to. She could hear the uncertainty in his tone. He could feel something was wrong, but he could not name it the way she could.

The Weave was doing something.

It was not scattering them anymore.

It was pulling.

Maya let her awareness extend, careful not to flare too hard. She did not reach for a jump. She listened the way Ethan had tried to teach her through flashes and nudges and that quiet white gold pressure that was never quite a voice.

There. A ripple. Two, maybe three signatures, arriving not like a car coming down the road but like a sudden knot in the net.

They were not approaching.

They were appearing.

Maya's pulse kicked. She rose just enough to see over the boulder.

Nothing at first.

Then, near the far edge of the basin, the air folded.

There was no bright tear, no green-white fracture like the tunnels had shown her. It was subtler than that. The world bent in on itself for a blink, like a sheet being snapped. Sound dropped out. The floodlight hum vanished. Even the distant sirens became a mute vibration.

The brush at the far edge shivered as if something had slammed into it from nowhere.

Then the air released.

Sound rushed back in, too loud for a second.

Maya surged to her feet. "Joe."

Alex was already moving, stepping out from cover with her.

Joe Biggs pushed himself up on one knee, swearing under his breath. Dirt streaked his jacket and blood smeared the edge of his mouth where he had bitten it hard on landing.

Beside him, Elara Whitcombe staggered, caught herself, and froze. Her hands came up instinctively, heat flaring around her fingers before she forced it back under control.

They stared at Maya and Alex like they were seeing ghosts.

"Okay," Joe said hoarsely. "Either I finally lost it, or we're not in Miami anymore."

Elara turned slowly, taking in the rocky basin, the cold air, the distant emergency lights. Her breath fogged in front of her mouth.

"This is not Miami," she said flatly.

Maya crossed the distance quickly, relief hitting her hard enough to make her dizzy. "You're real," she said, almost to herself.

Joe let out a shaky laugh. "That's comforting coming from you."

Alex stopped a few feet back, eyes scanning the dark on instinct. "What happened?"

Joe wiped his mouth with the back of his hand. "We were running in the industrial fringe and encountered a thin Residuum pocket. The air folded wrong and then we were... here."

"Rift-slip," Maya said. "Aftershocks. The Veil skips frames and people get caught in it."

Elara's gaze stayed locked on Maya. She swallowed. "I felt you before I saw you."

Maya nodded. "Me too."

Joe straightened, his expression shifting as his truth-sight brushed the scene. His shoulders eased a fraction. "No mimicry," he said quietly. "It's really you."

Elara exhaled, some of the tension bleeding out of her posture, though the heat never fully left her skin. "Good. Because I really didn't want to set anything on fire right now."

Alex huffed once, a sound halfway between a laugh and exhaustion. "Same."

For a heartbeat, they just stood there, the four of them, battered and breathing and very much alive. The motel room in Miami felt like another lifetime ago. A cracked mirror. Bad coffee. The uneasy truce of shared exhaustion.

Maya felt her own shoulders loosen by a fraction. Not trust. Not yet. But a tiny release of the instinct to run.

Then the ground under all of them shifted.

Not physically.

Harmonically.

A deeper tremor rolled through the basin, and the Residuum haze tightened like a held breath. Maya's senses sharpened involuntarily, her awareness snapping toward the source.

Something was coming.

Not from the road.

From the haze itself.

Alex stepped forward, placing himself slightly in front of Maya without looking back. His shield did not bloom the way it used to. It felt torn at the edges, brittle.

So he used his body instead.

Elara tensed, heat rising again.

Joe's eyes went unfocused for half a second, and Maya felt something flinch inside him, like his gift had been punched.

Then a figure stumbled out of the haze near the boulder line.

The man moved like someone dragging an anchor. One leg useless. Hands scraped raw. Clothes torn. Face streaked with dirt and blood. He almost fell, caught himself on a rock, and then froze when he realized he was not alone.

Maya's breath stopped in her throat.

Richard Barrett.

He looked nothing like the man she had felt in the tunnels. There was no confidence in his posture, no zeal in his eyes. Just pain and an alertness that felt newly earned.

Alex's stance went hard. He shifted, fully blocking the line between Richard and Maya.

"Stay back," Alex said.

Richard's hands lifted slowly, palms open. He did not smile. He did not speak right away.

Maya's skin prickled. She could feel his harmonic signature, quieter now, stripped down. Less performative, less layered.

Still contaminated.

Like a thread that had been dipped in ash and could not be cleaned without unraveling it.

Joe made a sound that was almost a gasp, then swallowed it back. He pressed a hand to his temple like someone had struck him.

"Jesus," Joe muttered.

Elara's eyes widened. "What is that?"

Joe did not look away from Richard. "That's a problem."

Richard's gaze flicked to Joe, then to Maya behind Alex, then away again as if he did not trust himself to hold her eyes.

"I didn't plan this," Richard said finally. His voice was rough, scraped thin. "I didn't plan any of it."

Alex did not move. "You planned enough."

Richard flinched, but he did not argue.

Maya forced herself to speak, even with Alex between them.

"Why are you here?" she asked.

Richard swallowed. His throat worked like it hurt.

"Because I couldn't stay there," he said. "Because it's different now."

Joe's breathing hitched. He blinked fast, then steadied himself. When he spoke, his voice was controlled, but the strain was obvious.

"He's not channeling," Joe said.

Maya's eyes snapped to Joe. "You're sure?"

Joe nodded once, sharp. "Right now. He's not actively feeding it."

Alex's shoulders did not loosen. "That's not comforting."

Joe's jaw tightened. "It shouldn't be."

He stared at Richard, and Maya could feel his gift working, a pressure in the air that made everything feel exposed.

"It hasn't let you go," Joe said.

Richard's eyes closed briefly, like the words were a confirmation of something he had been trying not to admit.

"No," Richard whispered. "It hasn't."

Elara's heat rose in a wave that made the air shimmer.

Maya lifted a hand slightly, not to stop her, but to ground herself. She reached for the Weave and felt it answer in small, tight vibrations.

Richard's presence made the threads around him twitch.

The Shadow Current had touched him deep.

But the touch was not moving the way it had before.

It was watching.

Waiting.

Richard opened his eyes and looked at Maya at last, past Alex's shoulder. His gaze held no triumph. Only a weary kind of honesty.

"I lied," he said. "I used it. I told myself it was the only way to see what was underneath. I told myself I was serving the lattice." He swallowed again. "I was wrong."

Alex's voice stayed hard. "You expect that to fix it?"

"No," Richard said immediately. "I don't expect anything."

Joe's eyes narrowed. "Then why come near her?"

Richard's gaze dropped. "Because I didn't choose it. I was trying to crawl out of a tunnel and the world grabbed me and threw me into the dirt." He let out a broken laugh that held no humor. "I don't even know if I'm lucky."

Maya felt the truth in his words, not as certainty, but as the absence of the old deception. His harmonic did not try to hide. It simply was.

Joe rubbed at his nose. There was fresh blood on his knuckles.

"It adapted," Richard said, voice low. "During the Surge. It learned from what happened down there. It learned from all of you."

Maya's stomach turned.

She had felt it too. The way Residuum had responded faster. The way the air in the tunnels had seemed aware.

She nodded once, slow. "He's right."

Alex glanced back at her, eyes tight. "Maya."

"I know," she said quietly. "I'm not saying we trust him. I'm saying the Weave confirms what he's saying."

Elara's gaze flicked between them all, like she was trying to build a map of a conversation she did not have time for.

Joe drew in a breath and let it out. "This is confirmation," he said. "Not forgiveness. Nobody's asking for that."

Richard's hands stayed up. He looked smaller than Maya remembered him feeling. Not less dangerous. Just less certain.

A distant sound rose on the wind.

Not the sirens from the road.

A higher, thinner whine that threaded through the night like an insect.

Maya's heart clenched.

Drones.

Alex heard it too. His posture tightened.

Elara's eyes sharpened. "That's not normal police."

Joe's voice went flat. "No, it's not."

Maya's awareness stretched and caught a faint harmonic ping in the distance, like a signal riding the Weave's disturbed threads.

HECATE.

They were close enough that the net of their equipment brushed the edges of the basin.

Alex spoke without looking away from the haze. "We move. Now."

Elara took a step toward Joe, instinctively. Her fire came up under her skin, not flaring outward, but ready.

Maya looked at Alex, then at Joe and Elara, then at Richard.

The pull in the Weave tightened again, subtle but undeniable. It was not harmony. It was alignment. Five signatures tugged toward the same axis as if the fracture itself had decided scattering them was no longer useful.

Staying separated was no longer viable.

Alex's voice was low, clipped. "If he comes with us, there are rules."

Richard's gaze lifted. He waited.

"No secrets," Elara said immediately. Her tone held fire even when her hands were still. "No solo actions. You don't disappear and come back with excuses."

Richard nodded once. "Agreed."

Joe added, "And nobody's alone with you."

The words landed heavy in the air.

Even Maya felt them like a boundary snapping into place.

Alex nodded. "Not even Maya."

Maya's chest tightened, but she did not argue. Not because she liked it. Because it was correct.

She looked at Richard. "Can you live with that?"

Richard's mouth tightened. He glanced toward the distant whine, then back.

"Yes," he said. "I can live with it."

Joe's eyes stayed on him for a long beat, then he nodded once, as if the truth in that answer was solid enough to stand on for now.

"Then we go," Joe said.

Alex shifted closer to Maya, and she felt his field try to settle again, thin but determined.

Elara moved to Maya's other side, not touching her, but close enough that Maya could feel the warmth of her presence through the cold air.

Richard limped, but he did not complain. He stayed where he was told, hands visible, posture carefully nonthreatening.

They started moving through the basin, away from the road, away from the floodlights, toward darker ground where the scrub grew thicker and the stone broke into uneven shelves.

The whine overhead shifted, tracking.

Maya did not look up. She kept her awareness on the Weave.

As they moved, the threads beneath them changed.

Not smoothing, not healing, not settling into anything like peace.

But aligning.

The net that had been yanked hard miles away began to pull into a shape around all five of them, as if their combined presence gave it something to brace against.

In the distance, far enough that it was only a pressure at the edge of her perception, Maya felt the Shadow Current react.

A subtle stirring.

A turning of attention.

It noticed them moving together.

Above and beyond, deeper than the sky, there was no Immortal intervention. No voice. No sudden radiance. No dream-touch.

Only the cold, quiet fact of consequence.

Maya kept walking, feeling the Weave shift with every step they took as a unit.

The fracture had scattered them across the world.

Now it was drawing them together, whether they were ready or not.

25

⚭

Visions Return

Maya learned to walk without looking up.

After the Surge, the sky felt like a lie anyway. Too wide. Too normal. Too willing to hold stars over ground that had been cut open and stitched back together wrong. Her life and refuge at the Wyrd Word Bookstore seemed like a lifetime ago.

They moved low through broken shelves of rock and scrub, keeping away from the road and its false safety, keeping away from any place that might funnel them into light. Alex set the pace when he could, but tonight his body did most of the work. His shield did not spread clean anymore. It came in ragged patches, a thin pressure that sometimes steadied the air and sometimes did nothing at all.

Joe walked on Maya's left, quiet for once, eyes flicking and narrowing as if he could see the lies hiding in the wind. Elara stayed close to him, heat tucked under her skin like a fist she refused to open. Richard limped behind them, keeping his hands visible, keeping his distance, keeping himself small without ever looking harmless.

The whine of drones had faded, but Maya did not trust that. She did not trust silence anymore.

The Residuum lingered in low pockets, a faint haze that barely showed unless she let her perception tilt. When she did, the world

207

gained an extra layer of wrong. Threads under everything. Strain lines. Sick little eddies that refused to flow like they used to.

But something else was there too.

Not relief. Not peace.

Direction.

It was subtle at first, like the Weave had decided to stop screaming and start pointing. The static that had filled her senses since the tunnels had thinned. In its place was pressure, like the air itself wanted to resolve into shape and could not quite manage it.

Maya kept her breathing steady and tried not to let her awareness flare. She had learned the hard way that the Weave noticed attention. The Shadow Current noticed it too.

Still, she could not stop the way the threads tugged at her perception as they walked. Not at her body, not like a jump. At her awareness, like faint taps on glass.

A pulse. Then nothing.

Another pulse, a half beat later, as if someone far away had tapped twice and waited to see if she would answer.

Maya slowed without meaning to.

Alex glanced back over his shoulder. Moonlight caught the sharp line of his jaw and the bruised exhaustion under his eyes. "You good?"

"Yeah," Maya said. She kept her voice low. "Just tired."

That was not a lie. Her muscles ached like they had been wrung out. Her head felt full of grit.

But the tiredness was not what made her slow.

The Weave was coming back.

Not the way it had been before the Surge, when she could blink and feel the net answer cleanly. Not the way it had been in the tunnels, when it throbbed with sickness and hungry echo. This was something between. A waking limb after it had been asleep too long.

It should have made her feel safe.

Instead, it made her feel watched.

Alex turned forward again, keeping his body angled so he was still half between her and Richard. Even now. Even after the rules. Even after the decision.

Maya did not resent him for it.

She only resented how right it was.

They climbed into a shallow crease between two ridges where the scrub grew thicker and the stone rose in jagged ribs. A good place to vanish for a few minutes. A bad place to stay if anyone thought to look.

Joe lifted a hand. "Hold."

They stopped. Everybody did, even Richard, though his breath hitched like the pause hurt.

Joe crouched and peered up through the branches. He listened. Then he nodded once, sharp. "No movement. No engines."

Elara leaned against a rock and closed her eyes for a moment. When she opened them, her gaze fixed on Maya. "You're pale."

Maya forced a small shrug. "I'm cold."

Elara's mouth twitched like she did not believe that, but she let it go. For now.

Alex shifted closer. His presence brushed Maya's senses, frayed but stubborn, like he was trying to wrap a blanket around her with his bare hands. "We don't stay long," he said.

Maya nodded.

Joe moved a few steps away, scanning the slope. Elara followed him, not far, the two of them keeping an angle on the ground behind. Richard stayed where he was told, on the far side of the crease, close enough to be seen, far enough to be kept.

Maya took one step deeper into the shadow and meant to breathe.

The Weave tightened.

It was not a pull like the convergence in the basin. It was a narrowing, like threads drawing inward around her alone, compressing into a point just behind her eyes.

Her skin prickled.

Light shifted.

Not the moonlight. Not the shadows.

The world itself dimmed by a fraction, as if someone had lowered the volume on reality.

Sound thinned next, the way it had when Joe and Elara had rift-slipped into Colorado. The faint rustle of leaves became distant. The scrape of Richard's boot on stone stretched wrong, like it had to travel too far.

Time skipped.

Not a jump. Not a blink.

A missing frame.

Maya's breath caught, and in that hollow moment the Weave rang.

Not like a voice.

Like harmonics layered over one another, tones braided into something too complex for her mind to hold.

They brushed the edges of her awareness and recoiled, as if the act of touching her hurt.

A single word surfaced through the tones, broken and incomplete, as if it had been forced through a crack too small.

Soon.

Maya's eyes went wide. Her pulse slammed once, hard, and she felt the echo withdraw immediately, snapping back like a hand pulled away from a hot surface.

Sound rushed in again.

Leaves rattled. Dirt shifted. Someone exhaled nearby.

Maya swayed.

Alex's hand caught her arm. He did not yank. He did not speak loud. He simply grounded her with contact the way he always had, the way he had learned to do when his power could not hold the world steady on its own.

His thumb pressed once against her sleeve. A quiet signal. Here. Now. Stay.

Maya blinked hard and forced her lungs to work.

Alex leaned in, his voice barely above breath. "Maya. Are you okay?"

She wanted to say no.

She wanted to tell him the visions were back, that the Immortals had brushed her mind like a warning and then vanished, that something old and bound and powerful was stirring again.

She did not.

She heard Ethan in the back of her memory, not as words, but as that steady white gold pressure that always felt like restraint and care at the same time.

Don't pull attention. Don't turn a spark into a flare.

Maya swallowed. "Just a ripple," she whispered. "It passed."

Alex held her gaze. His eyes were tired, but there was still that sharpness in them, that constant measuring of threats.

He nodded once, slow, but he did not let go immediately.

Across the crease, Joe looked back.

His eyes narrowed in the way they did when his truth-sight brushed something. Maya felt it as a pressure, like the air itself had decided to stop pretending and show what it was.

Joe did not flinch.

He did not call her out.

He only studied her for a long beat, then looked away again, scanning the slope like he could find the answer written in the dark.

Elara watched too. Her posture stayed casual, but Maya could feel the heat in her like a coiled spring.

Nobody spoke. Not about that.

Maya's answer had been true.

And not true enough.

They did not have time to sit with it anyway.

A faint buzz drifted through the night, so soft it could have been an insect if it had not carried that mechanical thinness that made Maya's stomach clench.

Joe lifted his hand again, sharper this time. "We move."

Elara straightened instantly. "That's a drone."

Alex's shoulders tightened. "Yeah."

Richard shifted his weight, pain flickering across his face. He did not complain. He did not argue. He simply started limping in the direction Alex indicated, like a man who had learned what happened when he tried to choose his own path.

They moved fast, staying under branches, cutting through narrow gullies where the stone rose high enough to hide them from anything scanning overhead. Maya kept her eyes forward and her mind split.

One part watched the ground, the terrain, the distance between cover and open space. One part listened to the Weave.

It was not screaming now.

It was whispering.

Taps brushed her awareness as she stepped. Not constant. Not rhythmic. Like someone far away testing the strength of a door.

Maya forced herself not to answer.

She mapped the terrain in her head without blinking, calculating vectors, angles, distances that could keep them out of sight if HECATE had thermal imaging. Elara's heat made them easier to see. Alex's weakened field would not blur them like it used to.

Joe murmured, "Left," and Maya adjusted without thinking.

The Weave tightened again.

Not as hard as before. Not enough to make the world dim.

Enough to make her skin crawl.

Maya kept walking.

They crested another low ridge and dropped into a narrow wash where dried stones filled the bottom like bones. Maya's breath fogged in the cold. Elara's did not, not as much.

The drone sound faded, then returned, sliding across the sky like a search pattern.

Maya's chest hurt with the effort of not reaching, not flaring, not blinking them away. A jump would leave a tear. A tear would leave residue. Residue would draw attention.

And now, apparently, the Weave itself was already drawing attention.

They reached a patch of thicker scrub and paused again, just long enough to listen. Joe crouched. Elara stood guard. Alex checked their back trail with his eyes because his shield could not do it for him.

Maya closed her eyes for a heartbeat, just to steady the burning behind them.

The second echo hit like a cold hand around her skull.

The Weave folded inward, quick and tight, compressing into a point that stole her breath. This time the world did not dim. It sharpened.

Every sound became thin and precise. Every thread underfoot brightened in her mind, not in color but in clarity, as if the lattice had decided she was allowed to see again.

Then she felt them.

Not fully. Not bodies. Not faces.

Identity without form.

Weight without light.

Judgment held in quiet restraint.

Kemen.

Not her radiance. Not her presence filling a space.

Just the unmistakable pressure of her attention, like standing beneath a sky that could choose to burn you alive and did not.

And something else beside it, softer and stranger, like a mirror held at an angle. Cylian. Not her voice. Not her sorrow. Only that unsettling sense of being seen through, of patterns and cycles and quiet inevitabilities.

A warning impression landed in Maya's mind, not spoken, not commanded, simply placed there like a truth too heavy to ignore.

Alignment precedes collapse.

Maya's eyes flew open. For a fraction of a second she thought she saw threads snap and reform in the air, like something trying to stitch the world and failing.

Then the echo tore away. Not withdrawing gently but breaking. Pain lanced through her awareness, sharp and sudden, as if a thread connected to her had been yanked until it snapped.

Maya stumbled.

Alex's hand caught her again, faster this time.

"Maya," he whispered, urgent now. "Hey. Talk to me."

She swallowed hard, tasting iron. "I'm fine."

It came out too quick, too practiced.

Joe looked up from his crouch. His gaze pinned her, and she felt that truth pressure again, probing.

Maya held his eyes.

She did not lie.

She also did not open the door.

Joe's jaw tightened. He looked away again, scanning the ridge above as if it was safer to fight an enemy you could see.

Elara stepped closer. "You're not fine."

Maya forced a shaky breath. "I'm not going to pass out," she said. "I'm just... getting hit with aftershocks."

That was true enough that it held.

Elara's eyes narrowed, but she did not press. Not here. Not with the drone sound still drifting in and out overhead.

Richard shifted behind them, and Maya felt it. Not him moving. The way the Weave twitched around him like it did not know whether to pull him closer or push him out.

Richard stared into the dark like he could feel something watching from behind it.

His voice came low, rough. "Do you feel that?"

Alex didn't look back. "Feel what?"

Richard hesitated, then shook his head once, like he didn't trust the words. "Like something's got its eyes on us."

Elara's heat spiked. "That's helpful."

Joe's tone went flat. "He's not wrong."

Maya kept her face still. Her heart hammered.

If Richard could feel watched, then it was not just her.

Or the Shadow Current.

Or HECATE.

It could be all of it.

They moved again, tighter now. Joe stayed closer to Maya than before. Elara kept pace on the other side, her warmth a steady presence in the cold. Alex stayed slightly ahead, scanning, choosing routes that kept them under cover.

Richard stayed behind, where he had been told. Nobody was alone with him. Not even for a minute. Maya felt the rule like a collar she had agreed to wear. She did not resent it.

She only resented that part of her wanted to tell Alex anyway, wanted to lean in and whisper, They're back. The Immortals. I can feel them again.

But if they were bound, if contact hurt them, if the echoes were reflexive and dangerous, then speaking it out loud might do more than comfort her.

It might pull the wrong kind of attention. It might turn those taps into pounding.

Maya watched Joe and knew his gift could not catch what she did not say. He could tear lies out of the air. He couldn't force her to offer the whole truth.

Elara glanced at Maya once, quick and searching, then looked away, jaw set like she had decided to wait until survival gave them the luxury of arguing.

Alex's hand brushed Maya's sleeve again as they crossed a narrow stretch of open stone. Not a question. A promise. I'm here. Stay with me. Maya stayed and kept walking.

The Weave underfoot shifted as they moved as a unit. Not smoothing. Not healing. Not forgiving.

Aligning.

Like the fracture had decided that scattering them was no longer useful, and now it wanted them in one place when whatever came next arrived.

The echoes did not return.

Not again in the next mile.

Not again as the drone sound finally faded into distance.

But Maya knew better than to believe that meant they were gone.

They had touched her twice.

Soon.

Alignment precedes collapse.

She felt those words settle into the back of her mind like stones.

Ahead, the terrain dipped into a darker line of trees, thick enough to hide them for a while. Joe signaled, and they slipped into the cover without speaking.

Maya followed, keeping her face calm, keeping her breathing steady, keeping her secret tucked behind her teeth like a blade.

The visions were back.

And this time, Maya understood why they were never meant to be shared.

26

Silent Protocol III

The operations center had no windows.

Senator Victor Hargreaves preferred it that way. Windows invited distractions. They invited weather, crowds, the illusion of normal life moving on beyond the walls. This place was built for what remained when normal life failed.

Banks of screens filled the room in a staggered curve, each one feeding a different slice of the same widening problem. Maps, waveforms, satellite overlays, thermal grids, time stamped camera feeds. The air smelled faintly of ozone and recirculated coffee. The hum of cooling systems never stopped.

Hargreaves stood with his hands clasped behind his back, shoulders square, expression set in the same calm he wore in hearings and photo ops. The difference was that here, no one asked him to smile.

A young analyst with a clipped haircut spoke without looking away from her console. "Senator, we've got another cluster."

On the primary display, the continental map pulsed with new markers, tight and ugly, blooming like bruises across the Rockies and then flickering in scattered points along the Midwest. The markers weren't places in the normal sense. They were moments. A coordinate and a timestamp that did not behave.

Hargreaves watched the dots appear, disappear, then reappear a few miles away.

"How many?" he asked.

"Seven in the last forty minutes," she said. "All within existing disturbance corridors. Most near Anomalous Field Residue zones, identified by elevated Persistent Interference Matter readings. Two near transportation routes. One near an emergency response perimeter."

He didn't need her to explain what that meant. The phrase they used in the first briefings had been blunt.

People had shown up where they could not have been.

On a secondary screen, video footage played in short loops. A warehouse lot at the industrial fringe of a city. A dim stretch of roadside. A drone camera sweeping a ravine. In every clip, there was a fraction of a second where the image tore without tearing. Not a glitch. Not signal loss. A skipped frame that made your eyes hurt if you tried to follow it.

Then movement where there had been none.

Hargreaves's gaze shifted to the timeline feed running along the bottom of the board. Each anomaly was paired with accompanying sensor data. Pressure dips. EM spikes. Thermal discontinuities. A brief, sharp distortion in the audio spectrum that resembled nothing in the library except other instances of the same problem.

"Aftershock behavior is accelerating," another voice said. A man in his forties, senior by posture if not by badge, lifted a tablet toward the central console. "The clusters are tightening. It's not dispersing the way it did in April."

April. That was when it started.

That was when the first reports came in from rural deputies and frightened civilians and a handful of internal assets who could be relied on to write down what they saw without embroidery. That was when HECATE had been born in a series of hurried meetings and closed door briefings that never reached the public record.

That was when Hargreaves understood the only honest truth about this country. If you did not define the threat, someone else would. If you did not build the cage, someone else would build it around you.

He stepped closer to the main board. A technician keyed in a new overlay and the map shifted into layers. Not geography now, but correlation. Red fields indicating PIM (Persistent Interference Matter) density estimates, derived from nothing more mystical than how often their sensors lost coherence in a given region. White marks showing rift slip events. Yellow hazard triangles where field teams reported persistent interference.

The red fields had thickened.

The white marks had begun to organize.

"Is there any sign these are independent events?" Hargreaves asked.

The senior man shook his head. "No, sir. That's the problem. The clustering isn't random. The probability models don't support coincidence anymore."

Hargreaves looked across the room. Eyes dropped. People pretended to focus on screens. Nobody wanted to be the one to say what everyone was thinking.

This was no longer a series of isolated incidents.

This was a convergence.

He had spent decades shaping policy around simple principles. Chaos spread unless contained. Uncertainty created fear. Fear demanded an answer, whether or not the answer was perfect.

He could work with imperfect answers.

He could not allow uncontrolled ones.

An analyst spoke softly, as if the room itself might be listening. "Senator, we're seeing multi source overlap."

"What kind?" he asked.

"Thermal profiles," she said. "Multiple. Human sized. Moving in proximity."

Another analyst added, "And we're getting repeated signature similarities across separate locations. Same distortion pattern. Same timing anomalies. Same pressure profile. It suggests the same mechanism, even if we don't understand it."

Hargreaves's eyes narrowed slightly. "Translate."

The woman swallowed. "It means it's the same kind of event occurring again and again, and now it's bringing multiple subjects into the same area."

Multiple subjects.

That was the part that mattered.

The danger of an unknown force was bad enough. The danger of unknown people gathering inside it was worse.

He did not care what they called themselves. Walker. Attuned. Asset. Threat. The label did not change the reality.

Group formation changed everything.

He watched as the diagnostics display updated on its own, the system pulling data and applying the newest correlation routine the engineers had built in a rush over the last weeks. A line of text appeared at the top of the board, stark and simple, the kind of language machines used when they had no patience for human denial.

MULTI SOURCE ANOMALY CONVERGENCE CONFIRMED

A few people stared at it as if it had spoken.

Hargreaves did not.

He had expected it. Not in this precise configuration. Not in this exact timeframe. But he had expected a point when the pattern would stop looking like noise and start looking like intent.

He glanced to the side where a smaller board displayed the protocol ladder, each tier locked behind specific conditions. The language was dry. Legal. Tactical. Designed to sound reasonable when read aloud in a room full of officials who wanted to believe they were still in control.

Silent Protocol I. Identification and monitoring.

Silent Protocol II. Containment trials, field disruption, denial options.

Silent Protocol III. Full operational deployment.

Silent Protocol III had been written months ago. Drafted in the first frantic weeks when the early reports came in and the agencies with more tradition than spine asked him what they should do.

He had told them what he always told them.

Prepare now. Apologize later.

The conditions were met. That did not mean it would work. It meant waiting would be worse.

He turned his head toward the senior man. "What's our confidence on location?"

"Moderate," the man said. "We can bracket the corridor. The convergence point is not fixed. It drifts along the disturbance field. But we can track it in real time with the latest sensor mesh."

The latest sensor mesh. A patchwork of repurposed technology, rushed prototypes, and field modifications built by people who understood engineering better than politics. It did not need to touch the phenomenon to be useful. It only needed to see the shadow it cast on the instruments.

"And Division Gray?" Hargreaves asked.

A woman in a dark uniform stood near the back, still as a statue. Her insignia marked her as internal security, but the way she carried herself said military.

"Ready," she said.

Hargreaves nodded once.

His thoughts did not go to morality. Morality was a luxury for stable worlds. His thoughts went to consequence.

If these individuals converged, if they stabilized each other, if they became coordinated, then containment would become exponentially more difficult. Not because of what they could do, but because of what they would inspire.

Panic did not need facts. Panic only needed a story.

He would not allow the story to be written by amateurs.

He faced the room. "You're telling me the anomaly field is behaving as if it's selecting for proximity."

A hesitation. Then the senior man answered carefully. "We're telling you the data supports non random clustering, sir. Whether that's selection, correlation, or cascading thresholds, we don't know."

Hargreaves accepted the uncertainty without flinching. He had built a career on acting when others froze.

He leaned slightly toward the board, eyes fixed on the confirmed convergence line.

"Containment is no longer preventative," he said.

No one spoke. No one moved.

"It's corrective."

The words settled into the room like a seal.

He turned toward the uniformed woman. "Activate Silent Protocol III."

She didn't ask if he was sure. She didn't tell him what it would cost. She only nodded once, sharp.

"Yes, Senator."

Hargreaves looked back at the screens as new windows opened and new permissions unlocked. Lines of deployment status scrolled down the side of the board. Units rolling. Air assets repositioning. Mobile sensor arrays shifting to bracket a corridor that still refused to behave like a normal place.

He watched the map tighten into a net.

"Division Gray to full operational readiness," he said. "No improvisation. No heroics. We proceed by the book."

The senior man hesitated. "Senator, if the subjects are together, collateral—"

Hargreaves cut him off with a glance that held no heat, only finality.

"Then don't miss," he said.

The room went very still. Somewhere, a printer began spitting out authorization forms that would be signed and filed and buried. Somewhere else, a technician's hands trembled as she adjusted a gain setting and tried to pretend she wasn't afraid.

Hargreaves was not afraid.

Fear was what happened to people who waited for permission.

He watched the convergence markers pulse again, tighter now, brighter in the corridor as if the country itself had decided to fold its problems into one place.

He had seen enough.

"Bring them in," he said quietly. "before the anomaly field shifts beyond our predictive range."

The briefing room sat three levels below the HECATE operations floor, sealed behind two iris locks and a checkpoint that did not acknowledge rank until it read intent. Senator Victor Hargreaves disliked the theater of it. He liked certainty, clean lines, and doors that opened because they were supposed to. Still, he let the system do what it was built to do. In a crisis, ritual kept people obedient.

The room was windowless by design. No clocks. No personal devices. The only light came from the wall display, a broad curve of muted blue filled with shifting data layers and static-heavy maps.

Victor Hargreaves stood at the center of the room, hands folded behind his back.

Division Gray commanders filled the tiered seating, uniforms identical down to the last matte seam. No insignia. No names displayed. That was intentional. Identity created hesitation. This protocol did not allow for it.

"Begin recording," Hargreaves said.

A tone sounded once.

"Silent Protocol III is now active," he continued. "This briefing defines your operational boundaries. There will be no deviation unless authorized directly by me."

The display shifted. A regional map resolved into focus, overlaid with faint geometric arcs and clustered markers.

"Target classification has been upgraded," Hargreaves said. "We are no longer pursuing individual anomalous actors."

A commander in the front row spoke. "Sir, confirm scope."

Hargreaves did not look at him. "You are not hunting people. You are containing a convergent event cluster."

The words settled heavily in the room.

"These signatures are not moving independently," Hargreaves continued. "Whether by intent or coincidence is irrelevant. What matters is that proximity increases instability. Separation is no longer a viable strategy."

The display zoomed in. Colored density fields bloomed across the terrain.

"This is what we classify as AFR," he said. "Anomalous Field Residue. It accumulates after high-energy spatial disturbances. We don't know what causes it. We don't need to."

One of the engineers cleared her throat. "Sir, AFR density margins are still theoretical. We're extrapolating based on—"

Hargreaves turned then. His gaze was calm, unreadable.

"You're extrapolating because reality doesn't wait for certainty," he said. "Continue."

She swallowed. "Yes, sir."

The display shifted again. Corridors appeared. Not lines, but volumes. Long, narrowing funnels of projected interference.

"Protocol III is not pursuit-based," Hargreaves said. "Chasing creates escalation. Escalation creates loss of control."

He gestured once. The corridors brightened.

"This system herds," he said. "Mobile suppression corridors restrict movement options without requiring direct engagement. You will guide the cluster toward a containment zone selected in real time."

A Division Gray officer leaned forward. "Rules of engagement?"

"Capture is the priority," Hargreaves said. "Lethal force is authorized only if containment integrity collapses. If that happens, command authority escalates immediately."

The officer nodded once.

"Dampener nets will deploy in layers," Hargreaves continued. "You will not rely on a single system. Assume redundancy failure. Assume adaptation."

Another hand rose. "Sir, what if they breach the corridor geometry?"

"Then you tighten the net," Hargreaves said. "You do not improvise. You do not pursue. You compress."

He paused, letting the silence stretch.

"These individuals are not hostile in the traditional sense," he said. "They are unstable variables. You are not soldiers in a firefight. You are a corrective mechanism."

The display changed one final time. A new overlay appeared, stark white text against blue.

MEDIA SUPPRESSION STATUS: ACTIVE

"Public-facing response teams are already staged," Hargreaves said. "Narrative control is in effect. If contact occurs, it will be explained as a hazardous materials incident or seismic aftershock response."

A commander asked, "Sir, confirmation on executive oversight?"

Hargreaves did not hesitate. "I'm assuming direct operational command."

A murmur rippled through the room, brief and controlled.

"I will notify the President after containment is secured," Hargreaves added. "Not before." The emergency delegation was already on file, signed during the first wave of anomalies. He was simply exercising it. He stepped back, hands folding again behind his back.

"Silent Protocol III exists for one reason," he said. "When uncertainty becomes fear, control must precede understanding."

His gaze swept the room.

"Deploy Division Gray to full readiness," he said. "Begin corridor alignment. You move on my word."

The tone sounded again.

Recording ended.

Hargreaves remained standing as the commanders rose in unison and filed out, already issuing quiet orders into secure channels.

Containment was no longer about delay. It was about outcome control.Bottom of Form

They did not deploy like a unit responding to an emergency. They deployed like a system completing a calculation. Across three states, gray doors opened at the same second. Hangar bays. Subterranean lifts. Highway depots disguised as utility hubs. No sirens. No shouted orders. Just the muted thrum of machinery cycling from dormant to awake.

An observer watching the feeds would not have seen urgency. They would have seen inevitability.

Division Gray moved.

In Nevada, a transport plane lifted without lights, its ascent smooth and unremarkable against the night. In Kansas, armored carriers rolled from a maintenance tunnel beneath an inactive rail yard, tires whispering over concrete. In Georgia, a helipad spun up inside a fenced industrial park marked as a weather research annex.

Every unit moved on the same clock.

Inside each carrier, the soldiers sat facing inward, hands resting flat on their thighs, eyes forward. No chatter. No last minute checks performed out of habit. Their gear had already been checked by systems that did not forget.

Displays flickered to life along the cabin walls.

No maps or satellite imagery, fields. Shifting density models rendered in pale wireframe, overlaid with pulsing probability cones. The terrain did not matter as much as the strain moving through it.

"Harmonic forecast updated," a synthetic voice announced evenly. "Deviation probability reduced to point four percent."

No one responded.

Each soldier felt the adjustment instead. A faint pressure under the skin. A recalibration along the collar line. Stabilizers tuned themselves, micro servos tightening and releasing with insect precision.

Flame resistance matrices spooled up first. Thermal absorption thresholds shifted upward without sensation, like a body deciding not to feel pain yet.

Shield interference counters followed. Field coherence disruptors synced to projected static patterns, ready to disrupt harmonic cohesion before it could settle.

PIM disruption protocols came last. Those took longer. A faint hum crept into the carriers, low enough to be felt more than heard. Some of the soldiers swallowed as it passed through them. Others flexed their fingers once and then went still again.

In one carrier, an operator blinked too hard.

It was nothing anyone else could see. A half second where his breathing hitched. A thought intruded where there should have been none.

He saw, just for an instant, the training footage they never showed the public. A body shaking on a concrete floor. A stabilizer glowing too bright. A scream cut short when the system compensated.

His jaw tightened.

The hum deepened.

The hesitation vanished as the system compensated.

Formation reasserted itself, not because anyone ordered it to, but because the system required coherence and the system always won.

Across the network, Division Gray units began to align their vectors.

They did not chase targets. They did not look for faces.

They responded to prediction.

Models updated in real time as anomalous field residue shifted and pooled. Corridors appeared on their displays, narrowing funnels of probability that shaped where movement could occur without a single visual confirmation.

The targets were not being tracked.

They were being guided.

A command node pulsed once.

"Target zone confirmed," the system announced.

Coordinates resolved across every display simultaneously.

A convergence point.

Not chosen for accessibility. Chosen for collapse tolerance.

In the command center, a confirmation light turned from amber to white. Division Gray adjusted course without comment. The net was closing and no one inside it would ever see the hands pulling the strings.Top of Form

The command chamber fell silent before Senator Victor Hargreaves said a word.

It was not the kind of silence that came from fear or respect alone. It was procedural. Systems recognized his presence the moment he crossed the threshold, rerouting permissions, shifting priority stacks, retracting layers of automated moderation designed to slow human impulse.

Hargreaves felt it happen. He always did.

The room was a tiered amphitheater of light and glass, screens rising in a shallow arc around a central well. Analysts sat at their stations, hands hovering over touch surfaces that now responded a fraction of a second faster. The air itself seemed to sharpen.

He did not pause to take in the room.

He walked straight down the central aisle.

A junior officer began to speak. "Senator, protocol recommends—"

Hargreaves lifted one hand.

The officer stopped mid sentence, words dissolving into the hum of processors and the distant ventilation system.

"I'm aware of the recommendations," Hargreaves said evenly. "I'm here to replace them."

He stepped into the command well and looked up at the wall of feeds. Rift slip aftershock clusters pulsed in pale overlays. Residual anomaly fields crawled across terrain models like frost spreading under glass. Predictive corridors narrowed and widened in slow breathing rhythms.

At the center of it all, five heat signatures moved together.

Not classified as individuals anymore.

A convergence.

Hargreaves folded his hands behind his back.

"Remove pacing safeguards," he said.

A beat of hesitation rippled through the chamber.

An analyst glanced toward the duty commander. "Sir, that will increase the probability of cascade responses."

Hargreaves did not turn.

"Yes," he said. "It will."

The safeguards dropped.

The system's gentle delays vanished. Feedback loops tightened. Prediction refresh rates jumped. The models grew sharper, less forgiving.

Hargreaves finally spoke louder, his voice carrying without effort.

"I want them contained before dawn."

No qualifiers. No conditionals.

A senior analyst cleared her throat. "Senator, civilian exposure increases exponentially if we compress the window. The corridor intersects two minor population bands and one emergency response zone."

"I know," Hargreaves said.

"And political fallout is likely if even partial footage leaks," another voice added. "There's also a non zero chance this forces permanent escalation among the anomalous assets."

Hargreaves turned then, slowly, and fixed the room with a level stare.

"I know," he said again.

He walked to the nearest console and placed his hand on its surface. The display shifted to acknowledge him, command authority blooming outward like a stain.

"We have been reacting since April," he continued. "Every adjustment we've made has been defensive. Careful. Measured. And every time, the problem has adapted faster than our caution."

He looked back to the feeds, to the five moving points.

"They are starting to believe movement itself protects them. That convergence creates inevitability."

His fingers tightened against the console.

"If they believe they're becoming inevitable," Hargreaves said, voice cold and precise, "we remind them they're not."

No one argued.

Orders cascaded through the chamber, clean and immediate. Division Gray vectors recalculated. Containment nets began to reposition. Suppression corridors aligned themselves with terrain that would force choices instead of escapes.

A live feed expanded across the central screen.

Infrared overlays. Probability contours. A thin white line marking predicted movement through broken ground and scrub.

Five figures moved along it, unaware of how precisely the path had been drawn.

Hargreaves watched without expression.

"Lock the corridor," he said quietly.

The system complied.

And the net tightened.

The first change was not visible.

It was procedural.

Across three states, Division Gray units shifted position without sirens, without chatter, without urgency that could be mistaken for panic. Vehicles altered routes by degrees, not turns. Boots touched down in places that had been empty seconds before. Men and women moved with the calm precision of people who trusted the math more than their instincts.

Ahead of the projected path, suppression zones came online.

At first they were only data points. Invisible volumes mapped over terrain where broken rock funneled movement and scrub narrowed lines of sight. Then the equipment engaged, and the air itself began to behave differently.

Drones adjusted altitude and spacing, abandoning broad search sweeps for something subtler. Their flight paths curved, overlapping just enough to create suggestion instead of pursuit. Light shifted. Sound dampened. Thermal gradients smoothed into false neutrality.

From the ground, it felt like weather deciding where you were allowed to walk.

In the HECATE operations center, a technician leaned closer to his console, brow furrowing.

"Sir," he said, not looking up. "PIM is increasing in suppression zones."

The display confirmed it. Pale bands thickened along the containment grid, pressure induced interference spiking where multiple fields overlapped.

"Expected," the duty commander replied.

The technician hesitated. "It's feeding back into the environment. Not just masking. It's pushing."

No one answered right away.

On the central screen, terrain feeds flickered as the suppression corridors locked into phase. The ground did not crack. The sky did not change color. But the models showed rising resistance where none had existed before. As if the world itself was bracing.

Out in the field, a Division Gray operator paused for half a second as his stabilizer recalibrated. His fingers flexed once. His breathing hitched. Then the system settled. He stepped forward and the formation moved with him, seamless, synchronized, the moment of humanity erased as efficiently as it had appeared.

Above them, drones slid into new patterns, their lights dimmed, their paths gentle and persuasive. Not chasing. Steering.

On the far edge of the containment grid, Residuum haze thickened, reacting poorly to the imposed order. It did not dissipate. It clung harder, pooling where suppression pressed against stressed geometry.

The Weave, unseen but present, tightened under the strain. Threads pulled taut. Directions narrowed. Choices collapsed into corridors that felt reasonable until they weren't.

Back in the command chamber, Senator Hargreaves watched the pressure curves rise and did nothing.

No order to slow.

No adjustment to relieve the load.

Containment was no longer a quiet thing.

It pressed back against the world, and the world began to notice.

Somewhere between the drones and the ground, between math and muscle, the hunt truly began.

And the cage started to close.

The room settled into a different kind of quiet.

Not the uneasy hum of anticipation, but the clean silence of commitment.

On the central board, a status field updated. Letters shifted from amber to white.

SILENT PROTOCOL III — ACTIVE

Below it, smaller lines of text cascaded down the display as the system executed its own authority.

Protocol I suspended.

Protocol II suspended.

Regional autonomy revoked.

Command priority elevated.

Hargreaves did not need to acknowledge it. The system had been designed to move faster than doubt.

He stood with his hands clasped behind his back, eyes fixed on the convergence marker representing overlapping anomaly returns hovered over a stylized map of broken terrain. Five signatures, compressed into a single pulsing symbol. It flared once, bright enough to draw the eye.

Then it stabilized.

Contained motion. Predictable vectors. Probability narrowing.

Hargreaves let out a breath through his nose, thin and controlled. Not relief. Satisfaction was too generous a word. This was simply the absence of uncertainty, and he had learned long ago to value that above comfort.

Around him, operators continued their work, voices low, movements precise. No one looked at him. They did not need to. The decision had already been made, and everyone in the room understood what followed.

He leaned closer to the screen, studying the steady pulse of the marker.

"Visibility creates inevitability," he said quietly, more to himself than anyone else. "And inevitability invites chaos."

No one contradicted him.

Hargreaves straightened, the faintest hint of a smile touching his mouth before discipline smoothed it away.

Silent Protocol III was never meant to fail.

It was meant to decide what survived visibility.

27

The Ambush

Maya learned to distrust quiet.

After the Surge, silence was never absence. It was a decision. A breath held too long. A room full of people pretending not to listen.

They moved for another hour under broken pine and jagged rock, keeping to the shallow cuts in the land where moonlight couldn't lay clean lines across them. The drones had faded into distance, the thin mechanical whine sliding away until it could have been wind. Maya didn't let herself believe it.

Ahead, the terrain softened into a low industrial fringe, the kind of forgotten edge where the mountains gave up and the world started pretending it was civilized again. Rusted fencing. A cracked service road. A line of old utility poles that leaned like tired men.

Joe slowed first, lifting a hand.

"Hold up."

Maya stopped with him, her boots crunching softly in gravel. Alex came up on her right, shoulders tense, eyes scanning as if he expected the dark to step forward and introduce itself. Elara kept close to Joe, heat tucked under her skin so tight Maya could almost feel the strain of it. Richard lagged a few paces behind, one hand braced against his thigh like it was the only thing keeping his leg from folding completely.

Joe squinted toward the structure half buried in shadow at the base of a slope.

It had once been some kind of maintenance outbuilding. Concrete block walls stained with weather. A corrugated metal roof sagging in the middle. A wide service door that hung crooked on its track, frozen half open like someone had tried to leave in a hurry years ago and never finished.

No lights. No vehicles. No movement.

"Looks empty," Joe said, voice low.

Elara's gaze flicked over the roofline, then the treeline beyond. "Looks like a place people dump bodies."

"Yeah," Joe said. "That's why nobody's here."

Alex exhaled through his nose, a sound that wasn't quite a laugh. "Perfect."

Maya felt the faintest tug in the Weave beneath her feet and stopped herself from leaning into it. The instinct was automatic now. Listen. Map. Reach.

She didn't.

Not yet.

"Low drone activity," Joe added. He rubbed at his temple like the motion might scrape the headache out of his skull. "If they've got anything overhead, it isn't close."

Maya watched him and saw the tightness around his eyes, the way he blinked a fraction too slow. His truth-sight had been working hard for hours, brushing everything they passed, checking the world for traps that didn't have to lie to be deadly.

"You're sure you're okay?" she asked.

Joe's mouth twisted. "I'm not dying."

"That wasn't what I asked."

He glanced at her, then softened by a hair. "I've had worse. It just feels like someone's trying to drill through my skull with a spoon."

Elara made a quiet sound of sympathy and anger all at once. "You should've said something sooner."

"And what," Joe whispered back, "so you can worry harder?"

Elara's eyes flashed, but she didn't argue. She shifted closer anyway, shoulder nearly brushing his arm. A wordless choice. Stay near. Be ready.

Richard reached the edge of their cluster and stopped, breathing shallow. Sweat darkened his collar despite the cold. His face looked carved out of exhaustion, as if the last few hours had sanded him down to something raw and unfamiliar.

"We stopping?" he asked.

Alex's head snapped toward him. The shield did not bloom. It didn't rise like it used to, clean and steady. Maya could feel it flicker at the edges, thin as a membrane, bruised and unreliable.

So Alex did what he had been doing since the basin. He stepped between Richard and Maya, not even thinking about it.

"Yeah," Alex said. "We're stopping."

Richard's gaze dropped, and he nodded once like he accepted being placed behind lines. He didn't complain. He didn't offer suggestions. He just stood there, hands visible, waiting to be told where to exist.

Maya hated that it felt necessary.

She hated even more that it still felt right.

They crossed the open stretch to the outbuilding in a staggered line, quick and quiet. The air around the structure was colder, not in a way that made sense. The cold sat heavy against her skin, as if the place had been storing it.

Inside, it smelled like dust and old oil. There were broken shelves along one wall and a collapsed table that had once held tools. Someone had spray painted a crude symbol on the far block wall years ago, faded now, flaking with the damp.

Elara moved automatically to the center of the room, eyes tracking corners, shoulders squared. She looked like she wanted to set something on fire just to remind the world she could.

Alex checked the door, then the narrow side window. His movements were slower than usual, not from caution but from cost. Every time he tried to spread his field, Maya felt the effort, the ragged push that didn't quite settle into place.

Joe dropped onto a low concrete lip along the wall and pressed the heels of his hands into his eyes.

"Don't do that," Maya said quietly.

Joe didn't move his hands. "It's either that or scream."

Elara crouched beside him, her voice barely a breath. "Let me."

"I don't need you to fix it," he said.

"I'm not fixing it," she replied. "I'm reminding you you're not alone."

Joe's hands fell. For a second his expression went bare, all fatigue and stubbornness and something that almost looked like gratitude.

Then his face closed again. "Fine. Just don't tell anyone I'm getting soft."

Elara's mouth twitched. "Wouldn't dream of it."

Richard sank carefully to the floor near the far wall, back against concrete, eyes closed. His leg trembled once, then stilled. Maya could feel his presence in the Weave like a stain that wouldn't wash out. Not active. Not feeding. But touched deep enough that the threads around him didn't know how to settle.

Maya stood near the doorway, listening.

Not for voices.

For the Weave.

Outside, the world should have felt frayed. The land around Colorado still carried strain like bruises beneath skin. Even when the Residuum haze was thin, Maya could sense it in the lattice, in the way threads pulled and resisted, in the way reality held itself too tight.

But here, at the edge of this forgotten structure, the Weave did something strange.

It went still.

Not calm. Not silent.

Held.

Like someone had taken a net and pulled it taut, then froze their hands in place.

Maya swallowed. She let her perception tilt just enough to feel the threads, just enough to test whether this was her exhaustion making patterns out of nothing.

The lattice was there, faint but present, a geometry beneath the concrete and stone.

And it was not moving the way it should.

It felt like a breath paused at the top of the lungs.

Alex glanced back at her, reading her posture the way he always had, even before he had the words for what he was sensing.

"You feel something," he murmured.

Maya forced her shoulders to relax. "I'm just listening."

He didn't look convinced. He stepped closer, keeping his voice low enough it wouldn't carry outside.

"This place is wrong," Alex said.

Maya met his eyes. "Yeah."

Joe lifted his head. "Wrong how?"

Maya hesitated. She didn't want to give shape to it. She didn't want to pull attention by naming it.

She settled for the truth that didn't open all the doors.

"It's quiet," she said.

Elara snorted softly. "That's the point, isn't it?"

Maya shook her head. "Not that kind of quiet."

Joe's gaze sharpened, and for a second she felt his truth-sight brush the air between them. Not accusing. Checking.

Maya kept her face steady. She wasn't lying.

She also wasn't explaining.

Alex's voice went softer. "Like the tunnels?"

"No," Maya said quickly. Then she slowed, choosing her words with care. "Not hungry. Not loud. Just... held."

Richard opened his eyes across the room. His stare fixed on the doorway, not the group. His jaw flexed.

"Held," he echoed, almost to himself.

Maya's skin prickled.

Alex's hand brushed her sleeve, a grounding touch that pretended to be nothing. "We don't stay long," he whispered.

Maya nodded, but her attention had already slipped past the door-frame, past the dark slope outside, into the space where the Weave should have been flowing.

It wasn't flowing.

It was bracing.

The stillness didn't sit around them like shelter. It sat around them like a lid.

And beneath it, she felt pressure.

Not inward, not tightening around her like the echoes had done.

Outward.

As if something beyond the ridge had started pushing on the lattice and the lattice was pushing back, building tension in a widening ring.

Maya's mouth went dry.

This wasn't safety.

This was the moment right before the snap.

She took a slow breath and tasted dust and old oil and the thin chemical bite that had been in the air since the basin. Borrowed quiet. Borrowed time.

Across the room, Joe shifted, his hand drifting back toward his temple. Elara watched the doorway with a feral patience. Alex stood half in front of Maya without even realizing he'd done it. Richard stayed where he was, small and contained and dangerous in ways none of them could afford to forget.

Maya stared into the dark beyond the threshold and tried to convince her body to believe what her mind already knew.

The net hadn't missed them.

It had simply stopped moving long enough to close.

Joe knew something was wrong because nothing was.

No static edges. No spike of fear bleeding off a passerby who didn't know why they were afraid. No nervous lies leaking into the air the way they always did around places people pretended were empty. The world outside the concrete walls felt scrubbed clean, not quiet like abandonment, but quiet like preparation.

He sat with his back against the cold block, eyes half closed, letting his breathing slow. His head still throbbed, a dull pressure that pulsed behind his eyes in time with his heartbeat, but the pain wasn't what caught his attention.

It was the absence.

Joe had learned early that his ability didn't just light up lies. It lit up intent. Fear left a residue. Guilt left a smear. Even people who believed their own stories left distortions behind them, tiny warps in the truth that his mind learned to read the way other people read faces.

Right now, there was nothing.

No anxiety from a bored security guard nearby. No distant irritation from a driver stuck on a service road. No stray human noise bleeding through the dark.

That didn't happen by accident.

Joe opened his eyes and stared at the crooked doorway. Beyond it, the night sat flat and empty, moonlight touching scrub and stone without hesitation.

Too clean.

He rubbed his forehead and muttered, "That's not good."

Elara glanced over from where she stood watch. "You say that a lot."

Joe didn't smile. "Not like this."

Alex shifted near the door, shoulders tightening. "What are you seeing?"

Joe shook his head slowly. "I'm not seeing anything."

Maya turned toward him, her expression already alert. "That's what's bothering you."

Joe nodded. He pushed himself to his feet, joints protesting, and took a careful step toward the doorway. Every instinct he had wanted him to stop moving, but curiosity had always been stronger than comfort.

He let his truth-sight widen, not flaring it, just easing it open enough to feel the shape of things.

The calm outside wasn't natural.

It had edges.

Joe stopped just short of the threshold. The air pressed faintly against his skin, not like wind, more like standing too close to a speaker you couldn't hear. His headache sharpened a notch.

"Anyone else feel that?" he asked.

Alex frowned. "Pressure. Yeah."

Elara's jaw tightened. "Like someone turned the volume down."

Maya didn't answer right away. Her eyes were fixed on the dark, unfocused in the way they got when she was listening to things nobody else could hear.

Joe swallowed. He focused again.

The calm had structure.

That was the part that made his stomach drop.

It wasn't peace. It wasn't emptiness. It was intent stripped of emotion, laid out in clean lines. Purpose without fear. Direction without desire.

Machines felt like this sometimes, when he brushed against a system that had been told what to do and did not care why. But even machines usually carried a human fingerprint. Someone's impatience. Someone's pride.

This didn't.

Joe felt a faint pinch behind his eyes, sharp enough to make him wince. He pressed his lips together and breathed through it.

"Guys," he said quietly. "We need to move."

Alex glanced back at Richard, then at Maya. "We just got here."

"I know," Joe said. "That's the problem."

Elara took a step closer to him. "Explain."

Joe shook his head. "I can't. Not cleanly."

Maya's gaze snapped to him. "Try."

Joe hesitated, then nodded once. "There are no lies out there. None. No fear, no panic, no curiosity. No human mess. Whatever's around us isn't reacting. It's waiting."

Alex's eyes hardened. "Waiting for what."

"For us to be where it wants us," Joe said.

The words settled heavy in the room.

As if on cue, the lights flickered.

Not a full blackout. Just a soft dip, like someone had briefly dimmed the world and brought it back up again. The hum of the distant power grid shifted pitch, then steadied.

Joe's head spiked with pain. He hissed and pressed his fingers to his temples.

Elara swore under her breath. "That wasn't normal."

The air changed.

Sound dampened, not disappearing but flattening, as if echoes had decided they weren't allowed anymore. Even their breathing sounded wrong, too close, too contained.

Joe felt the pressure behind his eyes deepen, a subtle squeeze that made his vision blur at the edges.

"This is it," he said. "This is the lock."

Alex stepped fully in front of Maya. "What lock."

Joe forced himself to focus through the pain. The truth-sight sharpened, and with it came understanding that made his chest tighten.

"We're not being watched," he said.

Elara's head snapped up. "What do you mean, not watched."

Joe laughed once, short and humorless. "I mean there's nobody on the other end of this. No one peeking through a scope or waiting for us to screw up. This isn't surveillance."

Maya's voice was very quiet. "Then what is it."

Joe swallowed. "Positioning."

The word tasted wrong in his mouth.

Outside, something engaged.

He didn't see it happen. He felt it. A ripple of intent snapping into place, clean and synchronized. Multiple actions unfolding at once without urgency, without haste.

Like a system completing a step it had already solved.

The pressure behind his eyes flared, then steadied, as if the world itself had decided this was the new normal.

Alex's shield twitched, tried to bloom, then faltered. He grunted softly and steadied himself with one hand against the wall.

"They're doing something to the field," Alex said. "I can't spread."

Elara's heat spiked in response, then guttered like a flame starved of oxygen. She clenched her fists, breathing hard. "That's new."

Joe nodded grimly. "Yeah. They're not reacting to us. They're shaping where we can go."

Maya took a step toward the door and stopped herself. Her face had gone pale, eyes dark with concentration. "The Weave feels... redirected."

Joe looked at her. "Like corridors."

Her gaze met his. "Yes."

That confirmed it.

Joe felt a sick twist of clarity settle into place. He'd chased liars for years. Con artists. Killers. People who thought they were smarter than the truth. Even the best of them improvised. Adapted. Panicked when something went off script.

This didn't panic.

This didn't improvise.

"This was planned," Joe said softly. "Not for tonight, maybe. But for this."

Elara stared at the doorway, heat trembling under her skin. "They knew we'd stop somewhere like this."

Joe shook his head. "I don't think they care where. I think anywhere would've worked."

Alex's voice was tight. "Then why now."

Joe closed his eyes for a second, then opened them. "Because we're together."

Silence pressed in again, heavier now.

Outside, faint clicks echoed through the night. Not footsteps. Not voices. Systems talking to systems.

Joe felt it then, unmistakable.

A perimeter.

Not marked by men, but by intention. A boundary where choices thinned and paths narrowed, where the truth didn't scream danger but quietly removed alternatives until only one direction remained.

Joe backed away from the doorway, shaking his head. "We need to assume everything outside is part of the same machine."

Maya's jaw set. "How big."

Joe exhaled slowly. "Big enough that we don't see the edges yet."

Another soft flicker rolled through the building. This one carried a faint vibration underfoot, too even to be seismic, too precise to be chance.

Joe met Alex's eyes. "They're not closing in."

Alex frowned. "Then what are they doing."

Joe felt the last piece click into place, cold and absolute.

"They're closing around," he said. "All at once."

Outside, multiple systems finished coming online in near perfect synchrony.

Joe straightened despite the pain and forced his voice steady. "Heads up," he said. "The net's locked."

And whatever had built it was done waiting.

Alex felt the field break before he understood why.

It didn't fail all at once. It came apart in pulses, like a heartbeat skipping under strain. One second his grounding held, thin but present, a familiar pressure pushing back against the chaos in the air. The next, it collapsed inward, snapping tight against his chest and leaving the space around them naked.

He sucked in a breath and planted his feet.

The ground hummed.

Not loud. Not violent. Just enough to make his teeth buzz.

Alex reached instinctively, trying to spread his shield, to lay that steadying pressure over the room the way he always had. The response came late and wrong. His field flared, then jittered, edges tearing as if something kept tapping it out of alignment.

He grunted and dropped to one knee before he could stop himself.

"Maya," he said, forcing the word out. "Something's interfering."

"I know," she said quickly. "I feel it too."

Another pulse rippled through the air.

Alex's shield snapped outward this time, uncontrolled, then collapsed again. The effort sent a spike of pain through his temples. He clenched his jaw and rode it out, breathing through his nose like he'd been taught.

Disruptors.

He didn't know the term yet, but he understood the effect. Whatever was hitting them wasn't shutting them down. It was shaking the foundation, making every attempt to stabilize feel like balancing on loose gravel.

"Short range," Joe muttered nearby. "Localized."

Alex forced himself upright, swaying for half a second before he locked his knees. He scanned the doorway, the windows, every dark angle where someone might rush in.

No one did.

That was worse.

Outside, the night rearranged itself.

Figures appeared at the edge of his vision, not stepping into view so much as resolving into place. One, then another, then more, evenly spaced, silhouettes locking into a ring around the structure.

No shouting.

No commands barked into radios.

They moved with the calm precision of people who trusted the plan more than their instincts.

Division Gray.

Alex didn't know the name yet either, but he recognized the posture. Military without the noise. Professionals who didn't need to prove anything.

They stopped at the same distance from one another, each position chosen with care. Not close enough to provoke. Not far enough to invite escape.

Perfect spacing.

Alex swallowed.

Behind them, heavier shapes moved.

Cinder teams.

He saw the armor first. Bulkier. Reinforced. Plates layered for heat deflection. The way their helmets angled told him everything he needed to know about who they were for.

Elara.

She felt it too. He saw her shoulders tighten, heat flaring under her skin in a reflex she crushed down with visible effort.

"They planned for you," Alex said quietly.

Elara didn't look away from the door. "I noticed."

Another pulse hit.

Alex's grounding shattered outward this time, not collapsing but blowing apart in fragments that stung as they snapped back into him. He hissed and braced himself against the wall.

The geometry snapped into focus then.

Not instinct. Not magic. Pattern.

The pressure wasn't random. It wasn't an attack meant to overwhelm. It was narrowing. Every pulse shaved options away, redirecting force, guiding motion the way a river guides debris toward the deepest channel.

Alex's eyes tracked the space automatically, mapping angles, exits, lines of retreat.

Every one of them was shrinking.

Not blocked. Redirected.

If they ran for the back, pressure would rise there. If they pushed left, resistance would thicken. Every choice funneled toward a central axis that wasn't a door or a road, but a zone.

Containment.

"They're herding us," he said.

Joe shot him a look. "You're sure."

Alex nodded. "It's geometry. They're shaping where we can stand without crushing us."

Maya's voice was tight. "That means they want us intact."

"For now," Alex said.

Another pulse hit harder than the last.

Alex's shield flared one final time, then broke completely. No response. No spread. Just a dull ache where his power should have been.

For the first time since Salem, since the caverns, since all of it started, he felt truly exposed.

He stepped forward anyway.

If his power wouldn't hold the line, his body would.

Alex moved between Maya and the doorway, planting himself squarely in the center of the narrowing space. He widened his stance, shoulders set, every muscle screaming in protest.

His role shifted in that instant.

He wasn't a shield anymore.

He was an obstacle.

Outside, one of the figures raised a hand.

Not a weapon. Not a signal flare. Just a quiet gesture.

The air at the threshold thickened.

Alex felt it before he saw it. A compression wave that made the hairs on his arms stand up and pressed against his chest like a held breath.

"Contact," he said, voice steady despite the strain. "They're about to test us."

Maya moved closer behind him. Elara's heat surged, then steadied, controlled and dangerous. Joe shifted to Alex's side, jaw clenched against the pressure.

Richard stayed back, exactly where he'd been told.

The doorframe creaked.

Not from force, but from tension, as if the space around it had decided to become smaller.

Alex lifted his chin and stared into the dark.

"Alright," he muttered. "Let's see what they do first."

Outside, boots crossed an invisible line in perfect synchrony.

The net had dropped.

And the first move was coming.

Elara felt the cage before she saw it.

It wasn't a wall. It wasn't a barrier you could hit and measure. It was pressure that told her where she was allowed to exist and where she wasn't, a narrowing of possibility that made her skin itch and her teeth grind.

Alex was in front of her, shoulders squared, body braced like he could physically hold the world back if it came down to it. Maya was just behind him, too still, eyes unfocused in the way that meant she was listening to something Elara couldn't hear.

Elara didn't wait for permission.

She stepped forward and let the fire come up.

Not a flare. Not a blast. She kept it tight, disciplined, the way she'd learned after Miami. A controlled arc of heat, focused and deliberate, pushed outward from her palms toward the doorway.

The air shimmered.

The flame stretched, brightened, and then did something wrong.

It didn't hit.

It thinned.

Like it had been poured into a space that refused to hold it.

Elara's breath caught. She pushed harder, feeding more heat into the arc, shaping it with intent instead of emotion. The flame responded, but sluggishly, like it was moving through syrup.

Then it bent.

Not back at her. Not away.

Sideways.

The fire slid along an invisible curve and peeled off, dispersing into harmless sparks that guttered out before they could catch on anything.

"What the hell," she muttered.

Outside, the figures moved.

Cinder teams advanced in steady steps, boots crunching softly on gravel. They didn't rush. They didn't brace. They walked straight through the fading heat like it was bad weather.

Their armor drank the warmth.

She could feel it happen, the way her fire bled into their gear and vanished, absorbed by layers designed to take exactly what she was giving and give nothing back.

Elara's jaw clenched. She shifted her stance and changed tactics, snapping her hands outward and driving a wave of compressed heat at knee height, aiming to disrupt footing, to force a reaction.

The wave hit the edge of the containment zone and collapsed.

Not explosively. Neatly.

Oxygen starved out of it in an instant, leaving behind a vacuum-cold pocket that made her gasp.

The fire recoiled.

So did she.

Elara staggered back a step, heart hammering. She reached for the flame again and felt it hesitate, not refusing her, but slipping, like her grip on it had gone numb.

Her emotions were still there. Fear. Anger. A rising, furious need to burn something until it made sense.

The feedback wasn't.

The suppression field cut across her internal loop, muting the response she relied on to shape her power. The flame flickered without rhythm, reacting late, responding wrong.

"Stop," Alex said sharply. "Elara, stop pushing."

She snarled, eyes locked on the advancing Cinder team. "They're walking through it."

"I know," he said. "That's the point."

One of the armored figures raised a device, its surface dull and unremarkable. Elara felt the shift before it activated. A tightening in her chest. A wrongness in the air that made her fire pull inward instead of outward.

She tried to force it.

The flame bucked.

Pain lanced through her arm, sharp and immediate, like she'd grabbed something too hot without protection. Elara hissed and dropped her hand, cradling it against her side.

Rage surged, hot and instinctive.

It didn't help.

The cage didn't react to her anger. It didn't care.

For the first time since her awakening, Elara felt truly outmatched, not by strength, but by design.

Rage won't save us, she realized.

Joe's voice cut through the haze. "Elara. Don't."

She looked at him, breathing hard. "Then what. We just let them walk in?"

Joe wasn't watching the soldiers. He was watching the space around them, eyes narrowed, face pale with effort.

"They're not here to fight us," he said. "They're here to move us."

Elara swallowed, forcing her breathing to slow, pulling the flame back under her skin where it belonged.

Outside, the Cinder teams closed another step.

Inside the cage, Elara lowered her hands.

And listened.

Joe had learned to trust the pain.

When his gift sharpened, it always hurt. A pressure behind the eyes. A tightening in the jaw. The sense that the world was about to peel back and show him something it didn't want him to see.

This was different.

This was like trying to force open a door while the room itself leaned against it.

Joe planted his feet and reached anyway.

The truth-sight flared.

For a heartbeat, the world fractured into layers. Not visions, not symbols, but impressions stacked too tightly to separate. The soldiers outside did not glow with lies. They didn't shimmer with hidden intent. There was no fear bleeding through their posture, no cruelty riding their breath.

There was nothing.

Joe sucked in a breath and nearly gagged.

His vision tunneled, the edges dimming as if someone had pressed thumbs against his temples. The pressure spiked hard enough that black spots danced across his sight.

"Joe," Maya said quietly. "Joe, don't force it."

He didn't answer.

He pushed deeper.

The truth didn't resist him. It simply wasn't shaped the way he expected.

The Division Gray soldiers resolved into focus, not as individuals, but as nodes. Reinforced points in a system that did not require belief or deception to function. Their harmonics were artificial, layered and braced, like steel wrapped around something already breaking.

They weren't being controlled.

They were being stabilized.

Joe swallowed, throat burning.

Orders didn't flow from a single source. There was no central command pulse to tear apart. Instead, intent was distributed across layers of protocol, overlapping instructions that reinforced each other until no one directive mattered more than the whole.

No lies.

No singular fear.

No point of leverage.

Joe's head throbbed. Blood trickled from his nose, warm and sudden. He wiped it away without looking.

"This is wrong," he muttered.

Elara glanced at him. "You just noticed?"

"No," Joe said, voice tight. "This was built for me."

Alex turned his head slightly. "What does that mean."

Joe laughed once, sharp and humorless. "It means there's nothing to break."

He looked back at the soldiers, at the way they moved in clean intervals, how their spacing never changed, how hesitation never rippled through the formation.

"There isn't a lie holding this together," Joe said. "There's no belief system. No fear narrative. It's math and redundancy and permission already granted."

His vision blurred again, the suppression field grinding against his gift like sand in a wound. He staggered and caught himself on the wall, breath coming shallow.

Truth without leverage is just noise, he realized.

He couldn't expose them. He couldn't shame them. He couldn't pull a thread and watch the whole thing unravel.

There was nothing human enough to crack.

Joe wiped his mouth again, hands shaking now. "They planned for this," he said. "They knew someone like me would try to look."

Outside, Division Gray adjusted position by inches. The cage tightened without urgency.

Joe lifted his head, eyes burning.

"We're not going to talk our way out," he said. "And we're not going to burn our way out."

Elara swore under her breath. Alex's shoulders set harder, like he could still will himself into being enough.

Then the air shifted.

Not the suppression field. Not the soldiers.

Something else.

Joe felt it before he understood it, a sudden spike of wrongness that cut clean through the system's careful balance. His truth-sight flinched, snapping toward the source on instinct.

"Wait," he started.

Too late.

Behind them, where Richard had been standing exactly where he was told, the Weave twisted.

Joe turned, heart lurching, just as reality began to bend.

"Richard," Joe said. "Don't."

Richard didn't look at him.

He looked at the wall.

Richard had spent his life learning when not to move.

You survived long enough, you learned the difference between pressure that waited and pressure that crushed. This was the second kind. He felt it in his teeth, in the ache behind his eyes, in the way the air itself seemed to lean inward as if the world were slowly deciding where it wanted them to be.

And it was deciding without them.

The containment geometry wasn't subtle to him. It never was. Where Maya felt direction and Alex felt collapse, Richard felt resistance. The Weave around them wasn't just strained. It was being shaped. Folded. Persuaded into narrowing choices until there would be none left.

They weren't being surrounded.

They were being compressed.

Richard shifted his weight and pain flared up his leg, sharp enough to make his vision blur. He ignored it. Pain was familiar. Cages were worse.

"This ends with us on the ground," he said quietly.

No one answered right away. The suppression field pressed harder, like it was listening.

Joe turned partway. "Richard, don't."

Richard didn't look at him. He didn't look at Maya either. If he did, he might hesitate, and hesitation was how the net finished closing.

"They've already solved us," Richard said. "They're not reacting anymore. They're executing."

Alex's voice came tight. "You don't get to decide this alone."

Richard nodded once. "I know."

That was the worst part.

He drew a slow breath and tasted metal and dust and the old, familiar wrongness that came just before everything broke. The pressure on the Weave surged as if it sensed intent. It always did. The lattice around him twitched, threads tightening like muscles bracing for impact.

"I'm sorry," Richard said.

Then he moved.

He reached into the wall beside him, not with hands but with intent. Stone resisted at first, dense and stubborn, the way it always did when the world wanted to stay solid. Richard pushed anyway, forcing the matter to forget what it was for just long enough to become something else.

The structure screamed.

Not audibly. Harmonically.

Stone softened, then warped, its internal bonds unraveling into a glassy slurry that peeled open like flesh under a blade. The wall buckled inward, forming a ragged oval just large enough to crawl through.

Richard staggered as the cost hit him.

The Shadow Current surged instantly.

Residuum bloomed along the torn edges, thick and hungry, clinging to the opening like oil on water. Echoes stirred inside it, not fully formed but aware, tasting the sudden violence done to the Weave.

Richard cried out despite himself. His vision fractured, doubling and tripling as something cold brushed his awareness, too close, too interested.

"Maya," Joe shouted. "It's spiking."

Richard dropped to one knee, breath coming in ragged pulls. Blood trickled from his nose and ears, warm against the dust.

"Go," he rasped. "Now."

Elara swore and grabbed Maya's arm. Alex didn't argue. He moved like instinct had finally won.

Maya hesitated for half a second too long, eyes locked on Richard. He saw the calculation in her gaze, the way she weighed control against consequence.

"This will follow us," she said.

Richard managed a crooked smile. "It was already following."

The suppression field surged, reacting late. Division Gray formations shifted, tightening in response to the sudden anomaly. Orders cascaded. Systems recalibrated.

Too slow.

Joe hauled Richard up by the collar, ignoring the way Richard's leg nearly gave out. "You're not dying here," Joe said. "You don't get to make this a martyr thing."

Richard laughed weakly. "Wasn't planning on it."

They dove through the opening.

The moment the last of them cleared the threshold, the warped stone began to snap back, the Weave screaming as it tried to remember itself. The exit collapsed in on itself, glassy matter shattering into jagged fragments that fused back into rough stone.

Residuum surged, then recoiled, denied purchase.

On the other side, the world tilted.

They spilled into darkness and debris and the sharp smell of old concrete, landing hard and tangled and breathing like they had outrun something with teeth.

The pressure didn't vanish.

But it loosened.

For now.

Richard lay on his back, staring up at nothing, chest heaving. Every nerve screamed. The Shadow Current lingered at the edges of his awareness, coiled and watchful, like it had been promised something and was waiting to collect.

Escape had a price.

He had just written the invoice.

Somewhere behind them, the net adjusted.

Ahead of them, survival waited.

And this time, no one argued when Maya said, "We move."

Maya felt the jump fail before it happened.

Not collapse. Not backlash. Just wrong. Like a step taken onto a stair that wasn't where it should be. The Weave under her feet shuddered, threads scraping against each other instead of aligning, pressure buckling outward in too many directions at once.

They didn't have time.

The suppression fields were recalibrating behind them. She could feel it like cold fingers combing the lattice, narrowing probability, sanding away options. Division Gray wouldn't rush. They didn't need to. The net would close whether it was fast or slow.

"On me," Maya said, already moving.

She reached for a vector that wasn't stable enough to trust and pulled anyway.

The jump tore.

Not wide. Not clean. Just enough.

Alex was there instantly, his hands on her shoulders, his field flaring in ragged bursts as he tried to hold the geometry together through sheer refusal. His grounding didn't spread like it used to. It punched. Collapsed. Reformed.

"Now," he said through clenched teeth. "Do it now."

Elara stepped in close, her fire pulled so far inward it hurt to look at her. The heat didn't vanish. It condensed, caged tight inside her chest like an animal that knew it was being muzzled. Maya felt it strain against the jump like a second gravity.

Joe pressed in last, his face pale, eyes bloodshot, jaw set in hard concentration. He wasn't looking at the world anymore. He was looking at them.

"I've got you," he said. "You're you. Stay that way."

Truth locked into place.

Not as power. As insistence.

Maya jumped.

The world split sideways.

There was no tunnel. No clean displacement. Just pressure and tearing sensation and the sickening feeling of being pulled through a seam that wasn't meant to open. The Weave screamed as they passed through it, threads snapping back too fast, too uneven.

Maya lost Elara's heat first.

Then Alex's weight vanished.

Joe's presence stretched thin, like a voice shouting through water, then cut out entirely.

Maya came out of the jump on her knees.

Stone bit through her jeans and into her skin, sharp and cold, but she barely felt it. Her lungs burned as if she had sprinted miles instead of folded through a broken piece of the world. The Weave around her was loud for half a second, then went muffled, like a scream cut off mid breath. Not gone. Smothered.

Alex hit the ground beside her, rolling once before catching himself on one elbow. He made a sound that was half pain, half breath, and then stayed very still.

Maya twisted, heart slamming, searching for the others.

No Joe.

No Elara.

No Richard.

The empty space where they should have been pressed in on her from every side.

"No," she whispered, the word tearing out of her before she could stop it.

Alex dragged himself upright, swaying. His hand came out on instinct, reaching for her shoulder. When it made contact, the world steadied just enough to stop spinning.

"They didn't make it through," he said quietly.

Maya shook her head hard. "I didn't let go. I didn't."

"I know," he said. His voice was thin but certain. "Something cut the vector. You felt it."

She had. A sideways wrench in the Weave, like a knot yanked too tight. She had finished the jump because stopping would have shredded all of them.

The knowledge didn't help.

Maya forced herself to breathe. In. Out. Counted. Controlled. She pressed her palms to the ground and listened, not for sound, but for alignment.

The Weave wasn't empty.

It was stretched.

Threads ran outward from her position, taut and trembling, pulled in three different directions. Not snapped or severed but displaced.

Alive.

Alex followed her gaze, even though he couldn't see what she did. "They're out there," he said.

"Yes," she said. "And they're moving."

They didn't jump again. Not right away. The air felt too tight, too watched. Maya anchored them instead, settling the pressure until her pulse stopped racing. Alex leaned heavily against a low rock outcrop, eyes closed, jaw clenched as he rebuilt what grounding he could.

Time passed in uncertain chunks.

Then Maya felt it. Truth, bright and painful, like a bell rung too close. Joe. Not his body. His signature. The hard, unmistakable clarity of him still being him. Alive.

She reached back, not pulling, just aligning. The threads answered reluctantly, shifting just enough to confirm direction.

Moments later, heat brushed her senses, restrained and tight, like a flame held under glass.

"Elara," Maya whispered.

They found each other in a dry wash lined with scrub and broken stone, close enough to smell dust and blood. Joe stumbled first into view, one hand pressed to his face, eyes unfocused but alert. Elara was right behind him, her shoulders rigid, her breath controlled to the point of pain.

Joe looked up and locked eyes with Maya.

"You didn't leave us," he said immediately.

"No," she said, her voice breaking anyway.

Elara crossed the last few steps and stopped herself just short of touching Maya, like she didn't trust her own hands. "We got shoved out sideways," she said. "Hard."

Joe nodded. "Suppression fields clipped the jump. Dumped us instead of tearing us apart. Dead subjects don't teach them anything."

Maya swallowed. "Richard?"

Neither of them answered right away.

Joe's gaze flicked to the dark behind them. "He didn't come with us."

The Weave twitched.

Maya felt him then. Not close. Not safe. But moving. Dragging something heavy behind him that didn't want to let go.

"He's alive," Maya said. "But he's hurt."

"Of course he is," Elara muttered.

They didn't argue. They didn't debate. They moved.

They found Richard collapsed near the remains of another service shed, the same forgotten utility sprawl as the outbuilding they'd tried to hide in. One wall still standing, the roof half caved in. He was on his side, breathing shallowly, hands clenched in the dirt like he was holding himself together by force.

Residuum clung to him in faint, ugly wisps.

Maya dropped beside him, careful not to touch too hard. His eyes fluttered open.

"I didn't mean to," he rasped.

"I know," Maya said.

Alex arrived last, pale and shaking, but upright. He leaned into the shed's support post and stayed there, breathing through the pain.

They were together again. Not cleanly, not safely, not without cost but alive. The Weave, stretched thin around them, settled just enough to let them breathe.

They didn't speak for a long time.

The rusted shed creaked softly as the wind moved through the broken panels, metal ticking as it cooled. Maya sat with her back against the wall, knees pulled in, hands resting uselessly in her lap. She could feel all of them without looking. Alex's presence was thin but stubborn, holding where it could. Elara's heat stayed locked down so tight it made the air around her feel brittle. Joe's certainty pulsed in uneven waves, like a headache that refused to fade. Richard lay where they had settled him, breathing shallow, the Weave around him frayed and restless.

Alive did not feel like victory.

It felt like something they had stolen.

Maya closed her eyes and let her awareness spread just enough to check the perimeter. No drones. No immediate pursuit. The suppression pressure had eased, leaving behind a dull ache in the world, like bruises under skin.

They weren't coming. Not yet.

"That was on purpose," Joe said quietly.

Maya opened her eyes. He wasn't looking at her. He was staring at the dirt near his boots, jaw set like he was afraid of what he might see if he lifted his head.

"They didn't mean to take us," he continued. "They meant to watch us try not to be taken."

Elara's hands curled into fists. "They could've grabbed us."

"Yes," Joe said. "But they didn't need to."

Maya felt it click into place, cold and precise.

The corridors. The spacing. The way the net had closed without urgency. The way it had cut her jump instead of stopping it. They hadn't been testing force.

They had been testing response.

"They measured us," Maya said.

Alex let out a slow breath through his nose. "And they learned."

Richard shifted, a small sound of pain escaping him before he bit it back. The Residuum around him stirred, agitated, like something listening too closely.

Maya's chest tightened. She had felt the Shadow Current sharpen its attention the moment he tore the exit open. It had noticed. It always noticed.

"He's worse," Elara said, her voice flat but not unkind.

"I know," Maya said.

The Weave around Richard didn't argue. It simply hummed with strain.

They sat with that truth, with the cost laid bare in front of them.

Joe wiped at his face again, smearing dried blood across his knuckles. "They won't rush next time," he said. "They don't have to."

"No," Maya agreed. "They'll build a better cage."

She looked at the others then. Really looked.

They were tired. Hurt. Frayed at the edges.

And they were still here.

Still together.

That was the part HECATE hadn't accounted for. Not yet.

But they would.

Maya let her gaze drop to the ground and pressed her fingers into the dirt, grounding herself in something simple and solid. The Weave shifted faintly under her touch, not resisting, not yielding.

Waiting.

"They think being seen gives them control," she said quietly.

Alex glanced at her. "Doesn't it?"

Maya lifted her eyes, resolve hardening into something colder.

"It gives them information," she said. "Control comes later."

No one argued.

Outside, the wind moved through the scrub, carrying away the last echoes of the fight. Somewhere far off, machines and systems adjusted models and logged data and congratulated themselves on a successful operation.

Maya did not feel safe. She felt marked. They hadn't escaped the cage. They'd just proven it could be closed.

SCATTERED

28

Maya came back to herself in pieces.

First was the ground. Cold, but not consistently so, like stone that could not decide what it had been poured from. It pressed against her shoulder and cheek in a way that felt familiar enough to be comforting, until she realized the pressure changed when she breathed. The surface flexed, not soft, not solid, responding a fraction of a second too late.

Then came the sky.

It should have been Colorado night. Stars sharp and distant. Thin clouds dragged across a wide black bowl. What she saw instead was a version of that, folded wrong. The stars were there, but their spacing felt off, like someone had nudged constellations out of alignment and hoped no one would notice. The clouds did not drift so much as hesitate, pausing between one shape and the next.

Maya pushed herself onto her elbows and stopped.

The Weave was visible.

Not flaring. Not summoned. Just there.

Threads ran through everything, faint but undeniable, crossing the ground beneath her, the air above her, even the dark between stars. They did not sing or pull or respond to her attention. They simply existed in a way they never had before, laid bare like nerves under skin.

Her breath caught.

This was wrong.

Maya sat up fully, heart beginning to race as understanding crept in sideways. She wasn't in the world the way she was supposed to be in it. The terrain around her was familiar enough to register as real, but every line felt slightly displaced, like she was seeing a memory instead of a place.

She turned her head slowly.

To her left, the land dipped into a shallow ravine that should not have been there. To her right, a stand of pines rose at an angle that made her stomach lurch when she looked too long. The trees were the right trees. The wrong arrangement.

The tear was nearby.

She felt it without needing to look for it, a presence that did not push or pull, just waited. It hummed at the edge of her perception, not loud, not hungry, but attentive. Curious, the way something living might watch a trapped animal without yet deciding what to do about it.

Maya swallowed hard and forced herself to breathe. This isn't separation, she thought. This is something else. Instinct kicked in before fear could catch up. She reached. Not carefully. Not thoughtfully. Just the reflex that had saved her more times than she could count. Blink. Fold the space. Get back to them.

The Weave resisted.

Not like a wall. Not like suppression fields or containment geometry. There was no force pushing her away. Instead, her vector slid sideways, skidding across threads that would not line up. It was like trying to step onto a stair that kept shifting half an inch out of place.

Maya gasped as the attempt collapsed, pressure snapping back into her chest.

"No," she whispered. "No, no, no."

She tried again, slower this time, shaping the jump with care, mapping a destination she knew as well as her own heartbeat. Alex's presence should have been a beacon. Solid. Familiar. Anchoring.

She reached for him and felt only absence.

Not gone. Not severed.

Distant.

The realization hit harder than the failed jump.

Her hands curled into fists against her thighs as panic flared hot and sharp. She forced it down through grit and training and the memory of every time she had survived by not giving in to the first wave of fear.

Think. Listen.

Maya let her awareness widen again, not to move, but to understand.

The threads around her were not tangled. They were arranged differently. This place sat between states, neither fully folded nor fully reasserted. A boundary. A seam that had not finished deciding whether it was a scar or a door.

A pressure brushed her mind.

It came without warning, without shape, and without mercy.

Pain lanced through her awareness, sharp and disorienting, not physical but harmonic, like a chord struck too close to the bone. Maya cried out and doubled over, clutching at her head as the resonance surged.

She felt them.

Not as voices. Not as faces.

Weight. Presence. Attention layered with restraint.

The Immortals brushed her consciousness like hands pulled quickly across a flame. There was no guidance in it. No message she could translate into words. Only the unmistakable sense of recoil, of something ancient and bound reaching too far and paying for it.

Then withdrawal.

The pressure vanished as abruptly as it had come, leaving behind a hollow ache and a certainty that settled deep in her chest.

She wasn't supposed to be here.

Not yet. Not like this.

Maya sucked in a shaky breath and pressed her forehead to her knees, grounding herself in the only way she could. The Weave did not answer her touch the way it once had. It did not resist either. It simply held, tense and undecided, like the world was waiting to see what she would do next.

"I'm not lost," she whispered aloud, as much to steady herself as to name the truth. Her voice sounded wrong in the air, too clear, too contained. "I'm displaced."

The word fit.

This wasn't distance. It wasn't scattering. It was misplacement, like she had slipped into the margin between pages while the story kept going without her.

Maya lifted her head and tried again to feel the others, not to pull them close, just to locate them. Everything came in blurred and indistinct, like listening through a wall that let sound pass but refused to open. Joe's truth felt like a faint pressure somewhere beyond the boundary, muted and distorted. Elara's heat was harder to miss, a tight, angry pulse fighting to stay contained. Richard was a wound in the lattice, moving and unstable, dragging attention he could not shake.

Alex.

She reached for him last, bracing herself.

For a heartbeat, she felt him. Not clearly, not the way she usually did, but enough to recognize the shape of his resonance. Familiar. Steady. Hers.

Relief surged.

Then it faded.

Not cut off. Not erased.

Just slipping farther away, like a light sinking beneath water.

Maya's breath hitched. "Alex," she whispered, knowing he couldn't hear her.

She tried to follow the thread instinctively and felt the boundary push back, not hard, but firm, like a hand on her chest saying not this way.

For the first time since her awakening, Maya understood what it meant to be unreachable.

Not hidden. Not blocked.

Out of traversal.

The realization hollowed her out in a way nothing else had. She had always been the one who bridged gaps, who refused distance and folded the world until separation became a choice instead of a sentence.

Now the gap held.

Now the world would not fold for her.

Maya sat very still, breathing through the ache, through the fear clawing at her ribs. The tear nearby pulsed faintly, curious as ever, threads shifting in small, testing adjustments.

She was inside a question the Weave had not answered yet.

Somewhere beyond this boundary, Alex's presence dimmed another fraction, not gone, but receding as he moved, lived, survived without her.

Maya closed her eyes and pressed her palm flat against the ground, anchoring herself to what little certainty she had left.

"I'm still here," she whispered to the unseen threads. "I just need to learn where here is."

The Weave did not answer. But it listened.

***

Alex woke choking.

Cold water filled his mouth and nose, thick with the taste of mud and rot. He jerked instinctively, coughing hard enough to scrape his throat raw, and rolled onto his side with a groan that barely sounded human. His ears rang, a high thin whine that made it hard to tell where the world ended and his skull began.

He lay there for a second, face pressed into wet grass, rainwater trickling past his cheek and into the shallow ditch that had caught him like a grave that missed its mark.

Move, he told himself. Don't go back out.

Alex pushed up on his elbows and nearly collapsed again as dizziness washed through him. The night tilted. Stars smeared. His stomach lurched, and he had to clamp his jaw shut to keep from vomiting into the mud.

Cold soaked through his clothes, seeping into places he didn't remember getting wet. His hands shook as he dragged one knee under himself and tried to sit up.

That was when he reached for his shield.

Nothing happened.

No familiar pressure. No answering resistance in the air. No sense of balance settling into place.

Alex sucked in a sharp breath and tried again, harder this time, pushing the way he always did when things were slipping out of alignment. He braced, focused, demanded.

Still nothing.

Panic flared hot and sudden, a spike that drove his heart into his throat.

No. No, no.

He planted his palms in the mud and forced himself to breathe, slow and deliberate, counting in his head like he'd been taught a lifetime ago. In for four. Hold. Out for four.

This isn't suppression, he thought. Suppression pushed back. This is absence.

That idea scared him more than anything else.

Alex squeezed his eyes shut and stayed upright through sheer stubbornness, refusing to let the dark creep back in. Passing out now felt too close to not waking up at all.

"Okay," he muttered hoarsely. "Okay. You're still here."

His voice sounded wrong in the open air, too small without the quiet reassurance of Maya's presence at his back. The realization hit him like a physical blow.

Maya.

Alex's head snapped up, pulse hammering. He turned slowly, scanning the roadside with unfocused eyes.

The ditch ran alongside a narrow two-lane road, cracked asphalt barely visible through the weeds. A bent guardrail leaned drunkenly a few yards away; its metal twisted like it had been grabbed and shaken. Beyond that, scrub and low trees pressed close, their branches snapped and scorched in places.

Scorch marks.

Alex stared at them, heart sinking. Blackened earth. Charred leaves still faintly warm, steam curling where rain touched burned ground.

"Elara," he whispered.

Memory came back in fragments. Pressure. Tearing sensation. The world folding wrong. Then nothing.

Alex forced himself to his feet, swaying hard enough that he had to grab the guardrail to stay upright. His legs felt hollow, like they were working on borrowed instructions.

He tried grounding again, quieter this time. Just a whisper of intent. Just enough to feel where he was.

The Weave did not answer.

The silence inside him was worse than the ringing in his ears.

Without Maya, his power felt like a limb that had been cut away without warning. He could still remember how it was supposed to work. He just couldn't do anything.

Alex pressed his forehead to the cool metal and breathed until the edges of panic dulled. "You're not broken," he told himself. "You're just empty."

The words didn't help much, but they kept him moving.

He followed the signs of disturbance away from the ditch, boots slipping on wet leaves as he pushed into the scrub. Bent vegetation marked a rough path, branches snapped outward instead of inward, like something had been thrown through instead of landing gently.

Violent displacement, he thought distantly. Not a clean jump.

His chest tightened. If Elara had landed near here, she would've come in hot whether she meant to or not.

Alex staggered out of the brush and stopped short.

Smoke drifted through the trees ahead, thin but unmistakable. Not the heavy black plume of a structure fire, but a low gray haze that clung to the ground and carried the sharp bite of burning pine.

"Damn it," he breathed.

He turned toward it immediately, body protesting every step. Without his shield, every sound felt too loud, every movement too exposed. He was just a man again, soaked and shaking and painfully aware of how fragile flesh was without the Weave smoothing the edges.

As he limped toward the smoke, Alex felt the weight of absence settle fully into place.

Maya wasn't just gone.

She was the balance he built himself around.

And without her, the world felt tilted, like it might slide out from under him at any moment if he didn't keep moving.

He squared his shoulders, gritted his teeth, and followed the smoke into the trees.

***

Elara woke choking on heat.

Not the clean burn she knew. Not the sharp, familiar edge of flame that answered her emotions like a mirror. This was thick and suffocating, pressing against her lungs and skin at once, air so hot it felt solid.

She rolled onto her side with a gasp, coughing hard enough to make her ribs ache. Ash smeared her cheek. Sparks drifted past her face like malignant fireflies.

Fire. Everywhere.

Elara pushed herself upright, heart slamming as she took in the slope around her. Trees burned uphill and downhill, flames racing through dry brush far too fast for the wind that barely stirred the smoke. Pockets of heat surged and collapsed in erratic waves, as if the fire itself couldn't decide how it wanted to behave.

"This isn't right," she whispered.

She staggered to her feet. The ground was hot enough to sting through her boots. Her head rang, not with pain exactly, but with a hollow pressure where the world still felt slightly out of sync.

Memory snapped back in pieces. The jump tearing. Pressure crushing inward. Her fire yanked loose, not from fear or rage, but from something deeper. Something structural.

The realization hit her like a punch.

"I did this."

Not deliberately. Not emotionally.

Her flame had reacted to the rupture itself. To the tear in the Weave. Like striking flint against a fault line.

Elara squeezed her eyes shut and reached inward, searching for the familiar loop. Emotion. Heat. Feedback. The subtle resistance that told her how much was too much.

It wasn't there.

The suppression fields were gone. She could feel that immediately. No Cinder dampening. No artificial drag. The cage had dropped away.

But instead of relief, there was only wrongness.

Her flame surged when she reached for it, flaring too fast, too eager, then guttering unpredictably like it was slipping out of her hands. She yanked her focus back, swearing as heat licked up her arm in a sharp warning.

"No," she hissed. "You don't get to do that."

The fire didn't listen.

Power without feedback felt like driving blind at full speed.

Elara forced herself to breathe, counting the way Maya had taught her. In. Hold. Out. Again. She couldn't fight the wildfire head on. She knew that instinctively. Trying to smother it would just make it push harder, especially now.

So she did the only thing she could.

She redirected.

Elara turned downhill, toward a darker line where the trees thinned and a narrow dirt access road cut across the slope. She focused on shaping heat instead of creating it, pulling flames sideways, thinning them just enough to starve one section while another burned hotter.

Not extinguishing.

Steering.

She moved through smoke and sparks like a conductor losing control of an orchestra, arms shaking as she carved channels of heat through brush and fallen branches. Sweat poured down her spine. Her lungs burned. Every correction felt late, every adjustment slightly wrong.

She gritted her teeth and kept going anyway.

"Not there," she muttered. "Not toward the road. Go that way. Burn there."

The fire responded, reluctantly, surging where she allowed it and easing where she pushed back. It wasn't obedience. It was negotiation under threat.

Minutes blurred together. Or maybe longer. Time felt unreliable inside the heat.

Elara stumbled to one knee near the edge of the road, chest heaving. The flames on the uphill side slowed, breaking into smaller fingers instead of a single advancing front. It wasn't safe. It wasn't contained.

But it wasn't racing anymore.

She dropped her hands, shaking.

"That's all I've got," she whispered.

The fire crackled around her, restless but momentarily redirected. Smoke drifted across the road in heavy waves, turning the world into shifting silhouettes and glowing embers.

That was when she saw movement.

Not the flicker of flame. Not a collapsing branch.

A shape moved through the smoke on the far side of the road, low and uneven, cutting across the fire's edge instead of following it. Too deliberate. Too wrong to be fire.

Elara's heart kicked hard.

"Hey," she called hoarsely, unsure why she bothered to whisper. "Who's there?"

The shape stumbled, resolved briefly into something human before the smoke swallowed it again.

Relief and fear hit her at the same time.

She pushed herself upright, ignoring the protest in her legs, and moved toward the road, flame coiled tight and unstable under her skin.

Because the fire crackled behind her, impatient and alive, and more than ever since her awakening, Elara was truly afraid of what her power might do next.

The fire crackled like it was thinking.

***

Joe figured out he was trapped when nothing tried to kill him.

The ravine narrowed ahead into a crooked slit between stone walls, scrub clinging to the sides like it had grown there out of spite. He slid down the loose gravel on his heels and came up short when the air changed.

Not colder. Not heavier.

Arranged.

The first drone rose into view without a sound, lifting from behind a rock outcrop like it had always been there and Joe just hadn't noticed. Matte gray. No markings. No visible weapons. It stopped ten feet above the ravine floor and held position.

Then another appeared behind him.

Then two more.

They spaced themselves with unsettling precision, not blocking him outright, just occupying the places he would need if he tried to move fast. High. Low. Angled. A geometry that said run if you want to prove the math right.

Joe's head throbbed in dull protest as his truth-sight flared automatically.

Nothing screamed danger.

That was worse.

The drones didn't lie. Not even a little. There was no hostility in their presence, no predatory intent, no satisfaction waiting behind their sensors. Just patience. Clean and unbothered.

They weren't here to hurt him.

They were here to see what he did.

Joe swallowed and forced his breathing to slow. "Okay," he murmured. "We're doing this again."

He took a cautious step forward.

The nearest drone adjusted by inches, maintaining distance without retreating. No warning tone. No escalation.

Containment without confrontation.

Joe closed his eyes briefly and let his truth-sight widen, ignoring the spike of pain behind his eyes. The ravine resolved into layers of intent and system logic, overlapping routines stacked like translucent sheets.

Distributed orders. Redundancy everywhere. No single lie to pry loose. No fear to amplify.

Built to withstand him.

"Figures," he muttered.

Joe backed up slowly until his shoulder brushed stone. Gravel crunched under his boot, loud in the unnatural quiet. The drones didn't react beyond micro adjustments, keeping the same angles, the same spacing.

He laughed once, breathless. "You're not even pretending to be scary."

The drones didn't answer.

His truth-sight told him something else then, something colder.

They weren't closing yet.

They were waiting for clarity.

For him to decide.

Joe wiped at his nose, smearing dried blood across his knuckles. The headache sharpened, but he leaned into it anyway, shaping his gift carefully instead of pushing it outward.

Truth didn't have to be loud.

It just had to be convincing.

He focused inward, on uncertainty. On all the questions still rattling around in his skull. Where Maya was. Whether Alex was alive. How bad the tear had been. He let that lack of resolution expand, muddying the edges of his intent.

Not a lie.

An absence.

The truth-sight bent around it, projecting hesitation instead of direction. No clear goal. No immediate threat. No decisive move to predict.

The drones shifted.

Not closer. Sideways.

Joe felt it like a pressure change, the geometry recalculating around a suddenly unhelpful variable. Pattern recognition stuttered when there was no pattern to grab.

He took advantage of the half second it bought him.

Joe dropped flat and rolled, gravel tearing at his palms as he slid under an overhang where the ravine bent sharply. He scrambled up on all fours, lungs burning, and ran the moment his feet found traction.

The drones reacted then.

Not firing. Never firing.

They repositioned, gliding smoothly to cut off the wider exit ahead. The ravine funneled him left whether he wanted it to or not, terrain and containment working together like they'd rehearsed.

Joe skidded to a stop again, chest heaving.

Smoke drifted across the opening.

Not dust. Not shadow.

Smoke.

Thick, acrid, and wrong.

Fire crackled somewhere beyond the bend, close enough that the sound carried through the stone. Heat licked the edge of the ravine like an uninvited thought.

Joe's heart jumped. "Elara."

The drones hesitated.

Just a fraction.

Joe felt it immediately, a ripple in their intent where the models adjusted for an environmental variable they hadn't fully owned yet.

Fire wasn't predictable. Not like people. Not like him.

Joe grinned despite the pain and leaned into the uncertainty hard, letting his intent fracture in a dozen directions at once. Should I run toward the heat. Away from it. Drop. Freeze. Lunge. Do nothing.

Truth scattered.

The drones recalculated.

Joe moved.

He bolted into the smoke without looking back, coughing as heat slapped against his face. Ash swirled around him, thick enough to blind sensors as well as eyes. He ducked low, slid down a slope of loose dirt, and vanished into the crackle and roar.

Behind him, the drones adjusted again, slower this time, their clean geometry blurring at the edges where flame and turbulence refused to behave.

Joe ran until his legs shook, until the smoke thinned just enough to breathe without choking. He stumbled into a shallow gully and collapsed against the bank, gasping and laughing at the same time.

Truth as evasion.

Who would've thought.

He wiped his face and forced himself upright, eyes scanning the firelit terrain ahead.

"Elara," he called hoarsely. "Alex."

The fire answered him with a sharp pop and a rush of heat. No one responded to his call.

Joe swallowed, heart pounding.

Whatever cage they were building, it hadn't accounted for wildfire. And neither had he.

***

Richard woke to the sound of the world deciding what it wanted to be.

The ceiling above him shuddered, not falling, not holding. Hesitating. Concrete beams hung at angles that made his eyes ache to follow, edges blurring as their internal bonds slipped in and out of agreement. One second the slab over his chest was solid and immovable. The next it looked like frosted glass, spiderweb cracks blooming and vanishing across its surface.

Richard lay very still.

Breathing hurt. Every inhale scraped his ribs like something sharp had lodged there and refused to move. Dust coated his tongue, chalky and bitter, and the air smelled wrong. Not just old cement and rot, but the metallic tang of stressed matter, of bonds being asked to do things they were never meant to do.

He tried to move his right leg.

Pain flared white and immediate, hot enough to steal his breath. His vision fractured, the room splitting into overlapping angles that refused to settle into one image. He squeezed his eyes shut until the double vision eased to something tolerable.

"Idiot," he muttered, voice rough and small in the unstable space.

The structure answered him with a groan.

Richard reached out with his senses before he reached with his hands. The Weave here was a mess, threads pulled and knotted and half melted together where his last act had torn through. Matter couldn't decide what state it belonged in. Neither could he.

And closer than all of that, pressing at the edges of his awareness like cold fingers on glass, was something else.

The Shadow Current didn't announce itself.

It never did.

It seeped.

The whisper wasn't a voice. It was a suggestion shaped like relief. A familiar resonance that wore his own patterns like a borrowed coat.

You're holding it wrong.

Richard swallowed hard and kept his hands flat against the floor.

You're tired. Let go. Let it settle. I can help.

Images flickered behind his eyes. The beam above him resolving cleanly, bonds reforging into something stable and strong. The pain in his leg dulling to a manageable throb. The walls choosing solid and staying that way.

Stability at a price.

Richard laughed weakly, the sound turning into a cough that left copper on his tongue. "You always say that."

The Current pressed closer, mimicry sharpening. For a heartbeat it felt like understanding. Like forgiveness. Like the quiet satisfaction of a problem solved elegantly.

Just a little more, it coaxed. You already crossed the line. Let me finish it.

Richard gritted his teeth until his jaw trembled.

"No," he said aloud, the word scraping his throat raw. "You don't finish anything. You erase it."

The pressure increased, not angry, not forceful. Patient. It always waited for him to get tired enough to agree.

The beam above him shifted again, this time cracking with a sharp report. Dust rained down, stinging his eyes.

Richard didn't have time.

He dragged one arm forward, fingers splaying against a section of wall that flickered between stone and something more fragile. He didn't shape it. He didn't force it to become anything new.

He nudged.

Just enough.

The stone softened reluctantly, bonds loosening like a clenched fist forced open one finger at a time. Pain lanced through his skull as the cost hit him, vision splintering into overlapping frames that refused to line up.

The Shadow Current surged in response, eager, excited.

Yes. Like that. You see how easy it is.

Richard screamed then, not in fear, but in defiance. He shoved his arm into the softened section and dragged himself forward, ignoring the way his leg screamed as it scraped against shifting debris.

The wall gave way in a jagged oval, not a door, not a clean passage. More like a wound the structure hadn't realized it could sustain.

He crawled.

Every inch cost him something. Sensation blurred. His left eye stopped tracking properly, images lagging behind reality like a bad transmission. His leg went numb, then flared again as unstable matter snapped back to solidity around it, pinching muscle and nerve.

Behind him, the Shadow Current recoiled, then pressed again, angry now, its mimicry cracking at the edges.

You're breaking it, it hissed. You're making it worse.

Richard laughed again, breathless and broken. "Yeah," he gasped. "That's kind of my thing."

He dragged himself free just as the structure decided.

The wall behind him collapsed inward with a roar, concrete choosing brittle all at once. Dust and debris thundered into the space he had occupied seconds earlier, sealing it completely.

Richard rolled onto his back and lay there, staring up at a sky that swam and doubled, stars splitting and recombining in nauseating patterns.

The Shadow Current lingered, circling the edges of his awareness like a disappointed predator.

This cost you, it whispered. You feel it.

Richard closed one eye to steady the world. His leg burned and then went strangely cold. When he tried to focus on the ground beneath him, the texture slid sideways, refusing to stay put.

"I know," he said softly.

Survival felt heavy in his chest, not relief but something closer to guilt. Every time he used his gift, the world paid. This time the bill felt permanent.

He pushed himself upright with a grunt and immediately had to brace against a twisted beam to keep from falling over. His limp was worse. Much worse. His depth perception was shot, distance turning unreliable and cruel.

He took one careful step.

Then another.

Smoke drifted across the ruined lot, gray and thick and unmistakable.

Richard sniffed, grimaced, and started limping toward it.

If the world was going to burn anyway, he might as well find the others before it did.

***

Smoke turned the world into a bruise.

It pressed low against the ground, thick enough to sting her eyes and scrape her throat raw with every breath. The fire had slowed, not because it was finished, but because Elara had forced it to. She had bent it away from the tree line, starved it where she could, driven it into rocky ground that gave it nothing to eat.

Her hands shook anyway.

The flame no longer listened the way it used to. It responded late, or too eagerly, reacting to pressure in the air instead of emotion in her chest. That scared her more than the fire ever had.

Elara moved downslope, boots sliding on ash and loose stone, senses stretched thin. The smoke carried pockets of heat that didn't belong to the fire itself. Movement. Intent.

She raised her hands on instinct.

A shape broke through the haze twenty yards ahead. Human sized. Upright. Moving fast.

Elara didn't hesitate.

Fire flared up her arms, hot and sharp, ready to snap forward in a killing arc.

"Stop," a voice shouted. Hoarse. Familiar. "Elara, don't."

She froze mid breath.

The flame bucked, fighting her grip, then collapsed inward with a painful snap that made her gasp. She staggered back a step, heart slamming, eyes burning as the smoke thinned just enough to resolve the figure.

Joe Biggs stood there, hands raised, face streaked with blood and ash, eyes wide in the kind of alarm that came from almost dying.

"Oh," Elara said stupidly. "It's you."

Joe let out a breath that sounded like it hurt. "Yeah. Hi. Great reflexes."

She dropped her hands and pressed them to her thighs, forcing herself to breathe. "I thought you were Gray."

"Fair," he said. "I almost thought you were a flamethrower."

She barked a short, shaky laugh that fell apart halfway through. "I almost burned you."

Joe stepped closer, slow and deliberate, like he was approaching something wild. "You didn't. You stopped."

"Barely."

"That still counts."

They stood there for a second, smoke drifting between them, the crackle of distant fire filling the silence neither of them wanted to break first.

Joe's gaze flicked past her, scanning the slope, the trees, the dark beyond. "You okay?"

Elara shook her head. "I'm upright."

"Same category I'm in," he muttered.

She studied him then, really looked. His truth-sight wasn't flaring. It wasn't doing much of anything. His shoulders were tight, posture guarded in a way that had nothing to do with enemies and everything to do with pain.

"Elara," Joe said quietly, "I can't feel her, not like before."

The words landed harder than any impact.

Elara swallowed. "Me neither."

They didn't argue it. Didn't soften it. The absence was too complete for denial. Maya's presence had always been there, a quiet pressure at the edge of Elara's awareness even when they were apart. A thread that hummed.

Now there was nothing.

Smoke shifted again.

A shape stumbled out of the trees downslope, gait uneven, breath ragged. Elara's hands twitched, fire stirring reflexively, but Joe caught her eye and shook his head once.

"Not Gray," he said.

The figure lurched closer, nearly falling, then caught himself against a rock outcrop.

"Alex," Elara breathed.

Alex didn't remember falling.

He remembered cold water, then nothing, then pain blooming everywhere at once as his body reminded him it still existed. By the time he became aware of his surroundings, he was upright only because someone had him by the arm.

"Elara," he rasped, recognizing her heat before his vision cleared. "Joe."

Joe tightened his grip. "Yeah. You're with us. Stay that way."

Alex nodded, though his head felt like it weighed too much for his neck. His shield was gone. Not quiet. Not resting. Gone in the way a limb was gone when it didn't answer at all.

He tried to ground anyway.

Nothing.

Panic surged sharp and fast, and he crushed it by force of habit. Breathe. Count. Stay.

Elara steadied him from the other side, jaw clenched, eyes bright with something that looked too close to fear. "You're freezing," she said.

"I'm fine," Alex lied.

Joe snorted softly. "Everyone says that right before they aren't."

Alex managed a weak huff of laughter and leaned more heavily into them. The ground smelled like ash and damp earth. Smoke clung to everything, making the world feel smaller, closer.

"Maya," Alex said. The name came out rough. "Where is she."

Neither of them answered.

He knew then.

The absence hit him like a structural failure. Not grief yet. Something colder. The sense that a load bearing element had vanished and the whole design was now suspect.

"She's not here," Alex said quietly.

Joe shook his head. "No. And I can't see her. Can't feel her. It's like she's... not on the board."

Elara crossed her arms, hugging herself without realizing it. "The tear's still active somewhere. I can feel the pressure from it."

Alex forced himself to straighten, spine protesting. "Then she's not dead."

They both looked at him.

"She's displaced," he continued, more certain now. "Out of phase. Somewhere bad. But not gone."

It wasn't hope. It was engineering. If Maya had been gone, it'd feel different, he'd know.

Footsteps scraped through brush nearby.

Alex tensed, then recognized the rhythm too late to do anything about it.

Richard emerged from the trees like something that had been chewed on and decided not to die anyway. His limp was worse, one side of his body moving half a beat behind the other. One eye didn't quite focus, gaze sliding past them before snapping back.

The air around him felt wrong.

Not active Shadow. Not feeding. But stretched thin, like a scar that hadn't decided whether it was done healing.

Elara swore under her breath. "You look like hell."

Richard smiled faintly. "You should see the building."

Joe's eyes narrowed as his truth-sight brushed Richard and recoiled. "You're changed."

"Yeah," Richard said. "That too."

They stood there together in the smoke, four figures ringed by damage and absence.

"No Maya," Joe said, stating it flat.

"No idea where she landed," Elara added.

"The tear's breathing somewhere nearby," Richard said. "I can feel it. Like a wound that didn't close."

Alex nodded once. "Then standing still is the worst option."

Joe glanced up as a low, distant thrum rolled across the sky. Not loud. Not close.

Rotors.

Elara's shoulders squared. "They're back."

Alex took a breath that hurt and forced his legs to cooperate. He stepped forward, unsteady but moving.

"We stick together," he said. "We stay off clean ground. We don't draw attention."

"And Maya," Elara said.

Alex looked ahead into the smoke and the dark beyond it. "We find her."

They moved as one, uneven, limping, altered.

A group again.

Just not whole.

They took shelter where the fire had already done its damage.

Blackened earth stretched in uneven swaths around them, trees reduced to skeletal silhouettes that creaked softly as heat bled out of their cores. Ash coated everything, muting sound and scent alike. Even the air felt stripped down, thin and cautious. Drones stayed high. Sensors hesitated. Fire made machines nervous.

Alex crouched behind the fallen trunk of a burned pine, knees drawn in, arms wrapped tight around himself. His breathing had steadied, but his posture hadn't. He kept glancing to his left, to the space where Maya always ended up without anyone deciding it.

She wasn't there.

Elara stood a few steps away, back to the wind, fists clenched so tight her knuckles had gone white beneath the soot. Heat trembled under her skin, restless and untrustworthy. She didn't let it out. She didn't dare. Every time her pulse spiked, the fire answered too fast.

Joe knelt in the ash with his head bowed, eyes closed, one hand pressed flat against the ground like he was steadying himself against a moving floor. He wasn't searching the perimeter. He was listening inward.

When he finally spoke, his voice was rough. "She's not gone."

Alex's head snapped up. "You're sure."

Joe nodded slowly. "Yeah. I don't feel a break. No absence spike. No echo collapse." He swallowed. "Her resonance is intact, just displaced."

Elara took a sharp breath. "Then where is she."

Joe opened his eyes. They were bloodshot, rimmed with exhaustion and something colder. "Elsewhere."

The word settled heavy between them.

Alex looked back at the empty space beside him. He reached out without thinking, his hand stopping short of where Maya's sleeve should have been. The motion cost him more than he let show. His fingers curled in on themselves.

"She should be here," he said quietly.

Elara turned away before anyone could see her face. Her shoulders shook once, then stilled. "I keep wanting to burn something," she admitted. "Like if I light up the sky enough, she'll see it."

"You'd light us up instead," Joe said gently.

"I know." She pressed her fists into her thighs until the urge passed. "I just hate not being able to do anything."

Richard stood apart from them, half in shadow, half in the firelight. He hadn't sat. He hadn't leaned. He kept his back turned, gaze fixed on the dark beyond the burned ground like it might judge him less if he didn't look back.

"This is my fault," he said quietly.

No one answered right away.

Joe shifted first. "It isn't."

Richard shook his head. "I was the fracture point. I drew it in. I felt it latch." His voice went thin. "If I hadn't..."

Alex cut him off, sharper than intended. "If you hadn't, we'd all be in a box right now."

Richard flinched anyway.

Silence pressed in again, thick with ash and unspoken fear. Above them, rotors throbbed faintly and then drifted farther away, unwilling to dip low over the burn scar.

Maya wasn't dead.

That should have been comfort.

Instead it felt worse.

Because somewhere nearby, the tear still breathed. Somewhere outside the rules they understood, a single thread had been pulled loose and not cut.

The tear hadn't taken Maya from them. It had taken her out of reach.

29

The Mass Jump

Maya knew they were out of road before anyone said it.

The land ahead looked open enough. A long slope of scrub and broken stone falling away into a shallow basin, moonlight laying everything bare. It should have felt like relief after the tight cuts and dead ground they had been forced through since the ambush.

Instead, it felt staged.

The Weave under her feet was wrong. Not torn. Not screaming. Held. Directional pressure had replaced pursuit, like invisible hands setting rails into the world and daring them to follow.

Alex stumbled beside her, caught himself, then forced his posture straight again. His grounding flickered in uneven pulses, no longer a field but a series of refusals. He was running on stubbornness and muscle memory now, not power.

Joe walked with his head slightly bowed, one hand pressed to his temple. The truth-sight wasn't gone, but it was blunted, like trying to see through frosted glass while someone leaned on the other side.

Elara kept her heat locked so tightly Maya could hear her breathing hitch when she inhaled. Every breath was measured. Controlled. Painful.

Richard lagged behind them, moving like gravity had decided he weighed more than he should. Residuum clung to him in faint, ugly wisps, barely visible but unmistakable to Maya's senses. And behind it, something else hovered close, attentive in a way that made her skin crawl.

They weren't being chased.

They were being shaped.

The faint mechanical rhythm returned then, distant but synchronized. Not engines. Not footsteps. Systems aligning. The sound of a net remembering how it was built.

Maya slowed, then stopped.

Alex noticed immediately. He always did.

"We're boxed in," he said quietly.

Maya nodded. "They're building the next one."

Joe exhaled, sharp and tired. "Field feels ready again. Like it did before the ambush. Like someone reset the board."

Elara looked from the open basin ahead to the ridgeline behind them. "So what, we keep walking until they tell us where to stand?"

Alex shook his head. "No. We stay low. Short bursts. Avoid strain nodes. We move like ghosts."

Maya turned to him. "We won't get another hour."

Alex met her eyes. He saw it then, the same conclusion he had been skirting around. "You're sure."

"Yes."

Joe swallowed. "She's right. Whatever they're doing, it's aligning faster now."

Elara dragged a hand down her face. "Then we move before we can't."

Richard didn't speak. He didn't need to. His presence alone made the Weave twitch, threads pulling tighter around him like they were bracing.

Alex's jaw tightened. "Next time they don't need to learn," he said. "They just close it."

Maya felt a faint pressure at the edge of her awareness. A whisper of resonance that was not hers. An Immortal echo brushing too close.

She shoved it down.

"No," she said. "Not now."

She turned back to the group. "I can take more than one person."

Silence.

Alex's eyes narrowed. "Not like this."

"I know," Maya said. "Not injured. Not with suppression residue in the air. Not with him." She didn't need to point at Richard.

Joe shook his head slowly. "Truth anchoring four people is hard. Five is dangerous."

"I won't scatter us," Maya said. "One vector. One destination."

Alex stepped closer. "Tight contact. Fixed order. Nobody lets go."

Elara met Maya's gaze. "If it goes wrong, you don't fix it mid fall. Promise me."

Maya hesitated, then nodded. "I promise."

Richard cleared his throat softly. "Can you carry contamination."

Maya didn't answer directly. "Hold on to me."

The Weave did the held breath thing again. Like the world itself was bracing.

Somewhere far away, a system flagged a spike.

Inside a HECATE operations node, AFR density climbed into warning thresholds. Spatial discontinuity probability spiked. Division Gray models shifted from herding to denial geometry, not to block movement, but to destabilize it.

A technician murmured, "High probability of mass displacement attempt."

The system adjusted. It did not try to stop it.

It prepared to watch it fail.

On the ground, the basin ahead narrowed into the only reasonable escape route. Clean. Open. Wrong.

Maya anchored the destination on instinct, on feel. A low strain pocket that hummed faintly beneath the noise, not safe but quieter.

Alex wrapped what shielding he had left around them. It felt thin, like a blanket held together by refusal.

Joe closed his eyes and forced coherence. "You're you," he said through clenched teeth. "All of you. Stay that way."

Elara pulled her heat down so hard Maya felt the absence like a pressure change.

Richard gripped Maya's sleeve. His hand trembled as something cold stirred just beyond him.

Maya jumped.

For one heartbeat, the Weave accepted it.

The vector aligned. The world folded. Relief flared sharp and bright.

Then the harmonics clipped.

Suppression geometry caught the edge of the jump, shaving stability away like a blade. Richard's contamination resonated instantly, drawing Shadow attention straight into the seam.

The load exceeded tolerance.

The seam tore. The Weave did not collapse. It split, edges grinding against each other like broken glass trying to remember how to be whole.

Maya felt it happen. The exact moment she stopped being a door and became a knife.

Reality split sideways.

Maya woke alone, and the absence hit harder than the stone. Stone pressed cold against her cheek. The Weave around her was not quiet. It breathed. The tear was nearby, a living boundary humming with strain.

A flicker brushed her awareness. Immortal resonance. Pain. Withdrawal.

She understood then.

Trying to save everyone had made a beacon.

HECATE would use the data. Close the next cage faster. Smarter.

Maya sat up, shaking, and forced a new rule into place.

No more mass jumps. Not until she understood what the Weave was becoming and what it would take in return. Not until she understood what the Weave was becoming. She hadn't moved them through the world. She'd torn the world to make room.

30

Scattered

Maya came back to herself in pieces.

First was the ground. Cold, but not consistently so, like stone that could not decide what it had been poured from. It pressed against her shoulder and cheek in a way that felt familiar enough to be comforting, until she realized the pressure changed when she breathed. The surface flexed, not soft, not solid, responding a fraction of a second too late.

Then came the sky.

It should have been Colorado night. Stars sharp and distant. Thin clouds dragged across a wide black bowl. What she saw instead was a version of that, folded wrong. The stars were there, but their spacing felt off, like someone had nudged constellations out of alignment and hoped no one would notice. The clouds did not drift so much as hesitate, pausing between one shape and the next.

Maya pushed herself onto her elbows and stopped.

The Weave was visible.

Not flaring. Not summoned. Just there.

Threads ran through everything, faint but undeniable, crossing the ground beneath her, the air above her, even the dark between stars. They did not sing or pull or respond to her attention. They simply existed in a way they never had before, laid bare like nerves under skin.

Her breath caught.

This was wrong.

Maya sat up fully, heart beginning to race as understanding crept in sideways. She wasn't in the world the way she was supposed to be in it. The terrain around her was familiar enough to register as real, but every line felt slightly displaced, like she was seeing a memory instead of a place.

She turned her head slowly.

To her left, the land dipped into a shallow ravine that should not have been there. To her right, a stand of pines rose at an angle that made her stomach lurch when she looked too long. The trees were the right trees. The wrong arrangement.

The tear was nearby.

She felt it without needing to look for it, a presence that did not push or pull, just waited. It hummed at the edge of her perception, not loud, not hungry, but attentive. Curious, the way something living might watch a trapped animal without yet deciding what to do about it.

Maya swallowed hard and forced herself to breathe. This isn't separation, she thought. This is something else. Instinct kicked in before fear could catch up. She reached. Not carefully. Not thoughtfully. Just the reflex that had saved her more times than she could count. Blink. Fold the space. Get back to them.

The Weave resisted.

Not like a wall. Not like suppression fields or containment geometry. There was no force pushing her away. Instead, her vector slid sideways, skidding across threads that would not line up. It was like trying to step onto a stair that kept shifting half an inch out of place.

Maya gasped as the attempt collapsed, pressure snapping back into her chest.

"No," she whispered. "No, no, no."

She tried again, slower this time, shaping the jump with care, mapping a destination she knew as well as her own heartbeat. Alex's presence should have been a beacon. Solid. Familiar. Anchoring.

She reached for him and felt only absence.

Not gone. Not severed.

Distant.

The realization hit harder than the failed jump.

Her hands curled into fists against her thighs as panic flared hot and sharp. She forced it down through grit and training and the memory of every time she had survived by not giving in to the first wave of fear.

Think. Listen.

Maya let her awareness widen again, not to move, but to understand.

The threads around her were not tangled. They were arranged differently. This place sat between states, neither fully folded nor fully reasserted. A boundary. A seam that had not finished deciding whether it was a scar or a door.

A pressure brushed her mind.

It came without warning, without shape, and without mercy.

Pain lanced through her awareness, sharp and disorienting, not physical but harmonic, like a chord struck too close to the bone. Maya cried out and doubled over, clutching at her head as the resonance surged.

She felt them.

Not as voices. Not as faces.

Weight. Presence. Attention layered with restraint.

The Immortals brushed her consciousness like hands pulled quickly across a flame. There was no guidance in it. No message she could translate into words. Only the unmistakable sense of recoil, of something ancient and bound reaching too far and paying for it.

Then withdrawal.

The pressure vanished as abruptly as it had come, leaving behind a hollow ache and a certainty that settled deep in her chest.

She wasn't supposed to be here.

Not yet. Not like this.

Maya sucked in a shaky breath and pressed her forehead to her knees, grounding herself in the only way she could. The Weave did not answer her touch the way it once had. It did not resist either. It simply held, tense and undecided, like the world was waiting to see what she would do next.

"I'm not lost," she whispered aloud, as much to steady herself as to name the truth. Her voice sounded wrong in the air, too clear, too contained. "I'm displaced."

The word fit.

This wasn't distance. It wasn't scattering. It was misplacement, like she had slipped into the margin between pages while the story kept going without her.

Maya lifted her head and tried again to feel the others, not to pull them close, just to locate them. Everything came in blurred and indistinct, like listening through a wall that let sound pass but refused to open. Joe's truth felt like a faint pressure somewhere beyond the boundary, muted and distorted. Elara's heat was harder to miss, a tight, angry pulse fighting to stay contained. Richard was a wound in the lattice, moving and unstable, dragging attention he could not shake.

Alex.

She reached for him last, bracing herself.

For a heartbeat, she felt him. Not clearly, not the way she usually did, but enough to recognize the shape of his resonance. Familiar. Steady. Hers.

Relief surged.

Then it faded.

Not cut off. Not erased.

Just slipping farther away, like a light sinking beneath water.

Maya's breath hitched. "Alex," she whispered, knowing he couldn't hear her.

She tried to follow the thread instinctively and felt the boundary push back, not hard, but firm, like a hand on her chest saying not this way.

For the first time since her awakening, Maya understood what it meant to be unreachable.

Not hidden. Not blocked.

Out of traversal.

The realization hollowed her out in a way nothing else had. She had always been the one who bridged gaps, who refused distance and folded the world until separation became a choice instead of a sentence.

Now the gap held.

Now the world would not fold for her.

Maya sat very still, breathing through the ache, through the fear clawing at her ribs. The tear nearby pulsed faintly, curious as ever, threads shifting in small, testing adjustments.

She was inside a question the Weave had not answered yet.

Somewhere beyond this boundary, Alex's presence dimmed another fraction, not gone, but receding as he moved, lived, survived without her.

Maya closed her eyes and pressed her palm flat against the ground, anchoring herself to what little certainty she had left.

"I'm still here," she whispered to the unseen threads. "I just need to learn where here is."

The Weave did not answer. But it listened.

***

Alex woke choking.

Cold water filled his mouth and nose, thick with the taste of mud and rot. He jerked instinctively, coughing hard enough to scrape his throat raw, and rolled onto his side with a groan that barely sounded human. His ears rang, a high thin whine that made it hard to tell where the world ended and his skull began.

He lay there for a second, face pressed into wet grass, rainwater trickling past his cheek and into the shallow ditch that had caught him like a grave that missed its mark.

Move, he told himself. Don't go back out.

Alex pushed up on his elbows and nearly collapsed again as dizziness washed through him. The night tilted. Stars smeared. His stomach lurched, and he had to clamp his jaw shut to keep from vomiting into the mud.

Cold soaked through his clothes, seeping into places he didn't remember getting wet. His hands shook as he dragged one knee under himself and tried to sit up.

That was when he reached for his shield.

Nothing happened.

No familiar pressure. No answering resistance in the air. No sense of balance settling into place.

Alex sucked in a sharp breath and tried again, harder this time, pushing the way he always did when things were slipping out of alignment. He braced, focused, demanded.

Still nothing.

Panic flared hot and sudden, a spike that drove his heart into his throat.

No. No, no.

He planted his palms in the mud and forced himself to breathe, slow and deliberate, counting in his head like he'd been taught a lifetime ago. In for four. Hold. Out for four.

This isn't suppression, he thought. Suppression pushed back. This is absence.

That idea scared him more than anything else.

Alex squeezed his eyes shut and stayed upright through sheer stubbornness, refusing to let the dark creep back in. Passing out now felt too close to not waking up at all.

"Okay," he muttered hoarsely. "Okay. You're still here."

His voice sounded wrong in the open air, too small without the quiet reassurance of Maya's presence at his back. The realization hit him like a physical blow.

Maya.

Alex's head snapped up, pulse hammering. He turned slowly, scanning the roadside with unfocused eyes.

The ditch ran alongside a narrow two-lane road, cracked asphalt barely visible through the weeds. A bent guardrail leaned drunkenly a few yards away; its metal twisted like it had been grabbed and shaken. Beyond that, scrub and low trees pressed close, their branches snapped and scorched in places.

Scorch marks.

Alex stared at them, heart sinking. Blackened earth. Charred leaves still faintly warm, steam curling where rain touched burned ground.

"Elara," he whispered.

Memory came back in fragments. Pressure. Tearing sensation. The world folding wrong. Then nothing.

Alex forced himself to his feet, swaying hard enough that he had to grab the guardrail to stay upright. His legs felt hollow, like they were working on borrowed instructions.

He tried grounding again, quieter this time. Just a whisper of intent. Just enough to feel where he was.

The Weave did not answer.

The silence inside him was worse than the ringing in his ears.

Without Maya, his power felt like a limb that had been cut away without warning. He could still remember how it was supposed to work. He just couldn't do anything.

Alex pressed his forehead to the cool metal and breathed until the edges of panic dulled. "You're not broken," he told himself. "You're just empty."

The words didn't help much, but they kept him moving.

He followed the signs of disturbance away from the ditch, boots slipping on wet leaves as he pushed into the scrub. Bent vegetation marked a rough path, branches snapped outward instead of inward, like something had been thrown through instead of landing gently.

Violent displacement, he thought distantly. Not a clean jump.

His chest tightened. If Elara had landed near here, she would've come in hot whether she meant to or not.

Alex staggered out of the brush and stopped short.

Smoke drifted through the trees ahead, thin but unmistakable. Not the heavy black plume of a structure fire, but a low gray haze that clung to the ground and carried the sharp bite of burning pine.

"Damn it," he breathed.

He turned toward it immediately, body protesting every step. Without his shield, every sound felt too loud, every movement too exposed. He was just a man again, soaked and shaking and painfully aware of how fragile flesh was without the Weave smoothing the edges.

As he limped toward the smoke, Alex felt the weight of absence settle fully into place.

Maya wasn't just gone.

She was the balance he built himself around.

And without her, the world felt tilted, like it might slide out from under him at any moment if he didn't keep moving.

He squared his shoulders, gritted his teeth, and followed the smoke into the trees.

***

Elara woke choking on heat.

Not the clean burn she knew. Not the sharp, familiar edge of flame that answered her emotions like a mirror. This was thick and suffocating, pressing against her lungs and skin at once, air so hot it felt solid.

She rolled onto her side with a gasp, coughing hard enough to make her ribs ache. Ash smeared her cheek. Sparks drifted past her face like malignant fireflies.

Fire. Everywhere.

Elara pushed herself upright, heart slamming as she took in the slope around her. Trees burned uphill and downhill, flames racing through dry brush far too fast for the wind that barely stirred the smoke. Pockets of heat surged and collapsed in erratic waves, as if the fire itself couldn't decide how it wanted to behave.

"This isn't right," she whispered.

She staggered to her feet. The ground was hot enough to sting through her boots. Her head rang, not with pain exactly, but with a hollow pressure where the world still felt slightly out of sync.

Memory snapped back in pieces. The jump tearing. Pressure crushing inward. Her fire yanked loose, not from fear or rage, but from something deeper. Something structural.

The realization hit her like a punch.

"I did this."

Not deliberately. Not emotionally.

Her flame had reacted to the rupture itself. To the tear in the Weave. Like striking flint against a fault line.

Elara squeezed her eyes shut and reached inward, searching for the familiar loop. Emotion. Heat. Feedback. The subtle resistance that told her how much was too much.

It wasn't there.

The suppression fields were gone. She could feel that immediately. No Cinder dampening. No artificial drag. The cage had dropped away.

But instead of relief, there was only wrongness.

Her flame surged when she reached for it, flaring too fast, too eager, then guttering unpredictably like it was slipping out of her hands. She yanked her focus back, swearing as heat licked up her arm in a sharp warning.

"No," she hissed. "You don't get to do that."

The fire didn't listen.

Power without feedback felt like driving blind at full speed.

Elara forced herself to breathe, counting the way Maya had taught her. In. Hold. Out. Again. She couldn't fight the wildfire head on. She knew that instinctively. Trying to smother it would just make it push harder, especially now.

So she did the only thing she could.

She redirected.

Elara turned downhill, toward a darker line where the trees thinned and a narrow dirt access road cut across the slope. She focused on shaping heat instead of creating it, pulling flames sideways, thinning them just enough to starve one section while another burned hotter.

Not extinguishing.

Steering.

She moved through smoke and sparks like a conductor losing control of an orchestra, arms shaking as she carved channels of heat through brush and fallen branches. Sweat poured down her spine. Her lungs burned. Every correction felt late, every adjustment slightly wrong.

She gritted her teeth and kept going anyway.

"Not there," she muttered. "Not toward the road. Go that way. Burn there."

The fire responded, reluctantly, surging where she allowed it and easing where she pushed back. It wasn't obedience. It was negotiation under threat.

Minutes blurred together. Or maybe longer. Time felt unreliable inside the heat.

Elara stumbled to one knee near the edge of the road, chest heaving. The flames on the uphill side slowed, breaking into smaller fingers instead of a single advancing front. It wasn't safe. It wasn't contained.

But it wasn't racing anymore.

She dropped her hands, shaking.

"That's all I've got," she whispered.

The fire crackled around her, restless but momentarily redirected. Smoke drifted across the road in heavy waves, turning the world into shifting silhouettes and glowing embers.

That was when she saw movement.

Not the flicker of flame. Not a collapsing branch.

A shape moved through the smoke on the far side of the road, low and uneven, cutting across the fire's edge instead of following it. Too deliberate. Too wrong to be fire.

Elara's heart kicked hard.

"Hey," she called hoarsely, unsure why she bothered to whisper. "Who's there?"

The shape stumbled, resolved briefly into something human before the smoke swallowed it again.

Relief and fear hit her at the same time.

She pushed herself upright, ignoring the protest in her legs, and moved toward the road, flame coiled tight and unstable under her skin.

Because the fire crackled behind her, impatient and alive, and more than ever since her awakening, Elara was truly afraid of what her power might do next.

The fire crackled like it was thinking.

***

Joe figured out he was trapped when nothing tried to kill him.

The ravine narrowed ahead into a crooked slit between stone walls, scrub clinging to the sides like it had grown there out of spite. He slid down the loose gravel on his heels and came up short when the air changed.

Not colder. Not heavier.

Arranged.

The first drone rose into view without a sound, lifting from behind a rock outcrop like it had always been there and Joe just hadn't noticed. Matte gray. No markings. No visible weapons. It stopped ten feet above the ravine floor and held position.

Then another appeared behind him.

Then two more.

They spaced themselves with unsettling precision, not blocking him outright, just occupying the places he would need if he tried to move fast. High. Low. Angled. A geometry that said run if you want to prove the math right.

Joe's head throbbed in dull protest as his truth-sight flared automatically.

Nothing screamed danger.

That was worse.

The drones didn't lie. Not even a little. There was no hostility in their presence, no predatory intent, no satisfaction waiting behind their sensors. Just patience. Clean and unbothered.

They weren't here to hurt him.

They were here to see what he did.

Joe swallowed and forced his breathing to slow. "Okay," he murmured. "We're doing this again."

He took a cautious step forward.

The nearest drone adjusted by inches, maintaining distance without retreating. No warning tone. No escalation.

Containment without confrontation.

Joe closed his eyes briefly and let his truth-sight widen, ignoring the spike of pain behind his eyes. The ravine resolved into layers of intent and system logic, overlapping routines stacked like translucent sheets.

Distributed orders. Redundancy everywhere. No single lie to pry loose. No fear to amplify.

Built to withstand him.

"Figures," he muttered.

Joe backed up slowly until his shoulder brushed stone. Gravel crunched under his boot, loud in the unnatural quiet. The drones didn't react beyond micro adjustments, keeping the same angles, the same spacing.

He laughed once, breathless. "You're not even pretending to be scary."

The drones didn't answer.

His truth-sight told him something else then, something colder.

They weren't closing yet.

They were waiting for clarity.

For him to decide.

Joe wiped at his nose, smearing dried blood across his knuckles. The headache sharpened, but he leaned into it anyway, shaping his gift carefully instead of pushing it outward.

Truth didn't have to be loud.

It just had to be convincing.

He focused inward, on uncertainty. On all the questions still rattling around in his skull. Where Maya was. Whether Alex was alive. How bad the tear had been. He let that lack of resolution expand, muddying the edges of his intent.

Not a lie.

An absence.

The truth-sight bent around it, projecting hesitation instead of direction. No clear goal. No immediate threat. No decisive move to predict.

The drones shifted.

Not closer. Sideways.

Joe felt it like a pressure change, the geometry recalculating around a suddenly unhelpful variable. Pattern recognition stuttered when there was no pattern to grab.

He took advantage of the half second it bought him.

Joe dropped flat and rolled, gravel tearing at his palms as he slid under an overhang where the ravine bent sharply. He scrambled up on all fours, lungs burning, and ran the moment his feet found traction.

The drones reacted then.

Not firing. Never firing.

They repositioned, gliding smoothly to cut off the wider exit ahead. The ravine funneled him left whether he wanted it to or not, terrain and containment working together like they'd rehearsed.

Joe skidded to a stop again, chest heaving.

Smoke drifted across the opening.

Not dust. Not shadow.

Smoke.

Thick, acrid, and wrong.

Fire crackled somewhere beyond the bend, close enough that the sound carried through the stone. Heat licked the edge of the ravine like an uninvited thought.

Joe's heart jumped. "Elara."

The drones hesitated.

Just a fraction.

Joe felt it immediately, a ripple in their intent where the models adjusted for an environmental variable they hadn't fully owned yet.

Fire wasn't predictable. Not like people. Not like him.

Joe grinned despite the pain and leaned into the uncertainty hard, letting his intent fracture in a dozen directions at once. Should I run toward the heat. Away from it. Drop. Freeze. Lunge. Do nothing.

Truth scattered.

The drones recalculated.

Joe moved.

He bolted into the smoke without looking back, coughing as heat slapped against his face. Ash swirled around him, thick enough to blind sensors as well as eyes. He ducked low, slid down a slope of loose dirt, and vanished into the crackle and roar.

Behind him, the drones adjusted again, slower this time, their clean geometry blurring at the edges where flame and turbulence refused to behave.

Joe ran until his legs shook, until the smoke thinned just enough to breathe without choking. He stumbled into a shallow gully and collapsed against the bank, gasping and laughing at the same time.

Truth as evasion.

Who would've thought.

He wiped his face and forced himself upright, eyes scanning the firelit terrain ahead.

"Elara," he called hoarsely. "Alex."

The fire answered him with a sharp pop and a rush of heat. No one responded to his call.

Joe swallowed, heart pounding.

Whatever cage they were building, it hadn't accounted for wildfire.

And neither had he.

***

Richard woke to the sound of the world deciding what it wanted to be.

The ceiling above him shuddered, not falling, not holding. Hesitating. Concrete beams hung at angles that made his eyes ache to follow, edges blurring as their internal bonds slipped in and out of agreement. One second the slab over his chest was solid and immovable. The next it looked like frosted glass, spiderweb cracks blooming and vanishing across its surface.

Richard lay very still.

Breathing hurt. Every inhale scraped his ribs like something sharp had lodged there and refused to move. Dust coated his tongue, chalky and bitter, and the air smelled wrong. Not just old cement and rot, but the metallic tang of stressed matter, of bonds being asked to do things they were never meant to do.

He tried to move his right leg.

Pain flared white and immediate, hot enough to steal his breath. His vision fractured, the room splitting into overlapping angles that refused to settle into one image. He squeezed his eyes shut until the double vision eased to something tolerable.

"Idiot," he muttered, voice rough and small in the unstable space.

The structure answered him with a groan.

Richard reached out with his senses before he reached with his hands. The Weave here was a mess, threads pulled and knotted and half melted together where his last act had torn through. Matter couldn't decide what state it belonged in. Neither could he.

And closer than all of that, pressing at the edges of his awareness like cold fingers on glass, was something else.

The Shadow Current didn't announce itself.

It never did.

It seeped.

The whisper wasn't a voice. It was a suggestion shaped like relief. A familiar resonance that wore his own patterns like a borrowed coat.

You're holding it wrong.

Richard swallowed hard and kept his hands flat against the floor.

You're tired. Let go. Let it settle. I can help.

Images flickered behind his eyes. The beam above him resolving cleanly, bonds reforging into something stable and strong. The pain in his leg dulling to a manageable throb. The walls choosing solid and staying that way.

Stability at a price.

Richard laughed weakly, the sound turning into a cough that left copper on his tongue. "You always say that."

The Current pressed closer, mimicry sharpening. For a heartbeat it felt like understanding. Like forgiveness. Like the quiet satisfaction of a problem solved elegantly.

Just a little more, it coaxed. You already crossed the line. Let me finish it.

Richard gritted his teeth until his jaw trembled.

"No," he said aloud, the word scraping his throat raw. "You don't finish anything. You erase it."

The pressure increased, not angry, not forceful. Patient. It always waited for him to get tired enough to agree.

The beam above him shifted again, this time cracking with a sharp report. Dust rained down, stinging his eyes.

Richard didn't have time.

He dragged one arm forward, fingers splaying against a section of wall that flickered between stone and something more fragile. He didn't shape it. He didn't force it to become anything new.

He nudged.

Just enough.

The stone softened reluctantly, bonds loosening like a clenched fist forced open one finger at a time. Pain lanced through his skull as the cost hit him, vision splintering into overlapping frames that refused to line up.

The Shadow Current surged in response, eager, excited.

Yes. Like that. You see how easy it is.

Richard screamed then, not in fear, but in defiance. He shoved his arm into the softened section and dragged himself forward, ignoring the way his leg screamed as it scraped against shifting debris.

The wall gave way in a jagged oval, not a door, not a clean passage. More like a wound the structure hadn't realized it could sustain.

He crawled.

Every inch cost him something. Sensation blurred. His left eye stopped tracking properly, images lagging behind reality like a bad transmission. His leg went numb, then flared again as unstable matter snapped back to solidity around it, pinching muscle and nerve.

Behind him, the Shadow Current recoiled, then pressed again, angry now, its mimicry cracking at the edges.

You're breaking it, it hissed. You're making it worse.

Richard laughed again, breathless and broken. "Yeah," he gasped. "That's kind of my thing."

He dragged himself free just as the structure decided.

The wall behind him collapsed inward with a roar, concrete choosing brittle all at once. Dust and debris thundered into the space he had occupied seconds earlier, sealing it completely.

Richard rolled onto his back and lay there, staring up at a sky that swam and doubled, stars splitting and recombining in nauseating patterns.

The Shadow Current lingered, circling the edges of his awareness like a disappointed predator.

This cost you, it whispered. You feel it.

Richard closed one eye to steady the world. His leg burned and then went strangely cold. When he tried to focus on the ground beneath him, the texture slid sideways, refusing to stay put.

"I know," he said softly.

Survival felt heavy in his chest, not relief but something closer to guilt. Every time he used his gift, the world paid. This time the bill felt permanent.

He pushed himself upright with a grunt and immediately had to brace against a twisted beam to keep from falling over. His limp was worse. Much worse. His depth perception was shot, distance turning unreliable and cruel.

He took one careful step.

Then another.

Smoke drifted across the ruined lot, gray and thick and unmistakable.

Richard sniffed, grimaced, and started limping toward it.

If the world was going to burn anyway, he might as well find the others before it did.

***

Smoke turned the world into a bruise.

It pressed low against the ground, thick enough to sting her eyes and scrape her throat raw with every breath. The fire had slowed, not because it was finished, but because Elara had forced it to. She had bent it away from the tree line, starved it where she could, driven it into rocky ground that gave it nothing to eat.

Her hands shook anyway.

The flame no longer listened the way it used to. It responded late, or too eagerly, reacting to pressure in the air instead of emotion in her chest. That scared her more than the fire ever had.

Elara moved downslope, boots sliding on ash and loose stone, senses stretched thin. The smoke carried pockets of heat that didn't belong to the fire itself. Movement. Intent.

She raised her hands on instinct.

A shape broke through the haze twenty yards ahead. Human sized. Upright. Moving fast.

Elara didn't hesitate.

Fire flared up her arms, hot and sharp, ready to snap forward in a killing arc.

"Stop," a voice shouted. Hoarse. Familiar. "Elara, don't."

She froze mid breath.

The flame bucked, fighting her grip, then collapsed inward with a painful snap that made her gasp. She staggered back a step, heart slamming, eyes burning as the smoke thinned just enough to resolve the figure.

Joe Biggs stood there, hands raised, face streaked with blood and ash, eyes wide in the kind of alarm that came from almost dying.

"Oh," Elara said stupidly. "It's you."

Joe let out a breath that sounded like it hurt. "Yeah. Hi. Great reflexes."

She dropped her hands and pressed them to her thighs, forcing herself to breathe. "I thought you were Gray."

"Fair," he said. "I almost thought you were a flamethrower."

She barked a short, shaky laugh that fell apart halfway through. "I almost burned you."

Joe stepped closer, slow and deliberate, like he was approaching something wild. "You didn't. You stopped."

"Barely."

"That still counts."

They stood there for a second, smoke drifting between them, the crackle of distant fire filling the silence neither of them wanted to break first.

Joe's gaze flicked past her, scanning the slope, the trees, the dark beyond. "You okay?"

Elara shook her head. "I'm upright."

"Same category I'm in," he muttered.

She studied him then, really looked. His truth-sight wasn't flaring. It wasn't doing much of anything. His shoulders were tight, posture guarded in a way that had nothing to do with enemies and everything to do with pain.

"Elara," Joe said quietly, "I can't feel her, not like before."

The words landed harder than any impact.

Elara swallowed. "Me neither."

They didn't argue it. Didn't soften it. The absence was too complete for denial. Maya's presence had always been there, a quiet pressure at the edge of Elara's awareness even when they were apart. A thread that hummed.

Now there was nothing.

Smoke shifted again.

A shape stumbled out of the trees downslope, gait uneven, breath ragged. Elara's hands twitched, fire stirring reflexively, but Joe caught her eye and shook his head once.

"Not Gray," he said.

The figure lurched closer, nearly falling, then caught himself against a rock outcrop.

"Alex," Elara breathed.

Alex didn't remember falling.

He remembered cold water, then nothing, then pain blooming everywhere at once as his body reminded him it still existed. By the time he became aware of his surroundings, he was upright only because someone had him by the arm.

"Elara," he rasped, recognizing her heat before his vision cleared. "Joe."

Joe tightened his grip. "Yeah. You're with us. Stay that way."

Alex nodded, though his head felt like it weighed too much for his neck. His shield was gone. Not quiet. Not resting. Gone in the way a limb was gone when it didn't answer at all.

He tried to ground anyway.

Nothing.

Panic surged sharp and fast, and he crushed it by force of habit. Breathe. Count. Stay.

Elara steadied him from the other side, jaw clenched, eyes bright with something that looked too close to fear. "You're freezing," she said.

"I'm fine," Alex lied.

Joe snorted softly. "Everyone says that right before they aren't."

Alex managed a weak huff of laughter and leaned more heavily into them. The ground smelled like ash and damp earth. Smoke clung to everything, making the world feel smaller, closer.

"Maya," Alex said. The name came out rough. "Where is she."

Neither of them answered.

He knew then.

The absence hit him like a structural failure. Not grief yet. Something colder. The sense that a load bearing element had vanished and the whole design was now suspect.

"She's not here," Alex said quietly.

Joe shook his head. "No. And I can't see her. Can't feel her. It's like she's... not on the board."

Elara crossed her arms, hugging herself without realizing it. "The tear's still active somewhere. I can feel the pressure from it."

Alex forced himself to straighten, spine protesting. "Then she's not dead."

They both looked at him.

"She's displaced," he continued, more certain now. "Out of phase. Somewhere bad. But not gone."

It wasn't hope. It was engineering. If Maya had been gone, it'd feel different, he'd know.

Footsteps scraped through brush nearby.

Alex tensed, then recognized the rhythm too late to do anything about it.

Richard emerged from the trees like something that had been chewed on and decided not to die anyway. His limp was worse, one side of his body moving half a beat behind the other. One eye didn't quite focus, gaze sliding past them before snapping back.

The air around him felt wrong.

Not active Shadow. Not feeding. But stretched thin, like a scar that hadn't decided whether it was done healing.

Elara swore under her breath. "You look like hell."

Richard smiled faintly. "You should see the building."

Joe's eyes narrowed as his truth-sight brushed Richard and recoiled. "You're changed."

"Yeah," Richard said. "That too."

They stood there together in the smoke, four figures ringed by damage and absence.

"No Maya," Joe said, stating it flat.

"No idea where she landed," Elara added.

"The tear's breathing somewhere nearby," Richard said. "I can feel it. Like a wound that didn't close."

Alex nodded once. "Then standing still is the worst option."

Joe glanced up as a low, distant thrum rolled across the sky. Not loud. Not close.

Rotors.

Elara's shoulders squared. "They're back."

Alex took a breath that hurt and forced his legs to cooperate. He stepped forward, unsteady but moving.

"We stick together," he said. "We stay off clean ground. We don't draw attention."

"And Maya," Elara said.

Alex looked ahead into the smoke and the dark beyond it. "We find her."

They moved as one, uneven, limping, altered.

A group again.

Just not whole.

They took shelter where the fire had already done its damage.

Blackened earth stretched in uneven swaths around them, trees reduced to skeletal silhouettes that creaked softly as heat bled out of their cores. Ash coated everything, muting sound and scent alike. Even the air felt stripped down, thin and cautious. Drones stayed high. Sensors hesitated. Fire made machines nervous.

Alex crouched behind the fallen trunk of a burned pine, knees drawn in, arms wrapped tight around himself. His breathing had steadied, but his posture hadn't. He kept glancing to his left, to the space where Maya always ended up without anyone deciding it.

She wasn't there.

Elara stood a few steps away, back to the wind, fists clenched so tight her knuckles had gone white beneath the soot. Heat trembled under her skin, restless and untrustworthy. She didn't let it out. She didn't dare. Every time her pulse spiked, the fire answered too fast.

Joe knelt in the ash with his head bowed, eyes closed, one hand pressed flat against the ground like he was steadying himself against a moving floor. He wasn't searching the perimeter. He was listening inward.

When he finally spoke, his voice was rough. "She's not gone."

Alex's head snapped up. "You're sure."

Joe nodded slowly. "Yeah. I don't feel a break. No absence spike. No echo collapse." He swallowed. "Her resonance is intact, just displaced."

Elara took a sharp breath. "Then where is she."

Joe opened his eyes. They were bloodshot, rimmed with exhaustion and something colder. "Elsewhere."

The word settled heavy between them.

Alex looked back at the empty space beside him. He reached out without thinking, his hand stopping short of where Maya's sleeve should have been. The motion cost him more than he let show. His fingers curled in on themselves.

"She should be here," he said quietly.

Elara turned away before anyone could see her face. Her shoulders shook once, then stilled. "I keep wanting to burn something," she admitted. "Like if I light up the sky enough, she'll see it."

"You'd light us up instead," Joe said gently.

"I know." She pressed her fists into her thighs until the urge passed. "I just hate not being able to do anything."

Richard stood apart from them, half in shadow, half in the firelight. He hadn't sat. He hadn't leaned. He kept his back turned, gaze fixed on the dark beyond the burned ground like it might judge him less if he didn't look back.

"This is my fault," he said quietly.

No one answered right away.

Joe shifted first. "It isn't."

Richard shook his head. "I was the fracture point. I drew it in. I felt it latch." His voice went thin. "If I hadn't..."

Alex cut him off, sharper than intended. "If you hadn't, we'd all be in a box right now."

Richard flinched anyway.

Silence pressed in again, thick with ash and unspoken fear. Above them, rotors throbbed faintly and then drifted farther away, unwilling to dip low over the burn scar.

Maya wasn't dead.

That should have been comfort.

Instead it felt worse.

Because somewhere nearby, the tear still breathed. Somewhere outside the rules they understood, a single thread had been pulled loose and not cut.

The tear hadn't taken Maya from them. It had taken her out of reach.

31

The Shadow Current

Maya opened her eyes.

Light existed here, but it behaved like a memory of light rather than the thing itself. Dim glows floated without sources, staining the space around her in muted colors that lagged when she moved her gaze. Reds bled into browns after she looked away. Blues stayed too long, ghosting the edges of shapes that refused to settle.

Nothing cast a shadow.

She pushed herself onto her elbows and froze.

The Weave was visible. She could feel the tear behind her now, not ahead, like a cut she'd fallen through.

Not flaring. Not responding to her awareness. Just there.

Threads ran through everything. Through the ground beneath her, through the air above her, through the dark between distant glows. They moved steadily in one direction, sliding past her like a river seen from underwater. No knots. No lattice. No structure she recognized.

A current.

Her heartbeat sounded wrong in her ears. Too far away. Like it was happening to someone else in the next room. She pressed her palm to the surface beneath her and felt the contact arrive late, sensation chasing intention instead of meeting it.

Her body was present.

But unreliable.

Weight flickered when she tried to stand. Gravity caught her, then let go, then caught her again like it was still deciding whether she qualified. She swayed, breath hitching, and the current around her thickened immediately.

Not in response to movement.

In response to attention.

Maya forced herself still.

The thickening eased, threads loosening their press against her skin.

Understanding slid into place cold and sharp.

This place reacted to awareness.

Not motion. Not force. Focus.

She swallowed and tried not to panic.

Blink, she told herself.

Fold the space. Get back to them.

The instinct rose whole and unfiltered, the reflex that had saved her more times than she could count. She reached for the familiar shape of a jump and felt the vector form, felt the world begin to slide.

Then it caught.

Not like hitting a wall. Not like suppression fields or containment geometry. There was no resistance pushing her away.

The motion slid sideways.

Her vector skidded across threads that refused to line up, slipping like a foot finding only air where a stair should have been. The jump collapsed inward, pressure snapping back into her chest hard enough to steal her breath.

Maya gasped and dropped to one knee.

"No," she whispered. "No, no, no."

She tried again, slower this time. Careful. Shaping the jump with precision, mapping a destination she knew as well as her own heartbeat.

Alex.

His presence should have been a beacon. Solid. Familiar. Anchoring.

She reached for him and felt only distance.

Not severed.

Not gone.

Distant.

The realization hit harder than the failed jump. Panic flared hot and sharp, flooding her veins. Her hands curled into fists against her thighs as she fought it down through grit and training and the memory of every time fear had killed people faster than enemies ever could.

Think.

Listen.

Maya let her awareness widen again, not to move, but to understand.

The threads around her were not tangled. They were arranged differently. This place sat between states, neither fully folded nor fully reasserted. A seam. A boundary that had not finished deciding whether it was a scar or a door.

Something shifted in the current.

Not movement. Attention.

The ripple she'd made back in the world had followed her here, and it carried her name like a scent.

Maya stiffened.

Something here knew who she was.

And it was listening.

The first voice was gentle.

"Maya."

It came from her left, perfectly pitched, perfectly timed. Alex's voice, low and steady, the way he sounded when he was trying not to scare anyone.

Relief surged before she could stop it. Her head snapped toward the sound.

He stood there, just beyond arm's reach. Dry. Whole. Shielding humming faintly around him like a second skin.

"Maya," he said again, smiling the way he did when he thought he'd finally convinced her to rest.

She took one step forward.

The current thickened instantly, threads pressing closer, the air growing heavier with expectation.

Maya stopped.

Alex did not move.

He did not breathe.

The smile did not change.

Her relief curdled into cold understanding.

"No," she said quietly.

The image didn't react. It simply waited.

The voice shifted.

"Maya, listen to me."

Joe's voice this time. Tired. Earnest. The way he sounded when he was telling a truth that hurt and needed to be said anyway.

"You don't have to fight this," the voice said. "You just have to stop resisting."

The space around her warmed slightly, pressure easing, the current thinning like a reward offered for compliance.

Small mercies.

Invisible strings.

Maya felt the pull of it, the temptation to let go, to stop holding herself rigid against a place that seemed willing to meet her halfway.

Then she noticed the perfection.

Joe's cadence was flawless. No strain. No hesitation. Elara appeared next, heat coiled neatly beneath her skin, eyes bright and unafraid. Richard stood behind them, unmarked, whole, Shadow absent as if it had never touched him at all.

Too perfect.

The world corrected itself around them, smoothing every flaw, every fracture.

Maya backed away.

"No," she said again, louder this time.

Cold pressure settled over her like a hand on the back of her neck. Not anger. Not punishment.

Correction.

The glows dimmed. The current slowed, threads pressing in close enough to make her skin prickle.

Behind the mimicry, she felt it then.

Not the voices. Not the images.

Something deeper.

Ancient. Patient.

Watching her choices instead of her body.

It didn't want her flesh. It didn't want her power.

It wanted her consent.

Maya clenched her jaw and held her ground.

"I know what you're doing," she said into the wrong air. "And I'm not playing."

The pressure eased, just a fraction.

Interest replaced insistence.

A steadier resonance cut through the current then, clean and unmistakably human.

The Residuum hesitated.

The air organized.

That was the only way Maya could describe it. The drifting glows pulled inward. Threads aligned, slowing their relentless slide just enough to form a pocket of stillness.

And then Ethan stepped out of the current.

Not flickering. Not half formed.

Fully present.

He appeared like a storm deciding to become a person, the space around him arranging itself instinctively to accommodate his existence. The wrong air moved aside for him. The current recognized him.

He looked real here in a way Maya did not.

Solid. Anchored. As if this place understood his shape and had been expecting it. The residuum recognized him the way it recognized contamination, only he didn't flinch from it.

"You're not supposed to be here," Maya said, fear spiking sharp and sudden.

Ethan's expression tightened. He looked older somehow. Not in years, but in weight. His eyes held a depth she hadn't seen before, like he'd been listening to something she couldn't hear for a long time.

"I didn't find you," he said. "You drifted."

"That's not an answer," she snapped.

"It's the only honest one," he replied. "This current leads to me."

He lifted a hand and the pressure around her eased further, a pocket of stability settling into place. Her heartbeat steadied. The delayed sensation in her limbs snapped closer to real time.

Control.

Not dominance. Understanding.

"How did you get here like that," she demanded. "Fully. Like this place knows you."

Ethan didn't answer immediately. His gaze flicked briefly to the surrounding current, then back to her.

"Don't bargain with it," he said instead. "It always asks twice."

Maya's breath caught.

"You've been here before," she said.

"Not like you," he replied. "Not without leaving parts behind."

The words settled heavy between them.

"What is this place," Maya asked.

Ethan hesitated, then reached for her hand.

The Residuum leaned in.

"This," he said quietly, "is older than our war with HECATE."

His fingers closed around hers, solid and warm, and the current surged.

The world tilted.

Not falling. Streaming.

The current caught them both and pulled, threads accelerating until the glows stretched into lines and then into something like stars dragged across glass.

Maya clung to Ethan instinctively as the space around them reshaped itself into memory.

The sky was wrong in the opposite way.

Pristine. Terrifying.

A blue so deep it felt endless arched overhead, unbroken by clouds. Light burned clean and sharp, casting shadows that cut like knives. Cities rose beneath them, vast and alien and familiar in the way of dreams that borrowed details from nowhere.

The Weave screamed.

Not audibly. Harmonically.

Maya felt it overload like a heart going into fibrillation, rhythm shattering into chaos. Pressure built across the landscape, bending matter in waves that rippled outward faster than sight.

Buildings twisted. Mountains sagged. Oceans rose into walls that forgot how to fall.

This wasn't destruction.

It was misalignment.

Matter behaved the way it had around Richard, but on a continental scale, bonds slipping, reasserting, slipping again. The first surge of the Shadow Current tore through the world like a flood finding a crack in a dam.

Maya staggered as sensation overwhelmed her.

"This is the shape of it," she whispered. "The same failure, just smaller."

Ethan's grip tightened. "This is what we did."

Figures moved through the chaos. Tall. Luminous. Immortals, though she could not see their faces clearly. Early Walkers stood among them, burning and breaking under the strain of power they barely understood.

And beyond it all, something watched.

Something patient.

The catastrophe locked into a single moment.

Five stood together.

Five chose a law.

The world stilled.

Five voices spoke, not aloud but into the bones of reality itself.

The vow cut deep, binding itself into the Weave with the precision of an engineer sealing a breach.

First clause.

Non interference.

Immortals would not rule. Would not correct. Would not shape mortal outcomes directly, no matter the cost.

Second clause.

Containment before salvation.

When fractures appeared, boundaries would be stabilized before individuals were saved, even if that choice killed millions.

Third clause.

Silence.

Certain truths must be smothered before they become levers. Not to protect power, but because knowledge became a weapon faster than wisdom ever could.

Fourth clause.

The anchor.

A mortal line would inherit guardianship. When Immortals could not act, mortals would stand in their place.

Fifth clause.

The unacceptable.

If the Shadow Current breached in full, an anchor would be sacrificed to reseal it. Sacrifice didn't mean dying. It meant being taken into the lock.

Maya felt the weight of it settle into her chest like a verdict.

This wasn't ethics.

It was architecture.

The covenant locked the world together with rules that could withstand truth and rage alike.

This was the Covenant of Silence.

Ethan's voice cut through the memory.

"It was broken once," he said. "That's why it remembers how to come back."

The memory dissolved into the present.

The Residuum shifted, replaying the mass jump rupture like a ripple still expanding. Maya watched the tear breathe, its edges flexing with every system that mapped it, every model that tried to understand it.

"They didn't just observe us," Ethan said. "They learned."

The cage was becoming a key.

Maya's stomach twisted. "I gave them this."

"You showed them the seam," Ethan replied. "They'll try to force it next."

The Current stirred, offering her friends again, whole and waiting.

The offer came softly.

A clean exit. A correction. Just let it ride her once.

Ethan shook his head. "It won't stop."

Maya closed her eyes.

She anchored to her name. To her limits. To the choice not to become a door again.

She aligned instead of forcing.

The Current recoiled, then leaned in.

Interest.

A corridor opened, thin and trembling.

"The last clause isn't metaphorical," Ethan said as the corridor pulled. "An anchor will be demanded."

Maya saw her friends, alive and hunted.

Then HECATE's systems, mapping the same ripple.

The Current didn't want her dead.

It wanted her useful.

32

❦

Judgment

The corridor Ethan had opened was still there, thin as a held breath, trembling in the current like a seam that hadn't decided whether it wanted to become a doorway. It didn't pull her through. It simply waited, patient and conditional, as if the next move wasn't about distance anymore.

Maya flexed her fingers and felt the delay. Not numbness, not weakness, but a lag between intention and sensation, like her body was half a step behind her mind. When she shifted her weight, gravity caught her late, then corrected too hard. The Residuum didn't resist her. It adjusted around her awareness, thickening when fear spiked, loosening when she went still.

She tried to touch the Weave and felt it answer wrong.

Not absent. Not broken.

Mis-tuned.

Ethan stood a few feet away, solid in a way the current recognized, watching her without urgency. He didn't look surprised by the distortion. He looked like he'd expected it.

"It's not your power," he said quietly. "It's your relationship."

Maya swallowed. "So what am I now."

Ethan's gaze shifted to the flowing threads. "You're a broken instrument in a system that doesn't do mercy repairs."

326

The words should've felt cruel. They didn't. They felt precise.

Maya stared at the corridor again, at the promise of escape that refused to become a command. "I can't brute force it," she said.

"No," Ethan agreed. "And that's not punishment."

He stepped closer, and the current softened around them as if his presence lowered the strain. "You can't be fixed," he said. "You can only be re-taught."

Maya nodded once, the motion small and careful.

"Teach me," she said.

Ethan did not answer immediately.

He sat down instead, folding himself into the current with an ease that made Maya ache. The Residuum parted around him, threads slowing, aligning just enough to cradle his presence without effort.

He belonged here.

That truth stung more than it should have.

"I didn't do this the way they did," he said at last.

Maya tilted her head slightly. "The Immortals."

"Or you," he added, not unkindly.

She did not argue.

"I never channeled the Weave," Ethan went on. "Never treated it like something that flowed through me. I didn't command it. Didn't shape it from the outside."

He looked down at his hands, flexing his fingers as if remembering something tactile and old.

"And I didn't ascend beyond it."

Maya felt the weight of that distinction settle between them.

"I merged," he said. "As a mortal."

The words were simple. The implication was not.

"When the Weave took me in," Ethan continued, "it didn't elevate me. It didn't crown me. It didn't grant permission. It changed how I perceive strain."

He looked back at her then, eyes steady.

"I feel its needs before its permissions," he said. "When the Weave is stressed, it's discomfort, not resistance. Like a joint being pushed the wrong way. Not a wall. A warning."

Maya absorbed that in silence.

"The Immortals know what the Weave allows," Ethan said. "They wrote rules around it. Built covenants. Engineered silence."

"And you?" Maya asked.

"I know what it needs."

The statement landed without arrogance. Without pride. Like a fact that simply existed whether anyone liked it or not.

Ethan gestured around them. "This isn't a power source. It isn't a lattice you climb or a river you dam. It's an ecology. Self correcting. Self preserving."

He met her gaze.

"You kept solving problems by overriding equilibrium," he said gently. "You chose outcomes over structure."

Maya flinched, just slightly.

"You saved people," he continued. "Over and over. But every time you forced the system to obey urgency, you taught it a bad habit. You trained it to tolerate damage."

Her jaw tightened.

"I didn't have time," she said.

"I know," Ethan replied. "That's why it didn't stop you. Not until now."

The realization settled slowly, like a weight lowering onto her shoulders rather than slamming into them.

"This isn't about technique," Maya said quietly.

"No," Ethan agreed. "It never was."

He shifted closer and held out his hand.

"Let me show you how to hear it."

Ethan did not stabilize the current.

That was the first surprise.

Instead of anchoring the space or shielding her from the flow, he asked her to do something that felt backward and terrifying.

"Lower yourself," he said.

"I don't know how," Maya admitted.

"I do," he replied. "Follow me."

He placed his hand lightly over her sternum, not pressing, just resting there as if reminding her where she existed.

"Stop trying to be significant," he said softly.

The words should have stung.

Instead, they loosened something in her chest.

Maya exhaled.

She let go of projection. Of reach. Of the instinct to matter.

The effect was immediate.

The Residuum did not recede. It did not brighten. It simply... settled.

Silence bloomed around her, not absence, but the quiet of a system no longer compensating for strain.

Pressure remained, but it was not threat. It was context.

Balance emerged, not as control, but as belonging.

Maya gasped softly as realization rippled through her awareness.

She could feel it now.

Where the Weave was under load. Where it was compensating for damage done elsewhere. Where a single intervention would create cascading fractures three steps down the line.

Every instinct she had relied on screamed to act.

And for the first time, she did not.

She stayed.

The Residuum watched.

It did not interfere.

Maya felt tears slip free, floating strangely in the wrong air before dissolving back into the current.

"Power was never the price," she whispered.

Ethan nodded. "Restraint was."

The current responded.

Everything stopped.

Not froze.

Aligned.

The current did not vanish. It cohered.

Maya felt it then. All of it.

Every jump she had ever taken. Every forced fold. Every moment she had ripped space open because someone was screaming and time was running out.

There was no accusation in it.

No condemnation.

Just accounting.

The Weave measured pattern alignment. Capacity for restraint. Willingness to accept limits.

Maya did not speak.

She did not justify.

She did not ask forgiveness.

She waited.

For the first time in her life, she allowed herself to be unnecessary.

The evaluation concluded without ceremony.

The answer arrived not as approval, but as access.

She was worthy.

Not because she was powerful.

Because she was correctable.

Ethan exhaled slowly. "That's judgment."

Rising did not feel like expansion.

It felt like tightening.

Her harmonic signature shifted, resonance pulling inward, resolving into cleaner, sharper lines. Less force. More precision.

She no longer felt like a door.

She felt like a keystone.

The Weave did not obey her.

It acknowledged her.

Mass jumps were gone. The brute force folds she once relied on simply no longer formed.

In their place came something quieter.

She could read stress. Anticipate fracture. Choose when not to act.

The Residuum loosened its hold.

Maya felt them.

Faint. Alive. Endangered.

Her resonance did not flare when she reached.

It threaded.

Ethan's voice was steady. "The Shadow Current will notice. So will HECATE. Eventually."

Maya nodded.

She accepted the cost.

She could not be what she was.

And that was the point.

The Weave hadn't given her more power.

It had trusted her with less.

33

Found

Alex felt it while he was still moving.

Not danger. Not relief. Not the sharp spike that meant run or the hollow drop that meant loss. This was something quieter, like a pressure change deep in his chest that didn't ask for action so much as attention.

He stopped without meaning to.

Ash clung to his boots and the air still smelled faintly of burned pine. Somewhere behind him, Elara and Joe were moving, careful and tired, and Richard's uneven footsteps marked the rhythm of damage that hadn't finished writing itself yet. Alex raised a hand without turning, a simple signal to hold.

The world didn't feel hostile. It didn't feel safe either. It felt aligned.

He closed his eyes and breathed.

Grounding came back in pieces. Not the old way. Not a shield snapping into place or a firm wall pushing outward. This was thinner. More precise. Like tension resolving along a line he hadn't known was twisted.

Less force. More clarity.

The dyad stirred.

Not a flare. Not a call. The bond didn't light up or pull hard enough to hurt. It settled, like a knot loosening when pressure was finally applied in the right direction.

Maya.

The certainty arrived whole.

She was alive.

Not hidden. Not fading. Not scattered across distance the way they had been after the jump. She was anchored.

Wrongly.

Alex swallowed and opened his eyes.

This wasn't a location problem. He understood that immediately, in the same way he understood load-bearing structures without thinking about math. You didn't fix a compromised beam by shoving harder. You fixed it by relieving stress from the right angle.

Maya wasn't lost in space.

She was caught in a state.

The bond didn't pull him forward like a rope. It didn't point. It oriented him. A direction that wasn't north or south, but inward, like something in the world had turned a few degrees and was quietly asking him to notice.

Alex exhaled and started walking.

Not faster. Not slower. Just truer.

The ground changed as he followed the pull. Ash gave way to soil that felt too smooth underfoot, then to stone that hummed faintly when he stepped on it. Threads flickered at the edge of his vision, not flaring, not weaving, simply present, responding to his movement the way water responds to a hull cutting through it cleanly.

His grounding adjusted with each step. He wasn't shielding against pressure. He was distributing it.

The bond tightened, not with urgency, but with certainty.

He was getting closer.

The terrain ahead bore the scars of the tear.

Not obvious damage. Not craters or broken earth. This was subtler. Lines that didn't quite meet. Slopes that should have leveled but didn't. A sense that the land had been folded, then unfolded without quite remembering where it started.

Alex slowed as the bond drew him toward a shallow rise.

That was when he saw the light.

It wasn't bright.

It didn't blind or glare or pulse. It didn't behave like flame or lightning or anything powered. It simply existed where light had no business being.

A soft glow hung in the air ahead, contained, precise, like someone had drawn a boundary and told illumination to stay inside it.

Alex's breath caught.

Maya stood at the center of it.

She wasn't floating. She wasn't radiant. She wasn't doing anything at all.

The glow didn't spill from her. It resolved around her.

No surge. No flare. No pressure wave. The aura was structured, harmonic, self-contained, like a chord held perfectly in tune. The threads near her quieted, not snapping to attention, not recoiling, but easing, as if they'd been waiting for her to stop struggling so they could finally rest.

The air around her felt lighter.

Alex took a careful step forward.

Nothing resisted him.

The Weave didn't tense. The pressure he'd been compensating for eased, just slightly, like the land itself had exhaled.

Recognition struck him harder than fear ever could.

The Weave knew her now.

Not as a door. Not as a breach. As something that fit.

Alex swallowed and moved closer, following the bond not with urgency, but with respect.

Maya felt him before she saw him.

Not as alarm. Not as relief that cracked her chest open and made her want to reach. This was alignment, clean and unmistakable, like two notes finally resolving into the same key.

She didn't turn right away.

She didn't pull.

She didn't reach.

She let him come.

The corridor behind her trembled faintly, still thin, still conditional, its edges breathing with the slow patience of a system that hadn't finished deciding what it would allow. The Residuum pressed close, curious but restrained, its attention sliding across her awareness like fingertips testing glass.

Alex stepped into view.

He looked wrong in the way everything else did here. Not displaced. Not distorted. Just human, carrying damage and stubbornness and the quiet ache of someone who refused to stop standing when the structure told him to rest.

Their eyes met.

No rush of words. No collapse into each other's space. No desperate confirmation that either of them was real.

Just recognition.

"You're here," Alex said softly.

Maya nodded. "You found me."

He shook his head once. "No. I matched."

The bond settled between them, not flaring, not tightening. It aligned.

Alex crossed the boundary because it permitted him to. Because the Weave, in its new quiet way, agreed.

Maya felt it acknowledge the crossing without reaction.

For the first time since judgment, something loosened in her chest that had nothing to do with power.

She could be reached.

But only like this.

Only through consent and precision.

Alex didn't need long to understand.

The corridor wasn't stable. Not yet. It wasn't a doorway. It was a condition. Forcing it would be like pulling a keystone from a half-set arch and expecting the rest to hold.

Maya stood calm inside her glow, the light tightening slightly as he drew closer, clarifying rather than expanding. He could feel the cost of haste the way he felt stress fractures before collapse.

"You can't leave," he said quietly.

Maya didn't argue. "Not yet."

"And if we try," he said, "we undo what just happened."

"Yes."

Alex looked past her at the trembling seam of the corridor, then back at her face. She wasn't afraid. She wasn't resigned. She was present in a way that made urgency feel almost inappropriate.

"I can go get the others," he said. "Tell them where you are. Bring them back slow."

She shook her head. "That would pull on things that aren't ready to move."

He frowned. "Then what do we do."

Maya met his gaze. "We wait until the system agrees."

Alex let out a short breath, half laugh, half disbelief. "You're asking me to leave you here."

"I'm not asking," she said gently. "I'm explaining."

He stared at her for a long moment, then shook his head again. "No."

Maya didn't tell him to stay.

She told him the truth.

"What the Weave is doing right now isn't healing," she said. "It's recalibrating. It's deciding what kind of access I get to have. Rushing would teach it the wrong lesson."

Alex absorbed that in silence.

"And if you leave," she added, "the boundary tightens again. Not because it wants to trap me. Because it would have to compensate for the loss of coherence."

He looked at the glow, at the way the threads near her moved more smoothly than anywhere else he'd seen since the tear.

"If the Weave thinks you're a keystone," he said slowly, "then you don't sit alone."

Maya's breath caught.

"This isn't romance," he went on, firm and clear. "This is load-bearing. You stay, I stay. That's the structure."

The bond tightened, approving in its quiet way.

Maya didn't argue.

She allowed it.

Alex's presence changed everything.

Not dramatically. Not explosively. The glow around her didn't brighten. It refined. The harmonic field tightened, lines resolving into cleaner shapes, like a system suddenly given the missing variable it had been compensating for.

The boundary state shifted.

The corridor steadied, not opening, but breathing easier. The Residuum adjusted around them, not alarmed, not pleased, simply accommodating the new coherence.

Maya felt it then, clear and undeniable.

The dyad wasn't power.

It was coherence.

She wasn't alone in judgment anymore.

Alex sat beside her at the edge of the corridor, close enough that their shoulders nearly touched, not reaching, not claiming, just present. The Weave held them without tension.

Somewhere far away, Elara and Joe and Richard were moving, hurt and determined. Somewhere deeper still, HECATE's systems were adjusting, learning. Somewhere beyond even that, the Shadow Current watched with patient interest.

None of it rushed them.
Alex stayed.
Maya allowed it.
The Weave didn't open because she called.
It opened because they aligned.

34

Resonance

Alex sat with Maya at the edge of the corridor and did nothing. That alone felt like work.

The seam hovered a few feet in front of them, thin and steady, no longer trembling but not opening either. It breathed in a way Alex could feel through his bones rather than his skin. Not alive. Not inert. Responsive. Like a structure under load that had finally stopped shifting but was still waiting to see if more weight would be added.

Maya sat cross legged beside him, posture loose, hands resting open on her knees. The soft glow around her did not expand or pulse. It held. A quiet geometry of light that made the wrongness of the surrounding space less sharp, as if the world had decided to behave better in her presence.

Alex felt the dyad steady between them, not tightening, not pulling, simply present. It was enough to keep the corridor from collapsing back into noise. It was not enough to finish anything.

He understood that now.

This was not a door they could open together. It was a structure they had stabilized just enough for something else to arrive.

The Weave shifted.

Not abruptly. Not as warning. A subtle tightening, the way a bridge does when new load approaches. Alex's grounding adjusted on instinct, distributing pressure instead of resisting it. His awareness widened, not outward, but sideways, tracking a familiar kind of presence that was not movement through space.

Truth pressure.

Maya felt it too. Her head tilted slightly, attention sharpening. "Joe," she said quietly.

Alex nodded. He did not turn. He did not signal. The system already knew what was coming.

Joe Biggs stepped into the edge of the field and stopped short.

He felt it immediately. The difference. The absence of hostility. The absence of invitation. The boundary did not brace against him. It did not recoil from his sight. It simply waited.

Joe swallowed and closed his eyes.

His truth sight rose out of habit and then stilled.

It did not flare. It did not burn. There was no spike of pain behind his eyes, no cascade of competing realities demanding interpretation. The sight narrowed instead, focusing down to something clean and quiet, like a lens finally ground to the right shape.

He opened his eyes and saw Maya.

Not idealized. Not fractured. Not mythologized by fear or hope.

Just Maya, seated in wrong space, breathing steadily, present in a way that made Joe's chest ache.

He took one step forward and felt no resistance.

Another.

The truth did not ask him to reveal anything. It did not demand analysis. It asked for alignment.

Joe stopped at the boundary, close enough to feel the hum of the corridor against his skin.

"You're not broken," he said aloud.

The words were not declaration. They were calibration.

The Weave responded by doing nothing.

No spike. No recoil. No surge.

A layer of tension simply... dropped.

Joe felt it like a knot loosening inside his own ribs. The boundary stopped bracing against interpretation. One entire band of harmonic uncertainty collapsed cleanly, leaving behind a quieter, steadier field.

"You're not done," he added, softer, mostly to himself.

Maya met his gaze and nodded once.

Heat entered the field.

Elara did not rush in.

She stopped well back, eyes narrowing as she felt the pressure of the Residuum slide across her awareness like a match struck too close to dry grass. Her fire stirred immediately, eager, reactive, wanting to answer the wrongness with force.

She clenched her fists and held it.

No suppression. No clamping down.

Refusal.

Elara drew her heat inward, tighter than she ever had before. Not banking it. Not smothering it. Compressing it into presence without expression. Warmth without flame.

The sensation made her teeth ache.

She stepped forward.

The fire inside her pushed once, sharp and insistent, and she denied it again. Her breath went shallow. Sweat broke across her brow. This was harder than burning. This was restraint under invitation.

The Weave noticed.

Volatility near the boundary dropped perceptibly. Alex felt it as a shift in load distribution. Joe felt it as clarity sharpening another fraction. The edge of the corridor stopped oscillating, its faint ripple smoothing into something closer to a straight line.

Thermal harmonics locked.

Elara reached the edge and stopped, hands trembling, eyes fixed on Maya.

"I'm here," she said quietly. "And I'm not lighting anything."

Maya's mouth curved, just slightly. "I know."

The space shuddered.

Not from heat. From stress.

Richard felt it before anyone else did.

He limped into the field slower than the others, each step a careful negotiation with pain and altered perception. The seam hurt to look at. Not visually, but structurally. His fractured vision saw micro misalignments crawling across its surface, tiny errors in matter state that wanted to cascade if given the slightest excuse.

And something else stirred.

The Shadow Current brushed his awareness, recognizing him the way a scar recognizes the blade that made it.

Richard did not answer.

He stopped short of the boundary and breathed through the pressure building behind his eyes. The temptation to do more pressed at him hard. To reshape. To force stability the way he always had.

Instead, he did almost nothing.

He reached out with the smallest adjustment he had ever attempted, nudging alignment by fractions too small to matter to anyone else. No reshaping. No assertion. Just correction.

Pain lanced through his skull, sharp and personal. His vision doubled and then tripled, stars breaking apart and recombining as something inside him gave way that would not come back.

He bit down on a cry and held the adjustment until the seam responded.

Structural coherence locked.

Alex felt it as the corridor gaining load bearing integrity. Joe felt it as the truth settling into place without effort. Elara felt the fire inside her finally stop straining against its cage.

Richard staggered and caught himself on one knee, breath ragged.

"That cost you," Joe said quietly.

Richard laughed once, thin and humorless. "Everything does."

The system finished evaluating.

Maya felt it all.

Not as people. As functions.

Alex at her side, steady and precise, distributing load without drawing attention. Stability.

Joe at the edge, truth narrowed into coherence instead of revelation. Alignment.

Elara holding heat without release, energy offered but not spent. Controlled potential.

Richard bearing cost to correct structure, leaving fingerprints on the world that would never wash out. Sacrifice.

The Weave did not open.

It reconfigured.

The corridor stopped trembling and became something else entirely. Not a pull. Not an invitation. A passage that existed because nothing in it needed to be forced.

Maya rose.

She did not step because someone reached for her. She did not move because the world asked her to hurry. She moved because her alignment allowed it.

The group held.

No one grabbed her. No one braced for impact.

She crossed the threshold under her own coherence and the Residuum receded just enough to let her go without complaint.

Her aura did not flare.

It integrated.

The shift rippled outward, subtle but unmistakable. The wrongness eased. The air felt heavier in a good way. Real.

They stood together in burned terrain and broken light and said nothing.

Somewhere far away, systems adjusted. Shadows watched. Friends moved, hurt but alive.

No one celebrated.

They all understood what had changed could not be undone.

They had not brought her back.

They had made room for her to return.

This was not rescue.
This was resonance.

35

The Awakening

Maya stood on blackened earth that still held warmth in its bones. For a few seconds she couldn't make herself move. Not because she was hurt, not because she was afraid of what might happen if she shifted wrong. Because the air had weight again. Real weight. Smoke still thinned the moonlight into a dull smear, but it was smoke that behaved like smoke, rolling and lifting with wind and heat instead of hesitating like a thought. Her lungs ached the way lungs ached after fire, not the way they ached inside the Residuum where every breath felt like asking permission.

Behind her, the corridor was closing.

She didn't turn right away. She didn't need to. She could feel it the way you felt a door latch in a room you weren't looking at, a small change in pressure, a quiet decision. The seam that had hovered in the air like a held breath was still there for one last moment, thin as thread, and then it wasn't. No flash. No sound. No rush of displaced wind.

It sealed with the same indifferent gentleness the Weave used when it corrected a mistake.

Alex's presence stayed beside her, steady and close, his shoulder almost touching hers, not holding her up but refusing to give the world any extra space between them. Joe and Elara were a few paces back, silhouettes in ash, both watching her like she might evaporate if they blinked. Richard stood farther off, angled away as if he was listening to something that had learned his name.

Maya expected relief to hit her like a wave. She expected her knees to go weak, her throat to close, her body to remember all at once that she had been somewhere wrong and had come back.

Nothing like that came. Instead there was a stillness that settled over everything, and it was so complete it made her uneasy.

The Weave felt quiet. Not absent. Not shut down. Not smothered by suppression fields or containment geometry. Quiet in the way a machine went quiet when it stopped vibrating because the load was finally balanced. Quiet like the last second after a storm when the air held itself, waiting to see if thunder would decide to speak again.

A held breath.

Maya looked down at her hands. She flexed her fingers slowly. Sensation arrived exactly when she expected it to, no delay, no chasing after intention. Her skin was smeared with soot, her knuckles scraped, her nails rimmed with ash. All normal.

But under that, something else held.

Her aura did not flare. It did not surge in response to fear or proximity or the simple fact that she was standing in a burned scar of land with the enemy somewhere above them in the dark. The glow she had carried through the corridor was gone as visible light, but its structure remained. She could feel it like a shape that belonged to her now, internal and self-contained, as if her resonance had tightened into something the world could recognize without being forced to.

The Weave did not lean away from her anymore.

It did not lean toward her either.

It acknowledged her and went still.

Maya swallowed, searching for the familiar hum she'd lived with since awakening, the quiet sense that threads were always near her skin, always ready to respond if she reached. She could feel the threads, yes, but they did not crowd her. They did not sing for her attention. They moved with the world, not around her.

She was grounded.

And she was hollowed.

It felt like standing in the center of a room right after everyone else left, still warm with bodies and voices, but suddenly too wide, too empty. Not loneliness exactly. Something more structural.

Like something was waiting.

Alex shifted slightly. The movement was subtle, careful, as if he didn't trust the ground to be honest under his feet. "You okay?" he asked softly.

Maya didn't look at him right away. She kept her eyes on the ash and the faintly glowing embers scattered in the dirt like dying stars. "I'm here," she said.

Joe let out a breath that sounded like it hurt. "That's a good start."

Elara took a half step forward, then stopped herself, as if she didn't want to bring her heat too close too fast. Her voice came out rough. "Is it over?"

Maya shook her head once. "No."

Richard made a sound that could have been a laugh or a cough. He didn't turn. "Nothing's ever over."

Maya finally lifted her gaze and looked around.

The burn scar stretched in broken patches, trees reduced to black spines against the night. Smoke drifted low, softening edges. Above, the sky was a dim bowl of cloud and star, and in the distance, far enough that sound came late and thin, rotors throbbed like a heartbeat that wasn't theirs.

They were still being hunted.

That should have made her adrenaline surge. It should have made her reach instinctively for a jump, a fold, a way to erase distance. Even now she could remember the old reflex, the shape of the vector forming, the sensation of the world bending to her urgency.

Her body did not offer it.

Not resistance. Not denial.

Simply no impulse to force the world anymore.

Maya felt Alex's attention on her, steady and quiet, like he was bracing a beam without making a show of it. The dyad bond between them sat in place without flare, a shared coherence rather than a tether. It didn't pull her toward him or him toward her. It aligned them and held.

The Weave stayed still.

And then, without warning, something touched the edge of her awareness.

It was distant. Faint. Not like a voice and not like a presence. More like a point of pressure far away that was not pain, not fear, not emotion. Just information.

Maya went rigid.

Alex noticed immediately. "What is it?" he asked.

Maya didn't answer. Not because she didn't want to. Because her mind was already reaching toward that distant point, not as a jump, not as a grab, but as recognition. She turned her head slowly, scanning the dark horizon like she could see through it.

The sensation did not fade.

It held.

And for the first time since she had stepped out of the corridor, anticipation finally arrived, cold and certain in her chest.

Something was coming.

Not a person.

Not a drone.

Not a threat in the normal shape of threat.

The world itself was about to speak.

Maya closed her eyes.

The burned ground beneath her boots stayed solid. Wind touched her face. Smoke scraped her throat. Everything physical insisted she was here, in Colorado at night, in ash and danger and exhaustion.

The pressure point held anyway.

She let herself lean into it the way Ethan had taught her to lean into silence. Not forcing. Not demanding. Not reaching for outcomes. She simply noticed.

The instant she did, the sensation clarified.

It wasn't a person.

It wasn't a place.

It wasn't even distance the way she'd understood distance.

It was a junction.

A point where threads did something different. Where currents converged and redistributed. Where strain became measurable, not because someone named it, but because the system required an accounting there.

Maya's breath caught.

A node.

She didn't know how she knew that. The word landed in her mind like it had always been there, waiting for the moment it became necessary. She could feel the node's shape in the Weave, not as geometry drawn in light, but as function. A hinge. A relay. A place where the world's coherence got negotiated.

She opened her eyes, startled by the sudden intimacy of it. The horizon did not look different. The burned trees did not lean toward the direction her awareness had turned. There was nothing in the visible world that pointed to the node's existence.

And yet she knew exactly where it was.

Not on a map.

In the network.

She swallowed, trying to steady her breathing. "I'm sensing something," she said quietly.

Joe's head lifted. His eyes were bloodshot, his posture tight with fatigue. "Like what?"

Maya hesitated. She searched for the right words and found none that felt safe. "A junction," she said at last. "In the Weave."

Elara's expression sharpened. "Is that like the tear?"

"No," Maya said, and the certainty of it surprised her. "This isn't a wound. It's... normal. It's part of how it holds together."

Alex's gaze stayed locked on her face. "Can you feel people through it?"

Maya shook her head. "No. It's not like that." She paused, listening inward. The sensation wasn't emotional. It didn't come with fear or hope. It didn't feel like a call for help. It felt like a measured stress reading on a system that had always been running, unseen, until now.

"It's information," she said, almost to herself. "It's telling me where the load is."

Joe's mouth tightened as if he'd bitten down on something he didn't like. "Is the Weave telling you?"

Maya opened her hands, palms up, studying the soot in the lines of her skin. "It's not telling me anything," she said slowly. "It's... letting me notice what already exists."

The words settled into place, and she felt them become true in her bones.

The Weave was not a person.

It was not a god.

It didn't speak.

It allowed.

And now, after judgment, it was allowing her to perceive structure the way she'd always perceived distance.

Maya's heartbeat accelerated, but not from fear. From the dawning awareness that this wasn't going to stop at one point of pressure.

The first node held steady, a faint anchor in her awareness.

And then another one surfaced.

And another.

Not because something moved toward her, but because her mind finally had the capacity to register them.

The sensation multiplied like stars appearing when clouds parted.

Maya inhaled sharply, eyes widening. The world around her did not change, but her internal map did. Points of tension sparked into being, scattered across an incomprehensible distance, each one a different junction, each one a different relay in the system's hidden architecture.

She raised a hand to her mouth, not trusting her voice.

Alex stepped closer, careful, as if he was approaching a skittish animal. "Maya," he said softly. "Talk to me."

Maya forced herself to breathe through her nose. "There's more than one," she said.

Elara's face went pale beneath soot. "How many?"

Maya didn't answer immediately. She didn't know how to count something like this. It wasn't a list. It was a network coming into focus.

"Enough," she whispered.

The first node clarified again as her attention brushed it.

The more she noticed, the more precise it became.

Maya understood then that she could never go back to not noticing.

She could close her eyes, turn away, refuse to listen, but the system would still be there. The junctions would still exist. The load would still move.

And she would still know.

More nodes surfaced simultaneously, not gently this time, but like a barrier giving way. Her awareness widened beyond what felt possible, and the Weave did not resist. It did not protect her from the scale of what it was allowing.

It simply opened the channel.

Maya's knees threatened to buckle.

Alex's hand hovered near her elbow without touching. He waited, the way he'd learned to wait for her consent, the way the Weave itself waited.

Maya clenched her jaw and stayed upright.

The next breath she took felt like stepping onto a ledge and realizing the ground beneath her had never been ground at all.

The nodes resolved into a lattice.

It didn't arrive all at once as a visual image. It arrived as understanding, the way you understood the shape of a city at night from the pattern of lights, even if you couldn't see the streets. The Weave's global structure came into focus around her awareness, not as threads drawn across a globe, but as a living distribution of strain and coherence.

Dozens of points became hundreds.

Hundreds became something she could no longer count.

Maya's breath caught in her chest and stayed there too long. She had to force herself to exhale.

The lattice pulsed, not with light, but with flow. Currents moved through it like blood through arteries, carrying load, correcting imbalance, rerouting around stress points the way a body rerouted around injury. She could feel where the network was strong and where it was thin. Where it carried too much and where it carried too little.

Cities appeared in her awareness as dense clusters of junctions, not because skyscrapers mattered, but because human mass did. The Weave bent around concentration, allocating coherence where reality had to hold against the constant pressure of billions of small choices.

Fault lines appeared as long, slow seams where the world already lived on the edge of disagreement.

Ancient sites surfaced not as landmarks, but as deep anchors, places where the lattice sank into older structure, older agreements written into the world's bones.

Human population centers glowed in the network not with warmth, but with strain patterns, each one a constant negotiation between order and chaos.

Maya stood very still, eyes open and unseeing, because the real vision was happening somewhere behind her eyes, in a place she didn't know existed until now.

She did not influence any of it.

That was the first mercy.

In the old days, noticing meant touching. Touching meant moving. Moving meant changing outcomes. Even when she tried not to, her presence had shaped the Weave like a hand in water.

Now, she could see without disturbing.

She could know without pulling.

She could register the system's state without becoming the problem.

The sensation was overwhelming but coherent.

It was like hearing an orchestra all at once and realizing it was out of tune, not because the musicians were bad, but because the hall itself had warped. Notes were still notes. Harmony still existed. The system still played.

But strain had introduced dissonance everywhere, subtle and constant.

Maya's throat tightened.

She could feel patterns moving through the network, waves of load shifting as events occurred. A surge somewhere as a Walker used power in fear. A dip somewhere as suppression dampened a node's capacity. A ripple where technology pressed into geometry and tried to model a thing it couldn't truly understand.

Her mind tried to categorize it, tried to name it, tried to do what it always did when confronted with too much.

Maya stopped herself.

Listening.

Just listening.

Alex's voice came from very far away, as if it had to travel across the lattice to reach her. "Maya," he said again, and this time there was more urgency in it. "Hey. Look at me."

She couldn't, not yet. Her eyes were open but her attention was somewhere else, caught in the global hum of reality holding itself together.

Joe's voice joined, quieter. "She's not gone," he murmured, more to Alex than to her. "She's... focused."

Elara made a small sound, something between a curse and a prayer. "What is happening to her?"

Maya heard them as if they were in the next room. The lattice was louder.

She became aware of her own heartbeat as a small, local rhythm inside a vast system. For a moment that made her feel insignificant in a way that could have been crushing.

Instead it made her feel terrified.

Because she understood what this meant.

The Weave had not simply corrected her.

It had repositioned her.

Not as a bridge that moved people from place to place, but as a point of awareness the system could route through.

Maya's fingers curled slowly against her palms. Her nails bit into skin. The pain was small and grounding, an anchor back to the burned world beneath her feet.

She forced herself to look at the horizon again, at trees and smoke and the faint smear of moonlight behind clouds. Ordinary reality.

The lattice remained.

It did not fade when she opened her eyes.

It did not fade when she tried to focus on the present.

It was there, layered under everything, a global architecture she could perceive now the way she perceived her own breathing.

Maya swallowed hard. "I can't... turn it off," she managed.

Alex's hand finally touched her elbow, gentle, firm. "You don't have to," he said. "Just stay with me."

Maya's eyes flicked to him, and for a heartbeat she clung to the simple fact of his face, his steady presence, his refusal to leave.

The lattice hummed behind him anyway.

She understood then that there were things you could not unknow. You could survive them. You could learn to hold them. But you could not return to the person you were before you heard the world's true music.

The strain patterns shifted again, and Maya felt it like a current changing direction in a river.

And then something else entered her awareness. A different kind of resonance, not a junction, not a node, not a load reading. Something living. Not one person. Not local. A new layer, sliding toward her perception like a shadow crossing a field of light.

Maya went still again, breath catching.

The lattice held.

The world waited.

And the next movement in the Weave was not about structure.

It was about presence.

The new resonance didn't arrive like a sound. It arrived like a realization that she had been listening to only half the world.

Maya's jaw tightened. Her eyes stayed open, fixed on burned trunks and drifting smoke, but her awareness tipped inward and outward at the same time, as if the lattice she'd just learned to perceive had turned and shown her another face.

People.

Not faces. Not voices. Not thoughts.

Harmonic signatures.

They lit up across the network like living stress points, each one a particular wrongness or rightness in the system's flow. Some were faint, barely audible in the global current, as if they'd learned to survive by keeping their resonance small. Others blazed with unstable intensity, bright enough to make the lattice around them shiver.

Maya's breath caught hard in her throat.

There were so many.

It wasn't a crowd. It wasn't a list.

It was a living field.

Each Walker registered as a condition rather than a person, and that was what made it terrifying. She didn't know names. She didn't see memories. She didn't feel their private grief like a hand inside her chest. She felt what their existence did to the Weave.

Fear threaded through many of them, not emotional fear she could sympathize with, but fear as a harmonic distortion, a high thin wobble that made their signatures unstable and their local nodes strain under the pressure. She felt suppression as a drag, a dull weight clamped over resonance so tightly it flattened it into something almost inert, like music forced through wet cloth. She felt wild, uncontrolled power as heat without shape, surges that shoved the lattice out of tune in sudden bursts, leaving echoes of stress that rippled outward into surrounding nodes.

And then there were the quiet ones.

Small, steady lines of resilience that held a clean tone despite everything pressing down. Not heroic. Not dramatic. Just consistent, the way a candle kept burning in bad air because it refused to die.

Maya's eyes stung. She blinked once and realized she was already crying.

The tears came without sobs, sliding down her cheeks in quick hot tracks. She didn't wipe them away. She didn't have spare attention for her own face.

Somewhere across the globe, a Walker flared in panic and the lattice around them bucked as if the world had swallowed wrong. Somewhere else, another Walker's resonance dimmed under suppression so complete it felt like a slow suffocation. In another place, a signature held steady under pressure that should have broken it, and that steadiness carried through the network like a tiny correction the system gratefully accepted.

Maya's stomach turned.

Empathy at this scale wasn't empathy anymore.

It was agony.

THE RECKONING

36

Maya tried, reflexively, to narrow it. To pull back. To focus on Alex's hand at her elbow and the burned earth beneath her boots and the fact that she was one person in one place.

The awareness didn't obey. It didn't push harder either. It simply remained. A system allowing her to notice.

Maya's lips parted. No sound came out at first. Her throat felt too small.

"I can feel them," she whispered.

Alex's voice was close, tight with worry. "Who?"

"All of them," she said, and the words sounded wrong even as she spoke them, too large to fit in language. "Every Walker."

Joe made a low sound, disbelieving. "That's not possible."

Maya shook her head once, eyes still fixed on the smoke. "It is. I don't know who they are. I can't hear what they're thinking. I can't..." Her voice cracked. She swallowed and forced it steady. "I can't reach them. I can't command anything. I can't do anything."

Elara's breath hitched behind her. "Maya..."

Maya's hands trembled at her sides. She clenched them into fists, nails biting into her palms, trying to anchor herself in pain.

It didn't change the awareness.

It only reminded her she was still a body trying to hold a world's worth of strain.

"I can't save them all," she said, and the admission tasted like blood. It wasn't guilt. It wasn't shame. It was fact. "I can't even save most of them."

Alex's grip on her elbow tightened, not dragging her back, not grounding her the way he used to with his shield, but holding her steady in the only way he could. He couldn't brace the world the way he used to, and he didn't try. His touch was a human anchor, not a Weave one.

Maya inhaled and felt the lattice move with her breath, as if the system itself registered that she was struggling.

She began to sense patterns in the suffering.

Not stories.

Not causes.

Patterns.

And that was worse.

The lattice wasn't random. It never had been.

Now that her awareness had widened far enough to include living signatures, the distribution made a brutal kind of sense. Walkers clustered around certain nodes as if drawn by gravity they didn't understand. Population centers. Old anchors. Fault lines. Places where the Weave already carried strain and the system's margins were thin.

She could feel suppression tightening in predictable corridors. Not everywhere. Not uniformly. Concentrated around points that mattered, around junctions that would create the most control if you could flatten resonance there. It wasn't just a net.

It was strategy.

HECATE's strategy, written into the network like a bruise.

Maya's throat tightened again as she recognized where fractures were most likely to occur. Not because she was guessing, not because she was imagining catastrophe. Because the system itself was showing her load and imbalance the way a trained engineer saw stress lines in a compromised beam.

She could feel the next break points as probabilities.

Hot spots in the lattice.

Places where one desperate surge or one containment miscalculation would tear a seam open wide enough for the Residuum to breathe through.

The Five Clauses from the memory corridor didn't return as words. They returned as structure.

Silence existed in the network as dampened zones where knowledge had been withheld, not by censorship, but by design. The lattice resisted certain kinds of awareness in those areas, as if it remembered what happened when too many minds knew how to turn the world into a weapon.

Containment was visible as routing, currents diverted around thin seams, stability prioritized over comfort, over individuals, over anything that would feel compassionate in the moment and disastrous later.

Anchorship was everywhere.

Mortal presence mattered. Not because mortals were important to the Weave in a sentimental way, but because mortal continuity was the only thing that could inherit pattern without breaking the covenant's rules. The system needed living hands that could act where the Immortals could not.

Maya felt it with sudden clarity that made her knees weak.

The Weave was not asking her to act.

It wasn't telling her to rescue. It wasn't begging her to fix. It wasn't offering her a crown or a mandate.

It was asking her to hold coherence.

To become a stable expression of what the Fifth Covenant had been engineered to accomplish.

Not a vow spoken aloud.

A behavior.

A state.

She realized then that she was not the Covenant.

She was its first stable expression.

Proto, not because she was first in importance, but because she was first in alignment.

A configuration the system could route through without damage.

The weight of it made her stomach twist.

If she reached too hard, she would teach the Weave the wrong lesson again.

If she refused to hold, the system would still strain, still route, still fracture, and there would be no stable reference point to correct around.

Maya's hands shook harder.

The lattice did not waver.

It waited.

The awareness hurt. Not like a headache. Not like harmonic pain from the Immortals brushing her mind.

This was pressure applied evenly across her entire sense of self, a steady, relentless force that made her body react as if it were being squeezed through a space too small. Her breathing went shallow, involuntary, ribs rising and falling too fast. A tremor started in her hands and spread up her arms, subtle at first, then undeniable.

Maya tried to inhale deep and couldn't. It felt like her lungs didn't have enough room.

Tears blurred her vision again. She didn't even register them as tears this time, just moisture, just overflow.

Alex stepped closer and put both hands on her, one steadying her upper arm, the other bracing lightly at her back. He didn't push his shield. He didn't try to ground her in the old way. He didn't force the Weave to quiet.

He anchored her physically, only physically, as if he understood that grounding her would be an interference she couldn't afford.

"Hey," he said softly, close to her ear. "Stay with me. You're here."

Maya nodded, but the lattice didn't let her be only here.

Joe's voice came from nearby, careful. "Maya, you don't have to hold all of that."

She almost laughed. It would have been ugly.

"It's not something I'm holding," she managed, throat tight. "It's something I'm allowed to notice."

Elara edged closer, heat tight and controlled, eyes wide with fear she was refusing to let become flame. "Can you turn it down?"

Maya shook her head, a tiny movement that cost her more than it should have. "If I narrow it," she whispered, "I go back to being a door. I go back to forcing. I go back to... urgent."

The last word came out like a curse.

She understood it all at once.

If she intervened everywhere, the system would collapse. Not because it would punish her, but because it would reroute around her interference until the lattice became a tangle of compensations too unstable to hold.

If she intervened nowhere, fractures would still occur. Suppression would still tighten. Wild surges would still tear seams. The Residuum would still press at the edges, patient and curious, waiting for weakness.

Worthiness felt like being trapped between mercy and ruin.

Maya's knees buckled half an inch. Alex tightened his grip and kept her upright without pulling her away from the awareness. He held her the way you held someone standing in strong wind, not blocking it, just keeping them from falling.

"Tell me what you need," he said. "Not what the world needs. What you need."

Maya swallowed hard.

What she needed was impossible. What she needed was to be able to care without being consumed. What she needed was to hold coherence without becoming stone. She closed her eyes and made herself do the only thing Ethan had truly taught her.

She listened. Not for pain. Not for threat. For need. The Weave's need was not salvation. It was stability. It was pattern. It was a coherent reference point it could route around when everything else shifted.

Maya felt the lattice hesitate, not in indecision, but in recognition of her attention. She understood then that this was the moment. Not a dramatic awakening. A choice.

Maya stopped trying to escape the scale of it.

She stopped trying to narrow it into something human-sized.

She accepted the awareness the way you accepted a weight you couldn't put down without breaking something underneath it.

Her breathing steadied by degrees. Not calm, not easy, but controlled. The tremor in her hands remained, but it stopped escalating. Tears still slid down her cheeks, but she didn't fight them.

She did not reach for solutions. She did not start naming targets or planning rescues or searching for the nearest crisis she could fix to prove she was still herself. She did not speak vows. The Weave did not ask for words. It settled. Not around her body, not like a protective shell, but around her alignment, as if the system had been bracing for her to flinch and, when she didn't, it finally let itself distribute load through her presence without harm.

Maya felt the lattice breathe, a subtle easing, a correction happening simply because a stable tone existed inside the network again.

She could still feel every Walker, every living stress point, every suppression clamp and wild surge and quiet resilience.

She could not save them all. That did not change. What changed was that the knowledge stopped feeling like a command. It became responsibility without orders.

Alex's hands remained on her, steady and human. "You're doing it," he murmured, and his voice was not praise. It was recognition.

Joe exhaled slowly, eyes closed, as if he could feel the field stabilize even if he couldn't see it. Elara's shoulders dropped a fraction, the tension in her jaw easing as if the air itself had stopped provoking her fire. Richard stayed turned away, but the sharpness in the space around him softened, like even the Shadow Current had paused to listen.

Somewhere distant, far beyond burned trees and rotors, the Immortals felt the shift and went still.

Maya didn't see them.

She didn't hear them.

She just knew the lattice had registered an old constraint returning in a new form.

Maya stood in ash and smoke and did the hardest thing she'd ever done. She held coherence. She did not rule the Weave. She bore its attention. And she understood then, with a clarity that hurt, that awakening was not ascension. It was exposure.

The lattice did not close around that realization.

It waited.

Something shifted at the edge of her awareness, not global this time, not diffuse. A single approach vector entered the field, heavy and deliberate, like a mass moving through water instead of light.

Alex felt it first, a pressure change that had nothing to do with danger and everything to do with consequence. His posture tightened, not defensive, but braced. "We've got company," he said quietly.

Joe's eyes snapped open. His truth sight flickered and then stilled again, narrowing instead of flaring. "That's not a drone," he murmured. "That's... intent."

Elara's fire stirred and immediately compressed inward at her command. She turned toward the treeline, jaw set. "I don't like the way that feels."

Richard stepped out of the smoke carrying the Talisman.

It was no longer dormant.

The metal surface caught what little light there was and bent it, not reflecting so much as organizing it. Lines etched into its frame glowed faintly, not bright enough to announce themselves, but too precise to be mistaken for ornament. The device hummed with a low harmonic that made the lattice around Maya tighten in recognition.

Not alarm.

Memory.

Maya's breath caught.

The Talisman wasn't a weapon the way she had feared.

It was a stabilizer.

She knew that instantly, not because it told her, but because the Weave reacted to it the way a damaged structure reacted to a brace being set in place. Load shifted. Stress redistributed. The lattice did not resist its presence.

It accommodated it.

Richard stopped a few paces away, holding the device like it weighed more than it should. His face was drawn tight, eyes too bright, like someone who hadn't slept enough because every time he closed them the world fell apart again.

"You shouldn't be doing this," Maya said softly.

Richard laughed, short and sharp. "Yeah," he said. "That's kind of my brand."

Alex stepped half a pace forward. "What did you activate?" he asked.

Richard didn't look at him. His gaze stayed locked on Maya, on the way the lattice bent subtly around her presence. "A failsafe," he said. "Or what's left of one. Turns out it still works if you feed it the right harmonics."

Joe swallowed. "You reactivated it."

"I didn't have a choice," Richard shot back. "None of us do."

The Talisman's hum deepened, syncing not with Maya, but around her, like a system trying to decide whether two stabilizers could coexist without tearing the structure apart.

Maya felt Richard then.

Not his power.

His trauma.

It hit her all at once, a dense knot in the lattice where his harmonic signature had never quite healed from the last time he'd let the Shadow Current touch him. She felt the memory of collapse, the sound of buildings deciding they were done standing, the certainty that if he didn't act fast enough everything would die and it would be his fault.

He wasn't afraid of Walkers.

He was afraid of inevitability.

"Richard," she said gently, and the sound of his name carried through the lattice like a tuning fork struck cleanly. "You think you're here to save humanity from us."

He flinched.

"Don't," he snapped. "You don't get to—"

"I can feel it," she said, not raising her voice. "You don't see monsters. You see uncontrolled variables. Systems without constraints. You see collapse waiting for permission."

His jaw tightened. The Talisman's glow spiked a fraction, then steadied.

"You don't feel what I feel," he said. "You didn't watch the world decide it was optional."

Maya took a slow breath and let the lattice carry her words instead of pushing them. "No," she said. "I feel what comes after."

Richard shook his head. "That thing," he said, gesturing with the Talisman toward her, "can lock the system. It can dampen global resonance. It can stop mass events before they start. We can contain this."

Joe's voice was quiet. "At what cost."

Richard rounded on him. "At the cost of not losing the planet."

Maya stepped forward one measured pace.

The lattice shifted to accommodate her movement, not resisting, not yielding, simply recalculating.

"You think the Talisman makes you the safeguard," she said. "Because that's the only way you know how to survive what you've already lived through."

Richard's breath stuttered. The Shadow Current stirred faintly at the edges of his awareness and then recoiled, like it didn't want to be seen right now.

"You think if you can just lock it down hard enough," Maya continued, "you won't ever have to choose who gets buried again."

The silence that followed was heavy and absolute.

Alex felt it as load redistribution. Joe felt it as truth settling without resistance. Elara felt her fire go utterly still.

Richard's shoulders sagged a fraction.

"You don't want to rule them," Maya said. "You want to stop the next collapse. You want the world to hold still long enough for you to breathe."

His voice came out rough. "You think that's wrong."

"No," she said. "I think it's human."

The Talisman's hum softened.

Maya reached out, not toward the device, not toward Richard's power, but toward the lattice around his trauma. She did not try to erase it. She did not try to heal it.

She aligned with it.

The Weave responded by doing nothing dramatic.

Which was the point.

"You can't save humanity from us," she said. "Because we aren't the fracture. We're the stress response."

Richard looked up at her, eyes wide and raw. "Then what are you?"

Maya held his gaze and answered honestly. "I'm the first stable place the system can stand without breaking."

The Talisman resonated once, deep and clean, like it had just been reclassified.

Richard lowered it slowly.

For the first time since she'd felt his signature, the lattice around him stopped screaming for correction.

Reckoning did not come with punishment.

It came with understanding.

And the world, for the space of a single breath, held.

37

The Breaking Point

The world moved again.

Not abruptly. Not violently. It resumed the way gravity resumed after a long fall where you had almost forgotten what down felt like.

Maya felt it immediately. The held breath ended, and the lattice she had been standing inside began to flow again. Load redistributed. Currents resumed their quiet negotiations. The Weave did not recoil from her awareness or pull it back. It stabilized around it, accepting her presence as a fixed point instead of an intrusion.

The sensation was grounding and terrifying all at once.

The Talisman's hum deepened.

It was subtle at first, a shift in pitch that slid under hearing and went straight to structure. The device was no longer waiting. It was searching, probing for equilibrium the way a brace tested stress points in a damaged building.

Maya knew the sound instantly.

Not as threat. As function.

A stabilizer seeking authority.

Alex shifted beside her without thinking, weight moving, posture adjusting as if he were stepping under a beam he knew was about to take load. His grounding did not flare outward. It redistributed pressure inward, keeping the space around them from buckling.

Maya didn't look at him. She didn't need to.

She understood before anyone spoke.

This was never going to be a fight.

Richard's presence grew heavier in her awareness. Not louder. Not brighter. Denser, like a mass increasing without expanding, bending everything around it simply by existing.

The Weave tightened slightly.

Not in warning.

In preparation.

Maya stayed still.

The air thickened.

Not heat, not pressure the way suppression fields felt, but something quieter and worse. Sub harmonic compression settled over the space like a blanket laid too carefully to notice at first. Threads in the lattice quieted too fast, harmonics muted mid resolution, like an orchestra cut off just before the chord could finish forming.

Maya felt the global lattice brace.

Walkers everywhere registered at once. Not injured. Not attacked. Compressed.

Alive, but flattened.

The sensation slid through her chest like ice.

Survival without expression.

Mercy by erasure.

Joe made a small sound beside her, breath hitching as his truth sight narrowed until nuance collapsed into blunt certainty. Elara's fire compressed inward so tightly Maya could feel the ache of it through the lattice, heat denied release, presence reduced to pressure. Alex's shield instinct flipped fully inward, distributing compression through his own frame rather than letting it crush outward.

Maya understood the horror immediately.

This was what safety looked like when fear was in charge.

Richard's voice cut through the thickened air, quiet and absolute.

"I'm stopping it before it gets worse."

Maya stepped forward one measured pace.

The Weave permitted it inch by inch.

The clamp brushed her alignment and failed to flatten it, sliding across her presence the way water slid around a stone instead of crushing it. She felt the reason clearly and without pride.

She was not variance anymore.

She did not turn toward Alex. She didn't raise her voice.

"Don't shield," she said calmly. "Don't push."

He obeyed without hesitation.

The stillness spread. Joe did not reach. Elara did not flare. The group followed Alex's quiet, and the space held because no one tried to dominate it.

Maya looked at Richard.

"Stop trying to make us smaller," she said.

The Talisman's hum spiked, defensive, reactive, like a system recognizing challenge and misclassifying it as threat. Maya felt global strain jump in response, a ripple of compression echoing through distant nodes.

She did not escalate.

She listened.

She reached for Richard's harmonic signature and found the trauma knot immediately.

It was impossible to miss now.

The clamp amplified fear, and his fear was ancient, layered, dense with memory. Collapse lived inside his resonance, not as metaphor but as lived experience. Buildings deciding they were done. Ground forgetting how to hold weight. The moment where speed felt like the only moral choice because hesitation meant burial.

The vow pulsed at the center of it.

Never again.

"You're afraid the world won't stop breaking," Maya said quietly.

Richard recoiled, not physically, but harmonically. The denial flared sharp enough to make the Talisman stutter.

"You don't get to psychoanalyze me," he snapped.

The Shadow Current stirred at the edge of his awareness, eager, curious, offering certainty in exchange for alignment.

Maya ignored it completely.

She aligned instead with Richard's strain pattern, not smoothing it, not correcting it, just matching the frequency of his fear without judgment. The lattice responded by reclassifying him.

Load, not threat.

Richard froze.

He felt it then.

Not accusation. Not condemnation.

Being seen.

Measured.

The Talisman desynced, its hum breaking into overlapping frequencies as it struggled to reconcile two stabilizers occupying incompatible authority. Maya felt Richard's vow surface again, raw and unshielded.

Never again.

"You made yourself the lock," she said gently.

Richard shook his head, jaw tight. "If they surge again, people die."

"If you flatten them," Maya said, "they die slower."

The truth landed structurally.

The lattice tightened around his fear, not crushing it, but holding it long enough for it to be felt. Richard's hands began to shake.

"No," he said, voice breaking. "You don't understand what I've seen."

Maya shifted her resonance a fraction.

Just enough.

She aligned with the Talisman's stabilizer harmonic, listening to its intent instead of its output. The device responded, confused, recalculating. Maya offered it a third option.

Calibration without suppression.

The Talisman hesitated.

Richard tried to force it.

The hum spiked violently, compression surging outward as he reached for control the only way he knew how.

Maya refused urgency.

She held coherence.

Alex anchored the dyad, silent and steady.

Joe's voice came soft and human. "Richard, you're scared."

Elara added, barely above a whisper, "So are we."

The Talisman's hum changed.

Lower. Slower.

The clamp released.

Pressure equalized instead of exploding, the lattice easing with a soundless sigh as flow resumed where compression had been choking it off.

Richard's knees buckled.

Maya felt the trauma hit unbuffered, raw and immediate. He dropped the Talisman into the ash, stone striking stone with a dull, ordinary sound that felt almost obscene in its normalcy.

"I can't do it again," he whispered.

Maya stepped closer, slowly, carefully, as if approaching someone standing on unstable ground.

"Then don't do it alone," she said.

The Shadow Current brushed him once more, weak and uncertain.

Maya did not acknowledge it.

It lost purchase.

Richard's breathing went ragged, ugly, real. He folded inward, not as a defeated enemy, but as a man who had finally set down something too heavy to carry anymore.

Joe approached the Talisman cautiously.

Maya nodded once. "Stabilizer," she said. "Not a weapon."

She felt immediately how it could be misused. How easily HECATE could learn from it. How closely Richard had followed a pattern the enemy already understood.

Richard looked up, eyes hollow. "They measured it," he said. "They're already adapting."

The implication landed like a fracture line.

Maya felt the global lattice ease, but she also felt the Shadow Current remember the clamp.

She looked at the Talisman differently now.

Not with fear.

With responsibility.

She hadn't defeated Richard.

She'd taken away the lie that he had to hold the world still alone.

38

Unclassifiable

Ash drifted in slow sheets across the burn scar, caught in rotor wash and thrown upward like gray snow that forgot how to fall. The air still smelled like scorched resin and wet mineral, a harsh, clean burn under the lingering smoke. Maya stood where she had stood through reckoning and breaking, feet planted on ground that did not care what names they gave it. The lattice kept breathing beneath everything, the global architecture humming with strain and correction, but here, in this pocket of burned trees and black soil, something more immediate was tightening.

The hunt.

Alex's hand hovered near her back, not touching, not pushing his shield outward, just ready in the way he always was when the structure around them started to shift. Joe was turned toward the dark treeline, eyes narrowed, his truth sight no longer flaring but sharpening into a quiet, brutal clarity. Elara stood with her shoulders square and her heat drawn inward so tightly it seemed to make the air around her shimmer without light. Richard was on one knee in the ash, breathing like he had been underwater and only just surfaced, one hand planted to keep himself upright, the other resting near the Talisman where it lay half-buried in soot.

No one spoke for a beat.

Maya could feel the difference before sound arrived. The lattice registered approach as load. As intent. As probability tightening into certainty. It was a pressure change in the world, the way a storm front announced itself long before the first wind.

Then she heard it.

Boots. Not far. Not careful. A rhythm of weight moving through brush and ash with trained confidence. Metal clicking against metal. A low murmur of voices that carried without trying.

Division Gray was close enough now that the night wasn't empty anymore. It was occupied.

Above them, rotors cut the air in slow circles, and the wash disturbed the ash so it lifted in spirals and slapped against the trunks of dead trees. The sound was not a single helicopter. It was two. Maybe three. The pattern was deliberate, overlapping. A net.

Maya's awareness tried to widen the way it had in the Awakening, to map the pressure and reroute, but she forced herself to hold still. Not because she was afraid of what she would find. Because she understood now that attention itself was load. A system that reacted to awareness did not reward panic.

"Drones," Alex said quietly.

They descended like insects, small silhouettes slipping between smoke ribbons. Their lights were muted, not bright enough to give away their positions to anyone without sensors, but enough to catch ash on their lenses. They moved in layered geometry patterns, precise arcs and stacked sweeps that did not look like searching.

They looked like measuring.

Joe's throat moved when he swallowed. His eyes tracked the drones for a second, then shifted to the ground, to the way the ash moved as rotor wash changed direction. His expression tightened into something that wasn't fear.

It was recognition.

"They're not searching anymore," he said. His voice was low, steady. "They're converging."

Elara's fingers flexed at her sides. She didn't let fire rise. She didn't let it lick the air. She held it inside herself like a promise she refused to break. "How long?"

Alex's gaze moved like a surveyor's, taking in the shallow rise to the west, the broken line of trees to the north, the ravine that cut across the burn scar like an old wound. "Minutes," he said. "Less."

Richard's breath hitched. He didn't look up, but Maya felt his resonance tighten, the trauma knot in him flaring against the approaching pressure like an old injury reacting to weather.

Maya looked at the Talisman.

It lay quiet in the ash now, no longer humming with clamp-harmonics, no longer trying to flatten the world. Its etched lines still held a faint glow, not bright, not dramatic, just precise, like a blueprint that refused to be forgotten. It pulsed once, softly, as if acknowledging the incoming load.

Not as alarm.

As function.

Maya's throat tightened. The lattice around her did not spike. It did not flare. It held. It waited. And somewhere under the immediate fear of being found, she felt something else settling into place.

A choice.

The last time they had been hunted like this, she would have reached. She would have folded distance. She would have forced an outcome. She would have ripped space open and prayed the tear did not remember her.

She did not do that now.

Instead, she listened.

The net was tightening because HECATE believed it knew what it was chasing. HECATE believed there was a target that could be isolated, classified, and contained. A single anomaly. A single spike. A single signature.

That belief was the net.

Maya's gaze moved to Alex, then Joe, then Elara, then Richard. Not because she needed reassurance, but because she could feel the functions each of them represented in the lattice. The Weave did not see them as names. It saw them as roles.

Stability. Coherence. Controlled energy. Structural correction. Coherence held without command.

Five notes that could either resolve into a chord or collapse into noise.

Alex met her eyes and understood without words. His posture shifted subtly, widening his stance, the way he did when he was about to distribute load across a structure that could not afford a single point of failure.

Joe's jaw set. His truth sight narrowed further, like a blade being honed.

Elara's breathing slowed, deliberate, the way it did when she forced her heat into stillness.

Richard's fingers brushed ash away from the Talisman, not picking it up yet, but touching it like you touched a tool you had once misused and were afraid of using again.

Maya did not speak vows. She did not give orders. She only said, quiet enough that it felt like speaking into the bones of the world.

"They can't classify what won't centralize."

Alex's lips parted as if he wanted to ask, then closed. He nodded once.

Joe's eyes flicked to the drones again. "They're going to lock the perimeter."

"Let them," Maya said.

Elara's voice came rough. "That doesn't sound like a plan."

Maya looked at her. "It is," she said. "Just not the kind you're used to."

A drone dipped lower, its sensors sweeping the ash like a hand searching for fingerprints. The air tasted metallic for a second, like ozone without lightning.

Alex leaned slightly toward Maya. "They're close enough to hear us," he murmured.

Maya nodded. "Then don't give them anything clean."

Joe let out a slow breath. "We're going to confuse them."

Maya's mouth twitched, almost a smile, but it didn't reach her eyes. "We're going to become unclassifiable."

The rotors shifted. The wash slapped ash against their faces. Somewhere to the north, a short burst of static crackled, then a clipped voice, too far to make out words.

Maya did not need the words. She could feel the intent.

The net tightened again.

And then, for half a page of time, the story belonged to someone who was not there.

HECATE's mobile command node sat in a hardened vehicle parked at the edge of the evacuation corridor, screens glowing pale in the dim interior. Dust and smoke filmed the air filters, but the systems ran clean, cooled, and precise.

On the primary display, a cluster of predictive models updated in tight loops, each one a different attempt to stabilize an anomaly signature into something actionable. The signature had been consistent before. A tear aftereffect. A mass-jump rupture. A recognizable harmonic distortion that could be tracked, triangulated, and met with geometry.

Now it would not settle.

A field report scrolled in a side window: Division Gray contact estimates, drone telemetry, rotor positioning, perimeter closure probability.

On the main display, a confidence graph dipped sharply.

Correlation confidence fell below actionable threshold.

A secondary module flagged a divergence alert.

Predictive model A suggested five harmonic sources within a forty-meter radius, overlapping, synchronized.

Predictive model B suggested five harmonic sources that could not occupy the same coordinates without collapse.

Predictive model C suggested a single artifact signature modulating local geometry in a way consistent with a stabilizer.

Then the artifact signature smeared.

Then it sharpened.

Then it became noise.

An analyst with tired eyes leaned forward, fingers hovering over a control pad. "The anomaly field broadened," she said, voice flat with disbelief. "We should be seeing spikes if they're exerting power. We're not. We're seeing distribution."

A second analyst, older, scarred, did not look away from the graph. "They're spreading the load."

"That's not possible," the first analyst said. "Distributed resonance requires coordination and a stable anchor. They don't have time."

The older analyst's mouth tightened. "Then what we're chasing has changed."

A third screen flashed a warning.

Asset classification error.

The system tried to assign a label and failed.

Walker cluster. Artifact. Environmental noise. False positive.

None met the threshold.

HECATE did not go blind.

It became uncertain.

And in a system built to act on certainty, uncertainty was paralysis.

A new line appeared, cold and simple.

Initiate escalation protocol. Increase sensor density. Expand containment radius.

The older analyst swallowed. "We're not hunting a target anymore," he said. "We're hunting a condition."

Maya felt the net tighten again and knew, without seeing screens or hearing radio chatter, that the enemy's certainty was beginning to fray.

She kept her breathing steady.

The lattice remained. It did not command. It did not comfort. It allowed her to notice.

She looked down at the Talisman again and the understanding that had been forming since Richard stepped out of the smoke finally clicked into place with the clean finality of a gear locking.

Richard had called it a failsafe.

He had treated it like a lock.

HECATE would treat it like a weapon.

Everyone who saw it would assume it was designed to shut things down.

But the Weave's response had never been fear. It had been memory. Accommodation. The way a structure recognized a brace.

Maya crouched slowly, careful not to spike urgency into the field. Ash stuck to her knees. She reached toward the Talisman and paused an inch above it, not touching yet, listening for what the system needed.

The device's hum was faint, barely audible, but her awareness picked up its harmonic shape the way she picked up nodes now. Not a blade. Not a clamp.

A load balancer.

It had not been meant to suppress Walkers.

It had been meant to prevent collapse by refusing centralization. To anchor distributed resonance into non-singular coherence. To keep the Weave from being forced into a single point of failure.

A stabilizer designed for plural voices.

Maya's throat tightened with a strange, quiet grief. Of course the ancient engineering solution would not be a weapon. Of course it would be architecture.

She lifted the Talisman carefully, palms flat beneath it like she was holding something fragile that might break if she tried to own it. The etched lines glowed slightly brighter, not because she commanded it, but because her alignment gave it permission to behave as designed.

Richard's breath caught. "Don't," he said, voice rough.

Maya looked up at him. "I'm not clamping," she said.

Richard swallowed. His eyes were too bright. "You don't know what it can do."

"I do," Maya said softly. "I just didn't know what it was for."

Joe stepped closer, cautious. "Maya?"

"It's not a lock," Maya said. She didn't raise her voice. She didn't need to. The lattice carried her words in its own quiet way. "It's a load balancer."

Alex's posture shifted, a subtle release, as if something in him had been waiting for that sentence. "It prevents collapse by distributing coherence," he murmured, more to himself than to anyone else.

Elara's eyes narrowed. "So it doesn't shut things down."

"It refuses centralization," Maya said. "It makes it harder to isolate a target because it makes the target plural."

Joe's mouth tightened. "That's why HECATE hates it."

Maya nodded.

Above them, drones dipped lower. The layered geometry patterns tightened, trying to slice the air into measurable segments.

Division Gray voices carried closer. A flashlight beam cut through smoke for a second, then snapped away.

The net was nearly closed.

Maya stood, holding the Talisman at chest height. She did not point it. She did not brandish it. She held it like a tool, not a threat.

"We don't run yet," she said.

Elara stared at her like she'd lost her mind. "Maya, they're almost on us."

"I know," Maya said. Her voice stayed calm. "If we run now, we give them a clean edge. They'll track the spike. They'll classify us and tighten the net."

Joe's gaze flicked to the treeline again. "We've got maybe sixty seconds."

Maya looked at Alex. "Stabilize local geometry," she said.

Alex nodded once. He didn't throw a wall. He didn't expand a shield. He shifted his grounding the way he'd learned in the corridor, distributing pressure through the land so nothing snapped and announced itself. His resonance moved outward in a thin, precise plane, smoothing the micro misalignments in the ash-scarred terrain without making them rigid.

The air eased by a fraction.

Maya felt the drones' sensor sweeps falter, just slightly, as the local geometry stopped producing clean reflections.

She looked at Joe. "Remove interpretive certainty."

Joe's jaw tightened. He closed his eyes for half a second, then opened them again. His truth sight did not flare. It narrowed into something almost gentle, and then it did something strange.

It refused to interpret.

It stopped trying to resolve the field into singular truths and instead allowed multiple possibilities to coexist without collapsing into a conclusion.

To Joe, it felt like letting go of the need to be right.

To HECATE, it felt like a confidence graph dipping into unusable territory.

Maya looked at Elara. "Controlled energy."

Elara swallowed hard. Her fire wanted to rise. It wanted to answer pressure with heat. She refused. She drew her warmth inward until her skin glistened with sweat and her teeth clenched with effort. She offered energy without ignition, a steady thermal presence that kept the field from going cold and sharp.

A stabilizing warmth, not a flare.

The lattice around them stopped bracing.

Maya turned to Richard. He was shaking, still half on one knee, eyes fixed on the Talisman as if it might turn into a weapon in her hands.

"Richard," she said.

He flinched. "I can't," he whispered.

"You can," Maya said. "Not by forcing. By aligning."

His breath caught. He looked at her, then down at the ash. The trauma knot in him tightened, then loosened a fraction, like a fist unclenching. He reached out, not to seize the Talisman, but to touch its edge with two fingertips.

He listened.

He felt the harmonic shape the way he had always felt micro-fractures in matter.

And instead of trying to clamp it into obedience, he guided it into coherence with the other four resonances.

A small adjustment.

A correction.

The Talisman hummed deeper, syncing with the field around them rather than trying to dominate it.

Maya held her own role last, because it was the only one she could not delegate.

Coherence without command.

She did not push. She did not reach for outcomes. She held her alignment the way she had held the Awakening, accepting the awareness without letting it become urgency. She let the lattice route through her presence without harm.

The effect was not a spike.

It was a broadening.

The anomaly field widened instead of sharpening. It became distributed, non-singular, refusing to collapse into a point HECATE could name. The drones' geometry patterns tightened, then loosened, then tightened again, trying to find an edge.

There was no edge.

To HECATE, it looked like five weak anomalies.

Or one unstable artifact.

Or background noise.

But never all at once.

Alex exhaled slowly. "They can't lock onto us."

Joe's eyes tracked a drone that dipped, hesitated, then rose again as if uncertain. "They're getting confused."

Elara's voice came out thin. "Are we invisible?"

"No," Maya said. "We're unclassifiable."

Richard's breath broke in a shaky laugh that sounded like pain. "That's worse," he murmured. "They hate that."

Maya's gaze lifted to the treeline.

A Division Gray flashlight beam swept the smoke again, closer now. She could hear a voice, clipped and confident, calling coordinates.

Then another voice corrected it.

Then another.

Confusion, not blindness.

Maya held the field steady.

"Now," she said.

Only after the reclassification did they move.

No teleport. No miracle.

Alex led them first, not running, moving with purpose through terrain already saturated by wildfire damage. They dropped into a shallow ravine where ash had settled thick enough to swallow footprints. Burned branches snapped underfoot, but Alex shifted his grounding so the sound dispersed, less a crack and more a dull crumble.

Joe followed, shoulders tight, eyes scanning not for enemies but for the moment truth would try to become singular again. He held his sight narrow, refusing interpretation.

Elara moved like a contained blaze, heat drawn inward so tightly it was almost cold. She kept her breath shallow to avoid steam, to avoid any sign that could be read.

Richard limped, jaw clenched, one hand hovering near the Talisman as if afraid to touch it too much. He did not argue. He did not try to take control. He followed.

Maya moved last, not because she was weak, but because she could feel the lattice's global pull and she refused to let it yank her into urgency. She kept her awareness wide enough to hold coherence and narrow enough to walk.

They cut toward the evacuation corridor.

Not the main road where headlights would announce them. The overlapping edges, the spaces HECATE would flag as low-value due to signal noise and human clutter. Burned terrain where drones saw too many false positives. Pockets where smoke and heat distortion made clean tracking impossible.

They slipped behind a line of abandoned vehicles half-coated in ash, then through a gap where a fence had melted and sagged. The smell of gasoline and wet plastic hung in the air, sharp and ugly.

A family's SUV sat open, doors gaping like a mouth. A child's shoe lay in the dirt.

Maya's awareness brushed the lattice and felt the ghosts of panic that had moved through here earlier, the human surge that had nothing to do with Walkers and everything to do with fire. She did not let herself drift into it. She kept moving.

A drone dipped low above the corridor, its sensors sweeping, then hesitated as the anomaly field smeared across the evacuation noise. It rose, searching for a cleaner signal.

It did not find one.

They moved with the crowd's shadow, not inside the crowd, but along its edges. Past posted signs and emergency tape. Past a National Guard checkpoint where soldiers watched the road with tired eyes.

Alex held his grounding steady so their presence did not create a ripple of geometry that could be read as unnatural.

Joe kept interpretive certainty low, letting them register as human movement in a human corridor.

Elara kept heat contained so no flare betrayed them.

Richard kept the Talisman aligned so it continued to refuse centralization.

Maya held coherence so the lattice did not sharpen around them and offer the enemy a clean edge.

Behind them, rotor wash shifted, then drifted farther.

Division Gray voices grew muffled.

The net did not snap shut.

It loosened, not because they escaped by speed, but because they escaped by changing the rules of what could be tracked.

They reached the far side of the corridor where the terrain dipped into a darker pocket of trees that the fire had skipped. The air here smelled less like ash and more like damp earth.

Alex signaled them to stop.

For a second, they stood in shadow and listened.

No boots. No voices. No immediate pursuit.

Not because HECATE gave up.

Because HECATE could not classify what it could not isolate.

Maya's breathing finally deepened. Not relief. Not triumph. Just the smallest easing of the held breath.

Joe leaned against a tree, eyes closed for a second. "They're not on us," he murmured.

Elara wiped sweat from her brow with the back of her wrist. "Yet."

Richard sat hard on a fallen log, head in his hands. The Talisman rested on the ground between his boots like a sleeping animal. He didn't touch it.

Maya watched him, feeling the trauma knot in his resonance still there, still raw, but no longer flaring into certainty. He had followed. He had aligned. He had not clamped.

That mattered.

Alex looked back toward the corridor, jaw tight. "They'll adjust."

Maya nodded. "They will."

The lattice shifted again, subtle, like a global system taking note. She felt the enemy's uncertainty as a ripple in the network, not emotional, not human, but structural. HECATE would not shrug and move on. It would escalate.

She could feel the moment the hunt changed shape.

From tactical to strategic.

From one team in one burn scar to a global mandate.

Joe opened his eyes. "They're going to widen the net," he said quietly.

Elara's voice went flat. "They're going to turn this into policy."

Richard's laugh was thin. "They already did," he murmured. "They just didn't have the math to justify it until now."

Maya looked down at the Talisman. She could feel what it could do. Not as a weapon. As architecture. As the first tool that made plural voices possible without collapse.

Responsibility sat heavy in her chest, not as guilt, but as inevitability. Somewhere far away, in a mobile command node, an analyst would stare at a graph and realize the confidence threshold had fallen below actionable. Somewhere else, someone would coin a new protocol name. A label for a condition that refused labels.

Maya didn't need to see the screens to feel the cold clarity of it.

Asset classification updated.

Initiate Covenant-level protocols.

She swallowed, eyes on the dark beyond the trees where the smoke still glowed faintly against the night.

This was not an end.

It was a reclassification.

And systems didn't tolerate what they couldn't contain.

Maya reached down and lifted the Talisman again, careful, steady. It hummed softly, not obedient, not dominant, simply aligned.

Alex's gaze met hers. "What now?"

Maya held the lattice without flinching and answered with the only truth that mattered.

"Now," she said, "we become what they can't trap."

Behind them, far beyond the evacuation corridor, rotors shifted direction, searching for a new certainty.

Ahead of them, the world waited, wide and strained and listening.

Maya did not hurry.

She moved with the system.

And that was how she knew, with quiet dread, that the next chapters would not be about running.

They would be about building something that could hold.

39

The Five

They stopped in a pocket of trees the fire had skipped, where the air smelled of damp earth and sap instead of ash. The canopy above them was thin, leaves curled and browned at the edges, but it held. Underfoot, the ground was soft with needles and old rot, and every sound was muted, as if the woods itself had learned not to shout.

Maya stood a few steps away from the others and listened to the world.

Not the wind. Not the distant rotors that still circled far off, hunting a certainty they no longer had. Not the low murmur of the evacuation corridor they had skirted and the exhausted human noise that filled it.

She listened to the lattice.

It was still there, layered beneath everything, a global architecture that didn't care whether she wanted it. The system held its tension the way a bridge held load. Corridors of suppression. Hot spots of probability. Junctions where coherence was thinning. Walker signatures scattered like living stress points across a planet that didn't know how to be quiet anymore.

The awareness had not receded since the Awakening. If anything, it had settled into her bones and made itself ordinary, which was more frightening than the first shock had been. There was no dramatic surge now, no moment of new sight snapping open. It was simply present, a constant that would not go away.

Alex stood near the edge of the trees, half turned toward the darker slope beyond, as if he could still hear Division Gray in the way the air moved. Joe leaned against a trunk with his arms folded, eyes open but unfocused, the look of someone forcing his mind to stay narrow when it wanted to interpret everything at once. Elara sat on a fallen log, elbows on her knees, hands clasped, heat drawn so far inward it made her skin shine in the cool shade. Richard sat on the ground with his back against a rock, knees up, head tipped back as if he was measuring how much sky was left to him. The Talisman rested in the needles between them, a dull piece of stone that hummed faintly like something asleep.

No one celebrated.

No one laughed.

No one even said they were safe, because it would have been a lie.

They had escaped the net, but the hunt had not ended. It had changed categories. That was what Maya felt most clearly, even more than the drones and rotors. Systems didn't give up. They adapted. And HECATE was not a person you could exhaust. It was a structure that grew more rigid when it failed.

Maya rubbed her thumb against the inside of her palm and felt the scrape where ash had embedded under her skin. The physical sensation grounded her, but it didn't shrink the lattice. Nothing shrank it now. Not pain. Not exhaustion. Not the simple desire to go back to being only a person on a hillside with friends and fear.

She inhaled and tried to do what she always did when a problem became too large.

She tried to solve it.

Immediately the world pushed back, not with force, not with resistance. With physics.

The lattice pulled, subtle and steady, attempting to route through her alignment the way a river sought the lowest channel. She felt the pressure gathering around her as if she was a convenient brace in a compromised frame. It was not asking permission. It didn't have intent. It was a system seeking a path.

Maya stood still and let it happen for three breaths.

On the fourth, the strain spiked.

She felt it as a tightening behind her eyes, a twist in her ribs, a subtle tremor at the edges of the global network. Load concentrated too sharply. Coherence thinned along distant seams. Walkers she didn't know flared in fear somewhere, and the ripple of their panic ran into suppression corridors like a wave into rock.

The lattice was showing her what would happen if it was only her.

No accusation. No moral weight. Just the blunt truth that a single anchor could not carry global strain without becoming a failure point.

Maya's throat went tight.

This breaks if it's just me.

She didn't reach to correct the spike. She didn't try to shove the load away. She didn't push her awareness narrower, because narrowing would turn her back into a door, back into urgency, back into forcing.

Instead, she stopped responding.

She became still.

The strain didn't disappear. It redistributed, searching for other paths. For a moment it surged awkwardly, like water hitting a sudden obstruction and spilling into channels that were not ready. The system didn't calm. It simply kept moving, relentless and honest.

Maya finally understood why the Weave had felt like it was waiting after Judgment.

Not waiting for her to become stronger.

Waiting for configuration.

Survival alone was not stability. Holding her alignment alone was not enough. If the system continued to route through her as a single point, the very thing that made her stable would become the reason everything else broke.

Maya turned back toward the others.

She didn't ask permission. She didn't offer a plan in the way plans had once mattered. She simply acknowledged necessity.

Alex noticed her movement first. His head lifted, attention sharpening like a beam finding its bearing. "What is it?" he asked.

Maya didn't answer with fear or urgency. She answered with certainty that felt heavier than either. "It's trying to use me like a single brace," she said. "That's a failure mode."

Joe's eyebrows drew together. "Use you how?"

Maya held her own hands up, palms open. "As the only stable reference," she said. "As the place it routes through because it can." She swallowed once. "It can't. Not alone."

Elara's gaze flicked to the Talisman and back to Maya. "Then what does it want?"

Maya's mouth almost formed the wrong answer.

It wants me to fix it.

She tasted the lie before it became words. The Weave didn't want. It didn't ask for salvation. It allowed perception and it followed structure.

"It's not asking for action," Maya said instead. "It's waiting for configuration."

Richard made a sound that might have been a laugh if it didn't hurt. "Configuration," he repeated, like he was testing the word against his teeth. "That's one way to put it."

Maya stepped closer until she stood near the center of their loose circle. She could feel them now the way she had begun to feel everything. Not just bodies in space, not just friends with histories. Functions. Harmonics. Structural roles that the system recognized even if they didn't.

Her awareness brushed Alex first.

He was not protection. Not in the old way. Not a wall. Not a force pushing outward. Alex was stability under load. A distributed grounding that spread pressure through structure instead of resisting it. A quiet correction that made collapse less likely simply by being present. His resonance didn't shout. It held.

Maya's gaze slid to Joe.

Joe was truth coherence. Not revelation, not exposure, not the violent act of ripping secrets into light. His truth sight had become something else since the corridor. It didn't flare. It narrowed. It removed interpretive certainty. It prevented narrative collapse by refusing to let a single explanation harden into a weapon. He didn't force the world to confess. He steadied it by refusing false conclusions.

Elara sat forward a fraction, and Maya felt her as contained energy. Heat without spread. Potential held under pressure. Elara's power didn't have to become flame to be structural. It could be warmth, it could be steady thermal presence, it could be the difference between brittle coherence and something that could flex without cracking. Control, not suppression. Refusal, not denial.

Richard's resonance was the hardest to look at without flinching.

He was structural correction. Cost-bearing and precise. Micro adjustments made at personal expense. The kind of function no one applauded because it was too small to see until you missed it and everything fell. Richard carried the memory of collapse in his signature, and that trauma had made him dangerous when he tried to become a lock. But the trauma had also made him sensitive to fracture, and that sensitivity, guided and held, could become the smallest corrections that saved a system from tearing.

And Maya felt herself.

Not control. Not command. Not authority.

Reference.

A stable tone the lattice could route around. A point of coherence that didn't demand obedience. A presence that allowed the system to distribute load without becoming a single point of failure.

She realized with a clarity that made her chest ache that none of them could replace another. You could not swap out stability for truth coherence. You could not replace contained energy with structural correction. You could not trade reference for control and still call it coherence.

They were not interchangeable. They were compatible. The Weave tightened around the group as a whole. Not in warning but in preparation.

Maya felt it like the subtle gathering of a net that was not meant to trap them, but to hold something heavier than any one of them could lift. The global lattice didn't surge. It didn't flare. It shifted its routing, attempting to distribute strain through a configuration that had not existed before.

Maya took a slow breath. "We can't do this as one," she said.

Alex's eyes stayed on her face. "We aren't," he said quietly.

Maya shook her head once. "We keep acting like it," she said. "Even when we don't mean to. Every time we look at one person and wait for them to pull us out. Every time we expect a single solution."

Joe's mouth tightened. "You mean you."

"I mean all of us," Maya said. "And I mean the system. It keeps trying to route through the most stable thing it can find. If it's only me, then I become the failure point."

Elara's voice was rough. "So what do we do?"

Maya looked at each of them, one by one. "We become plural," she said. "On purpose."

Richard's gaze flicked to the Talisman. "Is that what this thing was for?" he asked, and there was a careful edge in his voice, like he was afraid of being wrong again.

Maya followed his gaze. The Talisman lay in the needles, dull and quiet, humming with a patient harmonic that didn't ask to be worshiped. A tool. Architecture. A load balancer that refused centralization.

"It helps," Maya said. "But it's not the point."

Alex shifted his stance slightly, widening it. Not defensive. Structural. "Then what's the point?" he asked.

Maya exhaled and let the words come without ceremony. "Attunement," she said. "Not like a ritual. Not like a vow. Like a structure that locks because the pieces fit."

Joe's brow furrowed. "How do we do that?"

Maya didn't answer immediately, because she could feel the temptation in the question. The old pattern. Someone ask, someone lead, someone command. She refused it.

"We do it by not trying to synchronize," she said finally. "We do it by interlocking."

Silence settled.

Not the oppressive silence of hiding. The severe stillness of a system waiting to see if a new configuration would hold.

Maya stood in the center of their loose circle and let her awareness widen just enough to include them fully, not as people she loved, not as friends she feared losing, but as harmonic functions in a network that was too large for one spine.

She didn't tell them to hold hands.

She didn't tell them to speak.

She didn't draw sigils or raise the Talisman or ask the night for permission.

She simply held her alignment and waited for them to notice each other the way the Weave was noticing them.

Alex's resonance shifted first, a subtle adjustment that made the ground beneath them feel more honest. He didn't push his shield outward. He distributed load through the terrain, smoothing micro misalignments that would otherwise reflect into a clean edge for the enemy, or fracture under strain. His grounding became a plane, thin and precise, that gave the lattice a stable local surface to route across.

Maya felt it and didn't praise it. She only allowed it.

Joe's truth sight narrowed further, not to sharpen a blade, but to remove the need for a single story. In the presence of the others, his gift did something it had rarely done before. It stopped trying to resolve them into labels. It refused to collapse the field into one interpretation. It held multiple truths at once without forcing a conclusion.

Maya felt the lattice ease a fraction as interpretive certainty dropped. A system built on patterns didn't need a narrative. It needed coherence.

Elara drew a breath that trembled at the edges and then steadied. Her heat compressed inward, tighter than it wanted to go, until it became a consistent warmth rather than a flare. She offered energy without expression. Not fire. Not threat. Potential held so the field didn't go brittle under pressure.

Maya felt the thermal harmonics stabilize the local lattice, making it flexible without becoming chaotic.

Richard's fingers brushed the Talisman, and Maya felt his flinch before she saw it. He didn't want to touch it. He didn't trust himself not to clamp again. But he listened, and listening changed the shape of his fear. He set two fingertips on the etched edge and made the smallest correction he could, aligning the tool with the field instead of trying to dominate the field with the tool.

The Talisman's hum deepened, syncing with the other resonances. Not amplifying. Balancing. Refusing centralization by design.

Maya held her role last, because reference only worked when everything else had something to reference against.

She didn't push.

She didn't reach for outcomes.

She held coherence without command, accepting awareness without letting it become urgency. She allowed the lattice to route through her presence without turning her into a single choke point.

And then something happened that was so quiet it would have been easy to miss if she had been waiting for spectacle.

The harmonics didn't synchronize.

They interlocked.

Maya felt it like gears finding their teeth. Not unity. Compatibility. A closed system forming not because someone declared it, but because the functions fit together and created a loop that could carry load.

The local lattice stabilized.

Not in a bubble. Not in a dome. In the simplest possible way: strain that had been trying to route through Maya alone began to route through all five of them instead. The load didn't vanish. It redistributed. The pressure behind her eyes eased by a fraction, and she realized with a shock that it was measurable.

The global lattice shifted.

Far away, junctions that had been bracing against concentrated strain loosened just slightly. Suppression corridors didn't disappear, but the pressure they imposed began to route around them more intelligently, not because Maya commanded it, but because the system now had a plural reference. A stable configuration it could model and route through without collapsing into a single failure point.

The Residuum withdrew slightly at the edges of her awareness.

Not retreating in fear.

Recalculating.

Watchful.

Maya's throat tightened. She didn't smile. Awe was not joy. Awe was weight.

The Weave accepted the configuration.

Not approval.

Recognition.

It was the same indifferent gentleness with which it sealed corridors and corrected mistakes. A system acknowledging that a structure now existed that could carry load without tearing.

Maya understood then that this was the engineering solution the Covenant had always meant to be.

Not a crown.

Not a hierarchy.

Not an authority imposed from above.

A lattice.

An architecture of plural voices, each non-interchangeable, each necessary, each restrained enough to fit.

The old clauses Ethan had made her feel in the corridor surfaced again, not as words, but as behavior settling into place.

Silence emerged as damping. The refusal to shout the wrong things into the world.

Containment as routing. Load distributed away from seams that could not take it yet.

Anchorship as inheritance. Mortal continuity holding pattern where the Immortals could not.

Sacrifice as load acceptance. Pain borne in small corrections.

Non-interference as restraint. Action taken only when structure allowed it.

The system locked.

Maya felt it mark them.

Not with light. Not with a visible brand.

Structurally.

A subtle shift in how the lattice registered their existence. It was like the difference between a loose wire and a soldered joint. The connection was now part of the circuit. The network could recognize it, route through it, and measure it.

Which meant others could, too.

Maya's awareness flicked outward without her choosing it, and she felt distant attention go still.

Immortals.

Not voices. Not faces. Not gods watching from thrones.

Constraints tightening. Old agreements noticing a new configuration inside the rules they were bound to. A quiet, severe pause in places she could not see.

Maya also felt the cold logic of HECATE's future attention, not here yet, but inevitable. A system that had failed to classify would not stop trying. It would widen its models until it could.

And beneath it all, patient and curious, the Shadow Current recalculated.

The presence was faint, almost polite, but it slid along the edge of her perception like a hand testing the seam of a wound. It didn't attack. It simply noted the new lattice and adjusted its own probabilities.

Maya's stomach tightened.

This could not be undone without collapse.

They had not just survived a chase. They had become a condition the world would now route around. They were no longer just fugitives with powers and fear and a list of people hunting them.

They were load-bearing.

Alex looked at Maya, and she felt his internal register of it, not romantic, not emotional shorthand, but structural recognition. He didn't speak, but his stance held. He stayed in the configuration as if he understood that stepping out would not just leave her alone. It would change the system's math.

Joe's breath left him slowly, eyes widening a fraction as if he could feel the coherence settle even without seeing it. His internal register was blunt: this is real. This is true. And it does not care what he thinks about it.

Elara's jaw unclenched. Her heat didn't rise. It steadied. Her internal register was quieter and almost disbelieving: I can hold without burning. I can be part of this without destroying it.

Richard stared at the Talisman as if it had become a mirror. His internal register was the hardest to bear, because it was layered with shame and relief. He had tried to become a lock. He had almost flattened them all into mercy by erasure. And now, in the lattice, he felt something else: he didn't have to hold the world still alone.

Maya held all of it without flinching.

Not because she was strong.

Because she was reference, and reference meant you didn't get to look away when the structure mattered.

They stood together without touching.

No vow.

No proclamation.

No flare of light to announce the birth of something ancient.

The world didn't change visibly.

It steadied.

Somewhere distant, the global lattice held a fraction better than it had a moment ago.

The Fifth Covenant existed now.

Not written.

Not declared.

Active.

Maya exhaled and felt the system route through them as if it had been waiting for this shape all along.

The Covenant didn't begin with a promise. It began with five points that refused to break.

40

Global Resonance

The first warning wasn't loud.

It didn't come as a scream through the lattice or a surge that knocked Maya off her feet. It came as a subtle mismatch, like a note that should have resolved and didn't. A junction that should have taken load cleanly and instead held it, trembling, unwilling.

Maya opened her eyes in the dim pocket of trees where the five of them had become something load-bearing. The woods were quiet, damp air pressing cool against her cheeks. Rotors were far now, a distant mechanical thrum that no longer belonged to the moment. The world was doing what it always did after a near miss. It pretended.

The lattice didn't pretend.

It tightened beneath everything, not in warning, but in measurement. Maya felt its architecture like bone under skin, global and indifferent. Corridors of suppression still clamped down in predictable bands. HECATE geometry still existed out there, still being deployed, still testing. The Shadow Current still slid along the edges of probability with patient curiosity.

And then, as if those pressures had finally found the same beat, the load spiked.

Maya sucked in a breath that didn't go all the way down.

It wasn't one fracture point. It was many.

Three nodes in quick succession flared in her awareness. Not as lights, not as images. As thresholds. As structural readings turning red in a language that wasn't color. One sat in a dense human cluster she couldn't name, somewhere where millions of lives pressed on reality all at once. Another rode a fault line that had always lived on the edge of disagreement. A third was older, deeper, anchored to something ancient, something that had been holding strain since before her body existed.

They were all approaching failure.

Not because the Weave was weak, but because it was being forced to compensate everywhere at once. Suppression dampened resonance in one corridor and the system rerouted load around it, concentrating pressure somewhere else. A Shadow Current whisper brushed a seam and a Walker surged in panic and the spike echoed through a node that was already thin. HECATE deployed geometry to contain one anomaly and the containment created a new stress gradient that pushed another junction toward fracture.

Maya's mind tried to do what it always did. Find the nearest break. Solve it. Jump. Fix. Repeat.

It failed before it started.

Not because she couldn't move, but because the lattice was already telling her the physics. No single intervention would matter. Each correction would displace load into another failing point. Delay would mean cascade, a chain reaction of seams and stress that would turn the planet into a map of wounds.

Local containment was no longer viable.

The system needed a global correction.

Maya's throat went tight. She turned her head slowly and looked at the others.

Alex stood with his stance still widened, as if the ground itself was something he didn't trust to stay honest. Joe was upright now, not leaning, eyes focused the way they got when his gift narrowed into that brutal quiet. Elara sat very still on the log, hands clasped, heat so contained it looked like discipline carved into flesh. Richard was on his feet again, shakier than he wanted to be, gaze flicking between the trees and the Talisman resting in the needles like a sleeping piece of architecture.

They were all tired. They were all hurt.

And the lattice didn't care.

Maya felt the load trying to route through her again, testing the easiest path. For one heartbeat, she could have let it. She could have become the brace. She could have tried to be enough.

The strain spiked in response, immediate and punishing.

This breaks if it's just me.

She swallowed and stepped into the loose center of their circle. No ritual. No gesture. She didn't need to lift her hands or raise her voice. The Weave already knew where her alignment was.

"We're about to lose it," she said.

Joe's eyes flicked to her face. "Lose what?"

"The lattice," Maya said. "Not here. Everywhere."

Alex didn't ask how she knew. He didn't ask where. His posture tightened by degrees as if the words themselves added weight. "How close?"

Maya closed her eyes for a second and let the readings come. "Too close," she said. "Multiple points at threshold. If one goes, it pulls the next. It won't stop."

Elara's jaw worked once. "So we move."

Maya shook her head. "There isn't anywhere to move to."

Silence held for a beat, the kind that wasn't fear and wasn't denial. Just the severe pause of people whose bodies wanted to run and whose minds understood running wouldn't help.

Richard's voice came out rough. "So what do we do?"

Maya opened her eyes. The words that came weren't dramatic. They weren't a speech. They were a statement of consequence.

"We do what we were built for," she said.

Alex stared at her, and she felt his internal register shift. Not emotion. Structure. "Global," he said quietly.

Maya nodded once.

Joe exhaled through his nose like it hurt. "If we do that," he said, "the world will notice."

Maya didn't argue. She didn't reassure him. She didn't soften it.

"Yes," she said.

Elara's hands tightened together until her knuckles went pale. "That means there's no going back."

"Yes."

Richard's gaze dropped to the Talisman. His shoulders lifted on a breath and fell again. "HECATE will flag it," he said. "Division Gray will have it in every system they own."

"Yes," Maya said again, and the repetition made it feel like a nail being driven. "The Immortals will feel it. The Shadow Current will feel it. Anyone watching for a pattern will have one."

No one objected.

No one told her it would be okay.

Alex took a slow step closer, not touching her, not claiming her, just moving into position the way he would if a beam was about to take load and needed support from more than one side. "Then we do it right," he said.

Joe's chin lifted. "No lies," he murmured. It was not a vow. It was his function.

Elara's eyes went distant for a second, and Maya felt the heat inside her shift into something steadier, less reactive. "No burn," she said softly. "No flare."

Richard swallowed hard. "No clamp," he whispered, and the admission was a wound. "Not again."

Maya let the lattice feel their consent without turning it into a command. She did not become the leader of a ritual. She became the reference point inside an architecture.

The Weave tightened around them, anticipation without emotion.

Maya reached down and lifted the Talisman.

It wasn't heavy in the way stone was heavy. It was heavy like responsibility was heavy, like carrying a brace to the center of a structure you knew was failing. The grooves along its black surface pulsed faintly, ash-note humming beneath the skin of sound.

She didn't activate it.

She aligned it.

Maya breathed in and held coherence without urgency. She felt the lattice take her alignment as a frequency, a stable tone the system could route around.

Alex's resonance shifted outward in thin, precise planes. Not a wall. Not a dome. A local stabilization that gave the lattice a clean surface under their feet so the global correction wouldn't snap at the edges.

Joe's truth sight narrowed and did what it had learned to do. It refused to collapse the field into a single interpretation. It kept the resonance plural, preventing the system from hardening into a central spike.

Elara compressed her heat inward until it became presence without ignition. Energy offered without expression. A warmth that kept the field flexible under strain instead of brittle.

Richard touched the Talisman with two fingertips and listened past his fear. He made the smallest correction, guiding the tool's harmonic shape into coherence with the other four functions without trying to dominate it.

Maya held the last piece. Not power.

Reference.

A stable tone the planet could recognize without being forced.

The resonance began without spectacle.

No flash.

No pulse.

No wave of visible light.

It started as pressure equalization.

Maya felt it like a deep breath taken by something too large to have lungs. Load shifted through the lattice. Strain that had been gathering at distant junctions began to redistribute, not disappearing, not erased, but rerouted into channels that could take it. The planet's hidden architecture responded the way a structure responded when a brace was finally set correctly.

And then the sky answered.

At first, it was only a change in the air, a faint metallic taste at the back of Maya's tongue, like ozone that hadn't decided to become lightning. The canopy above them seemed to thin, as if the darkness itself was paying attention.

Then a thread of color appeared between the branches.

Not the green smear of ordinary aurora. Not the familiar curtains of polar light. This was a band of unfamiliar hue, something between deep blue and violet that didn't belong to any weather map. It moved with harmonic logic, shifting in patterns that felt like math made visible.

Maya's breath caught.

Beyond the trees, over the darker slope, the sky bloomed.

A curtain of color unfurled across the horizon, spreading upward in slow waves that didn't ripple like wind-driven light. They pulsed like a discharge finding ground. Lines formed and dissolved in geometries that made no human sense and perfect Weave sense.

Maya didn't see the rest of the world.

But she felt it.

Auroras ignited far beyond the polar regions. Over cities dense with junctions and human strain. Over oceans where the lattice ran deep and old. Over deserts where the sky was wide and the ground was ancient and the load had nowhere to hide.

The discharge was not decoration.

It was the system venting strain safely.

Maya felt the upper atmosphere respond as if it had been waiting for permission to release pressure it had been holding for years. The lattice moved, and where it equalized, the sky answered with light.

And then humanity registered it.

Not as thoughts. Not as words. Maya did not become a voice in anyone's mind.

She felt the response as texture, as a global shift in the way millions of bodies held themselves.

Across the world, people stopped walking.

Conversations trailed off mid-sentence.

Hands froze over phones. Forks paused halfway to mouths. Engines idled at intersections while drivers stared upward like they'd forgotten why they were moving in the first place.

Children looked up.

So did the exhausted. So did the skeptical. So did the ones who had trained themselves not to believe in anything they couldn't measure.

A shared sensation spread, not as belief, but as physiology.

Pressure easing.

Breath deepening.

A momentary sense of being held, not by arms, not by comfort, but by structure. As if something beneath reality had tightened its joints and decided it would not let the world slip apart tonight.

No one understood what they were feeling.

No one received instructions.

No one was changed directly.

Humanity was not saved.

It was stabilized.

Maya's eyes stung. She didn't know if she was crying again. She didn't have spare attention for tears.

The lattice absorbed the load, and the weight of it registered in her body like gravity increasing by degrees. Not pain. Weight. A vast compression of responsibility that made her ribs feel too small.

Alex's breathing changed beside her, a controlled exhale that said he could feel the strain even if he couldn't see what she saw. Joe's posture went rigid for a second and then steadied, his gift holding plural coherence under pressure that wanted certainty. Elara's jaw clenched, heat trembling under her skin as she refused to let it become flame. Richard's shoulders shook once, a silent shudder of cost-bearing correction, but his focus stayed on the Talisman, guiding without clamping, aligning without dominating.

Maya felt the lattice lock into a long-term configuration.

Not permanently solved. Not healed into softness.

Aligned.

The Immortals went fully still in the far places of her awareness, constraints tightening like ancient eyes opening. They did not speak. Their silence was not approval. It was recognition that something inside the rules had changed.

The Shadow Current retreated along the edges of the network, not vanishing, not defeated, but withdrawing the way a predator withdrew when the terrain shifted against it.

And HECATE, everywhere at once, would flag the anomalies.

Maya didn't need to see their screens. She could feel the cold logic ripple through the lattice like a secondary disturbance. Systems built on classification would choke on this. They would widen their nets. They would write new protocols. They would name what could not be named and then use the name as an excuse.

This could not be undone quietly.

Maya held the resonance until the planet finished venting the worst of the strain.

Then, slowly, the discharge subsided.

The auroras faded unevenly, like embers dying at different rates. Bands of color thinned into wisps and vanished. The sky returned to darkness in patches, as if it had to remember how to be ordinary.

People would start moving again.

Engines would start. Conversations would resume with confused laughter. News feeds would flood with shaky videos and frantic headlines. Scientists would argue. Conspiracists would feast. Governments would convene. HECATE would calculate.

The world would call it a phenomenon.

Maya felt the lattice hold without constant intervention, a fraction steadier than it had been a night ago.

She stood under a sky that was almost normal again, the Talisman humming softly in her hands, and she knew the point of no return had already passed.

The world did not change that night.

It aligned.

For the first time since the fracture, the planet breathed as one.

41

Shadows Across the Veil

The sky was empty again.

No curtains of color lingered at the edges of night. No unfamiliar hues bled through cloud or horizon. Wind moved the treetops the way wind always had, and the stars resumed their distant, indifferent patterns. Somewhere far below the canopy, an engine started. Somewhere else, a door closed. The world picked itself up and continued, slightly off balance, pretending nothing fundamental had shifted.

Maya felt the difference anyway.

She stood at the edge of the trees where the five of them had watched the auroras fade, boots pressed into damp earth that smelled of moss and old rain. The lattice beneath everything was quiet, but not loose. It held tension the way a drawn bow held tension, stable, deliberate, waiting. The planet was carrying a configuration it had never carried before, and every system inside it knew not to relax too far.

Stillness settled.

Not peace. Not relief.

Readiness.

Maya breathed and felt the lattice breathe with her, not because it needed her to, but because reference had become habit. The global strain that had screamed hours ago now sat distributed and balanced, routed through channels that could take it without tearing. The world was not healed. It was aligned enough to stand.

Humanity resumed motion in fragments.

Far beyond the trees, she felt the faint texture of people moving again, not as thoughts, not as voices, but as the low static of life restarting. Confused laughter. Uneasy silence. The strange need to talk about anything except the sky. Some would deny what they had seen. Others would cling to it. Most would file it away as a once in a life-time phenomenon and return to work in the morning with a headache they could not explain.

The lattice accepted all of it.

Maya let her awareness widen just enough to take in the aftermath without drifting into urgency. The Fifth Covenant held. The load didn't snap back. That, more than the auroras, told her they had crossed something irreversible.

Then she felt it.

Attention.

Not pressure. Not contact. Awareness at a distance so vast it barely registered as sensation at all, more like the way gravity announced a large body long before sight. It came from everywhere and nowhere, not converging, not intruding. Observing.

The Immortals.

They didn't arrive. There was no manifestation, no burning sigils in the air, no voices folding the night into declarations. Their presence was constraint made aware of itself. Old rules noticing a new configu-ration moving inside them.

Maya didn't look up. She didn't bow. She didn't offer explanation.

She felt them as measured stillness, as ancient attention recalculat-ing boundaries it could not cross. They didn't judge her. They didn't praise or condemn what the Five had done. Judgment implied author-ity. This was assessment.

The Fifth Covenant had been acknowledged.

Not approved.

The distinction mattered.

Their silence was not permission. It was recognition that something had formed without violating the laws that bound them. Mortal alignment. Plural coherence. No command issued. No hierarchy imposed.

The Immortals remained what they had always been.

Watchers constrained by their own oaths.

Maya felt the pause settle into the lattice like a held breath that would not be released yet. Whatever came next would unfold without their hands on it. The Covenant of Silence remained intact.

Above, attention held.

Below, something else stirred.

It was subtle at first, easy to mistake for aftershock or residual noise from the resonance. A faint warmth at the edges of her awareness where reality thinned. A slow thickening in places that had always been fragile.

The Residuum.

It didn't surge. It didn't push. It didn't test the lattice the way it had before, curious fingers probing for weakness. Instead, it behaved like a tide responding to a new moon, not rising yet, simply adjusting to a changed pull.

Maya's breath slowed.

Old thin places warmed, not opening, but becoming more receptive. Dormant fractures that had slept for decades shifted as if remembering how to stretch. The boundaries between worlds didn't weaken.

They became negotiable.

Alignment had not sealed the Veil. It had clarified it. It had turned chaos into approach vectors.

Maya felt the lattice register the change without panic. It didn't resist the awareness. Resistance would have been a declaration. Instead, it measured. Logged. Adjusted routing.

The Residuum was learning.

Not as a mind. Not as a singular enemy. As a process that adapted when the environment changed. It didn't fear the Fifth Covenant. It incorporated it into its probabilities.

A quiet dread settled in Maya's chest, not sharp, not overwhelming. Understanding without drama was heavier than terror.

Healing was not gentle.

Alignment invited contact.

The pressure came next.

Not harmonic. Not structural. Not hostile.

It pressed behind her perception the way the boundary state had pressed when she had first slipped between definitions, a familiar wrongness that was not pain. The Residuum didn't speak with sound. It didn't shape language the way minds did.

It transmitted intention.

Maya stilled completely and let it pass through her awareness without answering, without rejecting, without leaning into it. The lattice held with her, stable and alert.

The message arrived fully formed, not as a voice, not as a threat, not as promise.

"The Convergence begins."

No emphasis. No drama.

A statement of process.

Maya closed her eyes.

The screens in the command center had stopped flickering.

That alone was enough to make Senator Hargreaves uneasy.

He stood with his hands clasped behind his back, jacket folded over a chair he hadn't sat in for hours, eyes fixed on the central display where graphs stabilized into unfamiliar shapes. Confidence curves that should have rebounded after a transient event had instead flattened. Error margins widened instead of narrowing.

Nothing was resolving.

"Run it again," he said calmly.

The analyst nearest the console didn't look up. "We already did, sir. Three times. Different baselines."

"Then run it a fourth."

She hesitated. "The models aren't disagreeing. They're... failing to converge."

That got his attention.

Hargreaves stepped closer, studying the readouts without touching the glass. Global atmospheric anomalies flagged and archived. Auroral events tagged as non-solar, non-magnetic, non-random. Resonance signatures that didn't match any known Walker surge, artifact activation, or Immortal interference pattern.

Five overlapping traces appeared and disappeared in the same geographic window.

Then didn't.

A secondary display showed predictive failure rates climbing past acceptable thresholds.

"Explain," Hargreaves said.

A man with gray at his temples cleared his throat. "Sir, whatever caused the resonance wasn't centralized. There's no primary emitter. No command node. We can't isolate a source."

"Everything has a source," Hargreaves replied.

"Yes, sir," the man said carefully. "But this behaved like a distributed event. No spike. No decay curve. The system never found a dominant signal."

Another analyst added, "The strain redistribution was... selective. It avoided certain stress corridors. Like it was compensating."

Hargreaves's jaw tightened slightly.

"So it adapted," he said.

No one answered.

His gaze dropped to a final line of text that had appeared without commentary.

ASSET CLASSIFICATION UPDATED
INITIATE COVENANT-LEVEL PROTOCOLS

He exhaled slowly.

"So," he said at last, "they've changed behavior."

The analysts exchanged glances.

"They're no longer presenting as discrete anomalies," he continued. "Which means traditional containment won't work."

One of them spoke cautiously. "Sir, we don't know what *they* are anymore."

Hargreaves straightened, smoothing the cuffs of his shirt with deliberate care. "That's rarely stopped us before."

He turned from the screens and reached for his jacket.

"Escalate oversight," he said. "Global. Quiet. Increase monitoring thresholds and expand predictive modeling. No public language yet. Let this be weather. Let it be solar. Let it be anything that buys us time."

"And if it isn't?" someone asked.

Hargreaves paused at the doorway.

"Then," he said evenly, "we assume this wasn't an attack."

Silence stretched.

"It was a rehearsal."

He left the command center without looking back.

Containment had never been the endgame. Control had only delayed what was always moving toward coherence or collapse. The scale had shifted now beyond hunts and protocols and suppression corridors.

This was not about stopping something.

It was about surviving what came together.

Behind her, Alex shifted his weight slightly, feeling the change without knowing its shape. Joe's breath caught for half a second and then steadied as his truth sight refused to invent meaning where none had been offered. Elara's heat tightened, instinct bracing against a pressure she could not yet name. Richard stood very still, hands loose at his sides, as if some part of him understood that forcing anything now would shatter more than it saved.

Maya didn't turn to them.

Not yet.

This was not information to be shared like a warning. It was not something that could be acted on immediately without breaking the very alignment that had made it perceptible.

She held.

Above, the Immortals remained silent.

Below, the Residuum waited, patient and curious.

Between them, humanity slept, woke, argued, denied, and moved on, unaware that the rules beneath their feet had shifted just enough to matter.

The lattice held with Maya, taut and listening.

She didn't respond to the whisper.

She didn't signal the others.

She didn't hurry.

The world had been aligned.

Now it would be tested.

Silence held. Shadows gathered. The Veil waited.

What came next would not be a war.

It would be a convergence.

The lattice held. Above it, the Immortals remained silent. Below it, the Residuum waited. And between them, the distance that had once kept the worlds apart began to thin.

John discovered storytelling as a child navigating foster care, where books became both refuge and inspiration. After serving twenty-four years in the U.S. Army with three combat deployments, He returned to writing, drawing on a lifetime of resilience, discipline, and imagination. He now lives in rural Tennessee, where he writes full-time and spends time with his family.